LAND
of my
HEART

——— HEIRS OF MONTANA ———

LAND
of my
HEART

TRACIE PETERSON

BETHANY HOUSE PUBLISHERS
Minneapolis, Minnesota

Land of My Heart
Copyright © 2004
Tracie Peterson

Cover design by Ann Gjeldum/Cadmium Design

Unless otherwise identified, Scripture quotations are from the King James Version of the Bible.

Published by Bethany House Publishers
11400 Hampshire Avenue South
Bloomington, Minnesota 55438
www.bethanyhouse.com

Bethany House Publishers is a Division of
Baker Book House Company, Grand Rapids, Michigan.

Printed in the United States of America

ISBN 0-7642-2769-6 (Trade Paper)
ISBN 0-7642-2899-4 (Large Print)

Library of Congress Cataloging-in-Publication Data

Peterson, Tracie.
    Land of my heart / by Tracie Peterson.
        p.   cm. — (Heirs of Montana)
    ISBN 0-7642-2769-6 (pbk.)
    1. Women pioneers—Fiction. 2. Ranch life—Fiction. 3. Montana—Fiction. I. Title.
II. Series: Peterson, Tracie. Heirs of Montana.
    PS3566.E7717L36   2004
    813'.54—dc22   2003022919

To John and Kay Peterson
with thanks for your love
and for answering my
questions about steamboats

To Mike Parker
with thanks for answering
all my questions about ranching
the "old-fashioned way"

Books by Tracie Peterson

www.traciepeterson.com

Controlling Interests
The Long-Awaited Child
Silent Star
A Slender Thread • *Tidings of Peace*

BELLS OF LOWELL*
Daughter of the Loom • *A Fragile Design*
These Tangled Threads

DESERT ROSES
Shadows of the Canyon • *Across the Years*
Beneath a Harvest Sky

WESTWARD CHRONICLES
A Shelter of Hope • *Hidden in a Whisper*
A Veiled Reflection

RIBBONS OF STEEL†
Distant Dreams • *A Hope Beyond*
A Promise for Tomorrow

RIBBONS WEST†
Westward the Dream • *Separate Roads*
Ties That Bind

SHANNON SAGA‡
City of Angels • *Angels Flight*
Angel of Mercy

YUKON QUEST
Treasures of the North • *Ashes and Ice*
Rivers of Gold

NONFICTION
The Eyes of the Heart

*with Judith Miller   †with Judith Pella   ‡with James Scott Bell

TRACIE PETERSON is a popular speaker and bestselling author who has written over fifty books, both historical and contemporary fiction. Tracie and her family make their home in Montana.

PROLOGUE

New Madrid, Missouri
March 1864

HUMID AIR WARMED THE DAY CONSIDERABLY. DIANNE CHADWICK pushed back a loose strand of honey-colored hair and sighed, then glanced out the window of the store her father owned, noting heavy black clouds on the horizon. *Hope it's not a twister coming,* she thought as she stepped behind the counter of the New Madrid Emporium.

At sixteen, Dianne had proven to be her father's capable right hand when it came to running the store. Her efficiency, along with her genuine concern for their customers, surprised both herself and her father, who eventually agreed she could quit her formal schooling.

Her three older brothers had no interest in the store, which suited Dianne just fine. Her father had tried without luck to mold each of his sons into storekeepers, but they weren't the type to settle down to such a life. They craved adventure and the wild outdoors. Keeping a store inventory and watching the till did nothing but cause them grief and rebellion.

"Where are your brothers? We're going to need cash from the bank," her father announced as he came in from the back room. "I failed to take care of it yesterday."

"I haven't seen any of them since they left the breakfast table,"

Dianne admitted. "But don't worry about it. I'll go to the bank for you."

"No," he said, shaking his balding head. "I'd better just go myself. You know it isn't safe to have you out there without an escort. This war has ruined life for decent folk. I remember when things were much easier, more genteel. Why, your poor mother cries herself to sleep almost every night, longing for the good old days before the war."

Dianne nodded, knowing the truth of her father's words. Her mother wept often these days. Her worries over her boys, now almost old enough to go to war, were enough to keep her to her bed.

Dianne didn't argue with her father. She knew he'd eventually relent and allow her to go to the bank, for he seldom left the store these days. With his family living just above the Emporium, Ephraim Chadwick felt it his duty to stay close at hand. The increasing hostility he dealt with from his Southern-sympathizing neighbors, who failed to understand why he'd taken up trading with the Union soldiers who occupied New Madrid, made him even more tense.

Dianne failed to understand the fuss in any case. Business was business and the war was an infringement upon it. And she couldn't honestly say that she favored one side or the other. Her mother had been raised in a well-to-do Southern family, so naturally her loyalties lay with the South. But Dianne's father had strong ties with the North, and being a businessman, he tended to do whatever best served his livelihood.

She watched as her father fussed with several bolts of cloth before finally heading to the back room. He emerged through the curtain pulling on his coat, grumbling all the way.

"I don't know what good it is to have sons if they're never around to help with the business." He marched to the safe and pulled out the bag he always used for their money.

Dianne pretended to sort a box of medicinal remedies while her father stormed about the room. She knew he was only looking out for her best interests, but she felt no reason to fear being on the street. There were more than enough Union soldiers keeping watch over the town. Surely they were trustworthy and honorable enough to keep one young woman from harm.

"Are you sure you haven't seen the boys?" her father asked in an exasperated tone that told Dianne he was nearly ready to give in.

She wiped her hands on her apron. "Let me go check for you."

She made her way to the back door and opened it. Peeking out into the alley, she scanned the street for her brothers. Seeing that there wasn't a single soul stirring, she closed the door and returned to her father. "There's no sign of them."

He sighed. "I hate to leave the store. Especially with the state your mother's in."

Dianne came to his side and gently touched his arm. "I can go to the bank, Papa. I'll be just fine. It's early and most of the riffraff are sleeping off last night. There are soldiers patrolling and they'll look out for me. Most of them are your friends. They aren't about to let anything happen to me."

Ephraim sighed again and looked beyond Dianne to the door. "I suppose it would be all right, just this once."

Dianne hurried to the bank and conducted her business quickly. Mr. Danssen seemed rather surprised she'd come alone but said nothing. "Give your mother and father my best," he called as Dianne stepped to the door.

"I will," she replied, tucking the money bag inside her skirt. She walked at a quick pace back to the store, but her mind was on the sorry state of the town around her. Windows were boarded in several businesses, reminding her of friends who had moved away. Mrs. Simpson's dress shop had been burned to the ground only three weeks earlier. Her father said it was renegade Confederate soldiers, but Dianne figured it to be local folks. Mrs. Simpson was a Yankee of the most outspoken kind. No doubt there were folks who'd had their fill of her opinions.

As she passed a group of local men, a chorus of vulgar comments and whistles started up.

"Hey, that's Ephraim Chadwick's daughter," one of them called. "Her pa owns the Emporium."

"Yeah, he cozies up to those Yankees," another added.

"But her ma's a real daughter of the South," a third man threw in. "She ain't no Yankee lover."

"And she's real purty, just like her daughter."

Dianne tried to ignore their comments, keeping her head bowed and walking as quickly as proper etiquette allowed. But not ten feet from the store's front door, she found her process brought to an abrupt halt.

"Why don't you sit a spell and share some company?" a gruff character demanded as he took hold of her arm. "You ain't no Yankee lover, are ya?"

Dianne looked up to meet the burly man's gaze. His expression was one of hatred; he smelled strongly of whiskey, sweat, and manure. Apparently not all of the riffraff were still sleeping off the night.

"Excuse me," she said, trying to gently pull away. "My father is expecting me." Thunder rumbled in the distance as the storm moved ever closer.

He tightened his hold and grinned, revealing yellow rotting teeth. "And I'm expectin' some common courtesy. Ain't gonna hurt you none to show me some respect. That's the trouble with this war. Since the Yankees come to town, ain't nobody friendly no more."

Dianne stared at him hard. She knew many of the citizens of New Madrid. Her father had run the Emporium there for some time and Dianne had recently begun helping behind the counter full time. This scum was not someone she recognized. He had no doubt headed west to avoid getting killed on the battlefield. His boldness surprised her, however. Yankee soldiers were everywhere—protecting and defending New Madrid as a property of the Union. Rumor had it that skirmishes were being fought all over the state. If spotted, these men would no doubt be rounded up and questioned.

The man took her silence as acceptance. "There. Ain't so hard, is it? Just be nice to old Charley and he'll be nice to you."

Dianne drew a deep breath. "Unhand me."

Charley seemed surprised by this. He studied her for a moment, then began to laugh. His companions joined in as if Dianne had shared some joke.

She lifted her skirt slightly and kicked her captor hard in the shin. This caused him to release his grip long enough for her to move away. She reached the store's front door just as Charley reached out again and yanked at her long hair.

Dianne screamed out in pain, alerting not only her father but several soldiers who were inside the store.

"Let her go!" her father demanded as Charley played a sort of tug-of-war with Dianne. Lightning flashed in the sky and a light sprinkle of rain splattered the dusty street.

"You heard the man," a soldier Dianne knew as Captain Seager stated as he drew his revolver.

To Dianne's surprise, Charley did let go. Her father swiftly pushed her inside the store. Dianne nearly lost her footing but caught herself against the counter as thunder boomed outside. The storm was upon them.

"What's going on?" her mother questioned as she emerged from the back room.

"I . . . ah . . . well, there's some men out there and Pa—"

Lightning, more intense and brilliant, illuminated the darkened day as a dozen shots rang out. Dianne had no chance to finish her statement as her mother pushed past her and ran outside. Her pounding heart was heavy with fear.

"Who's shootin' guns?" her ten-year-old sister, Ardith, called out. The youngest in the family, Betsy, was right behind her. "Is the war here?"

"Both of you stay there!" Dianne commanded. "I'll see what's happened."

The boardwalk outside the store, so unassuming moments before, looked like a battlefield littered with the bodies of the fallen. The storm, churning and rolling, blotted out much of the sun's light.

Stunned, Dianne leaned back against the building for support. Thunder cracked again, shaking the very foundation beneath her feet. The rain began to pour in earnest and the soldiers hurried to clear the boardwalk of bodies. A few feet away her mother knelt beside her father. A trickle of blood spilled from a hole in the middle of his head.

"I'm sorry, ma'am," Captain Seager said as he crouched down beside Susannah Chadwick. "Your husband was caught in the cross fire."

Rain poured over her, matting her once-delicately styled hair to her face. "No doubt," Susannah said in a whisper. "But whose cross fire, I wonder?" Lightning streaked across the sky, the thunder exploding on top of it. Her gaze was fierce. "My husband's a victim of this war just as sure as if he'd been wearing a Southern uniform. Your people care for nothing but themselves." She then touched her fingers to the wound and began to sob. "Look what you've done. Look what you've done."

Dianne pulled her apron to her mouth and fought back her own tears. Her stomach cramped as she placed her hands over her eyes. *If only I hadn't gone to the bank—if only I would have taken Trenton or one of the other boys.*

She watched the soldiers lift her father's lifeless body and carry it into the store. They'd no sooner cleared the threshold when hail pummeled the streets. A twister was sure to follow.

CHAPTER 1

DIANNE ANXIOUSLY WAITED WITH HER SIBLINGS AROUND THE FAMily dining table as their mother considered their request. With their father gone nearly a month and store responsibilities mounting, Dianne had pursued the one idea that seemed to make sense.

"Move to the Idaho Territory?" Susannah questioned.

Dianne spoke with confidence. "I've been in touch with a wagon master who will lead a train west in about ten days. They'll head out from St. Louis, so we need to act quickly."

"But to just up and sell off everything and leave?" her mother asked, looking at each of her children.

"We can't leave New Madrid," Dianne's oldest brother, Trenton, spoke. "I don't mean to leave here until I've avenged Pa's death."

"Don't talk that way, Trenton. There will be no revenge," their mother declared, tears coming to her eyes. "I've already lost Ephraim; I'm not about to lose you too."

"That's why moving to your brother's place is so important, Mother. It will get the boys away from the war. You know how Captain Seager is constantly badgering them to join the Union as soon as they're of age. Before you know it, they won't have any choice but to choose sides."

"I wouldn't fight for the Union," Trenton declared. "I think they had more to do with Pa's death than they're letting on."

"But you can't be sure," his mother interjected. "No one is certain whose bullet took your father's life. I don't like the Union any more than you do, but I can't hold them wholly responsible for Ephraim's death."

Dianne's twin brothers, Morgan and Zane, exchanged a glance before commenting in unison, "We think the move would be good."

Betsy and Ardith, the youngest of the Chadwicks, began whispering back and forth as if trying to understand the full implication of the adult conversation.

Trenton scowled at the boys who were a year his junior. "It isn't right that a man's life was taken like that without anyone paying for it. Pa deserves better than that."

"They're calling it an accident of wartime," Dianne threw out. She knew if Trenton would listen to anyone, it would be her. "Trent, we can't bring Pa back—even if we put a bullet in every Union soldier in town. Or Southern sympathizers, for that matter. Nothing is going to bring him back."

"Maybe not, but at least we'll have done right by him."

"Stop it!" All gazes turned to their mother. Even Betsy and Ardith were silent. "There will be no more talk of revenge." A cloak of silence clung heavily to the air before she pushed her shoulders back and focused on her sons. "I think Dianne's idea to move west is a good one."

Dianne breathed a sigh of relief. Surely now things would progress forward. "We need to leave in less than a week," Dianne said, centering on her mother's careworn face. "We should sell the store. Pa had a couple of men interested in buying it at different times. We can get Mr. Danssen at the bank to check them out and see if they're still interested."

"I suppose that would be wise," their mother replied. "I certainly wouldn't want to trust someone else to run it after we left."

Dianne nodded. "Morgan and Zane and I have been talking. We'll take as much as we can in inventory to sell on the way at the forts, and when we arrive in Virginia City, we can sell anything left over. That should give us plenty of money to live on."

"Is Virginia City where Uncle Bram lives?" Ardith asked.

Their mother nodded. "Yes. Uncle Bram lives nearby."

"I've sent him a letter to let him know we're coming," Dianne said, surprising them all with her boldness. "I knew I would have to act quickly or we'd beat the letter there." She reached out and patted her mother's arm. "Look, there's been a lot of gold found in that area so a great many people are making their way to the territory. It should be an easy road, with good folk for company." She paused and looked at her siblings. "I've heard tell a good many Confederate folk are heading to that area."

"You just don't understand, do you, Dianne? Or maybe you just don't care. Moving away still doesn't change the fact that Pa was wrongly killed," Trenton declared.

"Do you think that fact has somehow escaped any of us, Trenton?" Dianne's irritation heightened with her brother's accusing tone.

Trenton's expression softened and he lowered his face. "No. I just can't bear to leave it undone."

"And I can't bear to see you hanged for murder. Or forced to fight for the Union." Dianne's words were blunt, but she knew it was necessary in order to completely win her mother to the idea. "Morgan and Zane are only two years from being old enough to be drawn into it as well. Would you have their blood on your hands, just because of foolish pride?"

"Enough," Susannah said, shaking her head. "I cannot bear any more deaths. I hardly know how to face the days as it is."

"You know I agree with going west," Morgan put in, "but how will we know what to do? We've been running the store and living in the city all our lives. How are we going to know how to live off the land and do what's necessary to survive on the trail?"

Dianne had wondered this as well. After asking around, she felt she had procured the answer. She produced a small book from her pocket and placed it on the table.

"This is the book that will teach us. *The Prairie Traveler*. This man tells how to do everything. He tells how to pack, how to handle the animals, what weapons and supplies to bring, and what to expect on the trail. I think we can follow his instructions and learn what we need to know. Listen to this." She opened the book to read randomly.

"'On emergencies, an ox can be made to proceed at a tolerable quick pace; for, though his walk is only about three miles an hour at an average, he may be made to perform double that distance in the same time.'" She paused and turned a few pages. "It says this about packing: 'Camp-kettles, tin vessels, and other articles that will rattle and be likely to frighten animals, should be firmly lashed to the packs.' Further down the page it says, 'One hundred and twenty-five pounds is a sufficient load for a mule upon a long journey.'" She smiled and closed the book. "There is all matter of information here. Details about packing and cooking, treating problems on the trail, fixing broken wheels—it's all right here. We need only study this to know better how to prepare and how to handle the situation once we're actually on the trail."

"I could go out and spend a day with Otis Wilby. He could show Morgan and me how to handle the wagon and how to care for the animals," Zane threw in.

"Yeah, he could probably teach us how to do just about everything we need to know," Morgan agreed.

Dianne nodded. "That would be good. You boys do that. I'll help Mama arrange things at the bank and then figure what inventory we'll take. Trent, why don't you go with them?"

"I'm not going!" Trent said, jumping up and overturning his chair. His blond hair fell across his face, causing him to frown and push it back in place. The action made him seem less sure—almost confused. "I'm nineteen years old—old enough to make my own decisions. I'm staying here until I make things right."

"You'll never make things right, Trent," Dianne said softly. She reached out to gently touch her brother. "Pa will still be dead. If anyone's to blame for that, it's me—not the soldiers. Pa needed money and I went to the bank for him. It's my fault."

Trent shook his head. "That's not true. You should be able to walk the streets without being attacked. You weren't to blame."

"She shouldn't have been out," her mother said, eyeing them both with a look of resentment. It was the first time Dianne felt, as well as heard, her mother's opinion of the matter. "But I cannot hold you responsible—not in full." Dianne felt the weight of responsibility settle on her shoulders as her mother continued. "I need you to be the man of the family now, Trenton. I need you to stop thinking of what you want and see us safely through to the Idaho Territory."

Trent shook his head. Dianne saw the sorrow in his expression. "I'm not going. You can't make me. I think you're ten kinds of fool to try to make this trip, but I'm sure Morgan and Zane will be men enough to get the job done."

Dianne watched her mother's face contort as she barely held back her tears. "You do this, Trenton Chadwick, and you're no son of mine."

Dianne gasped and put her hand to her mouth. Trenton seemed surprised by his mother's statement but refused to back down. "I have to do this, Ma. If you don't understand that, then you must not have loved Pa as much as you say you did."

Trent stormed out, not giving anyone time to reply.

Their mother stared at the door for several moments. No one dared to breathe or speak a word. Betsy pulled on one of her braids and began rubbing the hair between her thumb and first finger as she often did when upset. Ardith simply looked at the floor, while Morgan and Zane kept their gaze on the table. Only Dianne turned to their mother. And in that moment Dianne knew her mother truly blamed her for everything. The look on her face made it clear. Dianne sank back in her chair.

But then just as quickly as the look appeared, her mother's face relaxed and assumed an expression of resignation. "What do we need to do, Dianne?"

Dianne hesitated. "Well . . . I-I've made a list. I figure we should take at least three wagons. Each wagon will have four oxen each. We should also take several milk cows and some chickens and horses."

"With the war on, how will we be able to get those things?" Zane asked.

"Pa made friends with the Yankees. If you have enough money, you can buy whatever you need. I figure with the sale of the store, we should be able to get whatever we want."

"But who'd buy the store now? Especially with the Union holding the town? Those fellows who were interested before surely aren't going to want it now," Morgan stated.

"We'll just hope for the best. If not those fellows, then maybe one of the Yankee soldiers or their relation. Many of the men seem to like it here; even Captain Seager talks of settling here after the war."

Morgan and Zane seemed satisfied by this answer. "Ma, while the boys can go talk to Otis, I have some worries about how we'll learn what we need to know," Dianne began. "We don't know much about cooking on the trail and washing and such. The book talks about some of it"—her mother picked up the book and thumbed through as Dianne continued—"but I doubt we can learn everything there."

"Right here it talks about how to dry fruits and vegetables," her mother said matter-of-factly. "You press the juice out and dry them in the oven until they're rock hard. They pack tight then and won't spoil. When you go to use them again, you boil them in water and they are supposed to be as good as fresh."

Dianne thought it sounded reasonable. "But what about making campfires and cooking out in the open?"

"Dutch ovens are supposed to be great for cooking outdoors. We sell them here in the store," her mother replied. "Surely we can learn how to use one."

"Can I learn too?" Ardith asked.

Susannah smiled as if the tensions of the earlier moments were all but forgotten. "Absolutely. Everyone needs to learn." Her enthusiasm picked up, almost as if the idea to go west were hers. "Everyone will have to help. You younger girls will have to collect firewood as we go along the trail or we won't have a cook fire at night. It won't be easy, but we'll make it work."

Dianne heard the determination in her mother's voice. The decision was made, and there would be no turning back now.

"Can we have a dog?" Betsy, the animal lover of the family, questioned.

Susannah grew thoughtful. "A dog would probably be good once we get to Virginia City but less helpful on the trail. On the trail he might get bitten by a snake or killed by Indians."

Betsy's eyes grew wide. "Indians? For sure, Mama?"

Susannah nodded. "I've long heard your father and my brother talk about troubles in the West. That's something else we should consider."

Dianne nodded. "We all need to learn how to handle the guns. The boys have a pretty good knowledge of them, but the time may come when we ladies will have to use them as well."

"Pa didn't want his womenfolk handling firearms," Morgan said without thinking.

"Well, your pa isn't here to defend us," their mother replied. She frowned. "I think he'd understand."

"Ma, I'm glad about going west," Zane announced. "I've wanted to go west for the longest time. I read a book on Lewis and Clark going through that territory where Uncle Bram lives, and I've always wanted to see the headwaters of the Missouri."

Morgan nodded at his mother. "I'm glad too. You know I like to explore. I've always wanted to go west, just like Zane. We'll have a good trip—you can count on us."

"I'm happy too," Dianne said, smiling. "It sounds like a great adventure, and I know Uncle Bram will be happy to see you. He wouldn't want you living here without Pa—especially not with the war going on."

"Whether he'll be happy or not remains to be seen," their mother replied. "This will be a difficult journey. We'll have to help one another and learn as we go. No doubt some of the other women can teach us some of what we need to know. Other than that, we'll have to depend on our own ingenuity."

Dianne nodded, realizing that the trip would probably be hardest on her younger sisters. "I'll help the girls as much as I can."

"We're big enough to help ourselves," Ardith, the most headstrong of the Chadwick children, announced.

Dianne grinned. "Of course you are. I just meant that I'd give you an extra hand. I know you're strong and smart."

"What about school?" Ardith asked. "Come Monday, I was supposed to complete my report on George Washington."

"School's done for the year as far as I'm concerned," Dianne's mother said with a resigned sigh. "Are you sure this is the best time to go, Dianne—boys?"

"If we don't go now, we'll never get there by winter. The mountain passes fill up with snow early on. Like I said, I've been studying up on this," Dianne replied.

Their mother nodded and smiled at Ardith and Betsy. "You'll get by. I'll help you with lessons until fall. Maybe by then we'll be in Virginia City and there will be a school nearby."

"That's when we can get a dog," Betsy announced, dropping her hold on the pigtail. "I want to call him Shep."

Susannah picked up *The Prairie Traveler* and got to her feet. "That's fine, Betsy. We'll call him Shep. Now I've got some reading to do."

With her mother's clear indication that the discussion was over, Dianne and her siblings got up to tend to their various chores. Dianne still needed to dust their rooms upstairs as well as the store shelves, although she wasn't sure it was necessary if they were leaving next week. Living over the store made the Emporium a natural extension of their living quarters. It also doubled the workload—not that Dianne really minded. She enjoyed working with the customers, though she absolutely hated bookwork. Her father had always kept the ledgers so it wasn't any real concern to her, but now she was finding herself caught up with the unfamiliar task. She'd asked Morgan and then Zane for help, but neither one was interested. Trenton could have helped her, but he hated the store and refused to stay around any longer than he absolutely had to, preferring instead to be sent on delivery missions for his father.

"Do you think there will be other children on the trip west?" Ardith asked Dianne. Morgan and Zane slipped from the room while Betsy picked up the broom and began her job of sweeping.

"I'm sure there will be lots of children on the trip. Why do you ask?"

Ardith shrugged. "I just don't want to go to a place that doesn't have other children. I want to make friends, you know."

Dianne thought of her own beloved friends. Especially Ramona and Sally. How would it be to go so far away and not have them to talk to? What would it truly be like to live on the open prairie? Where would they sleep and tend to private matters? Where would they go to church?

A rush of other questions filled her head. Maybe she'd made a mistake in pushing for this change. How would they survive the trip? How would they manage it all? She picked up the duster and began to work.

I really don't know how to do much of anything for myself. How can I hope to help keep my family alive and well on such an arduous journey?

CHAPTER 2

DIANNE FOUND SLEEP IMPOSSIBLE THAT NIGHT. IT WASN'T UNTIL she heard Trenton sneak into the house that she could finally rest. She understood his anguish and resolve, but she couldn't comprehend his willingness to desert them, to leave them when they needed him most. Consoling herself with the thought that he might have changed his plans, Dianne got up and quietly tiptoed to the room he shared with the twins.

"Trenton?" she whispered.

He came to the door. "What are you doing up?"

"Waiting for you, of course. Come to my room and talk to me."

She pulled Trenton back to her room and lit a lantern. "Where have you been? I was worried about you."

Trenton pushed back his hair and shook his head. "You should know better than to worry. I'm a grown man."

"A grown man who sneaks in and out of his parents' house," Dianne chided. "Please, Trenton. Just talk to me. Won't you change your mind and come west with us?"

Trenton sank onto her bed. He looked emotionally drained. Dianne sat down beside him. "Please."

"I can't go." He seemed to struggle for the words. "You don't under-stand what it was like for me. I was always disappointing Pa. Here I am, his first son, and I never took any interest in the store or the things he thought important. He was always good in school; I can barely read and write."

"But he loved you dearly."

"I suppose I know he loved me, but I also know I disappointed him. I should have tried harder to please him. If I'd just been around that morning, I could have gone with you to the bank. I could have even taken care of the deed myself. He's dead because I was selfish. I left before breakfast so he wouldn't start harping at me about the inventory."

"But staying behind isn't going to change anything."

Trenton got to his feet. "You—" he lowered his voice—"you don't know that. I just feel that if I could do this one thing for him . . ."

"What one thing? Kill another human being? You know what Pa thought about violence. He didn't want you boys involved in the war, much less personal vendettas."

"I knew you wouldn't understand. You have your own ideas about how things should be. Well, this isn't one of those situations. I have to try to make things right. I have to ease my conscience in the only way I know how."

"By killing other men." Her statement was given with all the resignation and despair she felt.

"By killing the man who killed our father." Trenton walked to the door. "I'm sorry, Dianne. I guess I've disappointed you, just like the others."

Dianne thought to call out to him as he left the room but thought better of it. She'd let him get some sleep, then try to reason with him again tomorrow. Once he calmed down, surely he would understand why it was so important that he give up the idea of revenge.

The barest hint of light traced the curtains at Dianne's window. She sat up with a start, wondering what time it was and whether or not she might speak with Trent before the day demanded their attention elsewhere.

"I just know I can reason with him," she murmured. "We've always been close. He'll listen to me. I just know he will."

That was when she spotted the folded piece of paper. Someone had slid the missive under her door, and she was willing to bet that someone was Trenton. Shivering against the morning chill, Dianne wrapped her shawl around her nightgown and went to retrieve the note.

Picking up the paper, Dianne fought back tears. "Please don't be gone," she whispered as she stood and made her way back to her bed. Sinking back into the warmth of her goose-down comforter, Dianne unfolded the paper.

Dianne,

Don't be mad at me. I know you don't understand, but please try. I didn't treat Pa with the respect he deserved in life. I owe him this. It's important, and I wouldn't be much of a man if I didn't see this through.

I'll miss you. You'll always be my favorite. Just know that no matter where life takes us, I'll be thinking fondly of my little sister. Probably by the time I see you again, you'll be all grown up and married with kids of your own. I hope you'll tell them good things about their uncle.

Please be happy. Pray for me.

Love,
Trent

Dianne hugged the paper to her breast, then gazed again at the childish scrawl. Trenton—her mainstay. When Ma cried over the war and Pa made friends with the Yankees, Trent had always been there to help Dianne cope with the situation. When the war loomed ever closer and Dianne feared for her brothers and friends, it was Trent who had gathered her close.

"Who will comfort me now?" she cried softly into the thick folds of her covers.

Outside the rain began to pour, almost as if God understood her pain and cried with her. Dianne had been so hopeful that Trent would change his mind. She hated seeing her family go its separate ways. First Pa had died, and now Trent had gone. Who else would leave them?

Forcing herself to get up, Dianne couldn't help but take a mental inventory of all that she loved. Her room had been her sanctuary. It was small, barely large enough to fit her small bed, but it was all her own. Her mother had thought to make it a storage room, but Dianne had pleaded to turn the tiny room into her own place of quiet.

Trent had helped her paper the walls. The delicate rose pattern against a cream background had done wonders for the room. This, coupled with the oval rose-colored rug her father had acquired from one of the older women in the church, made the place quite cozy.

Dianne smiled at the memories. Her mother had even helped her polish the floor, and while it certainly wouldn't rival anyone's parlor, the wood was smooth and free of snags.

"I'll miss it," she murmured, fingering the lacy curtains her mother had ordered. They seemed to overwhelm the tiny window, but they finished off the room with a real touch of elegance.

With a sigh, Dianne once again read over her brother's words of farewell. *I can't bear for you to leave,* she thought. *It's bad enough to lose all of this, but I cannot lose you as well.* She thought of going out and finding Trenton—to talk him into changing his mind. Then the memory of what had happened to her father halted further consideration. Dianne had scarcely left the house since her father's death unless accompanied by the rest of the family. Her fear at repeating the scene while searching for Trenton kept her from pursuing her initial thoughts.

Going to her wardrobe, Dianne dressed for the day, choosing a serviceable day dress. Her mother had already warned them all that the days to come would be nothing but work. The black color seemed fitting, but Dianne was tired of wearing mourning colors. Her mother would wear black for at least a year, but Dianne hoped she'd allow her daughters to wear their pretty things much sooner. Of course, space would be at a premium. They might not even be able to take their colorful dresses with them.

Dianne pulled the shapeless gown over her head and quickly covered it with a black apron. Braiding her hair down the back, she hurriedly drew on stockings and shoes, knowing that her mother would be waiting for help with her corset.

Knocking lightly on the door, Dianne entered to find her mother sitting at her dressing table, staring into a hand mirror. "Mama, are you all right?"

Susannah Chadwick looked up and nodded. "I suppose as right as I can be. I was thinking—I'm only thirty-five. Thirty-six, come May. That isn't so very old, is it?"

Dianne shook her head. "No. It's not. Pa used to say you looked as young as the day he married you."

Her mother smiled wistfully. "Yes, I remember that." She fell silent and put the mirror on the table. Standing, she took off her robe, leaving only her cotton shift. She handed Dianne the corset.

"Don't make it too tight," her mother admonished.

Dianne marveled that her mother had maintained such a tiny frame after carrying eight children. Of course, two had been miscarried and there was one set of twins; nevertheless, her mother had managed to keep her figure trim. Finishing with the ties, Dianne helped her mother into her crinolines. Grateful that the fashion dictates of the day had flattened the sides and front of the undergarment, Dianne still found the hoop shape annoying. Her mother seemed not to care one way or the other. It was a Southern lady's responsibility to pay strict attention to proper dress, no matter the style.

After the crinoline came the petticoats, dyed black to match the mourning color of her gowns. Then finally, Dianne took up the dress her mother had laid out for the day. It was one of her finer Sunday dresses. No doubt her mother figured to look her best for her transactions at the bank.

Once dressed, her mother took on a somber expression and picked up some papers from her vanity. "I've looked over your lists. I think you and your brothers should begin packing the crates with as much goods as possible. The idea to take mostly food items seems sensible. People always have to eat, and even the army is in constant need of supplies."

Dianne took the lists and glanced at them for a moment. She

wondered if she should tell her mother about the note from Trent. It was possible, but not very likely, that he'd left a note for their mother. Dianne supposed she could wait and see if that were the case. After all, she didn't want to further upset her mother by sending her to the bank in a fit of grief.

"You'd best get me an apron," her mother stated as she put the finishing touches on her hair. "I don't want to splatter myself while I fix breakfast."

Dianne found her mother's aprons and brought her one quickly. "I can get breakfast if you like," Dianne offered.

"Nonsense. I've been cooking for this family since the day I married your father. I'll manage. You just see to getting your sisters dressed."

Dianne nodded. She went to work straightaway to get Betsy and Ardith into their clothes and ready for the day. She was surprised to find them already up and in the middle of an intense discussion.

"Why can't we take all our dolls with us?" Ardith pouted.

Dianne nodded sympathetically as she combed through Ardith's tangled hair. "I know it's hard to leave behind the things we love, but the load will be too heavy if we aren't wise about what we pack."

"But what about my tea set and my dolly's table?"

Dianne smiled. For all of Ardith's tomboy ways, she was still very much a little girl at heart.

Betsy nodded, adding, "And my baby's buggy. How will I take her for walks?"

Dianne worked to put her sister's hair into two even plaits as she spoke. "The wagons will be too full of other things. We have to be careful with how much we place in the wagons. Otherwise the oxen will suffer—maybe even die."

"Poor things," Betsy, ever the animal lover, bemoaned. "I don't want them to die."

Dianne nodded. "I don't either. So we'll do our part and take only a few of our treasures. At least we don't have to worry about having a houseful of furniture for when we settle at the other end. Uncle Bram should have all of that stuff."

"But I don't want to leave all my babies," Ardith said, jerking around as Dianne finished with her hair. "I'm their ma. I can't leave them behind. Who will feed them? Who will take care of my babies?"

Her impassioned plea did not fall on deaf ears. Dianne thought for a moment. "Why don't each of you take one doll and then see if one of your friends would be willing to take care of the rest of them for you. Then maybe someday we could send for them."

Ardith seemed to consider this a moment, then nodded slowly. "I guess so. Do you truly think we could send for the rest?"

"Of course," Dianne replied, imagining that once they sold the goods they'd take with them, they'd make a small fortune. Paying the postage on a shipment of dolls and their furnishings wouldn't be that costly at all.

Dianne went to work brushing out Betsy's long golden curls. It seemed a shame to braid it all up when it lay so pretty against her back. Still, there was nothing sensible about leaving it down to tangle and twist.

"How long will the trip take?" Betsy questioned. "Will it be longer than the time we visited Grandma?"

The last time they had traveled anywhere had been just after the start of the war. Their grandpa Chadwick had been sick—dying from some kind of heart failure. They had journeyed by riverboat to Memphis in order to say good-bye and wait out his passing. Not long after that, their grandma had followed her husband in death, leaving a sad void in Dianne's life. She'd always cherished her grandmother's visits.

"The trip will be much longer and harder than that," Dianne said, surprised that Betsy could remember anything about the trip. "We'll be several months trying to get to Virginia City. Idaho Territory is over a thousand miles away. Maybe closer to two thousand."

Betsy said nothing, but Ardith's eyes widened with surprise. "Months? We'll be traveling for months? Will I have my birthday on the trip?"

"Well, hopefully we'll be there before September," Dianne said, finishing Betsy's hair. "Morgan told me last night that it should only take until August at the latest."

"I'm glad," Ardith sighed. "I don't want to have my birthday in the middle of nowhere."

Dianne laughed. "I'm sure there are worse things to endure. Now come on, you two. Let's get our chores done. There's a long list of additional duties, and we need to show Mama our best faces. She's already sad about going, so we need not to worry her with our own problems."

The day passed quickly after that. Dianne and her sisters went through the neatly ordered lists Dianne had made. According to what Dianne had learned, they needed to figure at least two hundred pounds of flour and twenty-five pounds of sugar per adult, which seemed like an extraordinary amount. The list only got worse. Seventy-five pounds of bacon, ten pounds of rice, five pounds of coffee.

Well, she thought, *we can eliminate my share of the coffee. I can't abide the stuff.*

She packed and worked with the numbers until her head was spinning. By ten o'clock their mother had left for the bank and Ardith was ready for a break. Dianne had just begun to prepare her sisters some cookies and milk when the bells over the front door sounded, signaling customers.

Dianne hurriedly dished out the goodies to the girls, then rushed through the dividing curtain to meet Captain Seager. "Good morning," she said rather hesitantly. Dianne knew if her mother returned to find the man here she'd cause a scene.

"What can I do for you, Captain?"

"Is your mother in?"

"No, I'm sorry. She's out on business."

He nodded, glancing around the store. "Then it's true. She's selling the store."

Dianne had no idea how the man had learned of this, but the emptied shelves would speak for themselves. Still, she knew her mother would never allow for discussion of family business with Yankees. "Is there a message I can give her?"

He shook his head. "No, that's fine. I really only came to confirm that she was selling out. I heard you were all headed to the Idaho Territory."

Dianne felt little choice but to admit the truth. "Yes. My uncle lives there."

"I hope you'll be very happy, Miss Chadwick." He looked around the store again. "Why don't you . . . uh . . . give me a pound of peppermints. I have a bit of a sweet tooth."

Dianne hurried to do his bidding. She took his money and handed him the sack of candy, praying all the while he would leave before her mother's return. It wasn't to be.

"Dianne!" her mother called from the back room. At least she'd come in through their private entrance. Maybe Dianne could hurry Captain Seager out the front before her mother learned of his presence.

"I'll be right there!" Dianne smiled at the captain. "I'll have to bid you good day."

"That's quite all right. I'd like you to let your mother know I'm here. I'll wait."

Dianne frowned but nodded. She couldn't imagine her mother wanting anything to do with the man. "I'll tell her."

But before Dianne could reach the curtain that partitioned the storeroom from the store, her mother came into the room. "Dianne, there are still . . ." Susannah fell silent as her gaze fell upon Captain Seager. Stiffening, she nodded. "Captain."

"Ma'am, I'd heard it rumored you were selling out and leaving New Madrid. I wanted to come see for myself. Maybe offer you a bit of escort—at least for a short distance. There's been a lot of guerilla conflict of late."

"We need nothing from the Yankees," she stated flatly. "Certainly not protection from neighbors who love and respect us."

Seager seemed taken aback by her response. "Ma'am, there's a war of the worst kind going on in this state. We're facing the prospect of the battles being just as intense here in Missouri as in the East."

"And well I know it," she replied. "Why else would I take my family and flee? They might meet with the same fate as my husband, and then where would I be?"

Captain Seager glanced at Dianne as if for help. Dianne quickly bowed her head. There was no possible chance she would position herself in his defense. Not when her mother was suffering so much.

"Ma'am, I am sorry for your husband's death. He was a good man and a true friend to me."

"Please leave my store." The words were delivered with calm dismissal. Her mother wasn't generally given to losing her temper, but this might well be one of those times. Dianne stepped to her mother's side.

"Good day, Captain. Don't forget your peppermints," Dianne said, hoping he'd not make any further fuss.

Seager appeared to understand and for this Dianne breathed a sigh of relief. She watched him turn to go, glad there would be no further encounter.

"Well . . . safe travels, ma'am," he murmured and passed into the street. The bell jingled and echoed behind him, blocking out anything else he might have said.

"What was he doing here?" Mother questioned.

Dianne shrugged. "Just what he said. He'd heard we were leaving for the Idaho Territory and wanted to know if it was true. Then he bought some peppermints."

Her mother pulled off her black sunbonnet. "Gossips are everywhere. I wonder who told him." She put the hat aside and took down her apron from the hook where she'd previously left it.

"How did things go at the bank, Mother?"

"They went as well as could be expected. The Yankees are the only ones who have money enough to make it worth my while to sell. I hate dealing with them, but Mr. Danssen said it was the only way." She paused, a look of sorrow on her face. "I can't believe it will soon be gone."

"What? The store?" Dianne questioned.

"The store, your father's dreams. He chose New Madrid because it offered such hopes for growth. He was sure it would soon rival Memphis as a port on the Mississippi. Now he'll not be around to see that happen, and neither will I."

"But the boys will be safely out of harm's way," Dianne said, hoping this would help her mother put aside her sorrow.

"Yes, that's true," her mother agreed. "I know that would please your father. He couldn't abide the idea of them joining either side." She looked beyond Dianne to the door. "Have your brothers returned from Otis's farm yet?"

"No. They said they'd most likely be gone all day." Dianne put the lid back on the peppermint jar.

"I think we should go ahead and close the store," her mother said, surprising Dianne. "We'll have more time to complete our packing if we don't have to worry about customers."

"I think that's wise, Mama."

Her mother nodded and went to the door. Locking it, she turned the sign to *CLOSED* and squared her shoulders.

"You get back to work with your sisters. Oh, and pack your own things as well. I told your sisters this and now I'm telling you: take your woolen skirts. The book says they'll wear and travel better than anything else."

Her mother's ability to take charge took Dianne by surprise. She nodded, knowing it was important to let her mother do so. "How many skirts should we take?"

"I think we should pack four apiece for you and me. Most folks might think that extravagant, but I call it sensible. I don't want to be doing laundry every night. We can lay them flat under the mattress, as I plan to have a small bed in one of the wagons. I'm not of a mind to sleep outside as most folks will. The skirts will be added cushioning."

Dianne nodded and shifted uncomfortably at what she had to ask. "I don't have four black skirts, Ma."

"Well, I have no time for dyeing clothes. You and your sisters have paid your respects. It won't hurt for you to leave off with mourning. No one's going to care in the uncivilized West, and no one in the East will know."

Relief coursed through Dianne, but she said nothing. She wanted to take no chance at offending her mother. Not now.

"Take your best blouses," her mother continued. "Not your fanciest—just your best. The finer quality the material, the better. Our clothes will have to last the trip and not wear out on us before we make it through. We'll take bolts of material with us and if they don't sell, we'll have fabric for making new clothes."

"But neither of us knows much about sewing," Dianne spoke without thinking. "Just embroidery."

Her mother frowned. "Then we'll have to learn."

———————

Late that afternoon, Susannah Chadwick sat at her desk going over several lists of figures and information they needed for the trip west. She thought about the journey and what this would mean for her family. At first she'd thought the trip west to be a foolish idea, but the more Dianne reasoned with her, the more sense it made. She wasn't about to live her life in New Madrid without the protection of a man. The town had become much too dangerous, as proven by her husband's untimely death.

Yet she hated being left to make decisions and plans. Her upbringing had prepared her to run a household and manage a servant or two. Her family had never been wealthy enough to own very many slaves, but there had always been a cook, a housekeeper, and a groundsman when she was growing up. Her parents had wanted her to be a proper Southern lady, so she had never learned to cook very well or do the menial tasks their servants could do instead.

"I feel completely untrained for this venture," she murmured. Would she be able to handle the long days on the trail? Cook over an open fire? She'd learned to cook reasonably well in the last twenty years, but life in the wilds would be completely different from preparing meals on her thoroughly modern stove.

Is this the right thing to do? she asked herself, looking back to the information Dianne had gathered for her. The girl certainly had given this a great deal of thought. For someone who hated book learning, she'd done remarkably well at putting together the figures.

Taking up a pen and ink, Susannah added little notes to herself, additional items they needed that *Prairie Traveler* had not suggested. She thought of her children, trying hard to take into consideration what extra items they might require.

Morgan and Zane are happy to go, she mused. *But of course, they would be.* They had no desire to join in the war and they loved the stories told by those who'd been west to the wild lands beyond the state. *They'll need an extra pair of sturdy boots, no doubt.* She wrote their names and added boots to the list.

Then there was Dianne. She frowned at the thought of her eldest daughter. She couldn't even look at Dianne without seeing Ephraim dead in the street. It wasn't really Dianne's fault. As Trenton had said, decent folk should be able to walk the streets without armed escorts. Still, she had gone to the bank without protection and Ephraim might be alive now except for that one fact. Even Trenton—

Trenton.

She'd seen nothing of him at all that day. She needed to talk to him now that he'd had time to calm down. She needed to make him understand that she appreciated his desire to see justice done for his father, but she also needed him to realize it wouldn't be had in violence.

Tucking her papers into her apron pocket, Susannah climbed the stairs to the boys' shared room. She noted with satisfaction that each of the three beds had been made. She'd allow for nothing less and her boys knew the penalties for messiness.

Going to Trenton's corner of the room, Susannah felt something akin to fear overcome her. She opened the trunk at the foot of the bed and found it nearly empty. Going to his bed, she raised the covers on the side to peer under the frame. His rifle was gone—so, too, his revolver.

She dropped her hold on the covers and whirled around to sit down. "He's gone." She felt tears well up but refused to cry. *How could he do this to us? How could he desert us when I told him what it would cost him?*

Dianne peered into her cedar chest. She'd been storing household items here ever since her father and mother had given her the box on her thirteenth birthday. They'd said she was to save doilies and embroidered pieces of work for her own home some day, but Dianne had never worried overmuch about such things. She had received several pieces when Grandma Chadwick passed on, but they were more sweet reminders than useful household goods.

Taking Trent's letter from her pocket, Dianne reached up to her dressing table and pulled down a dried flower. The pressed blossom was from her father's funeral. Gently stroking the petals, she felt tears come to her eyes. Trent's leaving and her father's death . . . both were her fault. She placed the flower in the folds of Trent's letter and tucked it deep into the chest. There was no time for mourning now. She had far too much work to do. Dianne was determined to make her mother as happy as possible, and if that meant working her fingers to the bone, then that was how it would be.

"I'll drive oxen, cook and wash over a campfire, sleep on the ground—whatever it takes," she murmured, packing her blouses atop her memory pieces. She added undergarments, stockings, and a pair of satin dancing shoes she'd worn the first time she'd danced with Sally's brother Robbie.

"Whatever has to be done," she told herself aloud, "I must have the strength to do. If I work hard enough—if I give more than the others, then maybe, just maybe, Mama will forgive me."

"I'm so glad you stopped by before we left," Dianne told her friends Ramona, Sally, and Ruthanne, who had come to bid her farewell. They'd also come bearing gifts.

"Mama said I could give you this," Sally told Dianne. It was a small collection of *Godey's Lady's Book* magazines from 1859. "I know they're out of date, but since the war, Ma's had a hard time getting any kind of publication from back East."

"Oh, Sally, that's so sweet," Dianne said as she leafed through the first one. "Why, it shows how to knit these sweet little stockings."

"It has all sorts of wonderful stories and such too. There are fashion designs, patterns to crochet and embroider. . . . It even tells you how to set a proper table. You'll be out there in the middle of the wilderness and . . . well, you might forget."

Dianne laughed and closed the magazine. "Indeed, I might very well take to eating with my fingers."

Sally frowned. "Don't think me so ignorant that I would believe that of you."

Dianne gently touched her friend's arm. "I'm sorry. I truly wasn't meaning to suggest that. I'm so very touched that you'd share these with me." And honestly, she was touched. Sally lived for her copies of *Godey's*. Many an afternoon had been spent at Sally's, wiling away the hours poring through the pages.

"I brought you this," Ramona said, handing Dianne a small metal box.

Dianne opened the box to reveal sheets of writing paper and envelopes. "Oh, Ramona, this is a treasure to be sure. I'll write to all of you using this." She glanced up to meet their gazes. "I don't know how often I'll be able to write, but just know that I will as time allows."

They nodded somberly. Dianne felt an aching deep in her heart. What would she do without them to talk to? How would she ever abide the long, perilous trip across the plains without them to encourage her and bolster her spirits?

"This is from me," Ruthanne said, pushing a small cloth bundle into Dianne's hands.

Dianne unrolled the material to reveal a small wooden cross. "My pa carved it for me, but I told him you were leaving and that I wanted to give you something to remember me by. He said I could give this to you and he'd make me another one."

Dianne smiled. "I'll cherish it always." She put her things aside and reached out to embrace the three girls. "I'll miss you all more than I can say." The awkward hug ended to reveal them all in tears.

"I wish you didn't have to go," Ramona said softly. "I'll miss you so much."

"You'll miss Morgan just as much, I'll wager," Dianne said, trying to keep the situation from growing too maudlin. The girls giggled even as tears streamed down their faces.

"We're a sorry lot," Sally said, taking up a dainty handkerchief. "Just look at us. Our faces will be all red and splotchy."

"It doesn't matter," Dianne said. She studied the face of each girl, memorizing her features. How would she ever manage to say good-bye?

"I have some things for each of you," Dianne continued, trying to regain her composure. "You know we can't take many of our possessions, so I'm forced to leave them behind." She went to her wardrobe and opened the doors. "I want you to share what's left in here. The party gowns, the slippers, and such."

The girls were instantly animated with oohs and aahs over the bounty. While they shared the wealth among them, Dianne went to her vanity and opened a drawer. "I also have a special gift for each of you." She took up three small parcels wrapped in brown paper and brought them to her friends. "I wanted you to have something special to remember me by."

Sally was first to reach for the gift. She opened it even as Ramona and Ruthanne took their packages in hand. "Oh, it's beautiful." She held up a necklace—a delicate gold chain with a small heart hanging from the end. Ramona and Ruthanne found exact replicas in their packages.

"This must have cost you a fortune," Ruthanne exclaimed.

Dianne shook her head. "There are benefits to being a shopkeeper's daughter." She didn't bother to tell them her mother had found the entire lot tucked inside a box of useless bits of bric-a-brac. Dianne had declared an interest and her mother had shrugged and tossed the entire collection to her. It seemed preordained, as there were three necklaces of the same style and gold color.

"Now you'll each have something to remember me by, and I shall have these little treasures from you. I feel like the richest girl in the world."

"My father says your family is pert near the richest in these parts. If your pa hadn't made friends with the Yankees, like mine did, we'd probably all be poor as church mice."

Dianne knew that was most likely true. It was one of the reasons some people hated her family. They'd never understood her father's desire to work with, instead of against, the Yankees. Truth be told, Dianne wasn't at all sure she understood it either. She didn't understand much at all about the war. She'd read about slavery issues and such, but among her own people, no one owned slaves. At least not anymore, and when her mother talked of the servants her family had owned when she was young, they always sounded like extended family rather than slaves.

There were a bevy of other issues, like state's rights and taxation problems, but Dianne's father had never spoken much about such things with his womenfolk, and Dianne had never had the mind for such matters. And now with the move west, she supposed she wouldn't have to worry about it. Her uncle's letters assured her there was very little focus on war issues in the Idaho Territory.

"Promise me you'll never forget me," Dianne said, turning to her friends once again.

"Of course we promise," Ramona said, looking to each of her companions. "Don't we, girls?"

"Of course," they replied in unison.

Dianne nodded. "I know I shall never forget you for as long as I live. I don't know if we'll ever meet again, but if I can have one wish, that is it. I wish for us to be together again—friends forever."

The girls all clasped their hands together. "Friends forever," they pledged.

CHAPTER 3

A BRILLIANT LEMON SUN PUSHED STEADILY ACROSS THE SKY, BRING-ing spring warmth to the city of St. Louis. Susannah Chadwick hated St. Louis almost as much as she'd grown to despise New Madrid. The Yankees were in control here, and only yesterday she'd watched as they'd executed a Confederate soldier. There seemed to be no real trial or understanding of his punishment—just a systematic eradication of "vermin," as the nearby Yankee commander had told her.

Seeing the townspeople around her, Susannah wondered if they'd grown callous to such happenings. No one seemed eager to protest or raise a single claim in the man's defense. She was later told by the hotel owner that Confederates were executed almost daily—often led out of town on worn-out old horses and taunted to try and run for their freedom. The game was more cruel and heartless than Susannah could have ever imagined.

These images served their purpose, however. They solidified her resolve to leave the war and all its problems. She cared little for the plight of the black man. She cared nothing at all about the tariffs and political intrigues between the North and South. She wanted only for a chance to see her boys raised into men—to have them marry and produce families of their own. Dead men could do neither.

With all of these thoughts and images weighing heavy on her heart, Susannah cautiously slipped away from the hotel and made her way through the streets of St. Louis in order to finish her shopping. There were an amazing number of last-minute purchases to be made, especially in light of the news the doctor had given her yesterday. She was pregnant.

The very thought startled, frustrated, and delighted her all at the same time. It was completely unexpected and almost more than she could comprehend. Betsy was six and Susannah had been confident there would be no more children for her and Ephraim. In fact, even in seeing the doctor she had been confident he would tell her it was merely her change of life. Which, although early, would have been appropriate, given all the other changes she was making.

This baby added an entirely new aspect to life. It gave her new strength and resolve. Ephraim was gone, she couldn't change that, but a piece of him was growing anew within her. She would prove herself worthy of such responsibility. Susannah started her shopping knowing she would have to lay in a supply of white flannel and knitting materials for baby things. She'd have to see if she could buy a pattern or else find a ready-made gown that they could tear apart and trace. Susannah wasn't all that clever with a needle, but she'd do what was needed.

She browsed the aisles of one store, still contemplating the reality of her pregnancy. She certainly couldn't tell anyone. Daniel Keefer, the wagon master Dianne had signed them on with, would no doubt turn their application away should he learn of her condition. From what Dianne had showed her in a letter from Keefer, he was apprehensive enough about taking on a widowed mother, despite the fact she had three boys who could do the heavy work.

Of course, when Dianne had written the letter on her mother's behalf, she had believed Trenton would change his mind about accompanying them west. Susannah hoped the issue of Trent's absence wouldn't come up until long after they began their journey. Just as she hoped the issue of her pregnancy wouldn't come up until it was too late to turn her back.

Given that the baby wasn't due until December, Susannah felt there was no need to inform Mr. Keefer. They were assured they would reach the Idaho Territory before August ended. That would give her plenty of time. By the time she started showing, they would be in the middle of the prairie wilderness. Surely then Mr. Keefer would just have to allow for it. Besides, women of proper upbringing simply didn't discuss such matters with gentlemen. Mr. Keefer would just have to understand.

She toyed with some wool yarn dyed a pale yellow. The color pleased her senses, and she picked up several skeins and placed them in her basket. If any of the children asked, she'd just say that she intended to make a shawl.

That thought brought her to the idea of keeping the pregnancy from the children. She couldn't very well tell them without risking their accidental announcement to other people. Betsy could never keep anything secret; in fact, she had told everyone she'd encountered that her family was headed to Virginia. This in turn prompted Susannah to explain they were heading for Virginia City, in the Idaho Territory, and not the war-ridden state of the Southern Confederacy.

Betsy's excitement over their adventure west had no doubt filled her head with wild imaginings. She told people about Indians and about the dog they would have when the trip concluded. Most of the matrons laughed with amusement at the child, while men seemed to catch her animation and questioned Susannah about the gold possibilities and whether her brother had struck it rich.

"Can I help you with anything here?" a stern-faced older woman questioned.

The voice brought Susannah back into the present and she nodded. "I'd like to buy a bolt of white flannel. I'll also take a bolt of the white cotton and two bolts of the brown wool."

"You must be going to sew up a storm," the woman commented.

"We're heading west. I have a large inventory of goods and want to add this to it." Susannah caught sight of several sunbonnets and motioned. "I think I'd better have a look at some of those. I was sold out and couldn't get any more before coming to St. Louis."

The woman quickly complied. "These are the best," she told Susannah. "With the longer untrimmed brims you'll keep more sun off your face and not have to worry about the edging going bad or getting torn. And with the bavolet, your neck won't get burned. A lot of women forget about protecting their necks."

Susannah looked the pieces over and nodded. "I'll take these four. By the way, do you have anything that would fit younger girls? I have two daughters, six and ten, who would never be able to keep these on."

"I do have some. Wait right here." The woman disappeared into the back, and Susannah took the opportunity to continue her perusal. Nothing else struck her fancy, however. There were far too many trinkets designed for the happily settled homeowner. They would be nothing but burdensome for the long trip to Virginia City. Besides, as Bram had pointed out long ago, the territory was ninety-nine percent men. Of course, that had probably changed by now with the gold rush and all, but men would still outnumber the women, and men had no use for fancy doodads.

No, Dianne had been right. With men, food would matter more. Food and tools, even livestock, which was why Susannah was determined to focus her attention on those things more than others. They had one whole wagon loaded with mostly food—canned, bagged, and crated. Another wagon had tools—mining tools, farming tools—as well as heavy-duty clothing and boots. Wagon repair items, as well as spare harnesses and animal feed, topped off the freight. That left the third wagon for most of their personal things. How very small that wagon seemed once they'd loaded it with their belongings.

It's a different life from what we've known, she mused. Returning to the counter to wait for the storekeeper, Susannah couldn't help but wonder if she'd made the right choice. *We truly know nothing about what we're doing. We're unprepared for even the everyday needs of travel—cooking, cleaning, doctoring. We're worse off still when it comes to animals and their care.*

"Here we are," the woman announced. She held up two children's bonnets—one a red calico and one a brown solid. "This one," she said, thrusting the brown one forward, "should fit the younger girl just fine."

Susannah looked the piece over, noting the quilted brim. "Fine work. I'll take them both."

She made arrangements for the boys to pick up the cloth and made her way back to the hotel with the bonnets. She and Daniel Keefer were to meet in the lobby in just five minutes; already the day was getting away from her.

Coming through the hotel doorway, Susannah immediately spotted two men sitting to one side. Both appeared neat and orderly. Their trousers showed no signs of dirt and their faces were clean-shaven, with exception to the older man's mustache. They both rose as she neared. "Are one of you Mr. Keefer?" she questioned.

With a smile that lifted the corners of his mustache, the older man nodded. "And you'd be Mrs. Chadwick, I presume."

"Yes. I hope I'm not late for our meeting."

"Not at all. By the way," he said, motioning to the younger man, "this tall drink of water is Cole Selby. He's going to be my right-hand man on the train. Cole will inspect your wagons after we speak and make sure you have the proper provisions for the trip."

Susannah nodded. "Pleased to meet you."

"Ma'am." Cole barely looked her in the eye.

Susannah gave it no further consideration. Her own boys could be quite shy around strangers. "I read *The Prairie Traveler*," Susannah spoke. "I've studied it since deciding to move west."

"There's good information in that book, but there are also a lot of things you can't really know except for experiencing them yourself," Daniel replied. "I need you to keep this list of rules and study them up." He handed her a piece of paper. "It's important that your children know the rules as well. They'll help to make things run smoothly and to keep folks alive."

Susannah glanced down at the list for a moment, then returned her gaze to Daniel Keefer. He seemed like a dependable sort. He had an honest face, weathered and tanned from his life out under the sun. "I'll make sure the children understand."

"Most every rule on that list will be to your benefit. Curfews are established to make certain everyone is well rested. Can't be having a bunch of rowdies staying up all night keepin' other folks awake. Rules for how to treat the animals and where to arrange for them at night are for the sake of safety and order. Once we're on the trail, you'll see for yourself just how smooth things can run." He shifted and grinned. "Of course, these rules help when things aren't running as smooth too. Folks being folks—it's always hard to have some three or four hundred people with one goal in mind and not have someone wanting to do things their own way."

"I see you have a rule about alcohol consumption," Susannah said, noting her list again. "I'm glad to see that. I suppose, however, liquor for medicinal purposes is allowed?"

"Absolutely. I just can't be having my men drunk when there's a very real possibility of Indian attack."

"Is it truly that dangerous?" Susannah hugged herself to refrain from shuddering.

"It is indeed. There are a dozen or more tribes between here and Virginia City, and at any given time they can all be on the warpath. Pawnees, Crow, Cheyenne, and Sioux have all been giving us grief from time to time. They resent the whites taking over their hunting lands and killing off the game. They don't care how many people they have to kill—they just want us gone. Bringing a wagon train full of folks is just the same as insulting them—it wounds their pride."

"And causes them to retaliate," Susannah said, imagining the horror of watching her children die at the hands of such savages.

"It's just something to consider, ma'am," Keefer continued. "With the large number of wagons and families, I'm figuring we'll be fine. And things bein' what they are, you'll probably have more complaints with your fellow travelers than with the Indians. Now, if you don't mind, I need to have Cole check your wagons and gear. Can you advise him as to where you've liveried your animals and wagons?"

"Of course. We're just down the road at the Smith Brothers Livery."

Cole nodded. "I know where that's at. I'll get to it right away." He nodded to Susannah. "Ma'am."

Susannah waited until he'd gone before turning her attention back to the wagon master. "I'm sure he'll find everything in order, but please send me a message if anything is amiss. I tried to adhere to the book. I didn't want to make the ox teams work too hard. I mean to get to Virginia City in good condition, Mr. Keefer." And she did. Never before had she been more determined to accomplish anything.

He nodded. "I can appreciate that, Mrs. Chadwick. I think you'll do just fine. I don't generally allow widowed woman on my trains, but since you have three strapping boys to help, I'm sure you'll be all right." He started for the door, then turned abruptly. "I almost forgot. We'll leave for Independence day after tomorrow."

Susannah said nothing about his mistaken idea that three of her sons would accompany them. Let him suppose that was how it would be. Hopefully he'd be too busy to learn the truth of it until they were far enough west that he couldn't refuse them. She put her hand tenderly to her stomach. *Same for this matter. No one needs to know about the baby until it's too late to do anything else about it.*

———

Dianne looked at her brothers in sheer disbelief. "You really expect me to milk the cows? I don't know anything about it."

"That's why we're taking you down to the livery. You need to learn and quick. Milking is women's work," Zane told her with an air of authority.

Morgan nodded and added, "It's real simple, Dianne. Otis showed us how. It was kind of hard at first, because we had it all wrong in our minds. We figured you just pumped the teat up and down and the milk came out, but that's not the case. You have to kind of squeeze and roll your hand down, all at the same time."

Dianne frowned. "It doesn't sound all that simple to me. I've never been up close to those beasts—you know that." She stopped on the boardwalk, refusing to go any farther. "What if they decide to step on me?"

Morgan shrugged and Zane gazed heavenward as if completely

exasperated. "Just come on," Morgan encouraged. "If I can do it, you can."

Dianne wasn't convinced and as they made their way to the expansive livery stables of the Smith brothers, she felt even less confident that her brothers were right.

"Our stock is at the far end. We have the milk cows, the oxen, and the horses here. The chickens are kept elsewhere. The cows have to be milked twice a day. Once in early morning and once in the evening," Zane instructed as they moved toward the end of the stable.

"Are those our wagons?" Dianne asked, pointing to an open area opposite the stalls.

"Sure are," Morgan replied. "Ma paid extra to have them kept here. She thought they'd be safe from riffraff."

Dianne paused for a moment and looked at the wagons with a sense of disbelief. "Doesn't it seem strange to have our entire household packed up in those?"

"I think it's a good thing to be rid of so much stuff," Zane said. "I don't mind at all that we're starting over. I've always wanted to go west."

"But won't you miss having a table to sit down to for supper?" she questioned, looking first to Zane and then to Morgan. "Won't you miss having an indoor bathroom and a pump right in your kitchen? We'll have to haul water from rivers and creeks on the trip—it won't be easy."

Morgan laughed. "Doesn't matter how easy it is. It's going to be an adventure and a heap of fun. You girls might miss your fancy duds and conveniences, but I'd trade them all for a chance to explore where no white man has ever stepped."

Dianne went to the stall where the horses were kept. The mare she'd taken as her own moved toward the gate. No doubt she hoped for a treat, as Dianne had spoiled her over the last few days as they had become acquainted with each other.

"Sweet Dolly," Dianne said as she rubbed the buckskin's black mane.

"Come on, you can spend time with your horse later. We're supposed to teach you how to milk," Zane protested.

Dianne stepped over to the pen where the cows were nervously bunched together. Morgan grabbed a rope and fashioned a loop. Without any qualms about his task, he stepped into the stall. The cows moved away from him, as if uncertain as to whether he meant to do them harm. Dianne and Zane watched as Morgan easily laid the rope over the nearest cow's head and tightened the loop down.

"Zane, you open the gate real easy-like and keep the others back."

Zane did as instructed while Dianne moved to stand behind him, almost frightened of what might happen. What if the other cows decided to rush toward the opening? Would Zane be able to stop them from escaping? How in the world would she ever be able to do this task on her own?

Morgan moved out with the cow and walked her around to the far side of the stall. Roping her to the fence, Morgan threw a few handfuls of hay into a feeding trough and waited until the cow settled into eating.

"I'm not exactly sure how this will work on the trail, but I figure to ask around and see what other folks do to handle this." He reached around and took hold of a bucket and three-legged stool. "These both belong to us. I had Ma buy them yesterday. Up until today, Mr. Smith has been having a couple of the locals take care of the milking, but since we're set to leave day after tomorrow, I figure we'd better show you how it's done." He put the bucket down beside him, then placed the stool in position.

"If you touch her like this," he said, running his hand alongside the cow as he lowered himself to sit, "she knows where you are and doesn't get so nervous." He pulled the bucket under her udders and reached to take hold of two teats.

Dianne came around to better see what Morgan was doing. "Does it hurt her?" She couldn't bear to think that she might cause the animal pain.

"Nah. In fact, Mr. Smith says it hurts 'em if they aren't milked." The swishing sound of milk hitting the pail sounded almost melodic.

Dianne smiled. "She doesn't seem to mind it too much."

Morgan continued milking. "I told you."

Zane joined them. "Better have Dianne give it a try or she'll never learn just standing here jawing."

Morgan nodded. "You ready?"

"I don't know; it seems . . ."

"You'll do just fine," Morgan said, moving the bucket. He smiled up at his sister. "You always need to mind the pail—cows have a penchant for knocking it over."

Dianne swallowed the lump in her throat as Morgan moved aside and motioned for her to take his place. She went closer to the beast and gently touched her rump. The cow hardly seemed to notice. Dianne waited for a moment, just petting the animal with long smooth strokes.

"Work won't get done that way," Zane teased.

Dianne lowered herself to the stool and moved the bucket under the udders as she'd seen Morgan do. "Now what?"

"Take hold of her and squeeze and pull at the same time," Morgan told her. "You'll get the hang of it after a few tries."

At first nothing happened. Dianne squeezed as hard as she could but only a dribble of white liquid showed. She looked up to Morgan and Zane, feeling stupid and helpless. Morgan leaned down and took hold of her hand.

"Like this." He squeezed her hand and pulled down at the same time. The action caused a stream of milk to squirt out against the pail.

Dianne gave a tiny squeal, causing the cow to shift nervously.

Morgan laughed and admonished her, "You need to stay calm." He stood back up. "Now try again."

Dianne did and found complete success. "I see," she murmured. She milked the cow for several minutes, enjoying the rhythmic sound of the liquid as it hit the pail. Glancing up to smile at her brothers, Dianne caught sight of someone rummaging around one of their wagons. "What's he doing?" she questioned, forgetting the cow, the pail, and the milking. She jumped to her feet abruptly, causing the cow to skitter away, knocking the pail of milk over as she did.

"Oh, bother," Dianne said, noting the mess. Her brothers had both turned to see what had caused Dianne's alarm.

"You stay here," Morgan said softly. "He might be a thief."

Dianne felt her heart skip a beat as Morgan and Zane moved toward the wagons.

"What do you think you're doing?" Morgan called out in a gruff voice that sounded much deeper than his usual.

The man, who was crouching to inspect the undercarriage of the wagon, turned with an annoyed look on his face. "What does it look like I'm doing?"

"Looks like you're messing around where you have no business. Those are our wagons," Zane announced.

Dianne disregarded Morgan's instruction and came up beside Zane. She watched, somewhat amazed, as the man rose to his full height. He had to be at least six foot four, maybe even taller. But his height wasn't nearly as intimidating as his dark-eyed stare. She cowered and pulled behind Zane, wishing she'd heeded Morgan.

"I'm Cole Selby. I'm working with Daniel Keefer, your wagon master. I have to inspect the wagons to make certain they're in good working order and that the loads aren't too heavy or packed too loosely. Now, if you'll leave me to do my business . . ." He let the words trail off as he crouched down again.

"Anybody could say they were with the wagon master. We have no way of knowing the truth of it, mister. At least not until we talk to someone who knows you."

Mr. Selby didn't even look up at this. "Go ask the Smith brothers if you have any doubt. They can vouch for me."

Dianne saw Morgan and Zane exchange a glance as if questioning whether they should do this. They were saved having to make a decision, however, when Jeb Smith came walking toward them.

"Mr. Smith," Morgan greeted, stepping toward the older man. "This man claims to be working with our wagon master. He says he's supposed to inspect the wagons—is that true?"

Dianne watched the white-haired man for any expression that might suggest Mr. Cole Selby was a liar. Instead, he smiled. "Sure it's the truth. That's Cole Selby. He'll be looking your animals over too."

They all looked back at Selby, who seemed completely undaunted by their concerns. "I told 'em that, Jeb, but you know children. They'll fuss and fret."

Dianne watched her brothers stiffen. They would be eighteen come June, and she knew they considered themselves every bit a man as Selby.

Jeb Smith chuckled. "You folks don't have a thing to worry about. Cole is one of the best judges of horseflesh I've seen in these parts. Seems to have a natural way with it. He's good with the rest of the livestock too. You can put your faith in him."

"I'd just as soon keep my faith in myself," Morgan muttered under his breath.

At this Cole rose once again. He walked around the wagon, stopping not a foot away. Dianne felt her breath catch at the intensity of his stare.

"You'd do better to put your faith in those animals," Cole said dryly. "They'll be a whole lot more durable and reliable after a week on the trail than either of you—or the girl."

Dianne bristled at this. She was slow to get her anger up, but this man was just plain rude. "Come on, Morgan. Tell me more about milking," she said, reaching out to take hold of her brother. "You too, Zane. I'm sure to need you both."

Selby sent the briefest glance her way, and Dianne felt a chill up her spine. There was something about this man that suggested he was not at all happy—not with them . . . or with life.

CHAPTER 4

TRENTON CHADWICK PULLED THE COLLAR OF HIS COAT UP AND watched the torrent of cold rain as it pounded the Mississippi just up the river from New Madrid. The shack he shared with the Wilson gang, a group of Confederate guerillas, seemed poor shelter from the raging storm.

Lightning flashed, illuminating the river for just a moment. Trenton worried that a flood might ensue if the rains didn't stop soon. The plank-board cabin was sure to be engulfed if that happened; they weren't positioned but about twenty feet off the river. Thunder boomed, rattling the only window in the crudely made shelter. Trenton shook his head. Maybe they wouldn't have to wait to be flooded out—the lightning might well do its own damage.

The tiny porch on which Trenton took cover was of little protection. The wind blew the rain up and under the overhang, pelting his face. Still, being rain-soaked and cold beat having to deal with the drunken stupor of Jerry Wilson, leader of the gang of cutthroats.

Trenton had only teamed up with the men at the insistence of his best friend, Robbie Danssen. Robbie knew Jerry's younger brother, Sam, and had promised Trenton the men were as bent on revenge against the North as anyone around. Trenton wasn't sure his choice had been wise, however. Jerry Wilson had such a temper that he was likely to see someone killed just for looking at him the wrong way. Sam Wilson was so jealous of his older brother's power with the gang that he spent most of his time picking fights with his sibling. Within the last week alone, Trenton had witnessed three brawls, two of which ended with knives being pulled. The brothers were not of a peaceful nature, to be sure.

The rest of the gang was no better. Gustaf Johnson, or "the Swede," as they all called him, was a twenty-six-year-old silent type who knew his way around explosives. Having come west when the war started up, the Swede was from a mining family in Pennsylvania. Trenton didn't know what to make of the big man. He seemed reserved and cautious most of the time, but Trenton had seen him nearly strangle a man to death for pouring him a short glass of whiskey when he'd paid for a tall.

Then there was Mark Wiley. He was a hot-tempered gunman who had already earned a bad reputation by the time he was sixteen. Texas-born, Wiley was wanted in two states—his homeland and Louisiana. It was said he had killed as many as twenty men, and Trent could believe it. Just two days past when he'd gone with the Wilsons on a raid for horses and saddles, Trenton had seen Wiley put bullets into three different farmers without so much as a remorseful expression. There'd been no reason to gun down the men, but Wiley seemed to find it entertaining.

What have I gotten myself into? Trenton couldn't help but wonder. The storm of confusion within him was ten times worse than the raging storm about him. *All I want to do is avenge Pa's death. I just want to show the Yankees that they can't treat people that way and not expect retaliation.* Although he couldn't be sure, Trent felt confident that it had been a Yankee bullet that had killed his father. Robbie felt confident too. His father had heard talk. Still, there was some concern—some doubt. Trenton clenched his hands into fists. *I can't worry about it one way or another. This is my way of honoring Pa.*

"Not that I honored him that much when he was alive," Trenton muttered. But revenge for his father was a far cry from killing helpless old men whose only fault was being in the wrong place at the wrong time.

Trenton stood, then walked to the edge of the porch. He'd had a poor relationship with his father—especially after the War Between the States started. With the Union takeover of New Madrid, Trenton's respect for his father had shrunk each day. He had watched his father do business with the Yankees as if nothing had ever happened. He had heard his mother weeping late into the night and knew it was because her loyalties were torn. Little by little the war had taken its toll on Trenton's family.

His thoughts turned to Dianne. They'd always been close. Some of his friends couldn't understand this, but then, they hadn't grown up in the Chadwick household. Trenton had never been close to his parents and always felt like the odd man out with his brothers. As twins, Zane and Morgan always held more interest in each other than in him. He could remember working hard to pit them against each other when they'd been younger, but it never lasted long. Zane might come over to Trenton's way of thinking for a time, but in the end, he would return to Morgan for companionship.

He knew that Dianne understood this as well. She didn't fit in with the twins because she was a girl, first and foremost. She also didn't appeal to Zane and Morgan because she was younger. But Trenton hadn't cared—her company made life bearable. They talked, unlike many siblings he knew.

As if on cue, Sam Wilson hurled a string of obscenities at his brother as he came stalking out the front door. "A body oughtn't to have to tend to horses in this kind of weather," the small man grumbled, looking at Trenton as he stepped off the porch into the rain.

Trenton said nothing. It was best that way.

The storm appeared to be moving off to the east, but the rain showed no signs of letting up. Trenton went back to his chair and his thoughts of Dianne. She was his one real regret in leaving home. He wanted very much to protect her from the evils of the world. Dianne had the potential to marry well and make something of herself. Maybe that was why he didn't see sense in the family moving west. Dianne would have no chance to meet up with decent men in Indian country. Trenton was confident of this point.

"What are you doing out here in the dark?" Robbie Danssen asked as he stepped outside.

"I was tired of the bickering," Trenton told his friend. "Those two fight more than anybody I've ever seen."

Robbie laughed and took a seat on the chair next to Trenton's. "Yeah, that's for sure. They'll probably end up killing each other after they finish off the Yankees."

"I hope you know what you're doing, getting us involved with them," Trenton continued. The gang had plans to blow up a Union supply house the following night. "I'm not entirely comfortable with this, you know."

Robbie lowered his voice. "You don't want them hearing you talk like that. You know how Jerry is about things. He won't like it one bit if he thinks your loyalty is in question."

"It isn't my loyalty that's in question. It's his temper and nonsense with Sam. If they can't stop fighting long enough to spend a quiet evening together, what's going to keep them from jeopardizing our mission?"

"Money. That's the only thing Jerry cares about," Robbie replied. "That and the fact that he's as short as a stump. He can't do anything about his height, though, so he'll rob his way to happiness."

"He's going to get one of us killed if he's not careful. Fighting with Sam is no way to build my confidence in his leadership ability."

Robbie snorted a laugh. "I don't much imagine Jerry cares whether we have confidence in his leadership ability or not. He'd just as soon shoot his own brother as look at him—I doubt seriously he has any great affection for us."

"I suppose you're right."

They sat in silence for several moments until Sam Wilson came stomping back, still cussing and as mad as when he'd left only moments before.

"Now I'm wet clear through and cold as a dog left out on Christmas morning." He ignored Trenton and Robbie and threw open the door, letting out another string of curses. "Jerry, I'm tellin' you, I ain't going out again tonight, so don't even think of bossin' me around or I'll take my knife and——" He slammed the door behind him, muting the words.

"I sure could use a drink," Robbie said, ignoring Sam. "Too bad it's raining. We could ride into town and settle in for a night of fun."

"You know I don't go to saloons," Trenton replied. "My ma would ride all the way back from the Idaho Territory just to box my ears if she thought I was drinking."

"No doubt she'd highly approve of your joining up with Jerry's gang," Robbie said sarcastically. "You're a man now, Trent. Your mama ain't got any say over you now."

Trenton knew the truth of it, but still he hated that they'd all parted on such bad terms. "I know that's true," he said softly, "but I still respect some of my upbringing."

"Why? I remember my ma and pa dragging me to Sunday school to learn the Golden Rule. Then I watched all the rest of the week while folks tried to cheat my pa and my pa tried to cheat them. I don't see much good in any of it. Why respect a man who ain't never showed respect to anyone or anything—unless you count the bank."

"I miss Dianne. She always seemed like the voice of reason."

"I miss Dianne too. But not like you," Robbie said, laughing. "She was growin' into a right fetchin' young woman. I kind of thought we might end up together."

Trenton laughed at this. "Dianne is too good for the likes of you."

Robbie snorted again. "You're probably right about that. Especially given our habits of late. Neither one of us is fit to polish her boots."

That thought weighed heavier on Trenton than anything else Robbie could have said. What would Dianne say if she saw him now? No doubt she'd be horribly disappointed in him. She wouldn't approve of his choices, even if it was to honor their father's death.

Most likely, she'd ask him too many questions and make him think. Questions like, "When will you know you've done enough to avenge

Pa?" and "How can killing another man or taking what's rightfully his make Pa's death right?" Trenton always ended up thinking too much when he talked his problems through with Dianne.

"Robbie, are you sure about what your pa heard? I mean, thinking the Yankees are the ones who killed Pa."

"He said he talked to Captain Seager and he said your pa stepped out in front of Corporal Johnson's gun. I think that's pretty good evidence."

"But we can't be sure."

"I suppose not," Robbie said with a shrug. "But does it matter? I mean, you hate what the Yankees have done to the town same as me."

"Yeah, but I wasn't for the Union being destroyed. I can't say I honestly support either side."

"So don't join a side. I'm not planning on favoring anybody but myself."

They fell silent for several minutes before Robbie spoke again.

"Do you think you'll ever see 'em again?"

Robbie's question brought Trenton back to the moment. The rain had lessened and the thunder now rumbled off in the distance. "Who?" Trenton asked.

"Your ma and sisters. Morgan and Zane."

Trenton crossed his legs and toyed with the sole of his boot. "I don't know. There's a part of me that wants to join up with them when I get the chance. I feel bad for sending Ma off west without my help. Pa would never have liked that. Still, once Dianne made it clear they needed to move quickly, she wouldn't listen to reason and wait awhile. It was like Ma suddenly had a job to do."

"My pa said she was afraid you and your brothers would join up to fight the war."

"Yeah, I know she was worried about that. With things the way they are, the Yankees were always pestering my pa to put us boys into service. Pa wouldn't hear of it, and I guess I'm kind of glad for that. Everyone else was joining up, splitting into sides. Folks are never so mad at one another as when they're discussing politics and war."

"I know. My pa made a deal with the Union commander. I don't know for sure what transpired, but I knew I wouldn't have to worry about going to war. I think he paid him off."

Trenton smiled at his less educated friend. Robbie had infuriated his parents by refusing to continue his education after the tenth grade, and he still refused to be educated about the world. "You can pay three hundred dollars and send a substitute. Your pa probably found someone to go in your place. My pa didn't have to worry yet, 'cause the draft starts at twenty and I'm just nineteen. 'Course if I wanted to fight in the war I'd be wearing a Confederate uniform already. They take boys at seventeen now, you know."

"Still, it's right here in our own backyard."

"There haven't been any major problems since this time last year," Trenton threw out. "I doubt there'll be much interest here in Missouri. So long as the Union can get up and down the Mississippi, I doubt they'll pay much attention to us."

"That's not the way my pa hears it told. He believes there are major battles planned for this area within the year. Lincoln just gave over command of the troops to General Grant and Pa thinks that's signaling a change. Things have been quiet for a while, but that's probably just so they can build their forces. After they do, Pa says the Union will just make a clean sweep of things and crush the South. He thinks they'll come here in even bigger numbers because of all the guerilla activity."

Trenton didn't like the sound of that. He didn't like anything at all associated with the war, but he especially didn't like thinking the war might come their way in full force. "Then I guess it's a good thing we're planning to blow up that supply house tomorrow night instead of next month."

Robbie got to his feet and walked to the edge of the porch. "It's always a good time to blow up Yankees. I just hope there's a whole bunch of 'em that go up with the building. I want them to hear us loud and clear."

"I'm sure they will," Trenton murmured. The cold permeated his body to the very core. No doubt his friend's words didn't help. Robbie and the other members of the gang were intent on killing, just as if they had joined the ranks of a private army. Taking a life wasn't really what Trenton had planned when he spoke of avenging his father. He had only meant to make life miserable for the Yankees. Make them as uncomfortable and unhappy as possible, then see them retreat back to the North and leave Missouri for good. Now, listening to Robbie, he felt naïve and stupid. This group of cutthroats wouldn't be happy with merely wreaking havoc on the Union. They wanted blood. And if Trenton wasn't careful, his own blood would be spilled in the process.

CHAPTER 5

THE WAGON TRAIN LEFT ST. LOUIS IN A MISTY SPRING RAIN, SOME-thing Dianne thought rather quaint and almost fitting. At least for the first few miles. After that, the mist turned into a steady rain that drenched everyone in misery.

Betsy and Ardith rode with their mother in the wagon while Dianne struggled to keep her footing and guide the oxen. She followed behind Morgan's wagon, watching constantly for any sign of complications. Twice they forded small shallow streams, and Dianne's discomfort was complete as her leather boots became soggy with water.

The next day was somewhat better, although Dianne learned an important lesson about campfires. While her brothers tended the milk cows for her, Dianne worked to assemble some breakfast. Their mother lay in the wagon, sick with a stomach complaint, so Dianne made her first real attempt at cooking.

Taking the bacon, as she'd often seen her mother do, Dianne posi-tioned it in the cast-iron skillet and balanced the pan on some stones Zane had arranged for her at the fire's edge. Feeling rather proud of her ingenuity, Dianne then gathered eggs from the chickens, grateful to see they were still laying, and proceeded to scramble them in a bowl.

"That's a real waste," a male voice announced from behind her.

Dianne looked up from her work to find Cole Selby scowling at her. "What are you talking about?"

"You. Wasting eggs on breakfast."

"It's not a waste. My brothers and sisters are hungry. This won't even make a good portion."

"You could have fed them three times over and used half the number of eggs by making flapjacks. You'll have to learn sooner or later that life on the trail is all about making do and doing without."

Dianne stood up indignantly. "I think not." She whirled around so quickly she didn't even realize she'd edged too close to the fire. In moments the hem of her skirt was aflame, and she screamed out in panic.

Before she could take another step, however, Cole Selby picked up the blanket she had shared with her sisters the night before and wrapped it neatly around her legs. He beat at her as if trying to pound the dust from a cushion.

"You're going to have to learn about campfires too," he said, checking to see if the fire was extinguished.

Trying her best to hide her embarrassment, Dianne examined the scorched hem and sighed. "Thank you for your help," she said, biting back a sarcastic reply. The man might be infuriating, but he had saved her life.

He nodded, not offering her so much as a smile. "Where's your mother? Why isn't she taking care of this?"

Gone were any feelings of generosity Dianne might have had for the man. She stretched herself up to her full height and replied, "She's resting, not that it's any of your concern. Fixing breakfast is my job, and I'm fully capable of—" Just then the bacon burst into flames. Dianne's eyes widened in shock. "Oh no!" As she rushed to remedy the situation, she kicked over the bowl of eggs. Now caught between tragedies, she looked back to Cole, knowing he would have something to say about the matter.

He appeared for a moment to be trying to contain a smile. Once under control, however, he turned to go. "Like I said, it's a real waste."

Dianne's lessons on life on the trail had just begun.

The newspaper date read April 19, 1864, when the wagon train pulled into Independence, Missouri. Dianne felt a thrill she'd not ever known in her life. For the most part, the days spent in travel from St. Louis to Independence had been exhilarating, almost pleasurable. Although her feet ached and bore blisters from her time spent walking, Dianne thought nothing could have been more exciting.

They'd added a few families along the way, but Mr. Keefer had told her mother that they would add enough wagons and families at Independence to push their number into the hundreds. She couldn't even begin to imagine. Just the string of some twenty wagons heading west through Missouri had been marvelous to watch. At night, they'd practiced putting the wagons in a circle, their nights of sleeping on the ground or in a crowded wagon beginning in earnest.

Susannah Chadwick maintained a frugal attitude after their expenses in St. Louis and chose to stay with the wagons and animals. Dianne's first night sleeping under the wagon with her sisters had been a cold one to say the least, but they soon warmed up sharing one another's body heat. Their mother had instructed the boys to sleep one on either side of the wagon to protect their sisters, while she made sure the shotgun was loaded and by her side as she slept inside. The hardest part hadn't been the cold or learning to sleep on the hard ground, however. Dianne found it almost impossible to get used to all the noises going on around her.

Often Dianne would awake to find people walking nearby. Once she heard a mother chastising her child and then the unmistakable sound of the child being hit. Another time a man and his wife argued over his using too much tobacco. Then there were the kinds of sounds that came with the open night—hoot owls and the creaking of branches as the wind rustled through the trees. But even with these noises, Dianne managed to drift off to sleep with thoughts of how this would be her life for the next few months.

"It's not a bad life," Dianne told Morgan as she stirred the oatmeal. "It takes some getting used to, but I actually find it pleasurable in spite of the hard work."

"I could live like this the rest of my life," he commented as he took up a couple of biscuits. He bit into one and nodded. "Say, these aren't bad at all. A little burned on the bottom, but that's no problem. Where'd you learn to do this?"

"From a friend I've made—a black woman named Faith. She's really nice. She and her husband were slaves, but they were freed and decided to move west. They heard about the gold in the Idaho Territory."

"Ma won't think much of you associating with folks of color."

"Oh, I think Ma will have to put that behind her. The slaves were freed by Mr. Lincoln and even Pa said it was time for a change of heart."

"Just the same, I don't think Ma's heart is going to change that quickly."

Just then Zane came up with a bucket of water. "Smells good. Is breakfast ready?"

Dianne nodded. "I think so. Looks like the oatmeal is about as good as it'll get. It's a little lumpy—I'm still not sure what I'm doing wrong there, but I think it'll do. Sure wish I'd known more about cooking before we left on this trip."

"You'll learn by and by," Zane said, putting the water down. "At least that's what Ma says when I say something about wishing I knew more."

He sat down on the ground beside Morgan and grabbed some biscuits. Meanwhile, Dianne took up tin plates and dished the oatmeal. She handed one to Morgan and one to Zane. Wiping her hands on her apron, she looked to where their mother stood in the next camp talking to Griselda Showalter. Mrs. Showalter weighed at least three hundred pounds and had six children. Mr. Showalter was a mousy little man who seemed to absolutely adore his wife. To say he was henpecked was hardly the proper definition because Percy Showalter seemed not to feel in the slightest bit wronged. It made Dianne laugh to see them together—especially when Mrs. Showalter began bossing her husband around. He would just look up at her with the most adoring expression and reply in his high-pitched nasal voice, "Yes, dear." Even thinking about it now made Dianne giggle.

"What's so funny?" Morgan asked.

Dianne nodded toward their mother and the heavy woman. "I was just thinking about Mr. and Mrs. Showalter. They make such a funny pair."

"To be sure," Morgan replied with his mouth half full of biscuit.

"Ma told me he's an accountant by trade, but his missus wants to farm and so that's what they'll do," Zane threw in.

Dianne watched her mother momentarily, trying hard not to look like she was spying. "I wonder what Ma is saying."

Susannah Chadwick talked with animation while the older woman nodded and then appeared to reply. The Showalter children were obediently about their various chores, but even so, Griselda stopped from time to time to yell at one child or another. Watching now as Griselda paused to smack her eldest son with her wooden spoon, Dianne feared she was probably the one who had struck her child the other evening.

"James Showalter, you get down to the river and fetch me another pail of water. I can't believe how clumsy you are. Go on now, get!" she commanded, punctuating the demand with another smack of the spoon.

Dianne exchanged a glance with her mother, then looked away as her little sisters came to camp for their breakfast.

"I got to play with some baby pigs!" Betsy said, excitement causing her to dance around.

Ardith held up her hand to reveal a bloody streak. "And I cut my hand on their pen."

Dianne clucked in a motherly way and took her sisters in hand. "Betsy, go wash up, and Ardith, let's get that cut cleaned and bandaged. I wish you'd be more careful."

"It ain't my fault that the pen had a piece of wire sticking up," Ardith protested.

"Don't say *ain't*. You know Ma will skin you for lazy talk. Now let me wash your hand."

Dianne found the iodine and took up a strip of cloth for the bandage. Working quickly, she washed Ardith's hands, then noted the cut wasn't too deep. She touched the wound with iodine, amazed at Ardith's ability to bear the sting without crying. Her sister was such a tomboy, always getting herself into one scrape or another. If she wasn't falling off of something, she was getting stuck in places she oughtn't to have gone. Yet despite this, Ardith was a very tenderhearted girl who loved her dolls as though they were real babies.

Dianne tied the bandage in place, then lifted her sister's chin. "Do try to be more careful. We have a long way to go and we can't be having you torn up and bleeding all the way to Uncle Bram's." Dianne mothered her more by straightening her sunbonnet.

Ardith grimaced beneath the brim. "I'll be careful. Can we eat now?"

Dianne nodded. "Come on. I'll dish you some oatmeal."

They were just finishing breakfast when their mother came back to camp. "Mrs. Showalter says there's going to be nearly two hundred wagons in our train. Apparently the wagon master from another train here in Independence fell over dead yesterday. Mr. Keefer has agreed to allow them to travel with us as far as the cutoff for Salt Lake and Virginia City." She took up the bowl of oatmeal Dianne offered but didn't offer so much as a prayer or word of thanks.

"Mrs. Showalter said the additional people will make for extra protection against the Indians." She looked to Morgan and Zane. "We'll leave here tomorrow. In the meanwhile, you boys might want to scout through the camp and see what all you can learn about the trail and the journey. I know there's a great deal we don't know."

"Well, Morgan and I learned that the oxen need to be shod for the long trip. I didn't even realize they shoed oxen, but apparently it's the only way to get them across the rough terrain without making them lame. There's a man in town that can do the job. It's expensive, but I figure we'll be better off to spend the money now than worry about replacing an ox later."

Susannah considered this a moment and nodded. "Confirm this with Mr. Keefer or his assistant, that quiet man. Oh, what was his name?"

"Cole Selby," Dianne murmured, an edge to her tone.

Her mother looked at her oddly but nodded. "Yes, that's him. Check with one of them and make certain that we need to shoe the oxen. Find out about the milk cows too. I'm counting on you two to figure out the heavy work issues while Dianne and I will work hard to keep on top of the womanly chores. In fact," she said, pausing long enough to take a bite, "I have a couple of ladies coming by this afternoon to show us some tips on laundry and mending."

Dianne perked up at this. "Who's coming over?"

Her mother continued eating for a moment, then put the bowl aside. "Griselda Showalter and a woman named Charity Hammond. Mrs. Hammond is traveling with her preacher husband. She knows a great deal about nursing and such. Anyway, we'll learn what we can from them. Betsy, Ardith, I want you two to come with me now. I have some chores for both of you. Dianne, you get this mess cleaned up and put on something to cook for supper. Why don't you use the Dutch oven and make a stew? Make enough so that we can take it with us tomorrow for our nooning as well."

"Yes, ma'am." Dianne got to her feet and began to take up the dirty breakfast dishes. She would need to wash everything up before she could even begin to cook again. Taking her load of dishes down to the river, Dianne began to think about how she would put the stew together.

"Ya seem mighty deep in thought."

Dianne looked up to find Faith meandering her way with the same chore in mind. Dianne thought the woman very pretty. She bore herself in an almost regal manner, carrying her basket of dishes on her head. "Hello, Faith. I was just trying to figure out how to make a stew. Something really good, you know."

Faith smiled and her crooked teeth gleamed white against her dark chocolate skin. "I have some ideas if you're interested." She pulled the basket from her head and squatted by the river's edge.

Dianne nodded. "I'd love the help. This whole trip is going to be a real test for me. I can't sew or cook, either one. Although I did make some fairly edible biscuits this morning. I did it just like you told me."

"See there. You're a quick learner. I'd be pleased to help you as time allows."

Faith began washing her dishes and Dianne turned to do the same.

"I feel so silly out here," Dianne admitted. "I know it's probably wrong to say all of this to you, but I've been a city girl all my life. I've never had to worry about such things."

"Don't feel bad about it," Faith replied. "I've been a slave all my life, and I'm just learning how to be free."

Dianne looked up and met Faith's smile once again. In the wake of hearing Faith's confession, Dianne's problems seemed truly unimportant. "Was it awful—being a slave?"

Faith's expression sobered. "I had it better than most, which isn't saying much. I was a companion to my master's daughter from nearly the time I was born. I learned to speak proper-like and how to behave like a lady. When I was freed, my master even gave me a bit of travelin' money. That's how come we're here. My husband, Malachi, he didn't have it so good. He got whipped pretty regular by his master."

"Whipped." Dianne said the word and shuddered. "I can't imagine people being so cruel to one another. Beating a human being . . . like an animal."

Faith went back to scrubbing her plates and shrugged. "We weren't considered human. Still aren't by most."

Dianne had never given much consideration one way or another to the slave issues. Her mother and father had been born in border states and held varying views on the war. In the middle of hearing their debates, Dianne figured it wasn't any of her concern. It wasn't like she could do anything personally to help slaves have a better life, so she tried to just put such uncomfortable thoughts aside. She remembered when one of her teachers, a Yankee man who'd come south from Chicago, spoke nearly an entire hour about the plight of slaves in the Southern states. Dianne had been sickened when he'd talked of starving and beating the slaves on a regular basis. The teacher had offered graphic details about families being separated, babies ripped away from their mother's breasts, and children beaten to death when they ran away to rejoin their families. Dianne had gone to her mother with the stories only to have her reject what the teacher had said and then pull her children out of school when the school board refused to fire the man. They'd schooled at home for a time after that.

"You probably hate folks like us," Dianne said softly. The realization of her own naïveté settled on her shoulders like a heavy mantle.

Faith stopped what she was doing. "Why do you say that?"

Dianne met the woman's dark-eyed stare. "It's just that . . . well . . ." She fell silent, trying hard to think of the words she wanted to say. "I used to think the things they said about slavery were . . . well . . . lies."

Faith nodded. "A lot of folks do. Maybe that's why slavery was legal for so long." Her gentle accent was almost lyrical.

"Is it true that families were separated when they were sold?" Dianne asked, suddenly needing to know the truth of it.

"That and worse," Faith said, her expression taking on a faraway look.

"Like what?"

Faith shook her head. "You don't want to know, child." She leaned forward again and took up a small cast-iron kettle.

Dianne swallowed hard. There was a warning in Faith's voice that told her she was probably right. *I've lived in ignorance. Life hasn't taught me the reality of what's going on in the world. Poor Faith. What burdens she must bear.*

"The good Lord saw fit to free us. I try to put the bad times behind me, but sometimes it's hard. Folks are afraid of freed slaves."

"But why?" Dianne asked as she finished up the last of her dishes.

"Because folks generally fear what's different and unknown to them. And that's exactly what we are. Not only that, but a war is being fought over us."

"There are other things besides slavery that caused the war," Dianne replied. "Tariff laws and import problems. I heard my pa talk about it with my brothers."

Faith chuckled and gathered her things. Dianne began picking up her dishes as well. "People can say it's about other things, but it's slavery that's got them all up in arms." They walked up the bank and Faith added, "If there hadn't been black folks in chains, there might not have been a war."

Dianne was silent as they made their way back to camp. She didn't know what to say. It troubled her more than she could imagine that Faith might be right.

"You feel free to come on over later, and I'll show you how to season the stew. For now, just cut up some meat in chunks and put it in a kettle with a little water. Let it cook a spell till the water's gone, then flour it up good. You got milk cows giving, right?" Dianne nodded. "Then you can have a real rich stew. Put in some milk—don't bother to separate it. Let that simmer a while, and then add vegetables. While those are cooking, head on over and I'll—"

"Dianne, what are you doing?" Her mother's voice held an edge of irritation.

Dianne met her mother's stern expression and stopped in midstep. "I was washing dishes like you told me to do."

"What are you doing with her?"

Faith and Dianne exchanged a glance, and Dianne felt a flush creep up her face. "This is my friend Faith. I told you about her."

"You didn't bother to tell me she was a Negro. I won't have you associating with her kind—they cause nothing but misery and trouble."

"Ma, please don't say such things. Faith is very nice. She's teaching me some of the things I need to know for the trip."

"No she's not. I don't want you to be seen with her. Now come on. It's her and her kind that killed your father. The Yankees wouldn't have been in New Madrid if not for the slaves." She turned and began walking back to their campsite.

Dianne looked regretfully at Faith and followed; she could still see the expression on Faith's face long after they'd parted company. It seemed she hadn't been surprised by the condemnation in Dianne's mother's words. She'd taken it in stride with a look that seemed more weary than angry.

———

"I personally can't believe Negroes are being allowed to travel in the same wagon train as white folks," Griselda Showalter said as she took up a piece of quilting. "I suppose that's the way things will be now. Whites and blacks intermingling. It's one of the reasons I'm glad we're heading west. Percy and I can't have our children thinking it's acceptable to be making friends—even marrying their kind."

Susannah nodded. "I can't imagine such things. It's a complete abomination in the eyes of the Lord—I'm confident of that. At least they have the good sense to travel at the back of the train. Keep with their own kind."

Dianne said nothing but couldn't imagine what God would have against white folks being friends with blacks.

"There isn't a single one I'd trust. Don't you agree, Charity?" Mrs. Showalter paused long enough to let the older woman in on the conversation.

Charity Hammond was a gracious little woman. Dianne presumed her to be somewhere in her late fifties, for she spoke of a son who was nearly forty and lived in Oregon.

"I try not to let old prejudices give me cause to fear. I believe the good Lord has a plan in all things, even this. I've met some very nice people whose skin was darker than mine, and I've met some not-so-nice folks whose complexion was whiter than mine. I think we have to be careful about judging an entire group of people by the standards of fear and ignorance."

"I'm not ignorant about anything," Griselda replied hostilely. "I've had to deal with them too many times."

Dianne watched as Charity worked on her quilt block, seemingly ignoring the conversation. The tight clench of her jaw, however, made it clear that this wasn't the case. Dianne moved closer to watch Charity's stitches.

"I wish I could do work like that," she said, offering Charity a smile. She wished she could just blurt out that she didn't agree with her mother and Mrs. Showalter.

"The key is to put the needle straight down when you pierce the fabric. Don't slant it, or the stitches will be bigger. Here, you try on this block," Charity said, handing Dianne the piece.

"Oh no, I might mess it up."

Charity chuckled. "I'm not concerned about that, child. Nothing that's done can't be undone if needed. Every girl ought to know how to sew and make quilts for her home."

"There was never a need for such things when my husband was alive," Dianne's mother began. "I hated sewing as a child and have forgotten far more than I ever knew on the subject. We purchased our clothes and paid a seamstress to make what we couldn't order. She also did our mending."

Griselda harrumphed. "It must have been nice to have that kind of money."

Dianne remembered her stew and plans to see Faith to learn about seasoning it. "Ma, I have a stew cooking in the Dutch oven, but I don't know how to season it."

Griselda and Susannah both looked up. Charity reached out and patted Dianne's knee. "Seasoning is all a matter of likes and dislikes. There are all sorts of things you can try."

"I'll help you with the stew," Griselda said, looking at Susannah rather than Dianne. "I have come up with the perfect combination of herbs and spices. You'll love it, I promise."

And in this way the matter was taken from Dianne's hands. She watched as Griselda tossed aside her sewing and motioned for Susannah to follow her to where the Dutch oven sat in the coals.

"Never mind, child. It's just her way," Charity said quietly.

"I'd still like to know how you'd go about seasoning the stew," Dianne said, trying again to make a tiny stitch in the quilt block. "Oh, look!" she exclaimed. "I did it!"

"Yes," Charity said, offering Dianne a beaming smile. "I think you're going to find that you can accomplish most anything you set your mind to."

Dianne met the woman's gaze and heard the sincerity in her voice. "I wish I had as much faith in me as you seem to have."

"It's not faith in you, child," the older woman said softly. "It's faith in God."

CHAPTER 6

"You seem a bit preoccupied, Cole. Wanna talk about it?"

Cole looked up to find Daniel Keefer, his new boss, watching him from across the campfire. "Nothing much to talk about, sir."

Keefer took up his pipe. "I thought it a stroke of good luck to find you in Salt Lake, but you've been as silent as the grave. Not much of a companion across the empty prairie." He smiled, but his good nature did nothing to encourage Cole's black spirit.

"Will we be picking up any more families before we head out for Kansas?" Cole asked.

"I'm not expectin' to, but you can never tell," Keefer replied before lighting his pipe. He took several deep draws before continuing. "I have hired on a couple of new fellows to help out. They have nothing but the clothes on their backs and a bedroll, but they're desperate to get west. I've offered them good work, just like you. It never hurts to have an extra man on the trip." He chuckled and stretched out his legs. "They're all hungry for gold, but no matter. Throwing in with us will allow them the safety of numbers and the knowledge of how to get there. I hope Virginia City doesn't disappoint them too much."

Cole tried to focus on the conversation and forget the miseries of his past, but with statements like that he couldn't ignore his own disappointment with the territory. He thought often of the things that had happened in Virginia City, driving him away. Memories that burned in his heart and mind with pictures so vivid they made him long only to forget. Even now, as he talked with Daniel Keefer about the trip back, Cole felt his anger flame into an inferno. *Cursed country.*

"You sure you don't want to talk about what ails you, boy?" Keefer asked. "I've been around folks too long to be fooled into thinking you're just the quiet sort."

"Not much to tell. I guess I miss my family," Cole lied.

"Whereabouts are they?"

"Topeka. My mom and two sisters."

"But I thought you said you'd come from living with your pa in Virginia City."

Cole shifted uncomfortably and picked up the knife he'd started to put an edge on earlier in the evening. Running it gently across the sharpening stone, he tried to think of how to answer. "My pa is still in that area. When he went west for gold, I went with him while my ma and sisters decided to stay in Topeka. They'd had enough of moving around."

"Had you moved quite a bit before that?"

"At least four times that I can remember, in no more than a two-year period. My ma said it was time to settle down to one place and that she liked Topeka. My sisters were making good friends. None of the Selby women wanted to leave."

"That must have been hard on your pa. A man likes to have his womenfolk close at hand. He worries about their safety otherwise."

"Not my pa," Cole said, knowing the bitterness in his tone would make clear his feelings. "Pa thought of himself first and foremost. Said he was no good to anyone else unless he was happy with himself. The only problem was, Pa was never happy anywhere he went." Some of the anger left Cole as he remembered this. Somehow it seemed to unloose his tongue.

"I used to feel sorry for my pa. Ma was so hard on him at times. She would call him no-account and lazy, and I thought it pretty demeaning. When Pa came up with the idea to go to the Idaho goldfields, I knew Ma would never approve. I resolved to go with him so he wouldn't have to be alone. But sometimes . . . well, a lot of times . . . I think he would have preferred to be by himself." Cole glanced up to find Keefer nodding.

"Sometimes a man needs that. A fellow doesn't need company the way a woman does. He keeps his family close to make sure they're provided for and safe, but it's different than needing someone to talk to. That's why it's good for a woman to have her family and friends around her. I never did mind the missus having her ma and sisters around. She used to have the entire collection of church ladies to the house twice a month. Never bothered me at all." He grinned. "Of course, I mostly was gone during those occasions."

Cole gave him a halfhearted smile. "My ma did things like that as well. I usually made myself scarce."

"How did your ma fare with you and your pa away?"

Cole shrugged and went back to stroking the knife against the whetstone. "I guess she's done well enough. She started taking boarders before we even left. We had a fair-sized place that Ma had bought with money she'd come by when her aunt passed on. She saw boarders as good income. I couldn't abide the crowd, so any thought I had of staying in Topeka went right out the door."

"I wondered why you decided to take off; figured you might feel the need to take care of your ma."

Cole shook his head. "My ma never needed takin' care of. I think that was one of the reasons my pa felt so worthless around her. He knew she'd be just as well off, maybe even better, without him as with him. Seeing that, I guess I felt sorry for Pa. He never did seem to fit in anywhere." Cole remembered the way he'd actually hurt for his father. Townsfolk always seemed to scorn the man. He wasn't vital to any community, having a variety of skills but not being accomplished with any of them.

"Sometimes feeling sorry for a man only leads him to worse wear," Daniel said, breaking Cole's train of thought.

"I'm sure that's true. I really hoped Pa would strike it big in gold. I wanted him to be good at something." Cole fell silent and tried to refocus his thoughts on his mother. "Ma's last words to us when we loaded up to head north were, 'When you're done with this nonsense, I hope you'll be ready to earn a real living and settle down for once.' I knew she was upset with us running off, but at the same time, I think she was kind of relieved. We had a couple of letters from her while in Virginia City, but I haven't heard from her in a long while. I don't know for sure how she's been with the war moving ever westward."

"I suppose that's enough to make a fella down in the mouth."

Cole looked up again. "I don't mean to make my company unbearable." He had no idea of whether Keefer meant to console him or fire him.

"Isn't that so much as I recognize your misery. I've had my own share of it. I'm thinking, though, it would be possible to let you take a few days off when we bring the wagons north of Topeka. You could visit with your family and catch up with the train after a day or two."

Cole was surprised at the man's kindness. Daniel Keefer was the only person who had shown him the slightest consideration since he'd left his father. "I'd like that. Thanks, Daniel."

The man nodded and got to his feet. "Think I'll take a little walk and check on the camp before I turn in. I'm going to need you to help me tomorrow with checking out some of the wagons those new folks aim to take. We need to make sure they aren't new wagons made of green wood. Nothing sadder than seeing those things dry as the trip goes on and leave big old gaps and twisted frames."

"I'll be up early," Cole promised. "I'm just gonna finish sharpening this knife and then I'll turn in."

Keefer headed out, smoking his pipe as he went. Cole sat and stared at the fire for several minutes. He had to admit it would be good to see family again. His mother and sisters had never had much to do with him—a mystery to be sure—but he would be glad for their company nonetheless.

But then the thought came to him that he'd most likely have to explain his presence. How much should he say? A part of him longed to talk to someone about what had happened in Virginia City, but he really had no one. Would his mother understand or would it just give her one more reason to hate his father?

He remembered back a few years to an argument he'd heard his parents have. It was years before the war, and Cole had been just a boy. His mother had told his father that if he didn't settle down, he'd end up ruining Cole. "You'll teach him to be a rambling no-account, same as yourself, Hallam. The boy would be better off without a father as to end up like you."

The words had hardened him against his mother. She seemed so cruel—so hateful. He hadn't understood her misery, her longing for a place of her own and friends. Moving had been an adventure to Cole, an adventure that had given him new and exciting locations and friends. And while it was true that he never had a chance to rekindle those friendships or revisit those places, Cole felt he was no worse for the wear.

He couldn't say the same for his adventure to Virginia City. That nightmare had robbed him of all his hopes—all his tomorrows.

That night, Cole tossed restlessly in his bedroll. His mind betrayed him, leading him deep into the memories he'd sworn to bury. As if reliving the past all over again, Cole found himself back in the wilderness outside of Virginia City.

It was January and much had gone wrong in the community. Highwaymen ran rampant and many a good man had been robbed, even killed, while trying to live in the territory and make a living.

Cole Selby sat in silence atop his horse, away from the others. A heaviness hung in the air that could be blamed on more than the impending weather.

"You're gonna hang, Jeremiah," one of Selby's companions announced. "For your sins, the payback is death."

"You mean to leave my daughter—my Carrie—an orphan?" Jeremiah Gillham asked, stumbling over the words. No doubt the tightened noose around his neck made it more difficult to speak.

Cole hadn't wanted to be there. He had argued long and hard with his father only to have the man declare that when the law wouldn't deal with thieves and murderers, honest citizens had to take the law into their own hands.

"Sorry, Jeremiah, you decided her fate a long time ago. Long before we joined together to take this matter into our own hands," the man replied.

Cole shifted uneasily in his saddle. Why didn't they just get this over with before Carrie returned from her trip to town? Cole had arranged for her to ride into nearby Virginia City to meet with her best friend, Annie. He'd hoped it would give them time enough to hang and bury her father so that she didn't have to witness the event. It was the only thing Cole could give her. He knew her father was a low-down murdering thief. Jeremiah had been caught red-handed once, and twice his name had been offered by others who were about to suffer the same fate. Misery apparently loved company.

"What do you have to say for yourself, Jeremiah?" Cole's father, Hallam Selby, questioned. "You wanna give us the names of your cohorts?"

Jeremiah spit onto the ground, causing his horse to shift nervously. With a noose already around his neck, Cole couldn't imagine the man wanted to give his horse any reason to spook.

"You got the wrong man," Gillham said, eyeing them each individually. "You're gonna burn in hell sure as you're sittin' there."

Cole shifted uncomfortably, gazing at his father only to receive a look that suggested he'd better not move from where he sat. His father saw it as an honor to even be asked to join the group, and he wasn't about to have his son create problems for him. Cole, on the other hand, fully intended for this to be his first and only experience with vigilante justice.

He understood that something had to be done. Good, honest folk were terrified of coming to the territory because of the stories—stories that included putting the Virginia City sheriff at the head of this vicious group of highwaymen. Murders and robberies were commonplace along the trails outside the various gold camps of Virginia City and Nevada City and all along Alder Gulch. It was rumored the gang had killed over a hundred people. Maybe more.

Someone had to do something, to be sure, but Cole had wanted no part of it. Killings, even justified lynchings, were not his style. He'd not even wanted to be a part of the war going on back East, which was one of the reasons he'd happily joined his father on this frontier search for gold.

"Jeremiah Gillham, you were caught in the act of thieving and leaving poor Arnold McIntyre nearly dead to this world and without a horse in the coldest part of winter. Your friends identified you as being with them on at least a dozen other rides where murders took place. Are you still wanting to cover for those who would as soon turn you over to the devil himself as to look at you?" This time the speaker was a man Cole was familiar with. Paris Pfouts was the president of the vigilante committee.

"So if I tell you the truth, Pfouts, you gonna let me go? How 'bout we make a deal? I'll give you names and you give me a chance to get away."

"I'll make no deals with scum like you. I already know you're guilty. We have eyewitnesses."

Snow began to swirl around them. Cole glanced to the skies to see thick gray clouds spreading—smothering the land below. He felt the collar around his neck tighten as his gaze went back to Jeremiah. Funny, he could imagine the constricting squeeze of the rope. He drew a deep breath, almost to prove he still had that ability.

The sound of rustling in the brush behind the Gillham cabin caught everyone's attention. Paris held up his hand for silence. Cole's father drew his gun slowly and aimed it toward Jeremiah. Several of the other vigilantes did likewise.

The rushing form moving out from the shadows met their sight only a few seconds before the decidedly feminine scream rent the air.

There was no time to think about reactions. The men were nervous—worried that Gillham's associates would come to his rescue. Cole's father fired his gun without thought—a single bullet piercing the breast of Carrie Gillham. As she clutched her chest, two other shots rang out.

Cole was off his horse even as Gillham's mount reared and took off. Jeremiah was instantly hanged as his daughter crumpled to the snow-dusted ground.

Pulling Carrie into his arms, Cole took the handkerchief from his neck and tried to stay the blood that flowed down the bodice of her dress. Her eyes were glazed—lifeless. She was dead.

Moaning softly, Cole hugged her close and rocked back and forth under the swaying form of her father's lynched body. Tears came to Cole's eyes. She was the only woman he had ever loved. They had planned to marry in the spring.

"Don't die," he whispered, knowing it was pointless. He could feel the life had gone out from her. *Oh, God, why Carrie? I tried to save her from even seeing this. Why take her life when I loved her so? She wouldn't have wanted for anything—I would have seen to that.*

"We'd best bury 'em," someone said from behind Cole.

"Let me help you, son," Hallam Selby said softly.

"Don't even touch her," Cole said, looking up.

His father stepped back as if the very look on Cole's face had the power to keep him at bay. "Son, I never meant—"

"I don't want to hear it. You killed her. She never did anything wrong and you killed her. You all killed her."

Paris Pfouts came forward. "Cole, your father did what he had to. There was no way to tell who was coming to Gillham's aid. She could have been armed."

"Does she look armed?" Cole asked angrily. "She just looks dead to me."

"Now, Cole, you can't go takin' this attitude," another man added. "I was about to pull the trigger myself."

Cole got to his feet and lifted Carrie gently, almost ceremonially. "You're all a bunch of murderin' no-accounts. No better than the road agents you seek to put an end to. The woman I love is dead—there's no accounting for this." He looked directly at his father and added, "And no forgiving it."

Cole awoke from the nightmare with tears streaming from his closed eyes. He clutched his pillow and buried his face. When would it stop? When would the memories leave him to suffer in peace—to mourn her loss without the hideous reminder that he'd played a small part in her execution?

CHAPTER 7

COLE WAS GLAD FOR THE TIME AWAY FROM THE WAGON TRAIN. He'd had no idea that people could be so petty and quarrelsome. One family complained because they couldn't be at the front of the train each day. The husband explained that his wife didn't like the dust created by the other wagons and specifically requested they be moved. Daniel tried to explain that they would rotate wagons regularly so that no one wagon had to be at the back eating dust all the way west. That wasn't good enough for the couple, however. Then another group of travelers insisted the nooning stops were not long enough. Someone else wanted to know why they were required to purchase two more oxen before Daniel would allow them to travel. Never mind that they had their wagon so overloaded that the team already installed could barely move it.

And this was only the beginning of the trip. They were still near civilization, good water, and green grass. What would they do when they passed into the more arid areas of the country? How would they manage if the summer brought a drought?

As they passed north of Topeka, Cole had no regrets in leaving the train. It wasn't until he was several miles away that he realized just how consistently noisy that manner of travel could be. He wondered if he'd get used to it.

He quickly put aside such concerns as he approached the bustling city of Topeka. It had been over a year since Cole had been there. The town looked markedly changed by growth. There were far more buildings and a new ferry, and it seemed the population had tripled. Maybe all those eastern folks who were tired of the war had come west to Topeka.

He rode his horse up the main thoroughfare, gawking at the storefronts and dodging the freighters who seemed to have no mind for anyone but themselves. When he reached Sixth Street, he turned and rode west toward his mother's two-story boardinghouse.

Here, things looked much as they had when he'd left. The trees were dressed out in that brilliant state of emerald green, while spring flowers lined the walkway to the house. His mother had a natural affection for daffodils—it was one of the reasons she'd bought the house in the first place. Now she had an abundance of daffodils, all yellow and white, along with tulips in a riot of colors.

For a moment, Cole did nothing but stand staring at the house. His mother called it a Gothic Revival and delighted in the fact that it was less than three years old when she'd managed to buy it, and all its furnishings, from a dying old woman. The woman sold it to her on the agreement that she could live out her days in her own room. It turned out those days were only twenty in number, but Cole remembered his mother giving the woman very attentive care during that time.

His father had resented his wife pushing him into the house purchase. Mary Selby had inherited a nice bit of money from a childless aunt, and she was determined to settle down and plant roots—something his father knew nothing about. In fact, Cole had seen his father grow notably more restless after the sale was finalized and the old woman had passed on. Cole supposed it was because then the deal was final. The house was truly the possession of the Selby family, and his father could no longer just load up his family and move on.

But the fact was, Cole's father hadn't allowed even that to stop him. When news of gold in the Idaho Territory trickled into town, Hallam

Selby was ready to pack up and head north. Cole could still hear the ugly argument between his mother and father. His mother all but told her husband to never return. Anger permeated the household for days. It was most uncomfortable for the new boarders his mother had taken in.

Cole easily recalled the look on his mother's face the day his father came downstairs with his bedroll and saddlebags in hand. The look suggested betrayal—almost as if she'd caught him with another woman. In some ways, she had. Wanderlust was the name of this woman, and she clearly owned his father. By this time, Cole had already decided to accompany his father. His mother had never shown him more than a passing interest since his sisters demanded most of her time and attention. So why stay?

The memories left Cole feeling more empty and lonely than before. What kind of welcome would he receive now? He'd gone away with his father after what felt like a lifetime of his mother's indifference. Would he find that same emotion today? For the life of him, Cole had never figured out why his mother favored her girls and practically ignored her only son. He was her firstborn. Weren't mothers supposed to have a special bond with their first baby? It sure wasn't that way in the Selby family.

He tied his horse to the hitching post. The gelding was a replacement he'd picked up in Independence when his own mount went lame. He was sure going to miss that old boy. The liveryman thought with time the animal's leg might mend enough to allow him to carry a child or small woman, but never again would he be able to handle a healthy two-hundred-pound man such as Cole.

Cole ran his hand along the sorrel's neck. "We'll get used to each other by and by, eh, Buddy?"

The horse sidled away, intent on nibbling some fresh spring grass near the post. Cole smiled and headed toward the house. He knocked loudly on the door, then noted the time. It was nearly three o'clock. Hopefully his mother wouldn't be caught up in meal preparations. As he waited, he noted the list of rules posted beside the door.

No spitting or chewing of tobacco.
No cursing or rowdy behavior.
No drinking or drunken disruptions.
No admittance after 9 P.M.

Below this, a small placard read *Vacancy*.

The door opened and Cole stood face to face with his sister Cordelia. At fourteen, the girl was tall and slender, with a ruddy complexion and huge brown eyes. Her face bore a startled expression for a moment, then she broke into a smile. "Cole? Is it really you?"

Cole took the hat from his head. "It's me all right. How are you, Delly?"

She frowned. "No one calls me that anymore. That's a baby name. I'm almost old enough to court."

"At fourteen? I don't think so. Pa always said . . ." His words fell short. No one in this conversation cared what Pa had to say, so why bring it up? "Are you going to let me in?"

Cordelia laughed. "Sure, but where's Pa?" She opened the door and stretched around Cole to see if their father was on the porch.

"I don't know. I guess somewhere in the Idaho Territory."

His sister's frown told him she didn't understand. "Why'd you come back without him?"

"It's a long story. I can't even begin to explain it until I have something to wash the dust down my throat." Cordelia nodded and moved back. Cole stepped into the dimly lit hallway.

"I'll get you some lemonade. Come on in the parlor, and I'll let Mama know you're here." Cordelia showed him to the front room. He barely remembered it but knew it was for entertaining guests—not family. He wondered if Delly had done this purposefully or if she just hadn't thought about the implication.

"Mama!" she called out as she left Cole. "Mama, come see who's here."

Cole wondered again at the reception he might get. His mother hadn't been happy with his leaving to accompany his father. She'd wanted him to stay and help with the boardinghouse, but Cole had no desire to live with a bunch of strangers.

Running his fingers along the band of his hat, Cole suddenly felt silly for coming. His mother wouldn't care that he'd seen his whole world collapse back in Virginia City. She would simply remind him that she'd wanted him to stay in Topeka and that his disobedience had brought on his miseries.

"Cole?"

He looked up to find the tiny woman staring at him from the doorway. She was barely five feet in height—compared to his six foot four—and weighed barely more than his saddle. Her dark brown eyes searched his face as if for answers.

"Hello, Ma. I was in the neighborhood and thought I'd share your company a day or two. If you'd have me."

She frowned, causing her brows to draw together. "I suppose I can give you the room at the top of the stairs. I don't have a boarder there at this time, but if someone applies . . ." She left the words unstated, but Cole took her meaning.

Her lack of enthusiasm left a hole in Cole that seemed big enough to swallow him alive. "I can't stay but a couple of days at most. I have a job with a wagon train. I got special permission to come and see you."

"Why?"

He studied her hard, determined face. The severity of her expression furthered his feeling of hopelessness. "I guess because I thought since I was in the area, it'd be rude and thoughtless not to come by."

She nodded. "Very well. Take your things upstairs, then come back down and we'll talk."

"Where can I put my horse? I need to feed and water him."

"We've a small fenced-in stable in the back. You can put him there." She turned, leaving him to his business without another word.

Cole walked outside, wondering what had happened to the lemonade promised by Delly. His mouth felt like it was full of cotton. He took up the reins to his mount and walked him back around the house. The stable, as his mother had called it, was nothing more than a collection of stalls inside a fenced area of the huge backyard.

He took the sorrel into the first stall and unsaddled him. Searching for the pump, Cole filled a bucket with water and left it next to the hay box. Seeing there was plenty for the horse to eat and drink, Cole picked up his things and made his way back to the house. He'd curry the animal after he had a chance to speak further with his mother.

Shaking his head, he wasn't at all sure that would amount to much. *She hasn't changed,* he thought. *She still cares nothing about me.*

"Cole, come in this way!" Delly called from the back door.

"Why? Aren't I good enough for the front door?" he said, laughing.

" 'Course you are, silly. I just figured you'd want your lemonade. I had to make fresh, that's why it took so long."

Cole bounded up the back porch steps and wrestled his bedroll and saddlebags into one hand. Delly handed him the glass and watched in seeming amazement as he drained it. "Can I have more if I promise to wipe my boots?"

"Of course you can. Come on. Just leave your things here by the door."

She took the glass and led him into the house. Cole remembered the large kitchen with its huge iron cookstove. It had a homey, almost cheery feel to it. There were pleasant aromas of breads and spices in the air that served to remind him he hadn't eaten since breakfast. He put his things down and rubbed his stomach.

"I don't suppose a fellow could get something to eat, could he?"

Delly frowned. "Well, usually Mama doesn't allow for meals in between times. . . ."

"Gracious, just feed him," their mother interrupted from the doorway. "I'll not have it said I starved my own child." Even with this, there was no real affection in her voice.

"You come with me, Cole. We'll be in the dining room, Cordelia. Bring him a couple of ham sandwiches and some of that potato salad you and Laurel plan to take to the church social tonight."

"Thanks, Ma," Cole said, leaning down to kiss her cheek. He wasn't sure why he did it—it just seemed the right thing to do.

Mary Selby looked up at him rather shocked. Her hand went to the spot where he'd kissed her; then, as if realizing her action, she quickly turned to lead the way to the dining room.

Cole followed and took the seat she pointed to. "Cordelia will have your lunch in a moment." She took the chair across the table from him and sat down in her prim and proper manner. They sat in silence until Cordelia brought his food, along with another glass of lemonade.

"Cordelia, I want you to take your brother's bedroll and saddlebags upstairs. I gave him the empty room."

"But, Mama, I want to hear Cole's stories."

"Do as I say or you won't be attending the social tonight," her mother said rather harshly. Cole had never heard his mother so much as raise her voice to his sister. It seemed some things had changed.

Cordelia darted out of the room, biting her lip. Cole might have laughed if his mother weren't looking so serious. So rather than cause problems right from the start, Cole dug into the food. Never had anything tasted so good in all his life. The potato salad was creamy and cold, seasoned with just the right amount of spices. He had no idea what went into the dish beyond potatoes, but one thing could be said: his mother was an excellent cook.

"This is really good, Ma," he told her, hoping that the compliment might thaw her frigid mood.

"Thank you," she murmured, refusing to meet his gaze.

"The house looks really nice. The stalls for the horses are a good addition. I'm sure your boarders appreciate that."

"All of my boarders at present are women. None of whom have horses."

Cole took a bite of the ham sandwich and relished the flavor. His months on the trail would soon leave such luxuries behind. He figured he might as well enjoy it while he had a chance. If only he could find a common ground for discussion with his mother—but she seemed unreachable.

"Cordelia sure has grown up in the last year. She's pretty too. I suppose Laurel is just as pretty."

"Probably too much so for her own good." His mother met his gaze but only momentarily. "Without a man around, we've had our share of ne'er-do-wells come courting."

"I suppose that's to be expected whether there's a man around or not. So is Laurel here?"

"She's with friends." The stilted words made it clear there would be no further explanation.

Cole had had enough. He took a long drink and decided he would confront her once and for all. If she refused to speak on the matter, he'd simply collect his things and leave. After he ate, of course.

"Ma, I'm sorry that I made you mad by going off with Pa. But frankly, I didn't think you wanted me here anyway."

She looked surprised. "What? I asked you to stay."

Cole nodded and leaned back in his chair. "Yes, you did, but I didn't think it was because you wanted me personally so much as you needed a man to help with the heavy work."

"Why would you say such a thing? You're my son. Of course I wanted you to stay."

"You've been cool toward me ever since the girls came along. Every time I sought you out for conversation or even a simple hug, you made me feel I'd asked for far too much."

His mother looked away. "It was your father's doing."

"How so?" Cole had no idea what she was implying.

"He wanted it that way. He said I could have the girls to raise as I pleased, but you were his son and he would see to your needs. I wasn't to come between you two." She folded her hands and looked up. "He made it clear I was not to interfere." She repeated this as if Cole might have missed it the first time.

"But why? I needed you both."

His mother seemed taken aback by this. "I'm sure he thought I would sissify you."

Cole didn't know what to say. The silence engulfed them in a painful vise. Neither could move nor comment. Cole continued to look at his mother, her frail appearance making him wish he'd never said anything.

Finally he went back to eating, afraid to speak the thoughts on his mind. He'd hoped to talk about the past with his mother. To speak of what had happened to Carrie and why he'd come to hate his father. But hearing the bitterness in his mother's tone, Cole hesitated. He didn't want to give her any more reason to hate his father. They were, after all, husband and wife.

But even as these thoughts filled his mind, so too did his own indifference. Why should he care if his mother hated his father? If she divorced him, which she wouldn't, Cole would simply be rid of any chance of seeing the man when he came for visits.

"Your father thought nothing of dragging this family around the country," his mother began without warning, her voice bearing a sharp edge. "For years I lived with the dread of hearing him say, 'Pack up.' I couldn't bear to hear it again when he announced he wanted to go to the Idaho Territory to look for gold. It was too much for me to deal with. The girls were just starting to have friends. Laurel even had a suitor. I couldn't do that to them—or to myself."

"I guess I can understand that," Cole said after finishing off one of the sandwiches. He toyed with the second one, struggling to know what to say. The last thing he wanted to do was open his heart to his mother only to have her refuse him.

"What happened between you and your father?"

He looked up to meet her gaze. She knew.

"I . . . well . . . we had a falling-out, you could say." Cole still didn't feel it was right to tell her everything. "I felt like I needed to find my own way—see what life might hold for me. I don't intend to wander around all my life like he does."

"I'm glad to hear it. There's nothing good to be had of it. I can tell you that here and now."

Cole's heart went out to her. "I'm sorry you had to live like that, Ma. I never really thought about it. I saw Pa as the outsider all the time—the misfit. He wasn't good at anything—"

"Because he wouldn't stick with any one thing," his mother interrupted.

"I don't intend to be like that. I want to find what I'm good at. What I love."

"And do you love working with the wagon train?"

Cole shrugged. "I don't know. We've only just started and haven't really had to be too far removed from civilization. Our train is over two hundred wagons strong, and there is a kind of satisfaction in helping to guide those folks west to their dreams."

"Just don't spend your life going from one thing to another in order to figure what you're good at. If you find something you like, make it work. Learn to be good at it even if you aren't skilled to start out with. No one is born with the ability to do things perfectly. God has a purpose for your life and if you seek Him, you'll find it."

Cole frowned at this and turned back to the food. He didn't want to think about God right now. God had disappointed him and left him to face the future without the woman he loved. God seemed like a cruel and harsh master at this point—no different from the Southern masters who provided for their slaves with one hand and beat them with the other.

"Why don't you stay here with us?" his mother suddenly questioned. "I could use your help."

Cole considered the possibility for a moment, then shook his head. "I signed a contract with Mr. Keefer. I don't want to give my word and then take it back. I'll see this wagon train through. If I feel it's right to come home after that, then I just might take you up on your offer."

His mother got to her feet and motioned to the plate. "Do you want more to eat?"

"No, this is plenty. I'll finish this up and then if you don't mind, I'd like to take a bath. I've been on the trail a while and could sure stand to clean up."

"That would be fine. Supper is at six."

He went back to eating as his mother moved toward the door. He had the sandwich halfway to his mouth when she turned on her heel.

"How is your father doing?"

Cole swallowed hard and put the sandwich back down. "When I

left, he was fine. He managed to find enough gold to keep him in tobacco and food, but there was never any big strike of luck for us Selby men." He tried to smile, but it wouldn't come.

"There never has been," his mother commented dryly. "Why should it change now?" With that she turned and hurried from the room, leaving Cole to feel as though she'd passed some prophetic judgment on him as well as his father.

Maybe coming to Topeka hadn't been such a good idea after all.

CHAPTER 8

THE WEEKS SLIPPED BY FOR DIANNE. THERE WAS LITTLE TO DISTIN-guish one day from another. The work was hard, harder than anything she'd ever known. Her mother had taken ill and seemed weak most of the time, remaining in the wagon to rest. Dianne had charge over the wagon, driving the oxen along the trail behind her brothers' wagons.

Dianne didn't really mind the task. The oxen were good-natured and strong workers. They needed little guidance, as they seemed content to follow the wagon in front of them without fussing or balking. Each morning her brothers would take on the task of rounding up the animals and yoking them while Dianne prepared breakfast for the family and their little sisters gathered any spare firewood that could be found. They had all fallen into an acceptable routine.

"Look, Dianne," Betsy said, coming up from behind. "Mrs. Delbert's dog had puppies." She held up a tiny bundle of black and white fur.

"Oh, he's adorable," Dianne said, reaching out to stroke the downy fur. "And so soft." She smiled at her sister, noting the look of pure delight on Betsy's face.

"Mrs. Delbert said we could have him when we get to Virginia City. Do you think Ma would let us?"

"Ma did say you could get a dog when we got settled in," Dianne replied, turning back to the oatmeal. "I suppose you could take him to show her and ask for yourself."

"This one's only a week old. Mrs. Delbert said by the time we reach Virginia City, he'll be old enough to leave his mama."

Dianne smiled. Betsy was such a charmer; their mother was sure to agree to the arrangement.

Before they knew it, breakfast was finished and cleaned up and the wagon train was on the move once again. Eastern Kansas woodlands gave way to virgin farmland and prairie plains. Nebraska looked much the same, and Dianne seriously wondered how the leaders knew where one state or territory ended and another began.

She walked at a steady pace beside her oxen team. The tall prairie grass had been beaten down in this area from multiple wagon trains headed west. Deep ruts were formed in the ground where hundreds, maybe even a thousand wagons had gone before theirs. It put Dianne in deep thought as she considered the pioneers who had moved west to start new lives. These ruts represented their hopes and dreams. At the same time, a dead horse or the skeletal remains of an ox reminded Dianne of the frailty of life. Had the people traveling before her actually reached their destination? An occasional grave marker suggested that not all of them had. The graves always discouraged Dianne, but she said nothing to her family about it. The boys wouldn't understand, and her sisters were too young and would only be frightened. And there was no sense in talking to her mother—she'd seen enough death. To contemplate the graves alongside the trail would only cause her further pain.

Although hundreds of people moved west with them, Dianne often felt alone, isolated. There were people to talk to; there had even been a couple of times when men had shown interest in her, only to have her brothers tell them she was too young for courting. It was secretly a relief to Dianne that her brothers would handle the matter for her, but at the same time she couldn't help but wonder if the company might have been nice. A few times, Dianne had tried to seek out neighboring families who had daughters her own age, but everyone was too busy for lengthy socializing. Even when they rested on the Sabbath and didn't travel unless there was a threat to their well-being, there wasn't a whole lot of time for idle talk. Chores still had to be maintained in spite of it being the Lord's Day.

Washing was generally best kept for Saturday evening, for then the clothing had all night and into the next day to dry. The women sometimes got together and helped each other with the washing, talking and exchanging recipes as they performed the task. Dianne seldom joined them, however. Her mother seemed to prefer they keep to themselves. Susannah Chadwick considered it troublesome to share personal information with strangers, and she had no desire to make close friends.

Often on Sunday the clothes would be ironed or mended, and sewing and mending harnesses and wagons was generally reserved for that day as well. Together, the families had fallen into a pattern of seeing to duties and amazingly enough, it worked quite well.

Watching the ribbon of travelers, Dianne marveled at the very thought of what they were doing. The wagons stretched for what seemed like countless miles. She couldn't see where they began or ended, and it gave her a feeling of security. There was safety in numbers, her mother and father had always said, and nowhere did that seem more true than here. Zane had shown her a map of the country. He'd pointed to where they'd lived in New Madrid, then pointed to the Idaho Territory. The distance was impressive and frightening. There was very little in the way of civilization once they got past Missouri. A few forts would help ease the miseries and provide the possibility of extra supplies for some who'd lost or used up their goods. But other than that, there was nothing. Nothing but the vast wilderness.

Dust swirled around them as the train moved ever toward their goal. The Platte River offered them a constant source of refreshing water, but nothing could hold back the trail dirt. Of course, the rains and mud were just as difficult to deal with, but for entirely different reasons. Dianne preferred this dry stretch of ground to the muddy bog they'd fought back in northern Kansas.

Pushing her bonnet back just a bit, Dianne strained her gaze to the west. She noted a few wispy clouds and prayed they might offer just enough rain to lay the dust.

"Better keep that sunbonnet pushed forward," Griselda Showalter said as she walked toward Dianne. "You'll regret it if you let the sun burn you."

Dianne disliked Mrs. Showalter almost as much as she did the hated bonnet. Mrs. Showalter was always sticking her nose in where it didn't belong, as far as Dianne was concerned. However, her mother seemed to enjoy the gossipy woman's company.

"Ma's in the wagon lying down," Dianne offered, choosing to ignore the woman's scowl. Dianne slowed the team. "Do you want to step up for a visit?"

Griselda nodded. "I've come to discuss the Indian troubles."

Dianne felt her eyes grow wide and tried hard not to show her fear. "Is there trouble close by?"

"Close enough," Griselda replied. "Now stop this wagon. I can't jump aboard like some. It just isn't ladylike."

Dianne hid her smile as she brought the oxen to a standstill. She had no doubt Griselda's difficulty in mounting the wagon had more to do with her rotund waistline than her concern over etiquette. The other night they had joined the Showalters to share supper, and Dianne had never seen a woman eat as much food as Mrs. Showalter. In fact, Dianne had never seen any man eat as much.

Griselda hoisted her heavy body up onto the back of the wagon, talking the entire time. "Susannah, it's me, Griselda. I've come to see how you're faring. There's trouble aplenty in the west. . . ."

Dianne could hear her continued chatter even after she urged the oxen forward. Dianne felt sorry for the woman's poor little husband. He was probably no more than a third Griselda's size. He looked so frail that Morgan once suggested a good wind could blow him clear to Texas. Dianne had a hard time imagining how the couple must have met and married. They seemed so mismatched. Griselda was a talkative, pushy woman who insisted her thoughts and opinions were the only ones to be had. Percy, on the other hand, was so quiet and agreeable that he faded into the background anytime he was in the presence of his wife.

The Showalter children were obedient, to be sure. The only time Dianne had seen one of them step out of line, she'd been mortified to watch their mother take up a razor strop and beat the child soundly across the backside. Most of the time, because of the work their mother gave them, they were too exhausted to do much more than eat their dinner and fall asleep by the end of the day. She'd certainly never seen them at play as she did her sisters. Even the littlest one, a four-year-old boy named Brian, was constantly working to gather wood or chips to fuel their evening fire.

Dianne noted their pace had slowed considerably. Gauging from the sun overhead, she figured it to be time for the nooning. As the wagons in front of her stopped, she drew up her oxen and halted them as well. Pushing her bonnet all the way back, Dianne wiped her brow with the hem of her apron and sighed.

She liked the nooning. They would eat cold leftovers from breakfast and rest for about an hour—sometimes two, depending on the weather and condition of the train. She found it a great time to slip away and talk with her only friend—Faith.

Dianne's mother often slept at this time, grateful for the lack of motion. Today, however, it looked like she would be visiting with Mrs. Showalter, for Dianne never knew the woman to stay less than an hour.

As her brothers unhitched the oxen and led them away to water and feed, Dianne put out lunch for the boys and her sisters. Seeing Betsy and Ardith settled with their share of food, Dianne slipped down to the river to freshen up. Throwing the bonnet aside, Dianne splashed her face over and over. How refreshing it felt. She could feel the caked-on dirt wash away with each handful of water.

"It's pretty senseless to be out here without a sunbonnet on."

Dianne looked up to find Cole Selby twirling her bonnet in his hand. He tossed it to her. "I suppose you don't have the good sense to wear this, but I must insist."

Dianne was determined not to be bullied by this man. She set the bonnet aside and planted her hands on her hips. "You have no right to boss me around. I'm washing up, as if you couldn't tell from having spied on me. One hardly wears a bonnet when washing up."

"One does when dealing with the prairie sun." He scowled at her. "You're just a child, so I don't expect you to understand. But the sun is fierce out here. If you spend the day with it beating down on your head, you'll be sun sick before supper."

"Mr. Selby, just because you're older than I doesn't give you the right to treat me like a child and call me one," Dianne said, losing her interest in the previously quiet setting. "I'm old enough to know what's good for me." She climbed back up the muddy bank and stomped past him.

She hadn't taken three steps, however, when she was halted abruptly by Cole. With his ironclad grip on her arm, Dianne knew it was senseless to fight him, but she did nevertheless.

"Don't move!" he demanded gruffly.

Dianne didn't know why, but it seemed sensible to do as he said. She stilled, then shuddered as he drew a long knife from his boot.

He seemed to understand and softened his tone. "You might not want to look."

But Dianne couldn't help it. Her gaze followed down to where Cole had squatted, his hand still firmly holding her arm. There under her left boot was the firmly pinned but wriggling body of a snake.

"You're standing square on his head. He can't strike or hurt you. Don't move and I'll kill him."

Dianne began to tremble but quickly nodded and looked away as Cole went to work. *How silly he must think me,* she admitted to herself. *Here I just told him I wasn't a child—that I was old enough to take care of myself. Now he'll really think me daft.*

"Seems I'm always coming to your rescue," Cole said, releasing Dianne and standing. He held up the headless snake as though it were a trophy. "Rattlesnake makes good eating."

Dianne felt her stomach turn. She thought she very well might be sick. "You're going to eat it?"

"Sure. Why not? It's good meat. Would you like to try it once I fix it up?"

She shook her head slowly. "No. No, thank you." Dianne hesitated a moment. "May I . . . may I go now?"

"Sure. He can't hurt you. Go ahead and lift your foot."

Dianne did so quickly, almost jumping away. She turned to view the creature's head, not knowing why. It was just as Cole said. It couldn't hurt her now.

"Thank you, Mr. Selby," she said, then hurried from him before he could reply. She had no desire to hear another lecture about her childish inability to take care of herself.

There was still plenty of time before they resumed traveling, so Dianne made her way through the labyrinth of wagons to where Faith and Malachi rested. Malachi was just getting to his feet as Dianne approached. "I need to be lookin' in on dem beasts," he told Faith.

"Afternoon, Miz Chadwick. Ya looks like ya's seen a ghost," Malachi said with a smile.

"I just had a rather frightening experience," Dianne said, sitting down beside Faith. "I stepped on a rattlesnake and Mr. Selby saved my life."

"Gracious, child. A snake like that could kill you dead," Faith said, her hand going to her throat.

"I kilt me a snake just a few days back," Malachi said, shaking his head. "Weren't no rattler, it were a copperhead. 'Member that lake we camped by back in Kansas?"

Dianne nodded. "I remember."

"That be where I kilt it."

Faith shuddered. "I hate snakes."

"Useless creatures," Dianne agreed.

Malachi laughed. "Nah, some be good. Ya get ya a nice black snake in the barn and he be eatin' yar mice and rats. Bull snakes will even kill dem rattlers for ya."

"Well, no thanks," Dianne said, the memory still too fresh for comfort. "I want no part of any snake."

Malachi laughed again and continued chuckling even as he walked away. Faith couldn't help but smile herself. "This is all so new for you, isn't it?"

"I feel completely stupid some days. I try to mimic what I see others doing, but I fall so short of doing it right. I almost caught my skirt on fire—again—when I was fixing supper last night."

"But those things happen to everyone. I knew a woman who boiled laundry day after day at an outside kettle. She caught her skirt afire one day and burned to death. Bad things happen sometimes like that. It doesn't always matter what you know or don't know."

"What a horrible way to die."

Faith nodded and extended a plate with biscuits soaked in bacon grease. "Are you hungry?"

Dianne took one of the biscuits and nodded. "There was a time when we would never have eaten such things. Now they seem like a treat. I get so hungry and I eat as much as a horse. It's a wonder my clothes even fit anymore."

Faith placed a cloth over the biscuits and poured Dianne a tin cup of water. "You're probably working harder than ever before. You'll need to eat more to keep up your strength. Say, how's your mama? You said she was feeling poorly."

"She still is. All she wants to do is ride in the wagon. She gets so tired when she walks. I'm worried about her, but she won't talk. I think she still blames me for Pa's death. Truth be told," Dianne said, hanging her head, "I blame myself."

"Seems like folks are always blaming themselves for the wrong things and not taking responsibility for what truly should be counted against them."

Dianne looked up and met Faith's sympathetic gaze. "But my insistence on going to the bank started the whole thing."

"I've heard your account and I'll give you credit for that much. But don't forget that your pa allowed you to go. And the consequence of that was your encounter with those men. Your pa took care of that matter. He wasn't shot because he took you out of harm's way, now, was he?"

"No, I guess not."

"I thought you told me the ruckus was caused because the army got involved. Wasn't that right?"

Dianne remembered the scene as though it were yesterday. She could still see her father's blood pooling out around his head. "Yes," she finally managed to whisper.

"Dianne, it was an accident. Your pa was in the wrong place at the wrong time. Those men who accosted you could have walked away, but they chose to fight. Your pa should have come back into the store and let the army, or law, take care of the matter, but he chose to stay. It might have started with your poor choice—a choice your father agreed to—but it ended in free will. Those men made their choices and now you have to make yours."

Dianne shook her head. "I don't know what you mean."

Faith reached out and patted Dianne's shoulder. "Honey, you need to decide if you're going to go through life blaming yourself and letting others blame you for your father's death. You can't change everyone's heart on the matter, but you can change your own. And in doing so, you may help them to see it in a different way."

"I'll never change Mama's heart. She'll always blame me."

"She has to make her own choices. Give her time. When she sees that you've turned a page, maybe she'll be willing to do likewise."

Dianne nodded. She saw Malachi returning with the oxen and realized she'd spent way too much time with Faith. "Oh, goodness. The day's getting away from me. I best get back to the wagon and see what Ma might need from me before we start moving again."

Both women got to their feet. Dianne dusted off her dress, then searched around for her sunbonnet. It was nowhere to be found.

"Did I bring my bonnet when I came?"

"I don't recall seeing it," Faith said. "Guess sitting here in the shade of the wagon, I wasn't too worried about it." She smiled and motioned toward the river. "Maybe that old snake's wife is wearing it. You'd best go back and see if you left it by the water."

Dianne laughed. "I'll bet that's exactly what I did."

But her search of the riverbank turned up nothing. Defeated, she hurried back to the wagon and began to gather the lunch dishes. Already her brothers were hitching the oxen. A quick check on her mother found Griselda gone and her mother sleeping peacefully. Dianne decided against waking her. She'd just save her lunch and see if she wanted it later.

"You forgot this," a deep voice said as Dianne rushed around the corner of the wagon.

She stopped abruptly to keep from running into Cole Selby. She looked at the bonnet he twirled on his finger. Snatching it away from him, she pulled it on.

"Thank you." She knew her reply was curt and unfriendly, but she couldn't help it. He made her feel completely incompetent.

"I noticed earlier that your skirt looked a little scorched. Been standing too close to the fire again?" he baited.

His comment infuriated her and Dianne might have given him a piece of her mind, but Levi Sperry, Charity and Ben Hammond's ward, came into camp just then.

"Afternoon, Miss Dianne. Miz Charity thought you might be needin' some extra biscuits." He extended the pan and smiled.

Dianne thought him a sweet boy—close to her own age and such a gentle spirit. "Thank you. How kind."

Levi blushed and looked to the ground. He had a stocky, muscular build with ebony hair that fell casually over his left brow as he bent his head.

"Why, you're her knight in shining armor," Cole said with a laugh. "The family might well starve to death if left solely to Miss Chadwick's care. She has a habit of setting herself on fire, as you will note by studying the hem of her skirt."

"Oh!" Dianne exclaimed. She stepped forward to give Cole a piece of her mind, but already he was stalking away, his long legs covering the distance quickly. "That man makes me so mad. He's so rude! He doesn't care what he says or how it sounds."

"I wouldn't give him no mind, Miss Dianne. Men like him don't care what other people think."

She looked at the young man and nodded. He had a sweet face with dark brown eyes and thick black lashes. They seemed almost unnatural on a man, but Levi appeared no less masculine for their presence. "I'm sure you're right."

"Say," Levi said, suddenly seeming less shy, "have you heard the news?"

"I haven't heard much of anything news-wise for many days."

"They've changed the name of the territory where Virginia City is located. They're calling it Montana now. It's a brand-new territory because so many people are settling in up there and they need more law and such."

"Montana." Dianne tried the name, wondering at the meaning of it.

"Reverend Ben says it comes from the Spanish word for mountains. He says we'll see plenty of those once we get farther west."

"I like the name," Dianne replied. "I think Montana sounds just fine."

CHAPTER 9

RAINS FROM THE WEEK BEFORE HAD SWOLLEN THE PLATTE RIVER at Julesburg, leaving it impossible to cross. For three days, the travelers had waited impatiently, with several of the members trying to risk a crossing. The acts of bravery, however, were to no avail. The churning brown waters simply refused to allow passage.

Dianne didn't mind the delay. She was tired—weary of the constant routine—and desperate for something to break the monotony. She did take the opportunity to ride her horse and get better acquainted with the mare's needs. Dolly was a good-tempered buckskin whose mood seemed to alter to match her rider. If Dianne was feeling sad or over-whelmed, Dolly appeared to be more sedate. If Dianne felt an exuber-ance that left her giddy with excitement, Dolly picked up on that as well. They were a good match, Dianne decided. She'd overheard Cole Selby say that a horse and rider needed to belong to each other. Dianne figured that's how it was with Dolly as she fell more in love with the animal.

The delay along the Platte also allowed for overhauling the wagons and giving the animals the extra care that the trail didn't allow for. The rains had stopped and the cool weather had passed. Only a week before they were worried about snow, as the evenings had been so very cold. Now the temperatures were on the rise and it was quite comfortable to work outdoors.

The wagon master and his men took advantage of the suspension of travel to further inform the travelers about the troubles they would encounter west of Julesburg. Namely, Indians. Rumor had it that Indians had been sighted just downriver from where the wagon train had passed earlier. The word came via a post rider, but he couldn't tell the wagon master if they were friendlies or a war party.

To be on the safe side, Daniel Keefer set up training sessions where he taught the men how to properly take cover and fire their weapons at the same time. Dianne watched from a distance because only the men were allowed to be involved. She found the process fascinating and began to wonder at the perils they might meet in the weeks to come.

So far the Indians had been few and far between. From a distance they'd seen a few peaceful convoys—even one hunting party. It was as close as Dianne cared to come. Her mother had her positively terrified with tales of people being caught by the Indians, of their scalps being removed and kept as trophies, of unspeakable things done to women. Where her mother had heard these tales it was hard to say. Dianne guessed Griselda Showalter was probably to blame for some of the commotion, but everyone was edgy.

To Dianne's great joy, her mother's health appeared to return. Susannah Chadwick seemed more like her old self as she moved about the camp, fussing over Betsy's sniffles and Ardith's messy appearance.

"I swear you look like vagabonds," their mother declared as she worked to rebraid Ardith's hair. "A lady must always see to her appearance. Even on the trail in the middle of nowhere."

Dianne had to smile at this. They all had that same look to them. There wasn't a person traveling the plains who didn't wear at least a pound of dirt from day to day. Reverend Hammond joked that during his daily trek he'd eat so much dirt that he rarely needed supper.

"Dianne, I'm going to take the girls and go visiting. Since the laundry is done, why don't you start our supper? I'm sure that will keep you busy for a time."

Dianne wasn't sure why her mother was worried about keeping her busy, but Dianne had already seen to supper. She'd gotten rather good at planning ahead of time, and when the Hammonds offered her a small hunk of fresh venison, Dianne jumped at the chance to put together something special for supper. A fresh meat stew was already cooking and wouldn't need her attention for hours.

She said nothing about it, however, as her mother walked away with Dianne's sisters. Dianne wanted the time to visit with Faith. It was a defiance of her mother's wishes, but Dianne couldn't help it. Faith was her only real friend out here on the prairie. Besides, Faith was going to teach Dianne about making cobbler in the Dutch oven. Surely even her mother would be pleased with the results.

After washing up, Dianne filled a large jar with milk. They had more than they could use and generally they sold or traded it to keep from having to throw it away. Faith would enjoy the treat.

Dianne made small talk as she passed by other members of the wagon train. One woman asked if she'd heard when they might cross the river.

"I haven't heard anything today, but if I get any news, I'll let you know on my way back," Dianne replied. The woman, who had three small children clinging to her skirts, nodded.

"I'd be much obliged."

"Dianne," a gentle voice called, "how's your mother today?"

She looked to her right to see Mrs. Hammond waving. Dianne hated the delay in reaching Faith, but she liked Mrs. Hammond and appreciated the older woman's concern.

"Mother is doing much better. I think this rest has done her a lot of good." Dianne smiled and nodded as Levi came to stand beside Mrs. Hammond.

"Hello, Miss Dianne."

"Hello," Dianne said softly. She suddenly felt ill at ease in his presence.

"Levi has been a tremendous help to Mr. Hammond and me. I don't know what we'd have done without him when the wagon got stuck." Levi blushed furiously.

"It's always good to have an extra hand," Dianne replied, not knowing what else to say.

"I'm sorry he had to be orphaned but grateful the good Lord put us all together. Levi wants to settle in the West—maybe even in Virginia City, where you're headed. Wouldn't it be nice if you two were to get to know each other better?"

Dianne felt her own cheeks grow hot at this comment. "Ah, yes. I think that would be nice."

Mrs. Hammond seemed to understand their discomfort and dismissed Levi to return to his work. "He's not much older than you. Seventeen, to be exact. You never know, you might find yourselves courting before the trip is over."

"Courting?" Dianne shook her head. "No, I'm much too young according to my mother."

"Oh, nonsense—you're sixteen. I was married to Mr. Hammond when I was but fourteen. That was the way things were done in Kentucky, where I grew up. Mr. Hammond was only sixteen and green as grass. He had no idea yet that the Lord was calling him."

Dianne wasn't exactly sure what she meant by the Lord calling Mr. Hammond but decided questions would only delay her visit with Faith.

"I don't think Ma would smile on my courting—not just yet. She married at sixteen and has always told me it was far too much responsibility to take on at that age," Dianne said, hoping that would be the end of it. She held up her jar of milk. "I probably should be moving on. I need to deliver this."

"By all means, child. I didn't mean to keep you. Come back and visit when you're ready for another quilting lesson. I'm sure we can find loads to talk about."

Dianne realized she would very much enjoy getting to better know Charity Hammond. "I'll do that. My sewing still needs work, and with what I've heard of the cold weather up north, we'll be needing extra quilts."

"Come any time. If we're still waiting on the river, why don't you come tomorrow?"

Dianne nodded. "I'll do that if Ma can spare me." She bid Mrs. Hammond good-bye, then hurried off to where Faith and Malachi's wagon was positioned with the other handful of former slaves who had chosen to go west. Dianne thought it quite wrong that the Negroes were forced to keep to themselves but said nothing. Who would listen?

"Faith!" she called, waving. "I've brought you some milk."

Faith waved back and motioned Dianne into the camp. "I've soaked some dried peaches and they're ready for our cobbler lesson."

Dianne nodded. "I've been looking forward to this."

She spent the rest of the morning with Faith, laughing and learning. Dianne found herself telling Faith about her friends back in New Madrid and was fascinated by Faith's stories of her life before the war.

"Was it really against the law for you to learn to read?" Dianne asked as Faith handed her a wooden bowl of beans for lunch.

"Oh, it sure was. But I was Miss Deborah's companion. Where she went, I went. So when the tutor came to teach her and her brothers their lessons, I sat at Miss Deborah's feet and learned right along with them. They didn't know it. The whites figured we weren't able to learn such things anyway."

Dianne shook her head. "I never wanted to go to school. I was never that good at book learning. I mean, I can read and write. I can cipher math problems, but I don't enjoy any of it. Especially history. I hated that boring old stuff."

Faith laughed. "My history lessons came at the knee of an old house worker we called Granny. When the master and his family were entertaining, I was sent to be with Granny and the other house slaves. It was there that Granny would remind me who I was and who my people were. See, Granny remembered being stolen away as a girl in Africa. She was brought here and sold and sorely abused by first one master and then another, but she never forgot the old ways or her people." Faith's expression took on a faraway look. "Granny gave birth to fifteen children over the course of her life. She didn't know where a single one was because they'd all been sold off as they'd gotten older. That's the way things were done, depending on the master's need."

"How awful. I can't imagine having my children taken away."

Faith nodded. "I don't remember much about my mama. She wasn't sold off, though. She died of yellow fever when I was three. I never even knew my pa. But listening to Granny talk about her family, well, I liked to pretend they were mine too. I told her I'd be one of her daughters if she'd have me." Faith shook herself out of the sorrowful thoughts and added, "Granny taught me about Jesus too."

Dianne sampled her beans and didn't know when she'd ever tasted anything so good. "These are wonderful. What are they?"

"Black-eyed peas and a piece of salted pork," Faith said, checking the cobbler. "I think this is just about ready. We can have dessert with our lunch."

Dianne nodded. "I wish I could share this with my family. The flavor is just so different. It's always nice to have a change."

"I'll put the milk you brought into something else and send some black-eyed peas back in the jar."

"Oh, Faith, thank you. That would be wonderful!"

They finished their lunch and sampled the cobbler. Dianne was delighted with the simplicity of the recipe and knew beyond a doubt that she could make the dessert for her own family.

"I've had so much fun talking and cooking with you, Faith." Dianne took up the jar of beans and smiled. "I'll come again when I can."

"You do that. Next time I'll teach you how to make a rag rug."

Dianne stood amazed at the knowledge that Faith held. *I can learn so much from this woman,* she thought. *So much that will make our lives easier, especially when we reach Uncle Bram's house.* "Thank you again, Faith. I know my family will love these black-eyed peas."

But her family never had the chance to sample them. As Dianne put the finishing touches on supper and made certain that the venison stew had cooked to perfection, her mother appeared to oversee matters.

"What is this?" she asked, gazing into the small iron kettle Dianne had put the beans in to warm.

"Those are black-eyed peas. The flavor is so good. I just know you'll love it."

"That's darkie food. You got these from that woman, didn't you?"

Dianne had been squatting beside the fire but stood rather quickly.

"I got them from Faith, if that's what you're asking."

Her mother, mindless of the fire, kicked the pot over and spilled the contents onto the ground. "My family won't be fed such things. We're too good for the likes of that slop."

Dianne struggled with her emotions. "But it tasted wonderful. I thought you'd enjoy the change."

Her mother crossed to where Dianne stood. "You've been spending time with that slave woman, haven't you? Even after I told you not to. Even after I reminded you that they're responsible for killing your pa."

"But Pa's death was an accident," Dianne protested. "Besides, Faith and Malachi aren't slaves. They're free."

Her mother slapped her hard across the face, then stared at Dianne for a moment as if she couldn't believe what she'd just done. It was the first time her gentle-spirited mother had ever done such a thing. Getting over her initial shock, her mother stepped back.

"Get supper dished up. I'll call the boys." She turned to go, then stopped and faced Dianne again. This time her voice was gentle, almost loving. "Dianne, there are reasons why society has separated the races. It's not wise to dabble in things you know nothing about. I insist you have nothing more to do with that woman."

She didn't wait for a reply and for this Dianne was grateful. She could never have promised her mother that she wouldn't see Faith—wouldn't speak to her and learn from her. Her mother might not realize it, but she was benefiting as much as the rest of the family from Faith's lessons.

Supper was a somber affair. The venison stew brought praise from her brothers, but her mother said nothing throughout the entire meal. Dianne felt her sense of isolation grow. Her mother had never been one to share the thoughts of her heart, but at least she'd been willing to converse. Now it seemed she was struggling with something—something more than her earlier anger with Dianne. But what could it be?

As supper concluded, Dianne started to clear away the dishes, but her mother waved her off.

"Sit back down, Dianne. I want to talk to all of you."

Dianne sat down between Morgan and Ardith and waited. Perhaps her mother intended to talk about the earlier incident regarding Faith and the black-eyed peas. Dianne lowered her gaze to the fire and sincerely prayed that would not be the case. Her mother had a history, however, of using one child to make an object lesson with another. *Please just leave Faith out of this, Mama. She's a good woman and she's not to blame.*

"I have news to share. I know this has been a hard trip on all of us. I know you've had to work hard, and I appreciate it. I know you don't always agree with my opinions, but with your father now gone, I ask that you respect my wishes. Just as Mr. Keefer gave us the list of rules to help us keep safe, my opinions are often given for the same reason. You may not like them, but I expect you to follow them." Dianne looked up as her mother looked directly into her eyes.

"Now it's more important than ever. As we push west there will be the threat of Indian attacks. We've been blessed not to have encountered such things thus far, but you can never tell who might be the enemy. There's talk that Southern sympathizers have joined forces with Indians to attack Northerners. Personally, I do not believe this, but there are plenty of problems for us even without such alliances. Races do not mix. Indians do not live in peace with whites and neither do freed slaves. If it appears such things are possible, you must ask yourself what is motivating their actions." She paused and set aside her bowl, and Dianne wondered if this was why her mother held such bitterness toward Faith and Malachi. Maybe she believed the former slaves would rise up to kill them as well. But what would have prompted such fears? Had her mother been told things like this as a child?

"But the real reason I wanted to talk with you is to share something entirely different. I've known about this since we left New Madrid, but I didn't want to tell you until we were well on our way west," she began. "It will help explain why I've been so sick."

Ardith shifted and leaned over to rest her head against Dianne's shoulder. No doubt she was tired. Dianne knew their mother had kept the girls busy all day. Even Betsy was yawning.

"I'm going to have a baby," their mother suddenly confessed. At least it seemed sudden to Dianne. She jerked her head up, as did Ardith. "The baby will come in December, so we'll be long settled with Uncle Bram."

"A baby will be so much fun!" Betsy declared, clapping her hands.

"No it won't," Ardith grumbled. "Babies are a lot of work and they just get into your stuff and make messes."

Betsy frowned as if she'd been personally insulted, and in truth she had, for Ardith had no experience with babies other than with Betsy. Dianne reached out to soothe her sister.

"I didn't think you were a bother at all. I loved playing with you. You'll probably love playing with this new baby."

"No I won't." Ardith jerked away from Dianne and crossed her arms against her chest. With a frown on her face, she pouted as their mother continued.

"I didn't tell you right away because I was worried that Mr. Keefer would refuse to allow us to travel. It won't be much longer, however, that I'll be able to hide this condition from anyone, so I figured I'd better let you know."

"I don't want another baby around," Ardith said, getting to her feet. "I want you to send it away."

"Ardith Chadwick!" their mother exclaimed. "What a selfish child you are! How dare you suggest such a thing."

Ardith's lower lip quivered and Dianne saw her eyes fill with tears. "I don't want another baby around. You won't love us anymore—you'll only love the baby." She ran off across the camp and disappeared.

"I'll go after her," Dianne said, getting to her feet. She felt she should say something more to her mother. "Ma, I'm happy about the baby. It's like a special gift from God—since Pa can't be with us anymore."

Her mother nodded and for the first time since the tragedy in New Madrid, Dianne felt as though she'd reached her mother's heart with her words.

With that small moment warming Dianne inside, she hurried off to find Ardith. The poor girl was probably remembering how much less attention she had received when Betsy came along. To Ardith, it must have seemed that Betsy usurped her position as baby of the family. Another child would push her even farther from that place.

"Ardith! Ardith! Where are you?" she called, moving around the circled gathering of the wagons. But there was no reply. A couple of people mentioned having seen Ardith, but no one noticed which direction the child had gone. The sun was sinking toward the horizon, leaving streaks of red and lavender in the sky. Dianne knew the light would soon be gone altogether.

"Ardith!"

Dianne searched for over twenty minutes and still nothing. Then a commotion drew her attention. Maybe someone had found Ardith.

Making her way down to the river, Dianne heard one woman hysterically exclaiming, "A little girl just fell off the bank! The current's got her. I saw it myself but I couldn't save her."

Dianne felt sickened. She pushed her way through the crowd. "Was the girl wearing a blue dress and apron?"

The woman nodded. "As best as I could tell. She was crying, and I tried to talk to her. I thought maybe she was lost. She ran off from me and slipped on the riverbank."

"That's my sister!" Dianne cried out.

She took off running alongside the river, screaming Ardith's name. There was no sign of the child, however. Heartsick, Dianne pressed on. She had to find her. Ardith had to be safe.

"Ardith!"

Dianne turned to avoid a cluster of brush and found herself in front of a mounted rider. "What's going on?" Cole Selby demanded.

"My little sister Ardith has fallen into the river. Some woman saw her. The current swept her downstream, but I don't see her anywhere."

"Go back to your camp. I'll look for her, but—" he paused and Dianne met his expression in the dimming light—"don't get your hopes up. That river is fierce right now. A child would never be able to swim for the bank."

Dianne watched him urge his horse forward as an overwhelming emptiness washed over her. "Don't get my hopes up?" How could she not? How could she simply dismiss the matter?

Dianne slowly made her way back to the wagon. She could hardly stand the thought that she would be the bearer of this bad news. She neared their camp and prayed silently for strength. She wasn't normally given to talking much to God, but it seemed a good thing. "Please help us find Ardith," she murmured, "and please let her be alive and safe."

"Ma!" Dianne's voice sounded foreign in her ears. "Ma, you must come. Ardith has fallen into the river. Mr. Selby has gone after her."

Every member of her family jumped up from around the fire. Even Betsy rushed forward with questions.

"Come on. We can ask the woman who saw her fall in," Dianne suggested, not having any desire to relay the details. She kept hearing Cole's words over and over in her head.

"We'll ride out and see if we can help Mr. Selby," Morgan declared. He and Zane ran for the horses while Betsy, Dianne, and their mother rushed to the riverbank, where Susannah questioned everyone who had any knowledge of the incident. "Oh, this is all my fault," she whispered. "I told her she was selfish. I know it was probably nothing more than shock that made her say the things she did."

Dianne watched as her mother twisted her hands together. The agony in her expression was more than Dianne could bear, and she quickly looked away as if to gaze into the darkness of the landscape.

Fifty or more people gathered around them. Griselda Showalter held Susannah close and talked to her constantly. For once, Dianne thought, the woman's incessant chatter was probably a blessing.

"I just heard about your sister," Levi said as he came to stand beside Dianne and Betsy. "Is there anything I can do?"

"Just wait with us," Dianne said, not knowing what else to say.

"I will," he said softly. "And I'll pray."

Dianne met his compassionate gaze and nodded. "Thank you."

After an hour, Cole Selby and the twins rode back into camp. Their arms were empty, however. "We didn't see any sign of her," Cole said despondently.

Their mother tore away from Griselda and went to where Cole dismounted. "That's it? That's all you can do? My child is out there somewhere."

Cole frowned. "She's most likely been swept far beyond our reach. I'm sorry."

"But we can't just leave her. She'll be cold. She'll be afraid. Indians might find her."

Dianne heard the murmurs around her. "She's a goner," one man said.

"She's dead for sure."

Dianne watched her mother start to crumple to the ground. Morgan reached out to take hold of her and steadied her on her feet. "Come on," he said, "let's go back to the wagon."

Dianne stared after her family in disbelief. Surely that wasn't all they could do. Surely Ardith wasn't really dead. She looked to Mr. Selby, who by now had dismounted. "Can't we do anything else?"

"Nothing to be done," he replied. "I went down the river as far as I could. She couldn't have made it." As if realizing how harsh he sounded, his tone softened as he added, "I'm sorry."

Levi put his arm around Dianne. "Come on, I'll walk you back to your camp."

Dianne nodded but continued to look to Cole, as if he could give her something more to go on. He said nothing, turning away instead. The finality of it cut deep into Dianne's heart.

CHAPTER 10

THE WAGON TRAIN CROSSED THE RIVER ON THE TWENTY-SECOND of June. Dianne could barely comprehend that they were leaving the area.

Leaving Ardith.

Every day she'd taken Dolly and ridden along the swollen, swirling Platte, checking the banks with a critical eye, seeking with desperation anything that might prove Ardith had passed this way. Always she returned home defeated and discouraged.

Reverend Hammond, with Charity and Levi, had come to sit with them most every evening—sharing comfort and talking of God's ability to work this tragedy for good. But Dianne could see no good in the death of a child. The more Charity Hammond tried to share Scripture with Dianne, the more questions came to mind. Why would God take the life of her sister? Was He punishing them? Was He angry at their decision to move west? Or did He simply not care? With two deaths in her family, Dianne felt the latter was probably the answer.

God simply had better things to do. There was, after all, a war going on. No doubt God had His hands full with such matters. What was the life of one child compared to the lives of hundreds of thousands of men? Still, the very thought of this hurt Dianne in a way she couldn't begin to explain. Why were the Chadwicks not as important to God as other families?

In the back of her mind, Dianne remembered that other deaths had occurred along the way. A family here and there had lost loved ones as well. Travel was especially hard on the old and the young. But those were strangers. Dianne's need to understand was a much more personal matter.

As the days ticked by, Dianne carefully erected a wall around her heart. The pain was so great, she hoped she might contain it by isolation. Her brothers seemed to do the same, saying very little to anyone, while Betsy clung to their mother for understanding and comfort. But their mother had no comfort to offer and often Dianne found Betsy crying alone. It was the one chink in her armor that Dianne hadn't counted on. She could scarcely ignore her sister's tears.

So with great confusion, Dianne fought to work against the sadness that threatened to eat her alive. She tried to give of herself to Betsy while sealing off her feelings toward others. And that went for God as well. A cold indifference settled over her as she struggled to deal with her emotions. If it was God's plan to ignore her needs, then maybe she should just ignore God in return.

As they pushed west toward Fort Laramie, her spirits sank even further as Susannah took to her bed and refused to eat or speak. Even Betsy stopped making attempts to see their mother. Instead she stuck by Dianne's side. Her tears dried up, as did her questions and comments regarding Ardith. Dianne hated seeing Betsy become so sullen, but she barely had the strength to keep her own heart from plunging into darkness. How could she be responsible for Betsy's as well?

On the last day of the month, Dianne got her first close-up view of Indians. It was a peaceful clan, Mr. Selby had told them, although he didn't mention the tribe by name. Mostly they were nomadic, moving across the plains in search of food. Some even came to beg bread from the settlers. Dianne felt horribly sorry for them in spite of the way she'd attempted to put her emotions aside. Since her mother was nowhere around to suggest otherwise, she gave a jar of milk and a few pieces of fried bread to an Indian mother whose four small children looked nearly starved to death.

The woman smiled and offered Dianne a small leather pouch in trade. Dianne started to refuse it.

"Don't insult her," Cole Selby said from behind. "Take the trade. Otherwise her pride will be wounded."

Dianne didn't even bother to look around. She smiled back at the woman and took the pouch. She said nothing until after the woman and her children had gone. Fingering the fine craftsmanship of the pouch, she asked, "Why are they so hungry? We've seen antelope and other game. There have been berries along the way." She turned and met Cole's stern expression and asked again, "Why?"

He shrugged. "A lot of them have lost their men. That mother is probably alone, with no man to hunt for her. If you've noticed, a good many of the Indians we've encountered have been women and children and old folks. They don't have the ability to run down an antelope."

"Where are their men? What happened to them?"

"Some have died from sickness brought west by the whites. Others have died in the Indian wars. There's been fierce fighting out here over the last couple of years. There will continue to be more fighting as time goes on."

"When will it stop?" Dianne felt a deep sadness as she considered that those children were in the same position as she was: they had no father, and they would lose siblings just as she had.

"It won't stop until the Indians have been driven off the land," Cole said matter-of-factly.

"Do you agree with that idea?"

Cole shook his head. "No. But then, I don't recall anyone asking me what I thought, except you." He turned and walked away without another word and Dianne was left to contemplate yet another fact of life that she'd been blissfully unaware of—until now.

That night, a horrible windstorm blew up. There was no warning, no time to secure the campsite more than they'd already done prior to going to bed. As the wind picked up and the rain poured, Dianne gathered Betsy into her arms and abandoned their bed under the wagon for the safety inside. They joined their mother, who said nothing to either one of them. Dianne wondered if Morgan and Zane had gotten to safety. They were the ones who suggested the girls take cover. Meanwhile, they were going to help with the livestock.

As the wagon rocked back and forth, threatening to tip over at any moment, Betsy cried softly in Dianne's arms while their mother buried her face against her pillow and turned away from her daughters. Dianne immediately thought of Ardith. She couldn't help but wonder if her little sister was still alive—wandering around the countryside in the midst of the storm.

As if reading her mind, Betsy asked, "Is it storming on Ardith too?"

Dianne brushed back her sister's wild hair. "Oh, I don't think so. We've traveled quite a ways since Julesburg."

"Do you think she's with God?" Betsy then questioned, completely catching Dianne off guard. One minute the child spoke as if Ardith were alive, while the next she seemed to accept that Ardith was gone.

"I'm sure she's in God's care, no matter where she is."

"Will she understand why we left her behind? I mean, if she's still back at the river?"

"I'm sure she'll understand. And besides, lots of folks know about Ardith. We told everyone we could in Julesburg. If they find her, they know where we're headed. Mama left all the information with the sheriff. If they find her, they'll bring her to Uncle Bram's in Virginia City."

Betsy nodded and snuggled down against Dianne. "I hope they find her."

Dianne swallowed the lump in her throat. "I hope so too."

At some point, Dianne and Betsy fell asleep cradled in each other's arms. In the morning, Dianne awoke to find everything strangely calm. It was almost as if the storm had never happened. Some of the wagons had been damaged and several animals were missing—probably spooked off by the intensity of the wind and rain. Otherwise, everyone seemed fine.

Later that morning, they arrived at Fort Laramie. The fort sat amidst rolling hills and a lumbering river. There were very few trees, mostly small ones along the water. Dianne supposed that those who'd come before them had chopped down what wood could be had for fires.

They camped near the fort on the opposite side of the river. Here they would enjoy the protection of the soldiers and also learn whatever news was to be had at the sutler's store. Post riders, who were much quicker than wagon trains, had brought in mail from back East. Many families were delighted to hear news from their loved ones. Morgan went to check on behalf of the Chadwick family but found nothing.

Dianne was saddened by this, hoping against hope that Trenton might have taken time to write. She worried about him. She couldn't help herself.

Word swept through the camp on July 2 that three children in the train had come down with measles. Daniel Keefer made the decision to stay through for at least a couple of days and see how many others might show signs of the disease. It would also allow the travelers to celebrate Independence Day at the fort—where quite a party was planned.

Dianne went through the paces of her days, dreading the news of additional sick. She tried to occupy her time by seeing to the needs of the family. She took care of the laundry, washing it down at the river, then spreading it on a clothesline between two of their wagons. She cooked and cleaned up around their camp and tried to tend to any requests her mother made. Betsy was her constant shadow. She especially loved visiting the horses, and Dianne actually thought the animals helped to heal them both. Somehow stroking the velvet muzzle of Dolly and brushing the burrs from her tail gave Dianne a peace she found difficult to grasp anywhere else. Betsy, whose love of animals had always been evident, enjoyed such times as well.

In the evening, Dianne would listen to the sounds of the soldiers settling in for the night. The guards walking their posts were a comfort to her, even if they were across the river. Sometimes she watched them and wondered who they were and where they'd come from. Were they glad to be here in the West rather than back East where the war was raging? Did they have families who missed them? Did they worry about the Indians and the rumors of wars that would pit them against each other?

Then at night, Dianne would curl up in her covers under the wagon and marvel to think they were a world away from New Madrid and all that she had known. She fell asleep at night pondering the world that yet awaited them—praying it would be more merciful than the trail west had been.

By the fourth, Keefer's concerns were well founded. At least fifty families had someone ill with measles, and five people had died. Mr. Keefer wanted to move out on the fifth and leave the sick behind.

"There's another wagon train not but two weeks behind us. Anyone with sick can wait here and pick up with the other train when they come through," he told the travelers at a mandatory meeting. Standing on the seat of one of the wagons, he raised his arms as the crowd's murmurings grew to a fevered pitch.

"Everyone quiet down. I intend to move this train west come morning. I want those of you who have sick family members to speak with my assistant, Cole Selby. Let him know your family's name and he'll record it. Then he'll leave a list with the fort commander. It's the safest thing to do for everyone concerned. You don't want to get out in the middle of nowhere and take sick yourselves."

Dianne worried about Betsy. Whereas Dianne and the boys had already had the measles, Betsy had not. So far, she'd shown no sign of the disease, but Dianne knew these things took time.

"What if we don't choose to stay behind?" a tall man with a thick black beard questioned. He stood not two feet from where Dianne watched the ruckus.

"I'm the commander of this train. When you signed on, you agreed to do things my way. If you choose to do otherwise, you can leave the train, but so long as you're here, you'll do it my way."

The man muttered a curse but said nothing more. There were a few other questions, but overall, people seemed to understand the seriousness of the situation. They didn't like being left behind, but they comprehended there being no other choice.

Mr. Keefer ended his speech by urging those who could to join in with the Fourth of July celebrations. Some of the folks in the train had planned a celebration days in advance, not knowing they would be able to share in the fort's activities. Everyone who played an instrument was encouraged to come and join in the spontaneous band, while the women were asked to bake their sweetest treat.

Dianne had no desire to attend the party but found herself encouraged to do so at every turn.

"It would do you good to be with other people," Charity Hammond told her. "I can stay with your mama if you'd like, and if your brothers aren't going, I'm sure Levi would like to escort you."

Dianne shook her head. "No. That's all right. Ma would resent anyone coming to stay with her. She'll be fine. But maybe I will take Betsy over. She could use some fun, and I heard that the children are going to be playing games and having contests."

Charity smiled and patted Dianne's shoulder. "That's the spirit. It will do you both good. Tell you what. I won't sit with your mama, but I'll give her a visit during the evening. That way she'll not be alone and you'll know she's all right."

Dianne agreed and went in search of Betsy. Her sister was excited at the prospect of the party. Morgan and Zane approved the idea as well. They had already planned to attend, as Zane wanted to talk to the soldiers about life in the fort and Morgan had his eye on dancing with a particularly lovely blond-haired girl.

Dianne watched as Betsy participated in the three-legged race. With her leg bound to the leg of another little girl, the delight on her sister's face was evident as the race began. Hopping down the field, they giggled and struggled to coordinate their steps. Dianne laughed too.

"It's good to hear you laughing," Faith said as she joined Dianne.

Dianne met Faith's joyful expression. "It's the first time I've felt like laughing since . . ." Dianne's voice broke. She fell silent and looked away. "Sorry."

"Dianne, I know your heart is nearly cut in two, but you have to have hope and courage. You have to go on living in spite of what happened."

"I know, but I just can't figure out why such a thing happened. Did Ardith's fall into the river take God by surprise?" She looked to Faith, hoping—almost praying—the older woman would have the answer.

"Why do you ask that? God is never taken by surprise."

"Then He must not have cared."

Faith reached out and took hold of Dianne. It was a bold move, for people of color were not to ever touch a white person without their expressed permission.

"Child, do you honestly think God has forgotten you?"

"I don't know how else to see it. I mean, how hard would it have been to save one little girl from drowning?"

"Not hard at all. At least not for God. So that's why you think God must have been sleeping or looking the other way. God didn't save your sister from the river, so you figure He doesn't care about you and your family. Is that it?"

Dianne knew it sounded silly, but she couldn't help it. "I know God has much more important things to do than to worry over us. There's the war and all that's happening back East. It's much more important."

"Why would you say that?"

Dianne's throat constricted. "It must be true; otherwise Ardith would still be here." Tears came to her eyes. "My father would still be here."

Faith wrapped Dianne in her arms. "Oh, Dianne, God still cares. He hasn't forgotten you. We can't always understand His ways, but child, His eye is on the sparrow—He knows when even one little bird falls from a tree. Do you not imagine Him knowing and caring that Ardith fell into the river—or that your father was killed?"

Dianne let her tears spill. "But it hurts so much, and I don't understand."

"It doesn't always hurt less when we do understand," Faith replied. "Knowing the why of things doesn't always make it right."

"What are you doing to my child?" Susannah Chadwick screamed, pulling Dianne from Faith's hold.

Dianne was too stunned to say anything for several seconds. Her mother continued ranting, screaming for her children. Morgan appeared quickly.

"What's wrong with her?"

Dianne shook her head as her mother finally released her. Faith stood by silently. It was only another few moments before Malachi was at her side.

"What have you done with my children?" Susannah demanded of Faith and Malachi.

"Mama, they've done nothing wrong. Betsy is playing with the children over there—see?"

Zane came up behind Morgan. "What's wrong with Ma?" he asked, echoing his twin.

"Where's Ardith?" their mother asked. "What have these darkies done with Ardith?"

Dianne exchanged a look with her brothers. Morgan took the initiative. "Ma, don't you remember? Ardith fell in the river and drowned."

"What kind of nonsense is that? I'm telling you they have her." Their mother pointed her finger at Faith. "She's been trying to steal Dianne all along. She's a witch, I'm telling you. And now she's stolen my Ardith!"

Morgan took hold of their mother's arm. "Come on, Ma. Let's get you back to the wagon where you can rest."

"I don't want to rest. I want to find my daughter!"

Morgan looked to Dianne for help. "I'll fetch the doctor," Dianne said softly. By now a crowd had gathered around them.

"I'll get the doctor for you," Levi said from the sea of onlookers.

Morgan and Zane had to nearly carry their mother back to the wagon. Betsy had made her way to Dianne and stood clinging tightly to her sister as though something more horrible might yet happen.

Dianne looked to Faith and Malachi before following her brothers. "I'm sorry," she whispered. "I'm so sorry."

The army doctor and Levi arrived at the wagon at nearly the same time Dianne and Betsy did. The doctor went inside, shooing Morgan from his protective place at Susannah's side. He then worked to soothe

the woman as Dianne and her siblings watched from the back side. He poured a milky liquid into a spoon.

"I want you to take this now, Mrs. Chadwick. It will help you rest."

Reluctantly she swallowed the concoction. "I want to see my children."

"They're right here waiting, Mrs. Chadwick. No need to worry."

He gathered his things and exited the wagon, stopping only long enough to hand a bottle to Morgan. "See that she gets the rest of this laudanum. Give her a teaspoon every few hours. It'll help her sleep."

Morgan nodded and handed the bottle to Dianne as the doctor made his way back to the fort. "I think you'd better see to this."

Dianne looked at the bottle. "Laudanum's powerful medicine. I remember Pa keeping some hidden from the Union soldiers. He said folks in the town might have use for it if war came in earnest."

Morgan motioned to the wagon positioned in front of the one where their mother slept. "We brought a small case with us. Ma figured to sell it in Virginia City or along the way. She said it's good for all sorts of ailments. Guess we should have thought of it sooner."

Dianne nodded and tucked the bottle into her pocket. "Betsy, you get ready for bed. I'll be down shortly. I need to check on Ma and see if she needs anything more before we turn in."

Betsy reluctantly did as she was told while Dianne climbed into the wagon. "Ma? Are you asleep yet?"

"No. I want you to bring Betsy and Ardith here. I need to talk to all three of you."

Dianne felt tears form in her eyes. "Mama, Ardith isn't with us anymore. Don't you remember?"

Her mother sat up in the bed, her hair sticking out every which way. She looked rather like a madman—or in this case, a mad woman.

"I won't listen to such nonsense, Dianne. Stop it now before I take a switch to your backside."

Dianne didn't know what to say or do. Her mother was clearly out of her mind, unwilling to acknowledge Ardith's death and growing agitated with Dianne's every word.

"I'm sorry, Mama. Why don't you get some sleep and we can talk after that?"

Her mother yawned as the medicine seemed to take hold. "Very well. But I want to see all of you when I awaken."

Dianne left the wagon, a feeling of hopelessness washing over her. She couldn't help but wonder if God saw and understood this horror as well. Faith said He cared, that He saw everything. She gazed up at the star-filled sky, ignoring the sounds of revelry at the fort.

"Do you see this, God? Do you?"

CHAPTER 11

New Madrid

TRENTON, ROBBIE, AND GUSTAF CROUCHED IN THE BRUSH JUST
beyond the Union supply house. The hot July day had given way to an
equally steamy night. Lying in wait, Trenton wondered at the sensibility
of what they were about to do. He wiped sweat from his eyes and
watched for patrols.

He had it figured that the Union patrol was divided into two units.
One on foot, the other on horseback. The unit on horseback came
through every hour; the one on foot was a little less predictable. They
seemed to come in fifteen to twenty minute intervals, but sometimes
they took as long as thirty minutes. He guessed they were delayed by
checking out noises or other problems, or maybe even stopping to talk
to someone as they made their rounds. No matter what the reason, however, it made it difficult to gauge when the trio would strike.

The Swede worked preparing the black powder charges while Robbie and Trenton were to keep watch and figure out when they'd have
the best opportunity to move. The supply house was actually an abandoned residence. Trenton had never known the folks who lived there,
but it seemed a nice enough place. The war had no doubt caused them
to move away from the river, however. There was much to fear in living
near the Mississippi at a time when it was one of the most guarded and

essential water routes. And just as Trenton and his comrades were now planning, the risk of sabotage or invasion was a threat that no one wanted to deal with.

"Here they come," Robbie whispered back to the Swede. All three men ducked low into the brush coverage. Trenton found himself holding his breath as the Union patrol walked not ten feet away.

"I can't believe how hot it is," one soldier said.

"I can't either. It's not ever this hot back home," the other replied.

"Wish I were back home right now. I used to hate working with my father, but I'd give all I have to be there right this minute."

"My pa's dead, but my ma and grandma are still alive. They could sure use me at home helping out."

The conversation drifted down the path along with the men. Trenton let out his breath slowly. He just wanted to be done with the entire matter. Seeking revenge for his father was much more risky than he'd thought.

"I can't believe they don't have guards on the place all the time," Trenton said in a hushed voice.

"They've had no need to," Robbie declared in a whisper. "No one's threatened them until now, and most folks don't know about this place. With all the patrols, they figure they're safe enough. Which is to our benefit." Trenton nodded, though not completely convinced. He worried that they'd have hidden guards.

"Are you about done, Swede?" Robbie questioned, the nervous irritation clear in his tone.

"Ja, I'm finished."

"Good thing. Much longer and we'd have to worry about that horse patrol coming back."

Trenton struck a match to check his watch. "They'll be back in twenty minutes—about the same time as the two that just passed by." He pinched the match to extinguish the flame. "Let's get those charges placed and get out of here."

"Ja, I think dat's a gud idea." The Swede's heavy accent lingered on the air for a moment before he rose to his feet. "I can set the charges.

You two could be takin' some of the supplies for us. There's dat back vindow. You could climb through," he said, pointing to Robbie. "You could hand the guds to Trent, and he could hide them over here until we can load the horses. Ja?"

"That wasn't part of the original plan," Trenton argued. "We don't have a lot of time, Swede. We need to hurry."

"Ja, so get to it."

Robbie pulled on Trenton's sleeve. "Come on. We can at least get a few loads. It won't hurt anything. They'll never even know."

Trenton couldn't see the face of the big Swede, but he knew the man had the strength to kill him with a single blow. It was probably best if he kept on the man's good side. "All right. We'll get what we can."

Robbie and Trenton snuck to the back of the supply house while the Swede went to work setting his charges. The first problem Trenton encountered was the boarded-up back door and the locked windows.

"Now what?" he questioned, turning to Robbie.

Robbie took out his pistol, then pulled his felt hat from atop his head. "I'll just break the glass."

"What if they hear you?"

"They won't," he assured. Positioning his hat against the glass near the lock, Robbie took hold of the barrel of his pistol and smacked the butt against his hat.

The muffled sound of glass shattering seemed like a cacophony to Trenton. It seemed even louder as it hit the floor inside the house. He rushed to the patrol road and nervously peered up and down the trail. All was quiet, reassuring him that perhaps no one was any wiser to their exploits.

By the time he got back to the window, Robbie was already inside and ready to hand a box of ammunition out to Trenton. "Here, take this. Hurry."

Trenton did as he was told. He pressed through the blackness to where they had left the horses. Setting the box aside, he whispered a prayer that they wouldn't be caught. It seemed a strange thing to do. Why in the world would God listen to prayers that ask for a blessing on thievery and the likes? He remembered a time when he and Dianne had stolen cookies from where their mother had left them to cool. His only thought had been for the immediate pleasure and benefit. Now his only thought was to live to tell Dianne of this exploit. Of course, he doubted he'd ever tell her. It was too shameful.

Trenton hurried back to the house, where Robbie thrust a bundle of army blankets and more ammunition through the window. It went on like this for nearly ten minutes. Sweat soaked Trenton clear through. Partly due to his hard work, but mostly it was due to nerves. He just knew they were going to get caught.

He approached the house for the sixth or seventh time when the Swede showed up. "I'm finished. Let's go." The big man reached up and nearly lifted Robbie out of the window.

They went to where the horses were tethered and began to load up the goods. There were guns and ammunition, blankets, canteens, and other items that Trenton couldn't even begin to remember. With shaking hands, Trenton tied some of the goods to his horse. The patrol should be back in only a matter of minutes—not to mention the boys on foot. They still needed to make it to the main road and then to the path that cut off and headed along the river, and all of this before they ran into the cavalry.

"Let's go," the Swede instructed.

The trio mounted and picked their way through the blackness of the forest. The Swede seemed to know his way instinctively. When they reached the clearing, the big man halted his horse and dismounted. He handed the reins to Robbie. "Vait here. I'll light the powder."

Trenton's breathing quickened as his heart pounded. They were going to be caught red-handed at this. Then they'd be hanged for treason. He gripped the reins tight in his clammy hands. He grew a bit dizzy as he fought for breath.

The Swede came running back and yanked the reins from Robbie. "It's gonna blow for sure," he declared. Trenton couldn't be certain, but it almost sounded as if the Swede was laughing.

They urged the horses down the road, barely coming to the cutoff before hearing the patrol approaching. Just then, however, the sound of horses' hooves was drowned out by the explosion. The night lit up as the supply house burst into flames, blazing debris flying high into the air as one charge after another ignited. The Swede motioned them into the brush as the cavalry patrol passed by in a full run. As soon as they were gone, the Swede urged his mount down the path toward the river.

Trenton couldn't get away fast enough. His mind was filled with the horrors of the night. He hoped the foot patrol wasn't close enough to be harmed by the explosion. He had no plans to be a murderer or a thief, but being a thief was easier to swallow.

They split down three separate roads, just as previously planned. They would eventually meet back at the hideout, but for now they needed to make certain that no one could follow them. To Trenton's disappointment, he realized it would still be another hour before he could rid himself of the stolen supplies and feel truly safe again.

After splitting up with Robbie and the Swede, Trenton thought back on his actions, growing sicker by the minute. This wasn't about revenge for his father, he thought. This was just plain stupid. These were the actions of a foolish man who'd allowed himself to get caught up in the company of no-accounts. The thought sickened him. Why was he always so easily led astray?

The more he thought about it, the worse his stomach churned. "I'm a fool," he muttered.

He'd only gone along for about fifteen minutes before he jumped from the side of his horse and vomited. His stomach heaved and his entire body shook so violently that Trenton had to sit down. He felt like crying, something he'd not done since he was a boy.

Get ahold of yourself, he commanded his mind, but it didn't seem to help. *We could have been caught. We might yet be caught.* He rocked back and forth, willing his racing thoughts to still. His breathing slowed and the dizziness cleared. *We didn't get caught. We probably won't get caught.*

He breathed deeply and the steady pounding of his heart in his ears started to fade. In its place came the noises of the night—crickets and locusts, the gentle lapping of the water against the riverbank.

He felt so confused. He'd bragged to his mother and sister that he had a plan to make things right—to give his father justice. But this was no justice. There was nothing satisfying about what he'd done tonight.

Getting to his feet, Trenton looked down the road from which he'd just come. There was no sound, no disturbance to declare danger. He took up the reins and remounted his horse. He felt stupid for having gotten sick. *What kind of man am I if I can't keep my supper down just because things are . . . are . . . a matter of life and death?*

Tonight had been the first time that Trenton had taken death seriously. At least his own death. He wondered in silence, as the horse steadily progressed along the road, what it would be like to die now—in the youth of his life. He would regret never seeing his family again—especially Dianne. She would be sorely disappointed with him if she knew what he was doing with his life.

Of course, there were those among his friends who would have applauded his efforts tonight. They hated the Northerners and would just as soon see them all dead.

"But I don't feel that way," Trenton muttered. "I just wanted to show them up for what they did to Pa."

And now that he had done so and still had no feeling of accomplishment, Trenton began to ponder what his next move should be. He was all alone in the world—at least this part of the world. Dianne and the rest were far away by now—very nearly all the way to Virginia City. Hadn't his mother said they'd arrive in August?

The one thing he was sure of was his desire to leave the Wilson gang. He was tired of Jerry's threats whenever he messed up or misunderstood. He was tired of Jerry and Sam always fighting and of Mark's hair-trigger temper. No, after tonight, Trenton was determined to find another gang to associate with. Or else he'd head west and find his family.

When he arrived at the cabin, he had pretty much determined that the best way to leave would just be to do it. If he told Jerry of his plans, the man would probably shoot him. No, Trenton figured it'd be better to sleep off the exhaustion that threatened to leave him asleep in the saddle. In the morning, he'd gather his things and leave before the others awoke.

He unloaded the supplies he'd stolen and then gave the horse a quick rubdown with the saddle blanket. It wasn't much, but at this point it was all the energy Trenton had left to give. He noted Robbie and the Swede had already returned. Their horses were hobbled and grazing nearby.

After seeing to his mount, Trenton hoisted up the goods and made his way to the house. An attitude of celebration was already underway when he stepped through the threshold.

"And here's the last of it!" Jerry declared as Trenton lowered the box to the table. "You boys did all right tonight. This stuff is going to come in handy. Too bad you didn't take more."

"If we had, we would have needed a wagon," Trenton said, plopping onto the rickety wooden chair. He felt it give a bit but gave it no mind.

"Maybe that would be the answer," Jerry said, inspecting the lot that Trent had brought. "We could always steal it and sell it elsewhere." He pushed the box back. "But we can decide on that later. Right now we have plans to go over for tomorrow morning's bank job."

"What are you talking about?" Trenton asked. "I didn't hear anything about a bank job."

Jerry's scarred face seemed to harden as he stared Trenton in the eye. "I run this gang and I don't recall having to clear my plans with anyone. Especially not you."

Trenton knew the man would explode if nothing was done to defuse the situation. "I didn't mean nothing by it, Jerry. I'm just worn clear through. I didn't know we had other jobs to do." Trenton fought to keep his posture relaxed so it would seem nonthreatening to the small man.

"Well, see to it that you keep your mouth shut. Next time, I won't be so forgiving." He took out a piece of paper and spread it on the table. The other members of the gang took this as their cue to draw near. "We'll hit the bank first thing in the morning—before the town is awake enough to know what's going on."

Trenton exchanged a look with Robbie. His father was the president of the bank in question. Robbie shrugged. They both knew better than to say anything while Jerry was talking, but this was something that would endanger the life of Robbie's father. Something had to be said. Looking for an opportunity to speak, Trenton was relieved when Jerry asked if there were any questions.

"Why this bank? Why not one of the others? This bank is run by Robbie's pa. I don't want to see the man come to harm," Trenton spoke, waiting the consequences.

Jerry didn't seem in the least bit upset. "I picked that bank *because* of Robbie's pa. If Robbie tells us the secrets of the bank and keeps his pa under control, then there won't be any problems. It'll be a simpler job than trying to go into one of the other banks. Especially since we've got no time to study up and learn the layout of the other banks."

"But something could go wrong," Trenton protested.

Robbie seemed to find his tongue. "Yeah, I don't know about this, Jerry."

"I don't much care what either one of you think," Jerry declared. "We're doing this and you'll help me with it or you'll both be dead and so will Robbie's pa. Understand?"

Trenton swallowed hard and looked to Robbie. They'd really backed themselves into a corner this time. He slumped farther in the chair, hoping Jerry would take it as a sign of defeat. Maybe if they had the chance, he and Robbie could slip away in the night and warn Mr. Danssen about the robbery plan.

"Rob, you need to tell me everything about that bank. I want you to draw me a picture of the doors and windows and everything inside. I want to know about the routine your pa has when opening the bank and who else might be there."

Robbie reluctantly took the piece of paper and pencil that Jerry held out to him. He looked to Trenton as if for permission, then lowered his head and began to draw. Trenton felt sorry for his friend. They both knew Jerry would make good on his threats. He'd as soon kill the both of them as have his authority questioned.

Brooding over the matter as Robbie answered Jerry's onslaught of questions, Trenton still figured they'd have a chance to slip away before dawn. He tried to set a plan in his mind, but he found himself dozing off as Jerry continued to work Robbie over.

I never figured things to come to this, Trenton thought as his mind grew hazy. *I only figured to show those Yankees a thing or two and then be done with it. I never wanted to see anyone get hurt.* . . .

CHAPTER 12

THIS WAS ONE OF THOSE TIMES WHEN TRENTON WAS GLAD HE'D brought few personal belongings with him when he'd joined the Wilsons. Packing his saddlebags with his extra shirt and pants, he cautiously looked over his shoulder from time to time to make sure no one was watching.

In about an hour they'd be heading for the bank. Trenton wanted nothing to go wrong. He'd managed to whisper his plan to Robbie, who'd nodded enthusiastically in agreement. If they had a chance, they'd head out before the rest of the gang and warn Robbie's father. If even one of them could get away to alert him, it just might keep things from going horribly wrong in New Madrid.

"I hope you aren't gettin' ideas about goin' someplace," Jerry Wilson said as he surprised Trenton.

"I'm going to town with you," Trenton answered, hoping he sounded casual about the whole thing.

Jerry's lip curled, giving him the appearance of a dog about to snarl. "You don't need a change of clothes for that."

"You said we might not be able to get back here right away if a posse followed us." He continued packing, hoping Jerry would think nothing of his actions. Trenton wanted to make sure Jerry didn't think he was hiding anything from him.

Jerry rubbed his chin, then spit tobacco on the floor. "I've got my eye on you, Chadwick. You don't rub me the right way. If you and Robbie think about doing anything other than cooperatin' with me, I'll kill you where you stand."

"There's no need to take that tone with me," Trenton said, eyeing Jerry sternly. He felt a trembling run through his body but knew he needed to be firm in this matter. Jerry seemed to have a knack for sniffing out weakness in his adversaries, and Trenton knew there would be nothing but trouble if Jerry determined his feelings this time around. "You already said you'd do in Robbie's pa if we didn't stick to your plan."

The shorter man leaned forward in a menacing stance. "That's right, I did. And don't think it's not the truth of the matter." He spit again, then backed up. "You'd just better keep in my view the whole time or I swear I'll march into that bank and put a bullet in the head of Robbie's old man."

With that he turned and stomped across the worn wood floor. The sound echoed in Trenton's ears. *So what do I do now?* He glanced at his watch. They would leave for the bank in less than forty-five minutes. If he and Robbie were to make a break for it, they'd have to go now.

He grabbed his saddlebags and glanced toward the boarded-up window. He couldn't very well sneak out that way. He'd have to march right through the front room and the whole lot of them if he were going to get to his horse. But what could he say to make a plausible excuse for going outside? Jerry was already keeping a close watch. There was no chance he'd allow for Trenton to go anywhere.

I never should have come back here last night. I should have let them think I was captured. Then I could have just kept riding. He looked at the open door, knowing that if he made a run for it, they would gun him down in a matter of seconds. Then, without remorse, they'd probably kill Robbie as well.

Sweat trickled down the back of his neck—the saddlebag felt like a lead weight. He moved toward the door, but when he came within inches of the threshold, he stopped again. He could hear Robbie arguing with someone—no doubt Jerry. Robbie hadn't been at all happy about this arrangement, and who could blame him? Robbie and his father had had more than their share of arguments, but it didn't mean Robbie wanted to see the man dead.

"I don't want to do this. There's always a mess of Union soldiers at Pa's bank anyway," Robbie protested. "You go in there and we're sure to be killed."

"Not if you're with us. We'll just mosey in there like we're fresh-washed boys bound for Sunday school."

Trenton would have laughed at that thought had the situation not been so serious. He remained in the doorway, knowing that if Jerry turned around he'd see him there. It didn't really matter, Trenton figured. It wasn't like anyone in the house had secrets for long. The walls were thin and no one respected the privacy of anyone else.

"But if my pa gets hurt, my ma and sister won't have anyone to take care of them."

"They'll still have you," Jerry said rather snidely.

Robbie leaned forward and raised his fist. "No, they probably won't, because if you hurt my pa, I'm going to hunt you down and kill you."

Trenton knew Jerry would never stand for a threat of any kind. Why, he'd seen the man knock his brother Sam unconscious for less than that.

"Are we going to just stand around here arguing or are we going to get the horses saddled and ready to go? I don't want to be waltzing into town at noon!" Trenton declared with false bravado.

Everyone in the room stopped what they were doing and looked at Trenton, the tension and animosity suddenly focused on him. He gripped the saddlebags tighter with his left hand and rested his right hand on his hip. The feel of his gun gave him no comfort.

"I'm gonna deal with both of you once this is over with," Jerry said, narrowing his gaze. He motioned his younger brother to the door. "Get out there and saddle the horses. You keep an eye on Chadwick here and make sure he doesn't step out of line. Robbie will stay with me."

Sam pulled on his hat and headed for the door. It was one of the first times Trenton had ever seen him do anything without an argument.

"Come on, Chadwick," he muttered.

Trenton was torn. He hated leaving Robbie at Jerry's mercy, but he didn't know how else to handle the situation. The Swede watched him ominously. He'd been sharpening his knife and paused with the weapon in midstroke. Meanwhile, Mark Wiley slowly got to his feet and picked up his own saddlebag. From the way he slung the pack, Trenton could tell it was empty.

"You scared of an old banker, Chadwick?" he questioned as he came toward Trenton.

Trenton was barely conscious of fingering the grip of his gun. He frowned at Wiley but said nothing. The man might be Trenton's junior, but experience made him old and dangerous. Where Jerry was conniving and loved to argue, Mark was hot-tempered and held nothing sacred—not even life. Especially not life.

"Come on, Chadwick. I'll make sure you're safe," Wiley said, then laughed as though he'd just told the funniest joke. His laughter rang in Trenton's ears. Realizing he had no choice, Trenton nodded toward Robbie and Jerry and headed out behind Wiley.

The Wilson gang rode together as they headed toward New Madrid. Jerry had concocted a plan for them to each ride in from different directions so that no one would be suspicious. On the outskirts of town they all went their separate ways except for Robbie. Jerry kept Robbie close by his side, leaving Trenton with a feeling that something was bound to go wrong.

As Trenton made his way up the center of town, he nodded here and there to the shopkeepers he knew. His father had been well respected in the community—at least until he appeared to side with the Yankees.

Mr. Daniels stood leaning on his broom outside his small produce store as Trenton rode by. He waved enthusiastically. "Hey there, Trenton. Come by for a game of checkers," he called out. "You can give me all the news."

"I'll try to do that later on," Trenton said, knowing there was no possible way he'd be able to follow through on his statement. The old man nodded, then went back to his sweeping.

Down the street, Trenton could see Jerry and Robbie approaching the bank. The smaller man's dark brown gelding snorted nervously in the morning warmth. It was almost as if the animal knew what his master was about to attempt. Trenton drew his own mount to a halt and stepped down.

He watched as Sam tied his sorrel to a hitching post across the street from the bank. The man nodded to his brother, who in turn dismounted and tossed his reins to Robbie. It looked like Jerry planned for Robbie to wait outside. Trenton couldn't help but wonder what had brought on this change of plans.

"Mr. Chadwick!"

Trenton looked up to find Captain Seager coming from across the street. The dark blue uniform was a startling reminder of the events of the past twenty-four hours.

Swallowing hard, Trenton replied, "Good morning, Captain."

Seager shook his head. "Not so good, son. We had a bit of trouble last night at one of the supply houses." Trenton stiffened and waited for the man to continue. All the while he tried to watch beyond Seager to see what was happening at the bank.

"But that's not why I've stopped you. I wondered how your mother and family were doing. Have you heard anything from them?"

Trenton shook his head. "No. But then, I haven't really expected to. We didn't exactly part on the best of terms."

Seager nodded. "This war has made it difficult for most families. I'm sure your mother worries that you'll meet with harm once you join up."

Trenton pulled his gaze from the bank and looked to Seager. "Join up?"

"Well, that's the real reason you remained behind, is it not?"

Trenton didn't know how to reply. He could hardly tell the man he'd stayed in New Madrid to wreak havoc upon the Union Army. "Well, I can't really tell you why I stayed. I didn't feel the West calling to me, I can tell you that much. Ma had her heart set on moving in with her brother, and I just didn't feel the same."

Seager eyed him sternly. "Perhaps that's because deep inside you knew your country needed you more than your family did. You come by later today and we'll talk about getting you signed up."

Trenton's anger resurfaced as if newly born. "Why would I ever do that? The Union killed my Pa just as sure as they kill Confederates."

"Son, your father was killed in an accident—no one knows whose bullet took his life. For sure, no one on the Union side wanted to see him dead. He was a good man. I was sorry to see him die."

"Not as sorry as my little sisters or my mother," Trenton replied, his hands balled into fists.

"Now look, Chadwick—" Gunshots rang out. Trenton and Seager turned to see Robbie jump from the back of his horse and run toward the bank.

Seager immediately pulled his own pistol. "Stay here," he ordered.

Trenton gripped the handle of his revolver. His feet felt like they'd been nailed to the boardwalk as he watched the scene unfold in slow motion. There were more gunshots and then silence. Seager crossed the street and reached Jerry's horse just as he emerged from the bank with Sam in tow. Both men had handkerchiefs tied across their faces, concealing their identity. Sam's shirt revealed blood trailing down the sleeve.

"Halt!" Seager demanded.

Trenton mounted his horse, still not knowing what to do. He wanted to be there to help Robbie in case the gunshots meant that his father had met with harm. At the same time, he'd never been more afraid in his life. *I'm not a coward,* he told himself. *So stop acting like one,* his conscience seemed to argue back. He'd just turned his horse toward the fracas, however, when Seager called out again.

"Drop your weapons and put down those bags!"

Trenton reined back and watched as Jerry raised his pistol and shot Seager before the older man could react. The shot hit him square in the chest. Seager dropped his gun and clutched his coat as if to hold himself upright. Without waiting another second, Jerry fired a second shot, then jumped on his horse and sped off down the street. Sam followed suit, pausing only long enough to fire his own bullet into Seager. He was not to be outdone by his brother, after all.

Trenton saw people emerge from the stores and it was only another moment before a patrol of soldiers came rushing toward him. *I have to leave. I have to get out of here before they think I had something to do with this.*

But he did have something to do with it. And there were Robbie and his father to consider. Trenton knew he should go to his friend, but he couldn't seem to manage movement of any kind. The horse pranced in a sidestepping manner as the soldiers rushed by. Someone emerged from the bank and declared they'd been robbed and that Andrew Danssen had been shot.

Trenton thought he might very well be sick again. He gathered his wits and directed his horse down a side street. *What do I do?* He walked the horse in circles around the back streets. *How do I just leave Robbie there alone?*

The reasonable thing to do would be just to leave. Ride out of New Madrid and never return. Never face Jerry and Sam again. Never have to break the law in order to stay alive. But Trenton wasn't thinking clearly, and reasonable reflection didn't seem possible. Robbie might have escaped town and returned to the cabin to avenge his father. It was the kind of thing he could imagine his friend doing in the heat of the moment. The very thought of it caused Trenton's blood to run cold. Robbie wouldn't stand a chance against Jerry or any of the others.

He'll need my help.

Before he could stop himself, Trenton had urged the horse back in the direction of the river hideout. Maybe between the two of them, Trenton and Robbie would be able to stand up to the rest of the gang. Maybe then they could leave once and for all.

Jerry was tearing into the bags of Union gold when Trenton came through the door. Trenton's presence didn't even cause a stir. The Swede was on guard duty down the road, and if anyone approached who wasn't supposed to be in the area, the Swede would take care of business.

"We've hit the bonanza, boys!" he declared. He looked up and met Trenton's gaze.

"Where's Robbie?" Trenton asked, his voice low and tight.

Jerry laughed and poured the sack of gold onto the table. "Burying his old man, for all I know."

CHAPTER 13

Fort Laramie

MEASLES CLAIMED MANY MORE LIVES IN THE WAGON TRAIN, including two of the Showalter children. Griselda was an unmovable wall of self-composure as they gathered to bury her children.

"Do you suppose she doesn't care?" Dianne whispered to Zane as they joined others for the funeral. "I haven't seen her shed a single tear."

"Everybody grieves differently. She's probably in a state of shock," her brother replied.

"Mama sure didn't act like that and she had more reason to be shocked than Mrs. Showalter." Dianne watched as Griselda ordered her weepy husband and children to sit and be silent. The woman's attitude was almost disturbing. She was a rotund general with her little army—barking orders, frowning her displeasure.

Zane leaned over closer. "Mama sought her solace in a bottle of laudanum. Mrs. Showalter seems to find hers in running things."

As if to offer further proof, the large woman grabbed hold of Reverend Hammond and seemed to be instructing him on something—probably how she expected the eulogy to be delivered. Dianne thought it all very strange.

The funeral was a sad state of affairs, and Dianne would be glad when it was over and she could escape back to their camp. The

Showalter children weren't the only ones to die, although they were among the youngest. Little Brian was only four and Laurabelle was only five. The growing number of mourners put a heavy spirit of despair on the camp. Every day the travelers gathered to bury someone. Dianne figured that with today's count, the number of dead had reached at least fifty, and folks continued to get sick.

Even Daniel Keefer had contracted some form of summer complaint. He stayed in his bed for more than a week before the weakness finally passed. Someone thought he was afflicted with the ague, others said it was nothing more than a cold. Either way, it changed his plans for a quick departure.

Dianne was actually glad for the delay. The area around the fort was pleasant and the summer weather was enjoyable. And, in spite of the rampant sickness, she felt safe here. Safe from the Indians and safe from the dangers of the trail. She almost wished they could stay here forever instead of pressing into the vast unknown.

Reverend Hammond and his wife had their hands full with tending to the sick. Even Levi worked faithfully at their side, leaving him little time to visit Dianne. The Hammonds were a great comfort to those whose loved ones were suffering. The pastor would pray with people and encourage them, while Charity tended them with her nursing skills and tender love. Even Daniel Keefer benefited from their ministerings and asked the reverend to conduct a regular Sunday service for the entire wagon train.

Dianne wasn't sure what to think of the frontier style of worship. It wasn't like the quiet, reverent worship of their church back in New Madrid. Here on the plains, the need and enthusiasm of the pioneers gave church a spirit of anticipation. They sang hymns and prayed with great gusto, and some even offered up comments about how God had seen them through. After this was concluded and everyone ran out of things to share, Reverend Hammond would step up onto the back of a wagon and open his large black Bible.

Now Betsy snuggled close to Dianne, yawning in indifference.

Dianne had no doubt Betsy would rather be off running in the fields or playing with puppies.

"The good Lord has a plan for your life," the pastor began. "He sees His people in their suffering, just as we are now. Some of you are mourning the loss of loved ones. Some of you are sick and feel too poorly to go on. Some of you are just discouraged and want to head back where you came from."

Dianne definitely knew those who felt that way. She'd heard them grumbling for the last few days, and it was more than the routine complaints. Many of her fellow travelers were losing hope—losing sight of the goal. Hopelessness spread over the camp. Hopelessness that was fed on the worries and fears of the travelers.

"The good Lord has a plan for your life," Reverend Hammond again reiterated. "Some of you don't think much of the trip so far—you even doubt that God cares. I'm here today to tell you that He does and that He hears the cries of His people."

Dianne wished He'd hear her cries. Her fears weren't based on the measles or the Indians or any other concern of the trail. No, she was afraid of what was happening to her mother's mind and body. One minute her mother seemed perfectly normal and the next confusion overwhelmed her. Sometimes she forgot that Ardith was dead, like the night of the Independence Day celebration. Other times, she knew only too well and cried and sobbed, begging for more laudanum. The bottle supplied by the doctor had long since been used. Morgan and Zane had discussed the possibility of breaking into the case they'd brought. After all, what could it hurt to give her another bottle and ease her pain for a little longer?

Dianne thought it a bad idea, however. They'd already sold a portion of the laudanum to the fort doctor and also to some of the folks on the train. At this rate, they wouldn't have much of anything left should one of their own party get hurt or sick. Their mother might be grieving and wish to escape from the truth of what had happened, but was that truly the best way to handle the situation? Laudanum was dangerous medicine.

Dianne had heard the doctor's warning as he instructed Charity in her care of the sick.

"Laudanum can be a tremendous benefit, but too much can also kill," he had told Mrs. Hammond.

How much is too much? Dianne couldn't help but wonder. After all, their mother had used an entire bottle. Would their mother now die from having taken so much of the medicine? Why hadn't he been more specific? Dianne grew more fretful as she watched her mother's health deteriorate. What would they do if their mother died? How would the family survive and find Uncle Bram?

The pastor's voice broke through her thoughts. "I know some of you are tired and discouraged. I know you don't want to go on. You're afraid of what's to come and you're afraid of what's behind. But you don't have to be afraid. Your Father in heaven is watching over you. He has not forgotten you. He wants to offer you shelter from the storm and hope for tomorrow.

"Maybe you're wondering how you might have that hope." He opened the Bible and held it up for all to see. "The Good Book says, 'If thou shalt confess with thy mouth the Lord Jesus, and shalt believe in thine heart that God hath raised him from the dead, thou shalt be saved.' " He closed the Bible and smiled down compassionately. "Coming to the Lord isn't another difficult task to add on to your already overtaxed lives. Coming to the Lord requires only a confession of your heart. It requires that you believe in something bigger than yourself—that you believe in God and what He has done for you."

Dianne tuned out the words again. She'd heard such things since she was small. She knew all about God and Jesus, and she didn't want to hear the same thing over and over again. What she did want was an answer. An answer for what she was supposed to do in order to make things right again. An answer that seemed to elude her.

Later that afternoon, Charity Hammond stopped by to check on Susannah. Dianne and Betsy were seated on the ground beside the wagon when she arrived. Dianne had been showing Betsy how to sew a straight line and the little girl was quite pleased with herself.

"Look, Mrs. Hammond, I can sew!"

"I see that," the older woman said, lifting up the piece of cloth. "What fine tiny stitches you've made."

"Oh, and you know what else?" Betsy's animated voice was a song on the air.

Dianne got to her feet and admonished her sister. "Now, don't be bothering Mrs. Hammond." No doubt Betsy wanted to tell her something about the puppies or the horses she'd gotten to be with earlier in the day.

"She's never a bother," Charity said, leaning down. "Now, what do you want to tell me?"

"When Pastor Hammond was praying, I asked Jesus into my heart," Betsy said matter-of-factly.

Dianne couldn't have been more surprised. Betsy hadn't even mentioned this detail until now. Dianne said nothing but watched as a huge smile spread across Mrs. Hammond's face.

"Why, that's wonderful news, Betsy Chadwick. I'm so glad you shared that with me."

Betsy fairly glowed under Charity's comments, but Dianne thought the whole thing rather silly. "Betsy, you're only six years old. What do you know about such matters?" The child's countenance immediately fell.

"Don't be getting after her," Charity admonished gently. She straightened to meet Dianne's gaze. "Jesus said to let the little children come unto Him. She's not too young to hear the voice of God in her heart. We'd all do well to listen for Him so intently—and to act on that voice."

Dianne felt thoroughly chastised. She looked at her little sister and nodded. "If Mrs. Hammond says it's a good thing, then it is. I'm sorry I scolded you."

Betsy smiled, appearing to be satisfied with this.

"I've come to see if your mama needs anything," Charity announced. "I hope she's feeling better."

"Sometimes she is. She really misses Ardith. But I think a lot of times she forgets that Ardith is gone."

"That's probably natural, child. I wouldn't let it worry you too much. It's never easy for a mother to lose a child. It's worse than losing her husband or parents or friends. She'll get better by and by. Have faith."

Dianne thought of Mrs. Hammond's words later that night as she sat near the campfire with Zane and Morgan. "What did you think of the reverend's sermon today?" she asked her brothers.

"Seemed good enough," Morgan said, finishing off the last of the dried apple cobbler.

"Sure," Zane agreed. "He seemed to know the right things to say."

"Betsy said she asked Jesus into her heart. I was remembering when they made us pray that prayer in Sunday school."

Zane nodded. "We had that one old teacher who was mean as an old bear. What was her name?"

"Mrs. Cane," Dianne offered. "She told us we'd feel her wrath before God had a chance to take over if we didn't get right with the Lord. I just never thought about it until Betsy mentioned it this afternoon. No one forced Betsy to ask Jesus to save her—she just wanted to do it. Mrs. Hammond said that Betsy heard God in her heart."

Morgan shrugged. "Guess so."

They fell silent for several moments. Zane finally spoke as he added fuel to the small fire, poking at it with a stick and stirring up the embers. "I've been talking with the soldiers. They've been telling me about fort life and how they operate out here. I think when we get to Virginia City and we get Ma and you girls settled in with Uncle Bram, I'm going to join up."

"But why would you do that?" Dianne questioned. She watched Zane for any signs of his playful teasing. Maybe this was nothing more than a joke. "You know how Mama and Papa felt about such matters. That's why Mama wanted us to move west. She didn't want you boys involved in the war."

"This is different. Out here, the plan is to keep the peace—not make war. More and more settlers are moving through, and after the war, there will be an even greater number of folks. Anyway, my mind's made up."

Dianne shook her head and looked to Morgan. "I suppose you'll join up too? Seems like you twins are always following each other into one thing or another."

"Not me—not this time," Morgan replied, getting to his feet. "I'm too independent to be told what to do all the time. I don't want to be some dressed-up lackey. I've already told Zane I don't think much of soldiering. I'd hate for him to get himself killed by some warring Sioux or Cheyenne, but he doesn't listen much to me anymore."

"I'm a God-fearing man and I'm ready to do my duty to God and country. Besides, like the major in the fort told me, it's better to die on the field of battle as a Christian should die than to die as one careless of his relations to the great hereafter."

"What nonsense. Why should a Christian have to die on the field of battle?" Dianne protested.

"It says that in the *Military Handbook,*" Zane offered, as if that explained everything.

"And you believe it—just because some soldier said it's true?"

"Well, we take the word of pastors as Gospel truth. Why not believe the army might have a good understanding of things as well?"

Morgan shook his head. "I think it's all nonsense. I don't plan on trying to die for God or anyone else. I plan to stay alive and enjoy this great world." Just then a young woman with long blond hair walked by. Dianne had seen her making eyes at Morgan earlier in the day. She smiled over her shoulder and walked on. Morgan grinned and handed Dianne his plate. "And I plan to start right now." He walked away, hurrying to catch up with the pretty miss.

Dianne thought it rather funny that her very independent brother would want to attach himself to someone of the opposite sex. Did he not realize that a girl like that wouldn't be looking for a good time as much as she would be for a husband?

Zane yawned. "I'm going to bed. Will you be all right?"

"I'll be fine," Dianne murmured, not entirely sure it was the truth. So many questions rose in her mind. She wanted to know the truth of it, but no one seemed to have answers. Her brothers couldn't even offer her insight into the situation. It seemed strange to Dianne that a six-year-old could be so deeply touched by God. Didn't God speak only to white-haired old men?

She pondered these things all night long. In restless sleep she even dreamed of such matters. Who was she to say what was right or wrong in how God did business? If He could speak to Betsy, then maybe He could also speak to her. Hadn't Faith even suggested the same? Thoughts of Faith caused a deep longing for a friend. Her friends back home had one another, but out here, there was no one for Dianne to confide in. She didn't even have Trenton. Trenton would have understood her worries. He would have had answers.

Before morning light the soldiers in the fort were up and preparing for the day. Dianne couldn't help but snuggle down deeper in the covers with Betsy. They wouldn't need to rise for at least another hour. The wagon train wouldn't be moving out today—that much she was sure of. Daniel Keefer had called a mandatory meeting for the men—probably to announce when they would head out and leave the fort behind. But it wouldn't be today, so there was no rush to get up.

The night had turned chilly and a misty rain fell, making everything damp and miserable. The days could be quite warm, but as they neared the Rockies, the air had turned drier and the nights cooler. It was much more bearable than summer nights in New Madrid.

Thoughts of the town brought Dianne back to wonder how her friends were doing. Had the war intensified in New Madrid? Were there actual battles raging around them? So many people had suggested the fighting would soon come to Missouri in a major confrontation. Were there battlefields littered with the mortally wounded right there in New Madrid? Would Trenton be among the dead or dying?

Trenton came to mind more times than not. Often she would see something or hear a story and wish she could share it with her brother. When opportunity presented itself, she would write him a letter and share the details there. She'd been working on the same letter for the past three weeks, in fact. She'd had to share news of Ardith's death and of their mother's illness. It had taken a long time to figure out a way to put that information on paper without the facts just seeming cold and indifferent.

No matter how difficult, however, she would have to finish the letter today. Dianne figured Mr. Keefer would tell them they were leaving tomorrow—maybe the day after. She wanted to mail the letter before leaving and figured to make one more walk across the river to the sutler's store before they headed out.

"Is it time to get up?" Betsy asked, her voice groggy with sleep.

"Just about."

"When will we be in Virginia?"

Dianne chuckled. "Silly goose, it's Virginia *City*. Virginia is a state back East where the war is being fought."

"I keep forgetting. When will we be there?"

"I hope in another month—maybe less. We have to wait until the wagon train can travel again. I think Mr. Keefer plans for us to leave in a day or two, however."

Betsy yawned. "I'm glad. I want my puppy, and Mama says I can't have him until we get to Virginia City."

"Well, for now," Dianne said, reluctantly pulling back the covers, "we need to get breakfast. Let me help you with your hair and we'll get a fire going and start the oatmeal."

In spite of the night's misty rain, the morning brought clear skies and warmth. Dianne soon forgot her chill as breakfast was concluded and her brothers headed off for the meeting with Daniel Keefer.

"I need to try to get Mama to eat," Dianne told Betsy. She dished up the last of the oatmeal. "Can you stay here and play nice?"

"Can't I have a piece of apple for Dolly? She likes it so much when I feed her apple."

"We can go see Dolly later," Dianne said, pouring a bit of milk in with her mother's hot cereal. "It's not safe for you to go alone."

"Please. She's not far away and Morgan was going there before the meeting. I can just catch up with him. Please."

Dianne hated to deny Betsy anything. "Oh, all right. Just take one piece of dried apple. That's our food supply, you know. Dolly can eat the grass, but we can't."

Betsy danced around and clapped her hands. "I'll just give her one piece."

Betsy disappeared with the treat for Dolly while Dianne took up the bowl and climbed into the wagon, praying as she went that God might make things better for her mother.

"Mama?" She spoke softly, hoping not to startle her. "I've brought you some breakfast."

Her mother moaned softly and opened her eyes. "Why are you here?"

"I have breakfast. You need to eat."

"I'm not hungry."

"But, Mama, the baby needs for you to eat." Dianne worried about the unborn child as much as she did her mother. The excitement of another sibling helped her keep her mind off of losing Ardith.

The statement seemed to do the trick. Susannah sat up in the bed, yawning and wiping the sleep from her eyes. "I'm too tired to get up."

"Mrs. Hammond said you should get up and move around. She said it would help you get your strength back," Dianne suggested. She handed her mother the bowl of cereal and waited for her to begin eating.

For several moments, Susannah did nothing but stare at the bowl. "I can't believe she's gone. When I think about it, my heart hurts so much that I'm sure I'll die too."

"Oh, Mama," Dianne said, tears coming to her eyes.

"It was my fault. If I hadn't snapped at her . . ." Her mother pushed the bowl back into Dianne's hands. "How do I live with the guilt?" She looked at Dianne with such an expression of pain that Dianne burst into tears.

"It wasn't your fault, Mama. It was an accident."

"Just like with your father?"

Dianne looked into her mother's eyes and knew this was as close to an apology as she would get for all the blame her mother had heaped on her. Slowly, Dianne nodded. "Yes. Just like Papa."

For several minutes neither one said a word. Dianne dried her tears and composed herself. There was no sense in crying every time she remembered their losses. It served no purpose. She told herself this over and over, but for reasons beyond her understanding, her heart failed to listen to her. Maybe that's why she couldn't hear God either. Her heart had simply stopped listening to anyone.

"It's such a hard life out here. People die and get hurt. We should never have come. I should have stayed in Missouri. I should have kept the store." Susannah fell silent, her gaze glassing over.

Dianne stiffened. She hoped this wouldn't become something else her mother might blame her for. "Please eat, Mama. For the baby."

"Leave it here and go. I want to be alone." Gone was all sign of any softening or vulnerability. Her mother had firmly put her defenses back in place.

Dianne left the wagon wishing she could say something more. It was amazing that her mother had offered her what little she had. It comforted Dianne to know her mother didn't blame her anymore for Papa's death. Now, if Dianne could only forgive herself.

Dianne spent the morning washing dishes and tidying up their camp. She put together a dried beef stew and left it to cook in the Dutch oven while she went to work mending the boys' socks. It wasn't until an hour later that she realized Betsy had never returned from feeding Dolly.

A feeling of dread washed over Dianne as she cast the sewing aside. "Betsy!" she called out. Rushing to where the boys had staked Dolly and their other horses, she found no sign of Betsy. Dianne breathed a little easier. Maybe she had gone to see one of her friends. Betsy knew she wasn't supposed to go anywhere without permission, but maybe she'd forgotten in the excitement of feeding Dolly.

Dianne made her way back to camp, passing by their oxen and milk cows. Of late, Zane and Morgan had been helping her with the morning milking, leaving the evening session for Dianne to tend to on her own. She appreciated their help more than she could say. It allowed her to get a bit of extra rest before beginning the breakfast and other chores.

Up ahead, Charity Hammond waved and Dianne couldn't help but smile. "The meeting broke up a few minutes ago. We leave day after tomorrow." Charity seemed quite excited about this news. "So what has you out here, child?"

"I'm looking for my sister. Have you seen her?"

Charity frowned and shook her head. "She knows better than to wander off, doesn't she?"

Dianne nodded, but the look on Charity's face brought all her apprehensive feelings rushing back. "I'm not sure where else to look. I thought she might have gone to see one of her friends. What with the measles epidemic, we haven't let her be around other people for a while. I let her go feed Dolly some apple this morning, hoping it would help ease her boredom."

"Well, maybe she's gone to see the puppies. Mrs. Delbert's camp is just up the way. Why don't we walk over there and ask?"

It seemed like the perfect solution. Dianne knew her sister's love of the little dogs. No doubt she'd gone there. The two women walked side by side past the herds of camp animals. Two hundred wagons generated a lot of livestock, and the army had required they post them on the far side of camp. No doubt they'd need to push on soon or they'd have to stake the animals out even farther away from safety in order to see them properly fed.

"Mrs. Delbert!" Charity greeted. "Have you seen young Betsy Chadwick?"

The rosy-faced woman smiled and slapped a piece of wet laundry over her shoulder. "She was here about a half hour ago. She came to see the pups and then told me she was going to feed one of the horses. My boy Joseph told her he'd go with her and give our mules a treat. The mules are down over that way. They might still be together."

"Thank you," Dianne called as Charity turned in the direction of the animals.

"Your sister sure loves being with the little creatures. She'll probably be a good one to have on a ranch."

"She does love animals. She always has," Dianne said, smiling. "She was forever bringing home one stray or another. Mama used to get so vexed with her. At one time we had at least eight cats."

Charity laughed. "Well now, cats can be a great benefit. They eat the mice and make great lap warmers."

Dianne looked out across the field but could see nothing of Joseph or Betsy. "Where could she have gotten off to?"

Charity put her hand to her forehead to shield the brilliant sun. "I couldn't say. Maybe she's made her way back to your horses."

Dianne broke out in a cold sweat. She felt suddenly light-headed. "I'm scared, Charity." She looked to the older woman. "I think she's hurt."

Dianne rushed across the field to where a string of mules were stationed. She didn't know if these were the Delberts' mules or not, but she searched among them for any sign that Betsy had been there. Not finding any clue, she hurried on, checking here and there, still finding no sign of her sister.

She saw several men down by the river and for a moment she feared Betsy might have strayed too close to the water. But the men were laughing and seemed to be discussing something of great humor. They certainly weren't concerned about anything.

By now, Dianne had outdistanced Charity. The older woman had slowed considerably and was now making her way to where the men stood. Maybe she would get their help in searching for Betsy. Dianne welcomed the idea. The more people looking, the sooner they would find her.

But within a few more steps, Dianne had no need of other searchers. She had found Betsy. The child lay on her side, her eyes open, staring blankly. For just a moment, a very brief moment, Dianne thought her sister was playing a joke.

"Betsy?" she called sternly, but there was a tremor in her voice.

The child didn't move—didn't so much as blink. That's when Dianne knew the truth of it. She shook her head and began to scream. Rational thought left her mind. "Help me! Someone help me!" She couldn't even touch Betsy's still body.

The men came running, along with Charity Hammond. Two of the men reached Dianne first. They immediately saw the situation and one of them lifted Betsy into his arms. Blood marked the grass where her head had rested.

"She's dead," someone said.

Charity came forward and examined the little girl. She looked to Dianne with tears in her eyes. "I'm so sorry. It looks like she's been kicked in the side of the head."

It was impossible to breathe. Dianne's entire body began to shake so violently that her knees gave out. Someone took hold of her and lifted her into his arms. Looking up, Dianne met the pained expression of Cole Selby. Moments later, she lost consciousness.

CHAPTER 14

CHARITY HAMMOND HELPED DIANNE PREPARE BETSY'S BODY FOR burial. Dianne had initially balked at the idea of washing and dressing a dead body. It seemed almost unnatural . . . gruesome. Still, it was her sister—her Betsy. A tenderness within Dianne's heart pushed away all thoughts of the macabre. *This is my baby sister—she deserves my loving care,* Dianne told herself as she arranged Betsy's hair.

Their mother couldn't even comprehend the situation. Reverend Hammond had come to give her the news while Charity had cared for a hysterical Dianne. The life Dianne thought could surely get no worse had suddenly gone completely mad.

"Why did this happen?" she asked, glancing up from the bow she tied around Betsy's pigtail. "Why didn't that mule kick Joseph instead of Betsy?"

"Child, death and dying are a mystery to us all. The Lord giveth and the Lord taketh away. Blessed be the name of the Lord."

Dianne stiffened. "What is that supposed to mean?"

Charity smiled in a sympathetic manner. "It means that all of life is in the hands of God. The things He allows to happen are often beyond our comprehension. Still, we have to allow that He knows what He's doing and that there is a purpose in it. We have to bless His name in spite of our pain."

"That makes no sense," Dianne replied. She looked at Betsy, now dressed and prepared for burial. She looked unnaturally pale but otherwise seemed only to sleep. "How can I bless His name for this?"

"Oh, child, your grief is fierce—your pain overwhelming—but God understands that. He knows how you feel. He loves you, and He wants to share your burden."

"He gave me this burden," Dianne said angrily. "I don't see anything loving about that. He could have helped in this. He could have made Betsy feel the need to come home when little Joseph left her. He could have allowed Joseph to be there when the accident happened so that he could have come and got me. We might have saved her. God could have done so much, but He didn't."

Charity's expression irritated Dianne. She seemed to be at complete peace with everything. With Dianne's anger—even with Betsy lying dead before them—Charity could bless the name of the Lord.

Coming around the makeshift table, Charity put her arm around Dianne's shoulders. "Being mad at God won't change matters. It'll only make you feel worse. Then not only will you be mourning the loss of your sisters, you'll mourn the loss of His comfort. And, Dianne, the comfort you need in the wake of these tragedies is found only in Him. No person can offer it. Nothing can provide it."

"He seems so cruel," Dianne murmured. "How can I turn to Him for comfort when He seems to be the very source of my pain?"

Charity hugged her close. "It's that pain that is keeping you from seeing things clearly. I want you to think for just a minute." She pulled away and drew Dianne to face her. "You talked of the love you held for your father. You told me how much he loved you and how special he always made you feel." Dianne nodded but said nothing.

"Still, you told me about other times in your life when problems came. Didn't you tell me that you got hurt when you fell on the ice at Christmas one year?"

"Yes, but what does that have to do with this?"

"Did your father still love you even though you got hurt?"

"Of course he still loved me—he might even have loved me more."

Dianne suddenly realized what Charity was trying to say. "My father had no control over the ice. He couldn't keep me from falling. But God could have stopped this. He could have prevented Ardith from drowning. He could have kept Betsy from being kicked."

Charity nodded. "Yes. Yes, He had the power to do that."

"But He didn't," Dianne stated, as though Charity might have forgotten.

"No, He didn't." She reached up and gently touched Dianne's cheek. "And you have to decide for yourself what you will do with that knowledge."

Dianne pondered those words long after the funeral and into the following days when they were once again on the trail headed west. She walked alongside the oxen team, keeping them in line and contemplating all that Charity had said. Faith would no doubt have said something similar. Her ability to accept God's will and ways were a marvel to Dianne. But how did these women live with the horrors of life—the frailty of the human body and mind—and continue to bless the name of the Lord?

Still the days wore on with no real answers. The wagon train had been reduced by nearly seventy wagons. The train Daniel Keefer had said was two weeks behind them had shown up at the fort on the day they were to cross the river and head west. A man named John Bozeman was leading a train north through Sioux Indian country, and many of Keefer's people chose to leave Daniel's company and head north with Bozeman.

Morgan and Zane had discussed the situation with Dianne and had concluded that they were better off to stay with Mr. Keefer. When Cole Selby came by to find out if they would move out with the Keefer train or head north with the Bozeman party, Dianne had listened as her brothers confirmed they would stay.

"It's probably for the best," Cole had told them. "The Indians up north are not friendly to the wagons crossing their territory. Bozeman will be lucky if he doesn't get the entire party killed."

"What about our party?" Dianne had asked.

Cole had met her gaze with an expression that softened the hard edges of Dianne's heart. "We could still run into some hostiles, but Mr. Keefer feels the biggest dangers are behind us. He has friends among the tribes to the west. Hopefully that will keep us from trouble."

Now, walking with the oxen, passing by a fresh grave with a crude board marker, Dianne couldn't help but wonder if Mr. Selby's words would be true. Were the dangers really behind them? People were still dying periodically. A stillborn baby had been delivered only two nights ago. Death was their constant companion.

Dianne looked to the cloudless sky and then to the trail. The air was thick with dirt. She had long learned to wear a scarf around her mouth and nose and to pull her sunbonnet down tight against the dust, but today it seemed to offer little help. She coughed violently and slowed the oxen so that she could put a little more distance between her wagon and Zane's.

Would this journey ever end? Discouraged by the endlessness of it all, Dianne could well understand her mother's desire to do nothing but sleep. Dianne longed for it herself. The adventure had lost its attraction. She'd heard tales of people who went mad in the wilderness. She feared her mother might well be one of their number . . . but then again, perhaps Dianne would be too. The thought startled her. Was it possible she was losing her grip on reality—on life?

"I don't want to lose my mind." The very thought firmed up her resolve. *I have to be strong. Mama needs me to be strong. The baby needs me to be strong.*

"How are you holding up?"

Dianne startled out of her thoughts and met Cole Selby's gaze. He rode his horse at a slow, steady walk to keep even with her. "I guess I'm doing as best I can."

Cole nodded. "You've had to bear more than most."

Dianne noted sympathy in his words. Maybe Mr. Selby wasn't such a bad fellow after all. Maybe her pride had been the problem from the beginning. Now after losing so much, Dianne felt she had no pride left.

"I appreciate all that you've done for us. I guess I should have never encouraged my family to come west. If I hadn't, maybe my sisters would be alive now." She shook her head and pulled the handkerchief from her face. After wiping her brow, she shook the cloth in hopes of clearing some of the dust.

"Sometimes things happen," Cole replied, "things that we wish we could take back or keep from happening." He looked ahead down the trail, and Dianne got the distinct impression that he knew exactly what she was feeling.

"Well," Cole said, shaking off his contemplation, "we'll be stopping pretty soon for the nooning. Be sure to get the animals well watered. There'll be less water as we head out this afternoon."

Dianne nodded and repositioned her handkerchief as Cole rode away. He was such a complicated man, appearing to be helpful and knowledgeable but at the same time distant and aloof. Surely there was much more to him than met the eye.

The nooning offered little relief. The heat of the day bore down on them and with little in the way of shade, they were forced to endure the sun's punishment. Dianne's misery was further increased by Griselda Showalter's sudden appearance.

"I've come to see your mother," she announced.

"Mama hasn't been receiving visitors—" Dianne began to explain.

Griselda quickly interrupted her. "Never mind that. She'll be glad to see me."

"Well . . . I don't know. . . ."

"Child, you know nothing of a mother's grief. She needs another woman to bare her soul to. Now stop fretting and help me into the back of the wagon."

Dianne studied the determined look of Mrs. Showalter and decided to do as she'd instructed. The last thing Dianne wanted was to have an argument with the woman. She'd seen firsthand how Mrs. Showalter treated her children.

Half pushing, half supporting, Dianne helped Griselda up through the canvas entryway. Immediately the older woman began talking to Dianne's mother. Maybe she was right. Maybe her mother needed the comfort and shoulder of another woman who'd suffered the loss of a child.

When the nooning was nearly over, Dianne went to retrieve Griselda. She opened the back of the wagon just in time to see Griselda help Susannah take a long drink of something in a bottle.

"What are you doing? What are you giving her?"

Griselda put a cork in the bottle and helped Susannah lie back down before turning to Dianne. "I'm simply helping her deal with her grief. Be off. I'll see myself out."

Dianne bristled at the dismissal. After all, this was her mother, not Griselda's. "The nooning is over. We're heading out now."

"That's fine." Griselda moved to the back of the wagon. "I'll be by to check on her this evening."

"I'm sure you have your own family to worry over," Dianne stated, her anger at being denied an answer to her inquiry over the medicine building by the minute.

Griselda narrowed her eyes, her brows knitting together and arching up at the ends. "I won't have the likes of you dictating to me, child. Were your mother able to, she'd no doubt give you a good slap across the face for your lack of manners." She stomped off, leaving Dianne stunned by her words.

I'll speak to Zane and Morgan about this, she promised herself. *They can stand guard over Mama this evening and keep that woman from causing us more difficulties.*

That evening they reached Dry Sandy Creek. It was here they would separate the wagon train. Mr. Keefer would take the travelers who wished to go to Great Salt Lake City and head south, while Cole Selby was in charge of moving the rest of the group to Fort Hall and then on north to Virginia City.

The water here was brackish—barely drinkable. Wood was nonexistent and the grass supply quite poor. Dianne worried about the livestock. They'd worked hard that day and there was little food for them to forage.

"I've been thinking about you."

Dianne turned to find Faith standing not three feet away. She held a crock in her arms. "I brought you something."

Dianne smiled. "It's so good to see you. I've wanted to come find you—to talk about all that has happened. But Mama's taken worse and the work has been so hard."

Faith nodded. "I heard it from Malachi. He talked to your brothers. That's why I brought you this." She extended the crock. "It's smoked ham and beans. I took the last of the meat we purchased at that little store at Sweetwater."

"How in the world could you afford it?" Dianne took the crock and lifted the lid to breathe in the aroma. "I thought their prices outrageous. Zane actually did business with the man and sold him some goods. The fellow didn't want to pay much of anything, but then Zane pointed out the prices he had on his goods and the fellow relented and paid up."

Faith smiled. "Malachi helped out a bit. Since we laid over there, Malachi was able to help the blacksmith take care of the wagon train's needs. The man paid Malachi and so we had a nice bit of extra. The ham was just too good to pass up."

"I'm sure we'll enjoy it. We have some extra milk, although the cows aren't giving as much. I think all the travel and the poor feed has caused it. I'm happy to share it with you."

"Thanks, that would be nice," Faith said, her expression sobering. "I was sure sorry about your sister. I stayed away knowing that I'd probably just upset your mama. I've been praying for all of you, however."

Tears came to Dianne's eyes. "I still can't believe they're both gone. It was bad enough after Ardith was lost, but now Betsy. I mothered her as if she were my own and now she's gone too."

Faith nodded. "I know. It's never a simple matter to say good-bye."

Dianne thought of Charity's words the day they'd dressed Betsy for the funeral. "Faith, do you think God still loves us, even when He allows these bad things to happen?"

"I know He does, Dianne."

"How, Faith? How can you be sure?"

Faith smiled sadly. "Slavery."

Dianne shook her head. "I don't understand. How can slavery be proof that God still loves you?"

"Because in spite of the pain and suffering brought on by that horrible situation, I came to know that God really cared about me—me as a person. Knowing that, and knowing that He was there for me, allowed me to get through all of the bad things. I knew there would never come a time when anything could be worse than what I'd already endured. There's a liberty in that, Dianne. And a liberty in turning it all over to the One who knows the future. You can't change things by wallowing in the sorrow, but everything changes when you trust in Him."

Dianne took up a pan and poured the ham and beans into it so that she could give Faith back the crock. "You make it sound so simple."

"Does it have to be hard?"

"I suppose not. Guess I'm always making things harder than they have to be. I try not to, but things happen that concern me."

"Like what, for instance?" Faith asked softly.

Dianne sighed. "I'm worried about Mama, Faith. Mrs. Showalter came to see her at the nooning. I don't like that woman to begin with. She's so bossy and ill-tempered. She just forces her way in and doesn't pay any attention to what other folks think. Anyway, she gave Mama some medicine. I don't know what it was, but I suspect it was laudanum. I don't want to make this harder than it has to be. I don't want to overreact. Still, I feel like I should make sure that doesn't happen again, but I don't know exactly how to go about it. I heard the doctor say that too much laudanum can kill a person. I was hoping to keep Mama from using any more of it." Dianne knew she was rambling and stopped abruptly. "Sorry. What do you think I should do?"

"Well, did you tell Mrs. Showalter that?"

Dianne straightened and shook her head. "I can't tell that woman anything. She refuses to listen to honest concern."

"Maybe you should get someone to go with you when you speak to her. Maybe Mrs. Hammond?"

Dianne nodded. "That's a good idea. Could you come too? We could go talk to Charity while Zane and Morgan eat."

Faith's expression turned grim. "I doubt she'd listen to a woman of color."

"I don't care. I need you there for me, if for no other reason."

Faith smiled. "In that case, of course I'll come." She reached out for the crock. "Now, don't you go worrying about cleaning this out. I'll take care of it. Why don't you get your brothers set up and we'll just head right over. The Hammonds' wagon isn't all that far. I can get the milk from you later."

Dianne did as Faith suggested and moments later explained the situation to Charity Hammond. "I'm convinced it's laudanum or something equally as bad," Dianne said. "I've barely been able to rouse Mama. She just wants to sleep."

Charity considered Dianne's concerns, then pulled on her sun-bonnet. "Let's just go and have a talk with Griselda. I'm sure she means well, but she needs to understand your concerns."

The trio made their way along the wagons until they reached the Showalter camp. Percy sat working to mend a bucket. He dropped one tool after another and then fumbled around to pick them back up. He clearly had no skill at what he was attempting. The Showalter children—James, Glen, Grace, and Marysue—huddled under the wagon. It appeared they were eating their supper, but to Dianne they all resembled frightened animals.

"We've come to talk to your missus," Charity announced.

Percy looked up, frustration evident in his expression. "She's gone to see someone."

Dianne started to comment that it was probably her mother Griselda had gone to see, when the heavyset woman came storming into the camp.

"I've never in my life been so insulted. Percy, put that bucket down—it's not like you have any idea what you're doing anyway. I want you to go and speak with—" She caught sight of the women and paused in midsentence. "What are you doing here?"

Her gaze settled on Dianne. Dianne wished momentarily that the earth would just swallow her up. Griselda Showalter was a force to be reckoned with, and Dianne feared the real reckoning would be hers to bear alone.

Charity stepped between the women, however. "We've come to speak to you about Dianne's mother. Dianne saw you give her something from a bottle earlier today. She's concerned about it and I am too."

Faith gave Dianne a gentle pat on the back for support. Dianne needed the reassurance as Griselda's hostility grew.

"I was only helping Susannah. She's my friend and I know what she's suffering. None of you have lost a child, so you can't help her like I can."

Dianne stepped forward. "By giving her laudanum?"

"It won't hurt her. If she were a stronger woman like me, she wouldn't need it. But she's with child and she has a weak constitution."

"It's only going to be weaker if you keep drugging her," Dianne protested.

"You're a child. You know nothing."

By now, Percy had come to his feet and stood beside his wife as if to defend her, his devotion evident. There wasn't a time when they were together that Dianne hadn't heard the woman belittle him. *How can he love her and be so supportive of her when she does nothing but hurt him?*

Charity interceded again, glancing back at Dianne as if to warn her to remain silent. "Griselda, I know you to be a reasonable woman. I'm asking that you stop causing the Chadwick children additional worry. Susannah needs to wake up and face the reality of what's happening. She needs—"

"She needs her laudanum. She's the one who told me where to find it. She asked me to bring it to her, and that's what I did." Griselda crossed her arms defiantly and stared them down as if daring any one of the women to say otherwise.

Dianne remembered the remaining laudanum and sighed. How much had her mother already taken? Anger made her bold. Stepping forward, she nudged Charity aside. "Stay away from my mother. If you don't, I'll take this matter to the wagon master and demand you be removed from the train!"

"How dare you!" Griselda turned and stormed away, leaving Percy openmouthed and the children wide-eyed in surprise.

"What was that all about?"

Dianne turned to find Cole Selby standing behind Faith. "She's been drugging my mother," Dianne said, feeling shy and yet knowing he'd understand and help her in the matter.

"Why?" he asked, coming closer.

"She thinks she's helping Susannah deal with the grief," Charity said before Dianne could answer. "I think she'll stay away now. I don't think she meant any harm."

Cole continued to look at Dianne. The fading light made it impossible for her to see what color his eyes were, but it seemed she remembered them to be brown.

"I'm sorry for my wife's interference," Percy Showalter said. "I'll speak to her."

Dianne couldn't imagine that it would do any good, but she nodded to acknowledge his effort to make amends. He was such a gentle, soft-spoken man, and the last thing she wanted to do was hurt his feelings.

"Mr. Showalter, if you don't mind, I'll have you position your wagon closer to the front tomorrow. That way it will be more difficult for Mrs. Showalter to walk back and visit."

Percy nodded and pushed up his spectacles. "I understand."

There seemed to be nothing more to be said. Dianne bid them good-night and made her way back to their camp. Zane and Morgan were bent over a game of checkers as she approached. "She came here, didn't she?" Dianne questioned.

"I'll say," Morgan replied. "She ranted and raved when Zane and I wouldn't let her in the wagon. She even threatened to give us both a good spanking."

Zane laughed. "Yeah. I thought it might have been kind of fun to see her try, so I suggested she start with Morgan."

Morgan chuckled. "For a minute, I thought she might. Then she stomped off muttering and grumbling." He shrugged. "Guess she'll save the whupping for later."

Dianne shook her head. "I was at her camp when she came back.

She was as mad as I've ever seen anyone. She was going to have Percy come deal with you both."

The twins laughed even harder and went back to their game. "I have nothing but the utmost respect for that man," Zane commented as he made his move against Morgan.

"To be sure," Morgan replied as Zane jumped over several of his pieces. "Oh, bother. It's getting too dark to even see. Let's go check on the livestock."

"You're just a sore loser," Zane said, getting to his feet. He bent down and picked up the game. "Tomorrow night we'll start sooner and then you can't complain about the light."

They walked off to deal with the animals, leaving Dianne alone. She hugged herself to ward off the pain and stared into the small fire. Cole Selby had taught her brothers how to make a fire just large enough to cook and get warmed by. He said most folks were given to making their fires much too big. It was a waste they couldn't afford out here where wood and other fuels were so scarce.

She smiled at the memory of Cole's appearance at the Showalter camp. She'd really misjudged him. He'd been obnoxious and condescending the first few times she'd met him. Then when she'd stepped on the snake he'd treated her like a child while saving her life.

But tonight she again felt he recognized her pain and sorrow. She knew it as sure as she knew her own name. She saw the look in his eyes. He understood that Griselda's actions were out of line and needed to be stopped. She smiled faintly. Perhaps she had something of a champion in Cole Selby.

CHAPTER 15

THE WAGON TRAIN APPROACHED VIRGINIA CITY ON THE CORRINE Road. The mountainous beauty of the trail left Dianne with high hopes of a tranquil mountain village for their new home. But her hopes were quickly shattered with her first real look at the town. Nestled along the foothills of the Tobacco Root Mountains was a collection of false-front businesses and shacklike houses. Tents abounded down through the valley and along the creek, where mining efforts had torn up the ground, scarring it and leaving it longing for life.

The area was nearly void of trees. Dianne supposed the trees had been cleared in order to build and then maybe also for fuel. Either way, the landscape looked barren of vegetation. The dull, lifeless color of weathered wood, sluiced debris, and dried-out ground left Dianne wondering if anything good at all could come out of such a place.

Of those in the wagon train who had chosen to head north with Mr. Selby's party, most were coming for gold. There were only a few wagons of women and children coming west with male relatives in order to join husbands who were already hard at work in the pursuit of gold. The train had picked up stragglers along the Corrine Road coming north. Many men were coming from Colorado and California, where the gold seemed somewhat played out. They had a look of cautious anticipation in their eyes. Cole Selby had told Morgan it was a look of haunted hope—the desire to believe this just might be the one time they'd strike it rich, all the while remembering the other times when they didn't.

The Chadwicks, Showalters, and Hammonds were actually the only ones who had traveled to Virginia City with something other than gold on their minds. Griselda had heard the country was good for farming, but by the looks of it, Dianne figured someone had led that poor woman astray. Dianne seriously doubted you could grow much more than heart-break in this country. The Hammonds were actually heading west to Oregon to live with their son but, after praying about it, felt confident that they were supposed to lay over a time nearby and minister to the mining district. Their young companion, Levi Sperry, agreed with this as well. It was his desire to settle in the area, leaving the only mother and father he'd known for the last few years in order to start a life of his own. Charity had confided in Dianne that she felt certain Levi was developing an affection for her and that this had influenced his desire to settle in the area. Dianne had mixed feelings where Levi was concerned. He was sweet and well mannered, but she had no desire to be courted by any man. Her life was still too topsy-turvy, and with the events of the last few months, courting was the furthest thing from her mind. Nevertheless she was glad he was around—glad each of her friends were close by. Charity helped to keep things nicely balanced when Griselda was on the offensive. Dianne had a feeling she would need the woman's help if Griselda settled very close to Uncle Bram's house. The only other people from the wagon train that Dianne cared about were Faith and Malachi—but they had come for gold. Dianne could only hope that Uncle Bram wouldn't live too far from where the men were mining. Maybe that way she'd have a chance to slip down and visit Faith from time to time.

Cole directed the gold seekers to head down the gulch to check out the available sites. Daylight lasted until about eight o'clock in early September, so they would have plenty of time to look around and still set up camp before nightfall. As the rest of their company disappeared around the bend and headed deeper into the mining district, Dianne felt a bit lonely. The Hammonds and Showalters had even followed after the others, feeling more comfortable in making camp with folks they knew.

Susannah Chadwick had been positive her brother would be there to greet them, however, and chose to part company at this point. Somber— but sober since Charity's intercession with Griselda—she instructed her children to drive their teams into the heart of the town.

"We'll find Bram," she told them, "and then he can direct us to his home. Thank goodness we won't be like those fools."

Dianne's gaze followed her mother's blank stare as the last of the wagons disappeared from sight. It had been the hardest journey of her life and now it was over. Somehow it seemed almost anticlimactic, and Dianne was rather let down by the abrupt ending of it.

"Let's move on," Susannah called out from the wagon.

"Where do we go, Ma?" Zane asked as Morgan moved his wagon to the lead position.

Their mother looked about blankly. "I don't know. Just head into town. The folks there are bound to know my brother. He's a fine man and his reputation will be enough. He's been here a long time, after all. It's not like he showed up with those gold-fevered ninnies."

Zane exchanged a glance with Dianne. Worry etched his expression, but he only nodded to their mother and moved out to follow Morgan.

Dianne maneuvered her team behind those of her brothers as they slowly made their way down the dusty street. The noise built as they approached the collection of buildings. There was a bevy of saloons and dancehalls where music, if it could truly be called that, assaulted the senses of passersby. Several men, clearly drunk from the looks of them, whistled and called out to Dianne in a most unbecoming manner. It was amazing to Dianne that men could be drunk in the middle of the afternoon. She hurried to lower her gaze to the hooves of the oxen, all the while continuing to move forward.

I won't acknowledge them, she told herself. *I will ignore them and they will leave me be.* But she couldn't help but remember the day her father had been killed. She'd ignored those men, as well, and they hadn't left her alone.

By the time they'd reached the other side of town, Dianne liked

Virginia City no better. The streets were crowded with an amazing number of people, but no one seemed overly friendly.

Morgan and Zane drew their wagons to a halt on the side of the road and Dianne had no choice but to follow suit. If she'd been in charge, she would have just kept going. There was something about the area she just didn't like.

"Ma, there was a post office back a ways," Morgan called out as he came back to their wagon. "And Zane spotted the newspaper office. We've tied off the teams and will head over there and see if anyone knows where we can find Uncle Bram."

"Good. Find out where his house is and we'll just head right over," their mother agreed.

Zane had come up by this time and looked to Dianne. "Will you two be all right while we're gone? This place seems more than a little rowdy."

"We'll be fine," their mother answered before Dianne could speak. "Just go find out where your uncle lives."

Zane and Morgan nodded and hurried back down the street. Dianne looked up to see her mother craning around to watch the twins as they walked away. Her look betrayed her anxiety—her desperation. Dianne felt sorry for her mother. It had to be so very hard to have lost her husband and two daughters, have a son desert them, then endure the long trail to Virginia City, all while carrying a baby.

"Mama, are you feeling all right?"

Her mother turned back around and settled her gaze on Dianne. "I'm all right. I'll be better when we find Bram." She sounded almost afraid. "I could use a good strong cup of tea."

"I'm sure it won't take long," Dianne tried to encourage. Though she'd never been all that affectionate or endearing, now Susannah Chadwick was even more estranged than before. Dianne felt a coldness—almost a hostility—directed toward her and the twins. Did their mother resent them for living when the others had died? Did she hate them for enduring or even suggesting the hard trip when Trenton had refused to come?

They waited for nearly an hour before the twins returned. The news was not going to be good—Dianne could see that by their expressions.

"Well?" their mother questioned.

Morgan spoke first. "Folks know Uncle Bram but haven't seen him in months. They don't know where he actually lives, but it isn't here."

"One man said Uncle Bram has a place north of here, but he didn't know how far away it was or how to get there," Zane threw in.

Dianne was unprepared for their mother's response. Without warning, she came flying off the wagon seat and over the side. Morgan barely had a chance to help her. The baby hardly seemed to encumber her as anxiety gave her energy.

"He must be here. Dianne sent him a letter months ago. He should be here waiting for us. I'll go to the hotel we passed and ask there. He might very well be there right now."

"I'll go with you, Ma," Morgan said, stepping forward.

"No! I'll do this myself. You stay here and keep track of the wagons and your sister."

Their mother stormed down the street like a general about to take over the territory. Zane and Morgan looked to Dianne as if she had answers.

"What are we going to do when she doesn't find Uncle Bram?" Dianne questioned instead of offering solutions.

"I don't know," Zane replied. "What if he's moved out of the territory all together? What if he headed to Missouri when you wrote him with the idea of coming west?"

"Oh, surely he wouldn't have done that," Dianne said, wondering how they would ever deal with such a circumstance if it were true.

"Well, it sure looks like it could be possible," Morgan answered.

"So what do we do if that is the case?" Zane asked. "I don't hardly intend to go back to Missouri."

Morgan nodded. "Me neither."

"I don't think any of us could endure the trip back—at least not right now. Ma couldn't travel anymore and winter isn't that far off."

"Mountains get colder sooner. Plus we're farther north," Zane offered. "Seasons will change over the next few weeks."

"Be that as it may," Dianne continued, "we have to figure out what to do. We need shelter. If Uncle Bram can't be found, we'll have to search out a place to live. We have money, so paying rent shouldn't be a problem. We also have all these goods, plus the extra livestock. I think we're going to need to sell off the animals, except for our own horses and maybe a cow and some chickens. We can sell the wagons and such too. Maybe keep one."

"Do you think Ma will allow for that?" Zane asked seriously.

Dianne realized suddenly she'd again taken on a leadership role. "Look, she can't very well hope to feed the animals through the winter. We have grain for the horses and can probably purchase hay and straw. If not, we'll make do as best we can. But we can't keep all these oxen and milk cows alive until spring. Someone is bound to want them. I remember Mr. Selby saying that animals sell at a premium up here."

"Well, if Ma agrees to it, I think it's a good idea."

Dianne considered the idea of putting together some sort of sale. "I wonder if we can have an auction. Do you suppose that would be possible? We could auction the livestock and the wagons and all the other goods. That would give us a considerable size of money. It definitely should be enough with what we already have to last us till spring."

"We'll need to keep enough supplies to see ourselves through the winter," Morgan commented.

Dianne nodded. "So you'll both stay that long?" The boys exchanged a look and pushed back their hats in unison. Their actions were mirror images of each other.

"What makes you think we wouldn't?" Zane questioned.

Dianne sighed and leaned against the wagon wheel. "Look, you two have done nothing but talk about wanting to go your own way since we've been on the trail. Zane, I know you want to join up with the army, and Morgan, you seem bent on exploring and just moseying around. I don't blame either one of you, but neither do I have the liberty to make such decisions for myself. I'm going to have to stay put and take care of Mama and the baby, and that's fine with me.

"However, the winter is coming up fast and I don't know how we'll get through it if you two aren't here to help with wood and water and whatever animals we keep. I just want to know if you'll at least stay through the winter. Then, even if we don't find Uncle Bram by spring, you can go your own way and I'll make other arrangements."

Her brothers seemed surprised by her take-over attitude. Dianne was surprised by it herself. For reasons that eluded her, taking charge of the family just seemed the natural thing to do.

"I don't plan to leave you and Ma alone this winter," Morgan said firmly. "I don't think Zane thinks to do that either, do you?" He looked to his brother, as did Dianne.

"I can wait until spring to join up, but after that, I'd really like to make my own way. By then I'll be nearly nineteen. Old enough to be on my own for sure."

Dianne chuckled, but there was bitterness in the tone. "I'm nearly seventeen, and I think whether we like it or not, we are on our own."

As if to drive her point home, their mother returned at that moment. The rage was gone and in its place, Dianne could see that defeat and sorrow had taken over.

Zane helped their mother back up into the wagon. Once Susannah was seated she spoke. "I don't know what we're going to do. Bram isn't here. He doesn't live here; he just picks up supplies and mail here." She turned to go inside the wagon.

"Wait," Dianne called. She would risk her mother's ire and press forward to discuss the obvious needs of shelter and selling off the livestock. They had no time to waste.

"What?" her mother asked blankly.

Dianne could see tears forming in her mother's eyes again. She hated being the cause of any more pain. "We were talking—the twins and I. We figured if you didn't find Uncle Bram we would need to find a place to live. We need to sell off the oxen and some of the milk cows and maybe all the wagons except one."

Susannah shook her head. "I don't care what you do. Find a place or don't. I just don't care." With that she disappeared into the wagon—no doubt to forget about her misery in sleep.

Dianne turned to her brothers. They would have to act fast before their mother changed her mind. "Zane, go back to the newspaper office. Tell them we need to place an ad and that we also need some announcements printed up to post around town. Find out what it would cost. Morgan, go talk to the sheriff or whoever else is in charge and see what the law is about holding an auction. See if you can't also find out where we would be allowed to hold an auction."

"What are you going to do while we're gone?" Morgan questioned.

"I'm going to start going over the inventory, and I'm going to try to comfort Mama," Dianne said matter-of-factly. It seemed the die was cast and her job was to be the matriarch of the family. She felt her strength bolstered by the look of approval on the faces of her older brothers. "I'm also going to pen a letter to Trenton and get him out here. By spring the war will surely be over and his need to avenge Pa will be behind him. If he can come here by spring, you'll both be free to go your own ways."

CHAPTER 16

TRENTON STILL FELT THE NEED TO LOOK OVER HIS SHOULDER, even now, weeks after having escaped the Wilson gang's company. At night when he was all alone it seemed like he could almost hear Jerry's wicked laughter and ugly comments. The man cared nothing for anyone. He'd been glad to be rid of Robbie, saying that he was a simpleton who didn't know which end of his gun to shoot.

Trenton had tried to get Jerry to talk about what had happened at the bank, but all Jerry cared about was Yankee gold. Trenton had declared his desire to check up on Robbie and Mr. Danssen, but Jerry told him in no uncertain manner that he'd just as soon shoot Trenton as look at him. He was confident Trenton would bring the law down on them and demanded that Sam keep his eye on Trenton so that he couldn't escape into town.

Sam was a lazy man, however, and when he nodded off to sleep, Trenton made a hasty departure. He had no idea where he'd go. He had no money; Jerry refused to cut him in on the bank take until after he was confident of Trenton's loyalties. He had his horse, rifle, and pistol, and the only thing Trenton felt he could part with was the rifle. It hadn't brought him a whole lot of money when he'd sold it to a shopkeeper in Jefferson City, but it gave him a good meal and some money in his pocket.

Trenton made his way from southeast Missouri to Kansas City, where talk of the war was escalated. It seemed funny. The war was actually invading the town of New Madrid, whereas Kansas City seemed a safe piece away from battle. In New Madrid, people seemed to avoid even talking about the war. The threat was so very real that speaking of it seemed unnecessary.

But here, the newspapers proclaimed the threats and concerns, listing details of every battle as they became available. People discussed the war on every street corner and over meals and even in church.

Down to his last few pennies, Trenton was at a loss as to what he'd do next. There was no hope of getting a hotel or boardinghouse room.

He tried to find a job. Going from one business to another, he explained he was a shopkeeper's son and knew the business—that he could tote and fetch if nothing else—but no one would hire him. Due to Jayhawkers and other border ruffians, everyone seemed wary of strangers these days, and any spirit of generosity was lost in the wake of the war. At one dry goods store, an older woman did take pity on him and gave him some jerky and crackers. She told him she'd be praying for him, but Trenton wasn't at all sure God would listen, much less care about someone like him.

After a few days without food and with the cold weather setting in, Trenton was sure God wasn't listening. He thought about selling his remaining gear. He still had his pistol, saddle, and horse. But a man needed all of those things to survive. How could he possibly make his way to Montana Territory without them?

"*If* I go," he muttered.

For weeks now he'd figured to make his way north. At least he could check up on his family and know whether they'd arrived safely. He'd had no word from them, but then again, he hadn't bothered to check in with the post office in New Madrid before leaving. Dianne probably had written, but now Trenton would never know.

Leaving his horse tied at the end of the street, Trenton made his way down the boardwalk. He caught his reflection in the window of a greengrocer. *No wonder folks won't hire me. I look like an outlaw.* With a growth of whisker stubble and dust clinging to his clothes, Trenton made a rather ominous picture.

Maybe I can wash up in the river, he thought as he continued down the street. But even as the thought came to mind, Trenton's stomach rumbled loudly. He couldn't wait that long. He was starving, and now his Sunday school upbringing passed by the wayside altogether as he contemplated how to steal some food.

He stepped inside a general mercantile, glancing around to see what was to be had. He wanted jerked meat and maybe crackers or bread, but those things would be hard to slip off with. The store was crowded, so that helped his cause. Spying a bowl of apples atop the counter, he took two when no one was looking and quickly stuck them in his pocket.

Guilt washed over him as he thought of his mother. She would be horrified to know how low he'd sunk. Blowing up the Union supply house, doing nothing to stop a bank robbery, keeping company with killers, and now thieving.

He moved out of the mercantile and headed down the street to another store. Here he accidentally ran into a woman who was moving toward the door, scattering her goods on the floor. Trenton hadn't meant for the accident to happen, but it seemed like providence as he helped her collect her goods, managing to slip a wrapped parcel into his pocket. Surely it was either meat or cheese.

"Where are my buttons?" she questioned, looking around the floor. "I had a package of buttons.

Trenton handed her a spool of thread. "I'm not sure. I think something might have gone over there," he said, pointing behind her.

He pretended to crawl around looking for the missing buttons while another customer engaged the woman in conversation. They were deep in details about some woman named Mrs. Hancock when Trenton managed to slip out the door.

He made his way back to his horse, figuring there was no sense in pushing his luck. He'd go back to the woods by the river and see if he could shoot himself a squirrel or rabbit. Then he'd have a good supper.

As he rode, he unwrapped the package in his pocket and found it to be a wedge of cheese. Without waiting, he bit off a huge chunk. Nothing had ever tasted so good. He reached in his other pocket and pulled out one of the apples. Alternating between the two, Trenton finally started to feel satisfied. He couldn't help thinking, however, of days gone by and his mother's home-cooked meals. He thought, too, of his warm bed and the security he'd always known in his parents' care.

At nineteen, Trenton wanted very much to prove himself as a man, but so many times he felt helpless—childish. Like now . . . he would give just about anything for someone to take care of him.

As he neared the river, the air grew heavier with dampness. The cold permeated Trenton's thin coat, leaving him to wonder if it wouldn't be better to head south rather than north. He had no funds to buy anything warmer, and it wasn't going to be long before snow and chilled breezes were the routine of the day rather than precursors to the coming change of season.

Maybe I could head to Texas, he thought. He'd heard all sorts of stories about that area. There always seemed to be one ranch or another that would hire men to help with the livestock—not that Trenton had any experience. His hands were a bit callused and worn from his last few weeks at the reins but certainly nothing like those of a cowboy.

He found his camp and dismounted. Hobbling the horse's feet, Trenton pulled his pistol to check the ammunition and considered his choices. If he headed off to the west, the forest afforded better coverage and more possibilities for squirrels. If he went east, the land opened up a bit and would be prime ground for rabbits.

Figuring rabbits would be easier, Trenton headed toward the meadow. He walked for about thirty minutes without seeing so much as a single sign of life. The oaks and elms along the river rustled as the wind picked up. Trenton pulled his coat shut and secured the bottom buttons—the only two remaining.

He was about to give up and head toward the trees when a flash of white caught his eye. He followed the movement and saw a rabbit meandering through the tall grass. It stopped in a small clearing. Taking a bead on the animal, Trenton squeezed the trigger just as the rabbit raised its head to sniff the air.

The bullet shot clean through the neck. The rabbit gave out a death squeal and fell over. Trenton ran to where the animal lay, feeling quite delighted with his accomplishment. He could almost taste the meat.

Trenton immediately set to cleaning the animal, not wishing to have the mess at his camp to draw other beasts. Once he'd completed his task, Trenton went back to camp and immediately set to cooking his find.

In spite of his earlier meal of apple and cheese, Trenton was already hungry again. He'd just turned the rabbit over the fire when a rustling in the brush caught his attention.

"Hello the camp!" came the voice of a man.

Trenton reached for his pistol, still convinced that Jerry Wilson would run him down. "Who's there?"

An old man, looking even more tired and haggard than Trenton felt, emerged from the trees. He wore a knee-length coat that looked outdated by about twenty years. Atop his head was a well-worn, dirt-smudged top hat of what must have one time been fine beaver. "The name is Henry DuPont. I smelled your cooking. Ain't had nothing to eat in a month of Sundays."

Trenton relaxed a bit. "You're welcome to join me. I don't have much, just this rabbit."

"Sounds mighty fine." The man reached into his torn coat and pulled out a small cloth bag. "I'll provide the salt. Never travel anywhere without salt. I find a man can eat most anything if he has a bit of salt to go with it."

Trenton smiled. "I'm rather partial to salt myself. Come on and warm up." The old man limped into camp, favoring his right leg. Trenton didn't want to be rude and ask about it, so he said nothing.

"You headin' anywhere in particular?"

Trenton shook his head. "No, not really. I have a sister up in Montana Territory, but it seems the wrong time of year to head up there. How about you?"

"Nah, I'm just going wherever the wind takes me."

Trenton nodded and turned the rabbit again. It was browning nicely and the juices were dripping into the fire below—sizzling and releasing the most incredible aroma.

"Were you in the war?" Henry asked.

Trenton looked at the old man for a moment and then shook his head. "My pa didn't want me to join up." He shrugged. "I can't say I had any real desire to go off to war."

"Well, at least you're not a deserter. I can't abide a man who gives his word then runs off. Known too many of that type. If a man doesn't have his honor, he ain't got nothing at all."

Trenton nodded, feeling guilty afresh as he thought of his thieving that morning. "Hard times make a man desperate," he muttered.

Henry laughed. "Don't I know it. I wasn't raised to this life. I had a good wife and two fine daughters. Lost the wife to childbirth when she tried to give me a son. My own dear mother came to live with us after that. She raised the girls as if they were her own. I haven't seen any of them in years."

Trenton heard the loneliness in Henry's voice. "What happened to put you on the road?"

Henry shook his head. "I can't tell you. One day I just up and walked away and kept walking."

"You just left your home and family?"

Henry shrugged. "Like I said, I can't honestly tell you why. It just seemed the thing to do. I've been wandering around for the last twenty years."

"Seems a long time to be missing from the lives of your loved ones. I haven't been away from mine even a year, and I already miss them more than I like to admit. I miss the comforts of home too."

Henry stretched out his hands to the fire. The light was fading overhead as the sky thickened with dark clouds. "I know what you mean. Nothing beats a feather mattress and a warm quilt."

Trenton smiled at the thought. He took out his knife and tested a piece of the rabbit. "I think this is done."

They ate in relative silence, stripping the bones clean of meat.

Trenton remembered his second apple and offered it to Henry. It made him feel as though he were doing some small penance for having stolen the thing to begin with.

"No thanks. Can't chew it well enough to enjoy it. My teeth are pert near rotten."

Trenton put the apple back in his pocket just as the first few rain-drops began to fall. Henry glanced overhead. "I know a cave not but about a quarter mile upriver. It'll keep us dry if we hurry."

Trenton gathered his things and tied them onto his horse. Henry led them through the trees, sometimes having to wait while Trenton found a way to come through with his mount. Finally they reached the cave, grateful that the rain had still not begun to fall in earnest.

Trenton tied off the horse and took his things inside the cave. Henry was already gathering wood for their fire, and Trenton hurried to join him.

"Cave will be a mite warmer, especially with a good fire going."

"I've been cautious about fires," Trenton admitted. "I hadn't really built one until I needed it for the rabbit. I was afraid it might draw some of the border ruffians."

"Could at that. Them ol' boys know this area like the back of their hand. They could find us, that's for sure. But it ain't like we got much that they'd want. 'Ceptin' your horse."

Trenton nodded. "Is the cave big enough for him as well?"

"I'm sure we can squeeze him in," Henry said. "He might not like it, though. We can put him in first and then make our fire at the mouth of the cave. That shouldn't spook him too much."

They shared a companionable evening, talking of the weather and the winter to come. Henry pulled a deck of cards from his pocket and held them up. "Do you play?"

Trenton shook his head. "Ma thought cards were tools of the devil."

Henry began to shuffle the deck. "Lotta folks think that way, but I can't say why. A man never sits down to play but what he knows the odds are against him. Ain't like anyone's tricked him."

Henry dealt the cards. "We're not playin' for money, that's for sure, so why not go a few hands with me? It's a good way to pass the time."

"What will we play?"

Henry smiled. "Poker. What else?"

They played for several hours, stopping only long enough to add more wood to the fire. Outside the weather worsened and grew colder, the rain falling so hard at one point it was impossible to see beyond the opening of the cave.

Trenton seemed to have a natural affinity for poker. Once he understood the rules, he won hand after hand, surprising even Henry.

"You're good at this, boy. Maybe too good. You could probably make a decent living if you learned to read men good enough."

"What do you mean?" Trenton asked. He was enjoying the game. The strategy kept his mind occupied and helped him to forget about his worries.

"There are two kinds of men who play poker. Them that come expectin' to win and them that come hopin' to win. The hopers never get far. They don't understand the mind that drives those who expect to win.

"Now, there are a lot of professional gamblers out there. Used to be one for a time myself. You have your regular games where you might call it a good night if you make ten dollars. Then you have your high stakes games where thousands pass over the table."

Trenton perked up at the thought of all that money. "How can that be?"

Henry shrugged. "Guess there are a lot of rich men who don't know what else to do with their money." He snickered. "I could sure help them spend it."

Trenton laughed. "Me too."

Henry sobered and dealt another hand. "I know where you could get into a decent game. You might make thirty, even fifty dollars before the night was over. If you played this good."

"I couldn't do that. My ma would hightail it all the way back from Montana Territory to box my ears if I dared to gamble."

"I'm tellin' ya, it ain't the sin she makes it out to be. How can it be robbin' or cheatin' a man if he comes willingly to the table—knowing the odds are against him?"

Trenton let that information sink in for a moment. The man made sense, and the game *was* pleasurable. How was it any different from passing the evening playing some other socially acceptable game?

"Even if I wanted to give it a go," Trenton finally said, "I don't have any money."

"You got a pistol," Henry pointed out. "You even have a horse and saddle. You could sell one or all and then buy them back after you won yourself a fair pot of money."

Trenton shook his head and picked up the cards Henry had dealt. "I couldn't risk it. I might not win. After all, there are no doubt a lot of men out there who know a heap more about the game than I do."

"Well, sure. That's where I come in. I can teach you everything you need to know. How to read a man. How to keep track of the cards— this is especially good if you're playin' twenty-one."

Trenton began to see that the old man had something specific in mind. "And what would you want in return?"

Henry rubbed his scrawny white beard and raised a bushy brow. "Well, now, I think maybe twenty-five percent of the game would be fair. We could travel together and see what happened. If it didn't work out, there'd be no hard feelings."

Trenton wrestled with the idea for a minute. He knew how his mother would feel about her eldest son turning gambler, but he wasn't sure there was any other choice. No one would hire him for honest work.

Then he thought of Dianne and knew her disappointment would be more than he'd ever want to face. She had high hopes for him to make something of himself. So many times they'd talked long into the night about what he might try his hand at. Dianne felt he'd make a good business owner, but not in the mercantile or dry goods arena. She saw him more as owning a freighting company or working in delivery. That way he'd be outdoors most of the time, enjoying a life that at least had the pretense of freedom.

He looked down at the cards in his hand. Two kings, a ten, a six, and a five. Not much to go on, but a pair was better than nothing. Maybe he and Henry could make a good pair. It was something—which was more than he had right now.

"I guess it wouldn't hurt to give it a try. Something small to begin with, so I can be sure and get my pistol back."

Henry laughed and nodded. "I knew you'd see the sense of it."

CHAPTER 17

THE CHADWICK SIBLINGS SOLD OFF EVERYTHING THAT WASN'T NEC-
essary to getting them through the winter. The auction had gone well,
as there were numerous gold miners who were desperate for goods and
supplies. The auction lasted barely an hour, in fact, because people were
so bent on purchasing the items quickly.

Dianne even managed to speak to a woman at the auction who
knew of a place the Chadwicks could rent. It wasn't much, she told
Dianne, but it would be a heap better than living in a wagon all winter.
Dianne jumped at the chance but found it rather discouraging when she
actually saw the place for the first time.

It was just a one-room cabin, located on the north side of town.
There were no windows, but there wasn't any real need for them—the
holes in the walls from missing chinking were big enough to put a fist
through.

Dianne hadn't been happy about the situation, but there was nothing
else available. The hotel was full and the boardinghouses hadn't had
vacancies in months. With winter coming on and the baby due in
December, Dianne knew it was their only hope.

Working to make the cabin into a home, Dianne had tacked up
some of the wagon canvas to the walls in order to block out the weather.

Still, it was chilly, and the price of coal or other fuel to heat the small cabin left her worried that they'd soon run through their nest egg.

"How's Ma feeling?" Morgan asked as he and Zane came in for supper that evening.

"I haven't gotten her to talk to me all day," Dianne said, setting a batch of biscuits on the back of the tiny stove. They were burned on the bottoms, but it seemed impossible to regulate the temperature in the oven.

"Do you think she needs a doctor?" Zane asked. The boys sat down on the crudely made bench on the opposite side of the table.

"I wish I knew," Dianne said, bringing them each a bowl of stew. "How did work go today?" She was glad the twins had been able to find odd jobs around town. Both of them were now working for a freighting company, loading and unloading the various shipments of goods.

"It's a job," Morgan said.

Dianne put the biscuits onto a plate and brought them to the table. "Will they have work for you through the winter?"

Zane shrugged. "It's hard to say. I heard them talkin' about the gold not playing out like it should."

"They've struck gold up at someplace north. Last Chance Gulch, I think they called it," Morgan added.

Zane tore off a piece of biscuit. "One of the men figures this town won't be long running as a gold camp."

"I can't say that would grieve me any," Dianne declared as she took a seat opposite them. "I've never seen so many lowlifes in all my days. I went to the store to sell eggs this morning and was nearly accosted. It seems eggs are pretty prized around here." She glanced over to the corner where four rather content hens sat in crates stacked atop each other.

"You probably shouldn't go to town without one of us along. There are a lot of rowdies who give no thought to proper manners."

"I'm sure you're right, but honestly, some things can't wait. I mean— look—it's already seven-thirty. The store's been closed for over an hour. It wouldn't have done me much good to wait. I needed supplies for supper."

"Well, in the future," Morgan suggested, "if you can wait for one of us, it would probably be better."

Dianne nodded and began eating. She looked to the bed on the far side of the room where their mother slept. She worried about the situation more than she could ever let on to her brothers. Her mother seemed to have no interest in life. Dianne often had to force her to eat, sitting at her mother's side and spooning in nourishment until her mother absolutely refused to take another bite.

"I think that milk cow is going to calve come spring," Zane said, surprising Dianne. "That ought to bring us more milk."

"And a calf to sell," Dianne replied. She constantly worried about the money they'd need to survive. They had enough, even plenty at this point, but prices were outrageous and there was the possibility that they would never find their uncle.

"What are we going to do," she asked suddenly, "if Uncle Bram doesn't show up?"

Zane looked to Morgan and then to Dianne. "Well, we were talking about that the other day. Seems to me, you and Ma should go back to Missouri. Maybe not New Madrid, but somewhere with enough city and such to live comfortably."

"How would we get there and how would we afford a place to live once we were there?" Dianne asked frankly.

"Morgan and I would send you money. You might even be able to locate Trenton and he could take care of you both. It wouldn't be easy, but it would probably be a better situation than having you stay here."

Dianne thought of the long trip back to Missouri. "I don't think Mama could bear the trip. Especially with a new baby. I think we'll have to consider some other possibilities. Maybe we could build us a better cabin—away from town. You boys could learn how and we could set up a regular house. I can sew fairly well and can make us whatever linens or curtains we might need. We kept back quite a bit of cloth when we had the auction. Seems like there would be enough there for just about anything we'd need."

"I doubt it would be that easy," Morgan replied.

His dirty blond hair fell in matted waves almost to his shoulders. It was the first time Dianne thought of him needing a haircut. She looked at Zane. He was a mirror image of his brother. They both had lost the innocent boyish look to their faces. In its place was a hard, careworn expression.

"Well, maybe we won't have to worry about it. After all, the postmaster said Uncle Bram always comes in for mail and supplies this time of year. He stocks up before winter and then comes again in the spring. Anyway, the postmaster promised to give him the message that we've arrived." Dianne could only hope that he wouldn't forget.

"That's what we're counting on," Zane said, getting up to dish a second helping of the stew. "If Uncle Bram comes and takes control of the situation, then we won't have anything to worry about."

Dianne nodded. So much hinged on Uncle Bram—a man she'd never met—whose letters telling of the northern wilderness had fascinated her since childhood.

———

Dianne went through some of their personal belongings the next day. She hadn't realized how very little they actually owned. They'd brought very few household goods except for the few articles she had in her cedar chest. They'd not seen a need for it. They'd assumed Uncle Bram would have dishes and linens and blankets. Except for the things they'd used on the trip west and now used for everyday life, there was nothing that suggested this cabin was a home.

Dianne thought of taking some of her sisters' clothes and extra material and making some rag rugs like Faith had taught her. Originally, she'd thought to spread the wagon canvas on the floors, but they'd needed that for the walls. She'd even taken to stuffing the *Montana Post* in the cracks—after they'd read it from cover to cover—and still the cabin was unbearably cold at night.

She went to the trunk where Ardith's dresses had been packed and found herself moved by the sight of her sister's doll. The porcelain-faced beauty that Ardith had dubbed Miss Kilpatrick, after her third-grade teacher, was the one luxury Ardith had decided to bring on the trip. Dianne gently touched the gold ringlets that cascaded from beneath a velvet bonnet of pale blue.

She missed her sisters more than she could say. The pain in her heart overwhelmed her when Dianne allowed the memories to linger too long.

"Who will take care of my babies?" Ardith had asked in desperate concern.

Dianne could still see her worried expression as she sat amongst her dolls and tried to decide who could come and who would have to be left behind.

"I wish I'd given her space in my trunk to bring them all," Dianne whispered and clutched the doll to her breast. "Oh, Ardith—precious little sister. If only I could have found you."

She put the doll aside and pulled out Ardith's red calico dress. The gown had suffered much wear but would be good for tearing into strips for a rug. Next there was a plain brown print that Ardith had always hated but which was quite serviceable for everyday use. That left only her Sunday best, which Dianne couldn't bring herself to tear up. She placed Miss Kilpatrick atop the pale pink gown and closed the trunk lid.

Next she went to Betsy's trunk. It was smaller by half than her own but seemed large enough for the tiny six-year-old. Inside Dianne found Betsy's baby doll, Millie. She'd been given the doll on her second birthday and the two had been inseparable. Until now.

Dianne wiped at the tears that streamed down her cheeks. *They were just little babies. They did nothing wrong. Why are they dead?* She hugged Millie, as she had Miss Kilpatrick, as if the feel of these inanimate objects could somehow bring her closer to what she'd lost.

Farther in the trunk, Dianne found Betsy's three everyday dresses. They'd buried her in her Sunday best, so all three of these gowns, worn from the activities of a rambunctious child, would be perfect for her project. She put Millie back in the trunk atop Betsy's sunbonnet and shawl. There was also a little coat that Dianne remembered as a Christmas gift from the year before.

She closed the lid and looked at the gowns beside her. A part of her wanted to just put them back and not tear them up. Another part knew they were useless where they lay. They weren't good enough to sell and besides, Dianne couldn't bear to think of other little girls wearing her sisters' gowns. The rugs would serve to remind her of Ardith and Betsy every day—much better than wasting away in a trunk.

Days later, Dianne was sitting at the table tearing the material into strips for braiding when her mother let out a terrible moan and sat up in bed. Dianne put aside her work and got to her feet.

"Mama, are you all right? Do you need help?"

"What are you doing?" her mother asked groggily. She struggled to sit up on the rope bed.

Dianne went quickly to her. "Are you hungry? I have some potato soup. I've kept it warm on the back of the stove."

"No, I'm not hungry. Where are the boys?"

Her mother looked terrible. The dark half circles under her eyes had expanded to full circles and gave her a ghastly look against her pasty complexion. Her cheeks were sunken, leaving her face quite drawn.

"Morgan and Zane are working. They'll be home this evening."

Her mother barely seemed to register the information. "Have you heard from my brother yet?"

Dianne shook her head. "No, I'm sorry. I've checked at the post office, but there's no news."

"Well, go again," her mother said, her tone determined. She ignored Dianne and pushed past her to go to her trunk. She opened the lid, appearing to barely have the strength for the task.

Dianne came forward. "Let me help you. What are you looking for?"

"I don't need any help," her mother said, continuing her search. When she produced a dark brown bottle, Dianne felt her hopes fade that her mother might be on the mend.

"Mama, you shouldn't be taking that laudanum." Dianne had wondered where the bottles had gone. When they'd had the auction, a local doctor had offered to buy any and all medicines they might have brought with them. He was especially pleased to have laudanum, but Dianne had been shocked to find many bottles missing. She reached out gently and repeated herself. "You shouldn't take that."

"You shouldn't speak to me in such a manner. I'll do what I please." Her mother jerked away.

Dianne felt there was nothing to do but return to her work on the rugs. Her mother had strange lucid moments like this, and when they came, there was no sense in questioning her actions or deeds. She was in a world unto herself.

"I asked you before, what are you doing?" her mother said, coming to the table where Dianne was working.

"I'm making a rag rug. The dirt floor gets pretty cold and since the boys and I have to sleep there, I thought I'd do what I could to make it more comfortable. I don't have a lot of scraps yet, but I thought I'd check around town. I might even use some of the new material, but it seems a pity to waste it that way."

Her mother picked up the one dress Dianne hadn't yet rendered to strips. "What is this doing here? Whose is this?"

"It's Betsy's, Mama. Don't you remember it?"

Her mother took the dress to the stove and opened the door. "I don't know what you're talking about." She tossed the dress inside before Dianne could stop her.

Dianne sat in stupefied silence. Her mother closed the door and looked at her oddly. "You have a wild imagination, Dianne. You'd do well not to make up such nonsense."

"What nonsense? I merely told you the dress belonged to Betsy."

"Who is Betsy? Your imaginary friend?"

Dianne stiffened. She didn't know what to say. "Betsy, Mama. Don't you remember? My little sister Betsy."

"I don't know what you're talking about." Her mother turned to go back to the bed. She uncorked the bottle first, however, and took a long drink of the laudanum. "There, that will help my headache."

Dianne fought back tears, frightened beyond explanation. Seeing her mother fade away and lose her grip on reality was worse than losing her in a sudden death.

"Now get down to the post office and bring home Bram's letter," her mother declared as she curled up on the bed. "It's bound to be there. Or maybe he's even waiting there for us. Hurry up."

Dianne put her things aside and took up her coat. She knew it was senseless to go, but she figured she'd take a letter she'd been meaning to post. She hadn't written to Ramona since arriving in the territory, and she wanted very much to share all the news. Good and bad.

"I'll be back as quickly as I can," Dianne announced, taking up her purse. Her mother didn't acknowledge her in any way, but Dianne hadn't expected her to. Dianne checked the contents of her bag, finding nearly thirty dollars. She always carried this much because one could never tell when there might be a new shipment of fruit or some other rare commodity. And always the price was steep. She pulled the strings tight and looked again to her mother. Already she'd closed her eyes to sleep.

"I'll hurry, Mama."

Outside, the temperatures felt crisp, invigorating. It wasn't too cold yet, but at night it was a different story. Dianne could never seem to get warm at night. Even sleeping between Morgan and Zane didn't offer her enough warmth. She pulled her shawl close at the thought. Maybe she could get one of the boys to build another bed. They could surely spare money for something that important. Besides, having looked at the crude construction of the one their mother slept in, Dianne was almost certain she could build it herself.

The main street of Virginia City teemed with people. Most were men and many were drunk. It seemed a natural pastime in a mining town. Dianne made her way to the post office, hoping there might actually be a letter. She didn't have much reason to believe there would be, however, so when the postmaster shook his head, she wasn't really all that disappointed.

"I need to post this letter," she told the man behind the counter.

"I'll take care of it for you."

Dianne nodded. "Thank you." There seemed to be no other small talk necessary, so she turned around and started for home. Discouraged by the turn of events, Dianne fought to keep depression from setting in. She thought back to her conversation with Zane and Morgan. What would they do if her mother didn't recover? What if she had the baby and then slipped away—died? Dianne would have an infant to care for. She could hardly cross the distance to Missouri with a baby to provide for.

"Dianne! Oh, Dianne, it *is* you!"

Dianne looked up to see Faith coming toward her. The woman had been crying—still cried. "What's wrong, Faith?"

"It's Malachi. Some men beat him up. He's at the tent hospital right now and might not live."

"No!"

"He needs more care than I can pay for. I don't know what they'll do when I come back and can't give them the money they've asked for. Please pray for us."

"Surely they won't deny a man doctoring just because he can't pay. What kind of world would it be if that happened?"

"They can and will deny it to a black man," Faith said bitterly. "They don't care about our kind."

"Oh, Faith, I'm so sorry." Dianne hugged the older woman.

"He just can't die, Dianne. I need him. I love him." She pulled away. "Oh, I'm sorry. Listen to me. I know the Lord will provide, but the shock of this has been so great. I thought the worst was behind us, but . . ." She let the words trail off as she wiped her eyes. "The Lord will provide. I will find my strength in Him."

Dianne suddenly remembered the money in her purse. "I have some extra money. I'm going to give it to you for Malachi's care." She opened the bag and pulled out some of the cash. "Here. Don't tell anyone where it came from. If word gets back to Griselda and she tells my mother, there will be no end to the trouble it will cause."

"I can't take this," Faith said, trying to push the money back. "I can't be getting you in trouble."

"Look, we have enough to share. I don't know how far this will take you, but at least it will show them you're capable of paying for Malachi's care. Then they won't refuse to help him."

Faith began to cry afresh. "I can't pay you back. Not until Malachi gets well and is able to find gold."

Dianne shook her head. "That doesn't matter. What matters is that he gets well. Try to get word back to me and let me know how he is. You can always go to the freight company where my brothers work."

Faith nodded. "I will. I promise." She looked at the money and then back to Dianne. "No white person has ever been as nice to me as you have, Dianne. I'm going to pray God will bless you, like you've blessed me. This is an answer to prayer."

Dianne watched Faith hurry off in the direction of the hospital. Even now, with Malachi beat up, she still believed God was there for her—listening, helping. She could still hear Faith's comment—*"This is an answer to prayer."* Was that true? Was the real reason Dianne was out on the streets of Virginia City so that she could run across Faith instead of receive a letter from her uncle? The idea seemed most peculiar.

CHAPTER 18

BRAM VANDYKE HAD THE STATURE OF A MAN WHO COMMANDED attention. Standing nearly six foot three, with broad shoulders and thick beefy arms, he was the type of man that most other men either avoided or befriended.

Stalking into the post office, Bram slapped his hand down on the counter. "I've come for my mail," he told the postmaster.

"Mr. Vandyke! Why, we haven't seen you since the start of summer. How are things up north?" the man asked, bringing Bram only two letters.

"The cattle are well. I'm glad to say that much. Had trouble with a grizzly in June, but it was a sow and her cubs and I think they went off into the hills when she saw I was going to fight for my livestock." The postmaster laughed and Bram continued. "Not sure how the livestock will fair the winter, but we had a good season with them." He studied the letters in his hand, both from Missouri. He paid the postmaster and immediately opened the first one. Glancing over it quickly, he noted that his brother-in-law had been killed. The second letter was even more shocking. It was penned by his niece Dianne and told that the family had decided to come west—to live with him.

"Your kinfolk have been asking after you," the postmaster declared.

It was as if he'd been waiting for Bram to read the news before announcing this startling fact.

"So they came, eh?" Bram folded the letters and stuffed them into his pocket. "Do you know where they are?"

"Sure do. They made me promise to direct you the minute I laid eyes on you. I'd say they're feeling rather desperate."

Bram felt rather desperate himself. What was he going to do about this new turn of events? There was no possible way to explain his life over the last few years. His sister would never understand.

The postmaster gave him the details, explaining where he could find the family and the easiest way to get there. Bram left his other shopping plans and went immediately in search of the family. If he were lucky, they'd never have to know about his life. He could simply put them on a stage to Great Salt Lake City and then hopefully they could get back home from there.

He came upon the small cabin and grimaced. It was nothing more than a shack, hardly worthy of animals, much less his genteel sister. How it must have grieved her to settle into a place like this.

He knocked, apprehensive of what he'd find. He was sorry Ephraim had passed on, but he simply couldn't take on caring for his sister and her family.

The door opened and a young woman with blond hair stood looking at him as though he were there to rob her. "You must be Dianne," he said quickly. "I'm Uncle Bram."

Her face lit up. "Uncle Bram! Oh, but Mama will be so happy to see you. Everything will be fine now that you've arrived. Come in. Come in." Her animated chatter made him even more uneasy. Obviously she saw him as their savior.

Bram bent to step into the cabin. The lantern light gave the room a golden glow, but the air was chilly. He noted the dirt-packed floor and crude furnishings. Then he noted that his niece had crossed the room to where a woman lay on a bed. Surely Susannah wasn't sick.

"Mama, Uncle Bram has come."

"Bram? Oh, has he finally come?" His sister struggled, with Dianne's help, to get to her feet. That's when he saw that she was heavy with child. *Lord, what do I do now? How can I help her?* He fought back a grimace as Susannah walked over to him. She seemed to stumble, almost sway with each step. Was she drunk?

"Oh, Bram, is it truly you? I prayed you'd come. We've waited so long and I was so afraid."

He shifted uncomfortably. "What are you doing here?"

"Didn't you get our letter?" Susannah asked, seeming just a bit more clearheaded.

"I got it just now. I only come to town a couple times a year. I came back in May, but the letter wasn't there."

"Oh, well at least that explains why you weren't here to pick us up. We've nowhere to go but to your care. Ephraim is dead and Trenton deserted me. And, as you can see, I'm going to have a baby."

"Where are the others?" he asked.

Susannah shook her head. "I don't know."

Bram looked to Dianne. The girl seemed uncomfortable but answered, "The boys are working at one of the freight companies. The girls died on the way out here."

"I'm sorry to hear that. This is not a gentle land." He looked back to his sister. Odd that she had only mentioned Ephraim dying.

"Well, we'll be just fine now that you're here. I can take care of you after the baby comes. I can cook and clean for you and make you a nice home."

"Look, this isn't going to work. I only have a small cabin and it's a fair piece away from here."

Just then the door opened and two blond-haired men, perfect images of each other, bounded through the door. "We finished early," they declared in unison, then stopped, eyeing Bram. "Who's he?"

"This is Uncle Bram," Dianne announced. "He's just come."

The boys, men really, stepped forward and shook his hand. "Good to see you, sir. I'm Morgan Chadwick."

"And I'm Zane. Sure glad you finally came."

Bram shook his head. He had to make them understand. "I don't think you'll be so happy once you hear me out. I was just telling your mother that I can't be having you at my cabin. It's over twenty-five miles from here, and it's much too small for all of us to live comfortably." He turned to Susannah, who looked rather stunned. "Besides, with you like this," he pointed to her rounded stomach, "there would be no help for you, except for my wife."

"Wife?" Susannah questioned, sounding almost angry. "I had no idea you had married. All these years and you never mentioned her once."

"We just married about five years back. I'm sorry I didn't think to tell you."

Susannah shook her head and began to pace in an unsteady manner. "You can't turn your back on us. We've come all this way. You're my brother and you have to take us in. Where else would we go? What would we do?"

Bram looked to each of the children. Dianne seemed to watch him with such an intense stare that he couldn't help but address her. "I'm sorry, Dianne. If I'd known sooner, I probably could have suggested a better solution, but this isn't going to work."

Dianne stepped forward and put her arm around her mother's shoulder. "It has to work. We've rather run out of options. We have some money. . . ."

"Yes. Yes, that's it. We have money to give you," her mother interrupted. "Surely you can't complain that we wouldn't be pulling our weight. We can pay our way."

"I never said you wouldn't pull your own weight, Susannah. It's just not something I can explain or hope you'll understand. My life isn't something you'd favor."

"Why not? You said you'd decided to settle to one place and raise cattle. Why would I be against such honest business?"

"It's not the business, it's the conditions. You won't have the convenience you had back in Missouri. Things are hard here; provisions don't come in regular-like. I only make it over this way twice a year for supplies, and even then, I can only get what little variety is available. Not to mention the weather. Winters up here are cold. Real cold. The temperature can drop to forty below and it can snow something fierce. You'd never be able to endure it."

"You think we'll endure it any better in this cabin?" Dianne asked, surprising him with her boldness.

"I noticed it was in pretty bad shape," Bram admitted.

"Well, I don't think we'll find something better," Dianne continued. "I've had an advertisement posted at the general store, seeking a better place, ever since we moved in here."

"I have friends in town. I might be able to work something out. Why don't you let me check around? I don't want you to have to stay here, that's for sure, but neither can I take you with me. Come spring, we'll talk again and see what should be done. By then the baby will have come and you'll know better what you want to do. My guess is that you'll want to head back to Missouri."

"You can't be serious," Susannah declared, jerking away from Dianne's hold. "Take my sons back into the war? Risk their lives? Risk all of us on that Godforsaken prairie again?" She pummeled her brother's chest with her fists. Bram barely felt the attack through the thick buffalo coat he wore. Nevertheless, he took hold of her hands and stilled her fighting.

"I'm not doing this to hurt you but rather to protect you. You need to understand that and trust God with the rest."

Susannah began crying hysterically. "You can't leave me here. You can't! You can't just walk away—I'm your sister."

"I'm not deserting you," he said, looking past Susannah to where Dianne still watched him. She looked thoroughly disgusted by him. A quick glance at the twins showed they felt the same way. "You have to understand. None of the things you need are available in the area where I live. There's no doctor, no stores, nothing. You and the baby will need more care than you can get at my place. This is for your own good and for the good of your children. Now let me go see if I can't find you a better place to live. As I hear tell, a lot of people have pulled up stakes. Maybe the bank has something available." He released his crying sister and Dianne immediately took her mother in hand.

"Come on, Mama. You'll make yourself sick for sure. Let Uncle Bram go see what he can figure out."

Susannah said nothing but cried all the way back to her bed and continued to cry even after Dianne had tucked her in.

"The baby!" her mother moaned between sobs. "I think the baby is coming."

"Morgan, go fetch the doctor. There's a lady doctor I heard about, McNulty is her name, I think. She's down on Wallace Street. See if she can come. Tell her we can pay whatever she's asking."

Morgan ran for the door and was gone before Bram could offer to see to the task himself. He wanted only to be allowed to leave. Leave this sorry little cabin and his sister. Leave the accusing stare of his niece.

"I'll be back," he finally said, not knowing what else to do.

"Whatever you say," Dianne murmured.

Her tone suggested he was lying. He frowned. "I will be back. I promise that much."

CHAPTER 19

FLORA MCNULTY EXAMINED SUSANNAH WHILE DIANNE STOOD AT the head of the bed, ready to help in whatever way she could.

"I think she'll be fine," the doctor declared. "Sometimes these things happen. I think if she'll remain in bed and rest, the baby should be all right as well." She looked up and smiled at the crying Susannah. "Now, don't fret yourself so. You need to relax and stop crying." She noted the bottle beside Susannah's bed. "What's this?"

"Laudanum," Dianne said softly. "She's been taking quite a bit, ever since my sisters died on the journey here."

Dr. McNulty nodded. "It probably won't hurt her to continue taking it. If it helps her to rest, we might be able to prevent the baby from coming too soon."

It wasn't exactly the news Dianne wanted to hear, but she nodded.

"If she gets worse, send one of your brothers again. Otherwise, keep her in bed and see that she eats and drinks plenty. She's quite thin and that's not good. The baby needs sustenance, and so does she." The doctor reached out and patted Susannah's hand. "Now, you let your daughter take good care of you. Do you hear?"

Susannah looked at the wall, refusing to even acknowledge the doctor. Dianne handed the doctor some money. "Is this enough to cover it?"

The older woman nodded. "It's just fine. Thank you." She got to her feet and packed her equipment before pulling on her coat. The day had turned quite cold, and Dianne couldn't help but wonder if her uncle would have any luck finding them a warmer house.

After the doctor had gone, Dianne called her brothers in. They had waited outside, currying the horses and seeing to the other livestock to kill time.

"How is she? Did the baby come?" Zane questioned as they headed back into the cabin.

"No, the doctor believes if Ma takes laudanum and rests, the baby won't come until it's due. She's to remain in bed until then, however."

"That won't be hard for her," Morgan stated sarcastically. "She's hardly done anything else since Julesburg."

"Be that as it may, we have to stay here in Virginia City. Even if Uncle Bram wanted us, we couldn't go—not now."

"I don't understand him," Zane said, shaking his head. "I wanted to stomp him, but some of what he said made sense."

"I know. I can't help but think there's something more to this," Dianne declared. "He seemed so uncomfortable."

"Well, I have to admit, it had to be a shock to come to town and find all of us here," Morgan threw out. "I don't like what's happened, but I can't say that I blame him exactly. Maybe Zane and I can talk man to man with him later and see what's wrong."

Dianne nodded. "Maybe."

———

The next day, Uncle Bram reappeared around noon with Levi Sperry at his side. Dianne didn't know when the sight of someone had pleased her more.

"I didn't know you were still here. I'd heard that the reverend and Charity had gone on to Oregon after all," Dianne said as she greeted Levi.

"They plan to come back. I liked it here and wanted to stay. I knew

I'd like it here even before we made it this far. It just seemed like the kind of place for me."

"I've hired Levi to work for me," Bram announced.

"You can take Levi but not your own kin?" Dianne questioned, then turned without waiting for an answer. "I have hot coffee if you want some."

"No thanks," Bram replied. "Look, I've found you all a better house. It's bigger, warmer, and better designed. I've got my wife over there cleaning it right now."

"Your wife is here in Virginia City and you didn't bring her by to meet us?" Dianne questioned. "What's the matter, are you ashamed of us?"

"Not at all," Bram said, looking rather uncomfortable. "I just didn't want to burden your mother in her state. It's hard enough for her."

Dianne nodded but was still unconvinced. "So when do we move?"

"Right away—now," her uncle explained. "I've brought my wagon. I don't figure you have all that much to take." He glanced around the room. "Is this it?"

"Except for the livestock," Dianne replied.

"Shouldn't be hard at all." He turned to Levi. "You help the boys get those trunks and things loaded, and then I'll carry Susannah out and you can bring the mattress and put it down in the back of the wagon so she can rest on the trip over."

Dianne looked to her brothers to see what they might say or do, but everyone seemed satisfied with the decision. What else could they do? Her mother couldn't travel and Bram refused to have them anyway. She pushed back her anger and went to the makeshift cupboard where she kept their dishes. Without giving it much thought, Dianne put all of Ardith's things into Betsy's trunk, then used the empty trunk for the dishes and kettle. It was about the only packing she would have to do. Even the food sat in crates stacked against the wall.

The boys made short order of emptying out the house. Before Dianne knew what had happened, Levi had tied the chicken crates to the horses and the twins had secured the milk cow. Handing the reins of the horses to Dianne, Levi smiled.

"It's sure nice to see you again, Miss Dianne."

"It's nice to see you too, Levi. I just wish it could have been under better circumstances. How did you meet my Uncle Bram?"

"He put word out that he was looking for a hand. It only pays room and board right now, but he promised come next summer that there would be some money as well."

"I see. What does he need a hand with?"

Levi shrugged. "I guess the cattle. I'm not real sure what all he wants me to do."

Dianne nodded. "Well, I'm sorry we won't be there too. He wouldn't have had to hire anyone if he'd taken us in. My brothers would be more than happy to help with the cattle."

"I don't understand. You aren't going to live there? I thought that's why you were coming out here."

"I thought we were going to live with him too." She paused and looked to where her uncle was checking the load. "He thinks it will be too hard, especially on Mama. I suppose he has a point—at least until the baby comes. Still, I can't imagine it's much better for us to be here."

"Is that it?" Bram called to the couple.

"I would imagine so," Dianne replied. She looked to her brothers and at their nod headed back to the house. "I'll take one final look around while you get Ma."

She was glad to be leaving the little cabin, but her heart was in turmoil over staying behind in Virginia City. She longed to sit down and discuss the matter with her uncle, but there seemed to be no desire for that on his part.

She followed the men out of the cabin, Uncle Bram carrying her mother and Levi carrying the mattress. Her mother was in a deep stupor thanks to the laudanum, but it didn't prevent her from thanking Bram for changing his mind.

"I knew you'd come back for us," their mother murmured as Bram tucked her into the wagon.

"You rest here," he said. Dianne caught his eye as he glanced up at her. She refused to look away. She hoped he felt guilty for what he was about to do. Instead, he just shook his head as if there were no way to explain.

They headed west about a quarter of a mile, still keeping to the north side of town. Bram brought the wagon to a stop in front of a plain-looking box-style cabin. Dianne could see a small lean-to in the back that would be perfect for their livestock. Beside the front door of the cabin was a large stack of firewood—a surprise to be sure.

"It has two rooms and a back porch that's enclosed. The porch should be good enough for the chickens," he stated as he stepped down from the wagon. "There's a shack out back that's not real big, but I'm thinking if you boys put together a pole fence around it, the livestock will be just fine. I've arranged to get some hay and straw—not an easy feat in these parts, but I've got friends who owe me favors."

Dianne dismounted from Dolly and handed the reins to Morgan. "I want to stay with Mama," she told him softly. "Once she realizes Bram hasn't taken us to his place, she's going to be fit to be tied."

"I know," he answered. He moved away with the animals while Dianne went to her uncle.

"Are you sure you won't change your mind?" she asked.

"Dianne, I can't. I can't explain it except to say I'm sorry and to remind you that the doctor wouldn't allow for it anyway. You need to think of your mother's health. You'll be safe enough here. You have the twins, and a good number of the rowdies are leaving for Last Chance. This place will keep you warm and provide a good home through the winter. I wouldn't have taken it otherwise."

"What's it going to cost us?" Dianne asked, her voice flat and emotionless.

"It's not going to cost you a thing. I've squared for it already." He looked at her and his expression softened. "I do love her. I love all of you and don't want to see anything bad happen. Someday, I hope soon, you'll understand exactly why I had to do things this way."

With that, he went to the wagon and gathered Susannah in his arms.

"Are we there already?" she asked weakly.

"Yes," he replied. "Levi, you can worry about the mattress later; there's a bed already in place inside."

Dianne opened the door for her uncle, grateful that it felt much better made than the one at their last cabin.

Inside was a pleasant surprise. A great deal of care had gone into the place. Someone had papered the walls with newsprint and there was a rough puncheon floor instead of dirt.

"If you'll get that other door," Bram said, nodding toward the opposite side of the room.

Dianne went quickly and opened it, finding a small bedroom. There was a nice-sized bed, already made up with blankets, that she could share with her mother, and a nightstand that actually held a bowl and pitcher.

Bram lowered Susannah to the bed. "I'm going to help the boys unload."

Dianne said nothing, choosing instead to gently straighten the covers around her mother. Susannah smiled contently.

"I told you he'd come," she murmured, then fell back to sleep.

Dianne felt so sorry for her mother. When she woke up, it would be just one more disappointment in a long list of nightmarish events. How would she ever be able to handle this? She was already afraid and grief-stricken. If she thought her brother had deserted her as Trenton and the others had, Dianne feared what her mother might do.

Leaving her mother's side, Dianne went out into the main room and found that the men had made quick order of the work. The trunks were stacked neatly to one side and the crates of food were piled near the kitchen area. A sturdy, nicely finished table and chairs stood against one wall and not far from it was a small kitchen with two cupboards and a decent counter to work on. There was a washtub for dishes and a pail of water sitting ready to use. Beyond that, a large iron stove graced the room. It was no doubt used for both heating and cooking. The warmth it gave off was easy to feel, even from across the room. No doubt Uncle Bram's wife had thoughtfully seen to warming the house for its new occupants.

The rest of the room surprised her as well. There was a rocking chair and bench with a wooden back. And the room was quite spacious, large enough to accommodate Morgan and Zane sleeping on the floor—or even allow for another bed or two to be brought in. There was also a window with thick wooden shutters to seal out the cold or to leave open to let in the light. All in all, it looked like a very pleasant place to live.

She saw the door beside the stove and went to investigate, finding the porch Uncle Bram had mentioned. This was a very nice addition indeed. It would be a good place to keep the chickens and to wash and hang laundry in the winter. She opened the porch door and saw her uncle instructing the twins on how to construct a fence.

"It'll be expensive to find ready-made poles," he was saying, "but if you ride out northeast of here, you'll find some trees and can make your own poles. It'll be hard work, especially with winter coming on, but you'll need it to keep the animals contained." He said something else that she couldn't hear, then bid the boys good-bye and headed around the cabin to the front.

Dianne closed the door and leaned against it. She sighed, knowing that most everything they needed to do would be hard work. She wondered how they would ever keep enough coal and wood, how they would afford the feed for the animals without using up all of their savings.

Walking through the house to the front door, Dianne figured she should tell her uncle good-bye. She didn't want to say things she might regret, however, so she determined in her heart to say as little as possible. She opened the door and stepped out. There, on the opposite side of the wagon, she saw her uncle talking quite solemnly to a dark-skinned woman. The woman was much shorter than Uncle Bram and clearly of Indian descent. Dianne made her way toward them and both looked surprised when she approached.

"Uncle Bram, I've come to say good-bye," she stated without emotion. "Thank you for helping us find this place. I hope we'll be able to keep up with things until spring."

She couldn't help herself and pointed to the woman. "Who is this?"

She knew she was being rude, but Dianne didn't feel in the least bit charitable at the moment.

Bram looked to the woman and then back to Dianne. Before he answered he looked to the ground. "This is Koko. She's part of the reason I couldn't explain everything to you."

Dianne met the young woman's gaze. Koko had brown eyes that seemed to take in everything at once and a compassionate look that suggested she knew how difficult this situation was for Dianne.

"I'm Dianne Chadwick. I'm his niece."

Koko looked at Bram, who was still staring at the ground. "Koko is my wife, Dianne," he said in a clear voice.

"No!" The cry came from behind Dianne. Her mother stood just a few feet away, but how she had found the strength or sobriety to come outside was beyond Dianne.

"Mama, you're supposed to be in bed."

"You can't be married to a heathen squaw!" her mother declared, coming forward. "I won't have it. You must get rid of her."

Bram shook his head. "See," he said to Dianne more than to anyone, "this is why you can't come live with me. Your mother would never accept my wife, and I will never leave her."

Dianne took hold of her mother as she flung herself at Koko. "You aren't welcome here," she screamed. "You heathen! You've cast some kind of spell on my brother. Well, you can't have him! Dianne, go get your father. He'll deal with this." Dianne held tight to her mother's arm.

Morgan and Zane appeared just then. "Take Mama back in the house," Dianne commanded. Morgan came forward and lifted Susannah into his arms. She fought him and screamed.

"Ephraim, come here! You need to help me!"

"What's wrong with her? Why is she calling for Pa?" Zane asked as Morgan headed to the house.

"This is Uncle Bram's wife, Koko," Dianne said by way of explanation. Suddenly everything made perfect sense.

CHAPTER 20

CHRISTMAS WAS NEARLY UPON THEM BUT THERE WAS NO CHANCE for celebration. Dianne hadn't thought much about the season at all, except to wonder why God had brought her family to this end. In the back of her mind she couldn't help but remember better days, happy celebrations with a Christmas tree and presents. She could almost smell her mother's gingerbread cookies—taste the cranberry punch. And if she didn't mind the heartbreak so much, she could hear the animated giggles of her little sisters as they danced around the house in anticipation of what Christmas would bring.

Virginia City certainly held nothing of that account for her now.

With her brothers busy working as team drivers, hauling goods back and forth between Great Salt Lake City and Virginia City, Dianne found herself most often alone with her mother. It was a lonely life. She'd heard stories on the wagon train of women who went crazy living in the wilderness. She could understand it now. Hours upon end, day after day with no one to talk to, nothing to do but sew and cook and clean, gave Dianne nothing to look forward to.

She knew her mother would deliver the baby soon. Dianne had arranged for the doctor to come and check up on her mother, and everything seemed to be fine. Now they needed only to wait, which was a task Dianne didn't do all that well.

Working on a quilt that she'd designed for her brothers, Dianne thought about Christmas and sighed. There'd be no tree or presents. Well, she had made Zane and Morgan each a new shirt, but it hardly seemed like a real present. Dianne had made her mother a new nightgown, as well, but had given it to her early, as the old one was falling apart. Her mother hadn't even acknowledged the gift. But of course, she wasn't acknowledging much of anything these days.

Glancing out the window, Dianne noticed that it had started to snow again. She wondered if the livestock would have enough feed and water should the weather turn bad. She looked at the clock and decided to give it an hour or so and see what happened. She still wasn't sure how to figure mountain weather. In Missouri she would see certain signs and know it was going to rain or storm. She could determine very accurately how quickly the weather would be upon them. But here in the mountains the elements never seemed to do quite what she thought they would.

She sat stitching and thinking about her life. She wondered if her friends back in Missouri were safe. She'd heard nothing from them and worried that the war had taken its toll on their lives. She wondered, too, about Faith and whether Malachi had survived his ordeal. There'd simply been no chance to find out.

A knock at the door startled her. Dianne put her quilting aside and went to see who it might be. To her surprise it was Griselda Showalter. As much as she despised the woman's boisterous, pompous attitude, Dianne was actually glad to see her.

"Mrs. Showalter, how nice of you to come."

"I'm here to see your mother," she announced, pushing past Dianne in her usual fashion. "Where is she? Is she well? Has the baby come?"

Dianne closed the door, but not before she noted the thick collection of snow on the path leading to their door. With Griselda here she could leave her mother and go tend the animals—maybe even make a trip into town.

"No, the baby hasn't come," Dianne said. "Here, let me take your coat and hat."

Griselda parted with the items readily. "Well, you're doing quite well for yourself here. I know your brothers are working for the freight company, so I would imagine they're bringing in plenty of money. Of course, you had money to start with. Your family was probably the most wealthy on the train."

"Well, we've had enough to see us through, but we certainly aren't wealthy," Dianne said, not wishing to waste time discussing financial issues with the woman. "Come along and I'll take you to Mama. By the way, how did you find us?"

"I asked around. The postmaster knew where you'd gone, so he told me. I haven't had time to get away until now. Too much to do since Percy's been sick."

"I'm sorry to hear that Mr. Showalter is ill. I hope it isn't serious," Dianne said, knocking on the open door of her mother's bedroom. "Mama, I've brought you a visitor. Look here, it's Mrs. Showalter."

Her mother actually opened her eyes. "She's here?"

Dianne nodded. "Here, let me help you to sit up."

"Nonsense," Griselda said. "I can see to her. Go about your business."

Dianne hated being dismissed, but at the same time she needed to see to the animals. "I'll be out back tending the livestock if you need me," she told Griselda.

The woman made no reply to her, instead going immediately to Susannah and hoisting her up, plumping the pillow behind her and chattering on in her usual manner.

"Well, you certainly look worse than the last time I saw you," Griselda began. "I swear you're just bones. Doesn't that girl feed you? I should have thought to bring you some broth. A strong chicken broth would soon set you right as rain."

Dianne ignored the comments and hurried to check the chickens on the back porch. It was chilly out there, but the hens were still laying, and that was all that counted. Zane had suggested she stack the crates of food and firewood around the chickens in order to insulate them just a bit more. They seemed quite content with the arrangement, and although

Dianne had the unpleasant job of cleaning up after them, the porch made a decent coop. After giving the hens feed and water, Dianne hurried to pull on her outdoor things.

Outside, the snow was coming down heavier than ever and the wind had picked up. The skies had turned leaden gray and across the valley she couldn't even see town because of the snow and low clouds.

She worked to break the ice in the watering trough, a thankless, endless job that had to be done at least twice a day. If she didn't stay on top of it, the ice froze several inches deep and made it impossible to break without the heavy sledge.

Dianne forked hay into the manger, then checked on the milk cow and Dolly. Thankfully her brothers had taken their horses and oxen. The freight company paid the boys a handsome sum for the use of their team and wagon. It gave them a nice extra bit of money. It also meant that Dianne didn't have to worry about their feed and shelter.

Dolly whinnied softly and nuzzled Dianne's hand looking for treats. "Sorry, girl, I didn't bring you a thing," Dianne whispered against her ear. She stroked the mare's mane and gently hugged her neck. "You're my only friend in all of Montana Territory."

The snow blinded Dianne as she made her way back to the house. She figured it would be smart for Griselda to leave quickly or otherwise she might lose her way. She went into the bedroom, where the woman was talking softly to her mother.

"Mrs. Showalter, the snow is turning into a blizzard, I fear. You should probably head back home before visibility is impossible."

Griselda looked at Dianne and then, with a curt nod, got to her feet. "The girl is probably right."

"Mama, I'm going to fetch some water and heat it for tea. Mrs. Showalter, I'll get your things."

Dianne thought the woman might make some snide comment as was her way, but Griselda turned back to her mother instead. "Susannah, I'm sorry you aren't feeling well. I'll come again to visit."

"The Indians are everywhere," her mother muttered incoherently.

"They've taken my children, you know. I have to find them. I have to find my babies."

Griselda bid her good-bye, then followed Dianne into the front room. "Has she been like this for long?"

"Just since Uncle Bram refused to take us to his cabin and showed up here with his Indian wife."

"What! That's positively scandalous. Why would the man choose an Indian over his own kin?" She allowed Dianne to help her into her coat as she continued. "No wonder your mother has gone all addlepated. Are you giving her anything to help?"

"She's still taking laudanum. The doctor figured it would keep her calm."

Griselda nodded. "That's exactly what I would have done."

Dianne bit back a comment that perhaps her mother wouldn't be having delusions of Indians at all if she weren't taking the medicine. "I'm sure she enjoyed your visit. I hope you'll come back to see her." And in truth, Dianne meant every word. It would be nice to have Griselda come and relieve Dianne long enough to allow her to go into town and shop.

"I'll see myself out. You go about your business."

"I could walk part of the way with you," Dianne suggested, hoping she wouldn't take her up on the offer.

"No, I'm just fine. I've been making my way all over this place. I don't need anyone to hold my hand."

Dianne didn't wish to further offend the woman, so instead she picked up her pail and headed outside. She shook her head sadly as she remembered her mother's comments. Dianne longed for the days when her mother's mind was clear and wondered if her sanity would ever return. Dianne wondered, too, what she would do if her mother remained in her stupor.

"Maybe it's just the laudanum," she told herself as she struggled to get the pump working. "Maybe once the baby comes, she won't be sad anymore—she'll want to face life and live for the sake of the infant." But Dianne wasn't sure she could take hope even in that idea. Her mother didn't seem strong enough to sit up in bed without help, much less take care of a child.

When the pail was finally full, Dianne trudged back through the snow to the cabin. She was grateful to have the chores done and to know she'd given it her best. If the cow or Dolly suffered, it wouldn't be because Dianne hadn't tried to keep them safe.

She entered the mud porch, shivering from the icy wind that pelted her back. Closing the door, she put the pail down and shed her coat and boots. She hung her heavy wool bonnet by the back door next to the coat. Zane had thoughtfully driven pegs to allow for just such purposes. It made it much easier for Dianne when folks left their muddy things on the porch rather than traipsed through the house. It would also be easier to clean up melted snow from this room than following paths across the cabin.

That thought brought Griselda to mind. The woman had tracked a good amount of snow into the house. Dianne remembered seeing the prints the heavy woman left as she made her way to the bedroom. She sighed. She supposed it wouldn't hurt to just mop the entire house since the floor would already be wet.

Dianne took the water to the stove and put it on the back to warm. She turned to judge the job at hand and noticed that the front door stood wide open. Snow had already begun to accumulate in the threshold.

"How strange." She brushed the snow out with her broom, then secured the door and latched it tight. The room was very cold and, spying her mother's open door, Dianne figured she'd better take in another blanket lest she catch a chill.

Going to the trunk, Dianne pulled out a thick wool blanket. It was one they had used on the wagon trail and was in worse shape than some of the others, so Dianne had packed it away until they needed it. She took it in to her mother, then froze in place. The bed was empty.

"Mama!" Dianne tossed the blanket aside and looked around the small room, even looking under the bed in case her mother had fallen from the bed and somehow rolled beneath.

There was no sign of her mother. Dianne went quickly to the front room and looked around. She wasn't here, that much was clear. The mud porch revealed the same disheartening fact. Going slowly into the front room again, Dianne caught sight of the front door.

"Oh no," she said, looking outside. "She couldn't have!"

CHAPTER 21

TRENTON STOOD LOOKING IN THE MIRROR AT THE OUTFIT HE'D just tried on. The crisp lines of the black wool suit fit him as though it had been tailored just for him. The gray striped vest and new white shirt added a special look of refined dignity to the man who only weeks earlier had been so down on his luck he'd had to steal to eat.

"The suit was clearly designed with you in mind, Mr. Chadwick," the store clerk announced as he appraised him from behind. "It will require very little in the way of adjustments."

Trenton couldn't have agreed more. "I'll need a couple of extra shirts."

"But of course. Wait here and I'll see to it."

Trenton watched as the man disappeared into the back room. Henry had suggested Trenton buy a new wardrobe in order to get into some of the better games. There was a great deal more money to be had in poker than Trenton could have ever imagined. It amazed him that in a time of war so many people would be so willing to part with their cash. But part with it they did. Most of the time Trenton didn't have to do anything but play well and pay attention. Henry had been right. Most men could be easily read. They would make certain little moves or actions when their hand was good and another set when they held nothing at all.

At the same time Trenton had needed to learn how to read other men, he'd had to practice hard with Henry to learn how to disguise his own reactions. It hadn't been easy, to be sure.

"Don't look away from them," Henry had said, "but when you stare the other players down, do it with such an attitude that suggests you'd just as soon be home takin' a bath. Look bored, disinterested—it makes them wonder what you're about, and while they're busy worrying about what you're really thinkin', they won't be able to pay much attention to their game."

Trenton thought it an awful lot of nonsense, but he'd become accomplished in a relatively short time and in doing so had doubled his winnings. The extra money changed his mind rather quickly about Henry DuPont.

"Here we are, sir. I've wrapped them for you. You can either take them now or come back after we've tailored the suit."

Trenton shook his head. "No, I'm leaving town and don't have time for tailoring. This fits well enough as it is."

The clerk, a portly fellow with a balding head and gold-rimmed glasses, nodded. "If that's what you desire, it's perfectly fine."

Trenton smiled. "That's what I desire." He liked saying that and getting his way about things. He felt important for the first time in his life. People paid attention to him, seemed to know that he was a force to be reckoned with. Now the clothes would help even more.

He paid for his purchases, pulled on the broad-brimmed black hat he'd purchased only the day before, and nodded to the man. "Thank you for your help."

Feeling like a new man, Trenton made his way back to the hotel. Henry awaited him there, also dressed in new clothes.

"Well if we ain't a pair," Henry announced as Trenton walked through the door. "I swear you could sit down to play a hand with the president himself."

Trenton laughed. "I seriously doubt President Lincoln plays cards."

"If he played with you, he'd lose. Of that I am sure." Henry sauntered over to the window and glanced out. "I have tickets for the riverboat. Had to pay extra for that nag of yours but finally arranged for it."

"When do we leave?" Trenton questioned, tossing the parcel of shirts into his carpetbag.

"Midnight," Henry replied. "Enough time to play a few hands up the street if you want. I know of a game going on at the Seymour Hotel. Stakes are high—it's by invitation only."

"And we've wrangled an invitation?"

"Yes, sir," Henry answered, looking quite proud of himself. "I let it get around that you're the grandson of a New York state senator."

"Ah, I see. A wealthy, naïve grandson who's just taken up an interest in poker, no doubt."

Henry laughed. "Is there any other kind?"

Trenton looked at the two men who hadn't yet folded. The one on his right had a nervous tick in his cheek that started up every time he held more than a pair. The man directly across from him was a bit trick-ier. He generally kept his head down and eyes to the cards. He seemed to try overly hard to keep from revealing himself.

"Well, will you call or fold?" Trenton asked, yawning as if it made no difference to him.

Both men fidgeted a moment before finally giving up the game. Trenton revealed his hand of three nines and pulled in his winnings. It was just too simple. He hadn't even needed to cheat or use a marked deck.

"You know," the man at Trenton's left said to his companions, "there's news on the plans for the transcontinental railroad. Good money to be made if you get in on some of the small towns going up along the line. I have a large amount of money tied up in a couple of the loca-tions."

"How did you find out where those locations would be?" the man opposite him questioned. "The line hasn't even been finalized, as far as I know. Complications keep them changing things here and there."

"I'm smart," the first man replied, laughing. He leaned forward as if to share some deep secret. "I'm telling you, the railroad is the future."

Trenton tried to imagine rails joining the country together. It seemed an impossible task, especially in light of discussions he'd heard about the mountains to the west. How would they ever manage to put a railroad over the Rockies?

The idea of traveling from one end of the country to the other in less than a week instead of months fascinated Trenton. He imagined himself going to Montana Territory to visit Dianne, riding in style on rails instead of stages or horseback.

If I ever get to Montana, he thought. He honestly hoped to head that way by spring. Henry had his heart set on going to Omaha in spite of the fact it would no doubt be colder up north. The first part of winter had been mild—some rain and cold temperatures, but not much snow and certainly not enough cold to freeze the waterways. Trenton hadn't argued with the idea of Omaha; after all, it was closer to Montana. But when Henry started talking about heading to Chicago and New York after that, Trenton flat-out refused.

Henry dealt the next round, laughing and telling tales of his days when he'd been a boy working on some canal line back East. Trenton didn't pay too much attention to him. The others didn't know they were traveling companions, and Trenton would just as soon keep it that way.

The round went as easily as the others until they were down to just Trenton, Henry, and the man with the tick. Trenton had nothing of any use in his hands, not even a pair, but he'd learned from Henry that bluffing would often get the pot up.

"Well, boys?" Henry questioned. "I raise you twenty dollars."

"Well, that's mighty steep, mister."

Henry shrugged and Trenton watched the man at his right to see what his response would be. The minutes clicked by as the tick grew more noticeable and perspiration beaded on the man's upper lip.

Trenton figured him to have a flush. He figured it that way because he'd seen the man's hand at one point when he'd accidentally moved to accommodate the waiter bringing drinks. There were three hearts in the original hand, and since then Trenton was pretty sure the man had drawn his additional hearts. He figured Henry knew this, or had a good idea of it, but the old man wasn't backing down, so Trenton figured Henry's hand had to be even better.

"I'll call," the man finally said.

"Fold," Trenton declared. "This game's too rich for my blood."

Henry laughed. "Shouldn't let babies play with cards." The men at the table laughed, except for the man with the tick.

Henry turned over his hand. "Cowboys and ladies," he said, revealing three kings and two queens. "Full house."

The man lost all color in his face as he turned over his hand. Trenton noted the flush was complete, but it wasn't a straight flush and it wasn't a royal. Henry had won the hand.

"You're cheating!" the man declared, standing abruptly. He reached for Henry's arm and yanked at the French cuff. The cufflink flew across the table, and to Trenton's disappointment, two cards fell out from the open sleeve. "I told you so!"

The men at the table, all fairly wealthy businessmen, were in no mood for a cheat. "Call for the police. Have this man taken to jail."

Trenton got to his feet. "I'll take him there myself. Stupid old man."

The waiter had already gone to rally the law, however, so the men at the table were in no hurry to turn him over to anyone.

"He can wait," the man with the tick announced. "I want to make sure the officer hears my side of the story."

"You've got me all wrong, boys. I wasn't cheatin'. Honest. This is the first hand I've won. You know that."

They looked at each other, almost as if considering his words, then shook their heads collectively.

An officer appeared in no time at all and took down the names and addresses of each man at the table. As he took Henry into custody and headed down the back stairs, Trenton got to his feet. "Well, I must say this game had more excitement for me than anything in a long while, but I need some sleep. I have an important business meeting in the morning."

The men bid Trenton good night, seeming no more interested in what he was about than they were in what would happen to Henry DuPont. Trenton raced through the lobby of the hotel and out onto the street, meeting up with the officer just as they rounded the front corner of the building.

"I wonder if I might talk with you a moment," Trenton said as he approached the man. He'd learned enough from Henry to read something in the officer's expression that made Trenton sure beyond doubt that the man was approachable.

Fifteen minutes later, Trenton was twenty dollars poorer and Henry was free. They raced for their hotel as fast as the old man could move.

"We'd better get down to the boat," Trenton told Henry. "I doubt we'll be able to come back to St. Joseph again."

"I'm sorry about that, boy. I'm gettin' old. Slippin'." There was sorrow in his voice.

"It doesn't matter now, Henry. What matters is that we hightail it out of here and not get caught. I assured that fellow we'd be long gone by sunup, and I intend to see to it."

Once on the boat, Trenton parted company with Henry. The old man was given to moments of drink and tonight was certainly no exception. No doubt the close encounter with the law had shaken him up and he wanted the alcohol to steady his nerves.

It wasn't surprising to find the riverboat full to overflowing in spite of the enormous ticket price. Sometimes the boats were allowed to travel without any trouble and sometimes they weren't. Trenton had even read of one boat facing the threat of being blown up by border ruffians. The tragedy had been averted by Union soldiers, but the threat was there nonetheless.

Over the months that had passed since his father's death, Trenton had come to look at the war and the world with new eyes. He'd grown up some—perhaps not enough, but his experience had taught him something about himself. Namely, he had no purpose or goal for his life. His friends had talked proudly of joining the Confederacy. They were excited to march off to war—to live or die for what they believed in.

Trenton had no such aspirations. He also had no intention of going back to shopkeeping. Gambling suited him, but the guilt of it made him feel the need for daily penance. Trenton always tried to help some poor unfortunate, giving away coins or food to soothe his own conscience. But even this didn't help. There was no purpose for his future. He had no plans to go to any particular place at any particular time. He was just drifting along in life—not knowing what tomorrow would bring. Some men might cherish the freedom, but Trenton found it a millstone around his neck.

Dianne would no doubt have laughed at him. Once she got over the initial shock of what he was doing, that is. Dianne always had goals and plans—whether for the games they played or their talks of the future. She was a natural-born leader; pity she hadn't been born a man. No one cared much for the opinions of a woman—not even one as smart and capable as his sister.

He felt another rush of guilt, realizing that Christmas was nearly upon them and he'd made no attempt to contact his family. He'd not even bothered to check up on them and learn whether they'd arrived safely. He knew he had no one to blame but himself for that, but he always tried to assuage his conscience by promising himself he'd write soon—even send them money in case they were down on their luck. But he never did. And now their first Christmas apart would come and they'd not know where he was or how he was and he'd not know any-thing of them. No wonder Henry drank.

"We've got the South on the run," Trenton overheard a man at the bar announce. "The war is bound to be over soon. I'm guessing just after New Year's. Those rebels can't hang on much longer. Not after the way we crushed them at Nashville."

"I heard there were over twenty-three thousand of those rebels and still we whopped 'em," the other man replied. "And Sherman is march-ing right through to the sea, killing every one of those Dixie boys as he goes."

The first man nodded. "South should have known better when we reelected old Honest Abe. There's not a Confederate out there that doesn't know they're done for."

Trenton wondered if it were true. If the war came to an end, what would it mean for him—for the country? He enjoyed Henry's companionship for the most part, but when the man got drunk like he was doing now, Trenton could scarcely abide him. Then there was also the very real fear that Jerry Wilson and his gang might still find Trenton if he remained too close to New Madrid.

The thought of that always made Trenton feel like a fool and a coward. He'd never even found out whether Robbie's father had lived after the bank robbery. He hated not knowing, but he couldn't risk so much as a letter to question the family. He never stayed long enough in one place to get an answer anyway, but he could just see Jerry getting ahold of the information and somehow tracking it back to Trenton's exact location. Jerry was cunning that way.

"Well, here's to victory," the man behind Trenton said in a loud voice. "Long live the Union." Cheers went up in the room as Trenton made his way to the door.

He looked back at the people in the celebratory spirit. Then an image of Captain Seager clutching his chest and falling dead on Main Street came to mind. This, coupled with the picture of his father in a simple pine coffin, gave Trenton little reason to want to join in the festivities. War was not decided by words like *victory* and *defeat*. It was affixed in the blood of men who believed they were fighting for something important. But in the end, what they believed in no longer mattered. They were dead and someone else would live on to start a new cause.

Fools, Trenton thought as he left the room. *And I'm the biggest fool of them all.*

CHAPTER 22

THE BLIZZARD CONTINUED INTO THE NIGHT AND DIANNE HAD NO choice but to stay put in the cabin. She hoped her mother might have regained her senses enough to take shelter with neighbors, but she doubted it. She kept hearing her mother's last words over and over: *"I have to find my babies."*

Dianne added wood to the stove and turned up the lantern to dispel some of the gloominess. Outside, the wind howled, rattling the shutters, even shaking the cabin itself. Everything held fast, but Dianne's desperation grew. How were Dolly and the cow? How were her brothers faring? Where was their mother?

By ten o'clock, with no end in sight to the blizzard's rampage, Dianne took up the family Bible and sat down at the table. She had wrestled with her conscience all night. Words that Faith had shared on the trail came back to haunt her.

"Oh, Dianne, God still cares. He hasn't forgotten you. We can't always understand His ways, but child, His eye is on the sparrow—He knows when even one little bird falls from a tree. Do you not imagine Him knowing and caring that Ardith fell into the river—or that your father was killed?"

"Or that Mama is lost in a snowstorm?" she questioned, flipping through the pages of the New Testament. She paused and looked to the front door. "If only she would come walking back through—safe and happy. If only Ardith and Betsy would return to us, whole and healed." She shook her head. *If I'm going to wish for anything, I might as well start it all back with Papa.* She sighed and looked back to the Bible.

The words of the twenty-fourth chapter of Luke drew her attention. *And they entered in, and found not the body of the Lord Jesus. And it came to pass, as they were much perplexed thereabout, behold, two men stood by them in shining garments: And as they were afraid, and bowed down their faces to the earth, they said unto them, Why seek ye the living among the dead? He is not here, but is risen.*

Dianne reread the passage, not sure why it stirred her so. Was she seeking her life among the dead? Were the things that haunted her—the mistakes of the past and the losses she'd endured—binding her heart so that she might as well be dead with the others?

"I don't know what to do to make it right," she said aloud. "I feel so lost and alone. I'm so afraid."

The men in the Scripture had been afraid too. Dianne thought for a moment of the Christmas season and of the Scriptures her father used to share with the family each year. Those, too, had been in Luke. She gently turned the pages back until she found the verses in the second chapter. She'd heard them so many times she almost knew them by memory.

Fear not: for, behold, I bring you good tidings of great joy, which shall be to all people. For unto you is born this day in the city of David a Saviour, which is Christ the Lord.

A savior, she thought. Someone to save her. That's what she needed. That's what they all needed—each one of them. They needed to be saved from the endless tragedies that life thrust upon them. They needed a savior to rescue them from the adversity of sickness, famine, hardship, and death.

Could Jesus be that savior? Was it really that simple?

He'd come as a baby, so little and pure. The angels declared his birth—shepherds came to see him, even though they were afraid.

Dianne thought back on all her childhood Bible stories. She knew the mission of Jesus . . . His love of the people . . . His desire to show them the truth.

His truth.

God's truth.

"Why do I seek the living among the dead?" she murmured.

"I've asked Jesus into my heart." Betsy's words rang clear in Dianne's memory. Was it really that easy? Could she just ask Jesus into her heart— her broken heart? Would He even want such a heart?

Tears came to Dianne's eyes as she slipped from the table and knelt on the floor beside her chair. "Oh, God, I don't know how much more we can stand. I don't know how much more *I* can stand." She cried softly, her face buried in her hands. "Please help me. Please take my heart and make it whole. I can't bear this pain—this sorrow. I don't wish to seek the living among the dead—I wish only to seek you. To know you."

Dianne remained there praying for some time. With each passing moment she felt the burdens of her life lift slowly away. Faith and Charity had been right. God did care—He really did.

The night wore on and Dianne eventually took herself to bed. Exhausted, she fell immediately to sleep and didn't awaken until an eerie silence bore down on her. She opened her eyes with a start and sat up. The storm was over.

Having slept in her clothes, she hurried to put on her coat and boots. She would go look for her mother and hopefully bring her home to safety. Opening the door, however, Dianne found a drift nearly three feet high blocking her way. Even that seemed unimportant. She hurriedly swept at the snow, pushing it back into even higher drifts on the side of the walk.

"What are you doing out so early?" Zane's voice called out as he and Morgan made their way up the road.

"Oh, I'm so glad to see you both!" she declared, forgetting her task. She threw the broom aside and ran to their arms. "I'm so glad you're safe."

"We almost got caught full in the face of that blizzard," Morgan admitted. "We took refuge just outside of town, however, when we couldn't see to go any farther."

"I thought it would never stop snowing," Zane added.

Dianne stepped away from them. "Mama's gone. I hate to just tell you like that, but it's the truth of the matter and we have to find her."

"Gone? How? Where?" Morgan asked.

Dianne shrugged. "I don't know. Griselda came to visit her, so I went out back to see to Dolly and the milk cow. That went well and by then the snow had picked up, so I suggested Griselda leave. I told Mama I'd get some water for tea and be right back and then I saw Griselda out."

"Did she take Mama home with her?" Zane questioned.

"No. I know she didn't because I offered to walk home with Griselda, and Mama was in her bed. When I came back from getting water, the front door was open. I think Mama went looking for Ardith and Betsy. I'm worried sick. I know she didn't take her coat or put on shoes." Tears fell anew. "Oh, Zane, Morgan . . . I don't know what to do. I don't even know where to look."

"We'll ask the neighbors. We'll talk to the sheriff and get some men searching for her if she isn't nearby. You stay here and wait."

"But that's all I've been doing," Dianne protested. "Can't I come look too?"

"Someone needs to be here, Dianne," Zane said, taking the lead. "We'll check in periodically. Just wait here."

Dianne nodded, knowing there was nothing to be gained by arguing. "You'll let me know as soon as you . . . find her."

The twins nodded solemnly. "We'll let you know."

———

Cole Selby gritted his teeth as his father approached him at the general store. He hadn't seen the man in nearly a year and he certainly wasn't looking to share his company now.

"Cole, you're a sight for sore eyes. Where have you been, boy?"

"Why? Are the vigilantes after me for desertion?"

Hallam Selby took hold of his son and pulled him to the side of the store, away from other customers. "Don't be talkin' about it. You know better."

Cole scowled. "What do you want?"

"I want to know what's going on. Why haven't you come back to the claim? Where have you been?"

"I've been busy working. I hired on with a wagon master last spring. I saw Ma and the girls, and now I'm spending the winter doing what I can until I join another wagon train come spring."

"You saw your ma? How is she?"

"Why? What would you care?" Cole's words were sharp—bitter.

"Don't take that tone with me, boy. I'm your pa and you should have some respect for me."

Cole's eyes narrowed. "We both know Carrie changed any hope for that."

"Now, don't go getting ugly about it. You know that was an accident. Nobody feels worse about her passin' than I do."

Cole doubled his fist, then thought better of carrying through with his desire to punch his father square in the face. He took a deep breath and forced his hands to relax. "All I know is Carrie is dead. It really doesn't matter how you feel."

His father shifted uncomfortably and scratched his bearded chin. "So is your ma doing well?"

"Well enough. She's happy, which is more than I can say I've ever seen before. The house looks great and the girls have beaus. They're all very happy—so leave them alone."

"Don't be telling me what to do, boy."

Cole turned to go, but his father grabbed his arm. "I could use you at the claim. Why don't you come help me?"

Cole stared for a moment at his father's hand, then returned his gaze to the older man's face. "I'm surprised with all the hangings I've heard about that you have time for gold mining."

His father leaned in and said in a hushed voice, "I'm telling you not to take that attitude with me."

"Cole!" Zane Chadwick approached from across the store. "Our ma's gone missing and we're raising a search party. Can you help?"

"Of course. What happened?"

"Ma and Dianne were at our cabin last night and Ma wandered away when Dianne went for water. We've asked the neighbors, but no one's seen her."

"Let's get to it, then."

"I can get some of my friends to help," Hallam Selby offered.

"I'd be much obliged, mister," Zane said, turning to go.

"Just make sure they don't hang her," Cole muttered only loud enough for his father to hear. He didn't wait for any reaction.

Cole searched for hours with the other volunteers. In the small community, when word went out that someone was in jeopardy, folks were good to rally round and see what could be done. This was evidenced by all the people combing the streets, gently prodding drifts, and shoveling aside mounds of snow that had formed against fences and walls. Murmurs circulated that there wasn't much hope for the Chadwick woman. Cole didn't like to take the comments seriously, but he knew the truth of what a night in a Montana winter, exposed to the elements, could do to a body. Living on the mine claim had been bad enough. He'd had the comfort of a tent and plenty of blankets and still he almost froze to death. No, the Chadwick woman was most likely dead.

It seemed natural that Cole's thoughts went to Dianne Chadwick. Her sisters had died on the trail, and each time he'd most uncomfortably played a part in their search or discovery. Still, in spite of her adversity, Cole had never seen anyone as strong as Dianne. She took the blows life dealt her and managed through them. It wasn't that she could just accept anything that came along; it was more that she possessed an incredible ability to reconcile each situation and realistically recover enough to proceed with forward momentum. It was a lesson Cole would have done well to learn.

Cole moved out across the open field and began climbing toward Boot Hill. He didn't believe Susannah Chadwick could have made it this far, but there was always that possibility, and as long as a chance existed, he had to check it out.

With a gentle sweep of his feet, Cole studied each mound, each rounded drift, but to no avail. The snow grew deeper, making it even harder to maneuver, and with the light fading and night coming on, Cole decided to head back to town and see if there had been any word.

His stomach rumbled loudly as he realized he'd not eaten since breakfast. He made his way to Armstrong's Store, where everyone had agreed to check in. He hoped there might be word of Susannah's rescue—he found himself close to praying that she had been located at a neighboring cabin or even taken to the hospital.

"Found her yet?" Cole asked as he entered the small store.

"Not that I've heard," the clerk replied.

Cole nodded and glanced around. "You got any of that jerked beef they brought up from Salt Lake?"

The man shook his head. "'Fraid not. Sold out of that almost as soon as I offered it for sale."

Cole decided to forego eating. As soon as they called off the search for the night, he'd make his way over to the small café at the end of the street and have something hot. That would set better anyway, he reasoned.

Pulling his collar up, Cole again braved the winter air as he stepped back into the street. He'd no sooner walked to the end of the block when he heard a commotion coming from down the way. He hurried, hoping it might mean good news.

"They found her," an old-timer told him as he approached the gathering crowd. "Froze to death."

Cole's heart sank. He immediately thought of how hard this news would be for Dianne.

"They took her to the undertaker, but it'll take days to thaw her out," the man said, dribbling tobacco juice as he rambled on. "I saw that happen a few years back. Never could get the man to thaw. They built a fire and—"

"Thanks," Cole muttered and made his way around the old man.

He knew he had to find Zane and Morgan and let them know if they hadn't already heard. He walked the short distance to the undertaker's and found the boys already there.

"I just heard," he told them as he pulled the hat from his head.

Zane nodded. "We were just getting ready to go tell Dianne." His face was void of emotion, but his voice cracked even as he spoke.

"She's going to blame herself," Morgan said, shaking his head.

They walked outside and Cole found it a natural thing to just walk with them. "I'm sorry it couldn't be better news."

Zane shrugged, but Cole wasn't sure if it was from the cold or his indifference to the comment.

They walked on in silence to the little cabin. Cole felt a growing misery in his heart. Why did this country have to be so hard on folks? Why did people have to suffer and lose the ones they loved?

The door to the cabin opened and Dianne stepped out. Cole figured she'd been watching or else someone had already come with the news. She looked at each of them, meeting their eyes, studying their faces. It was enough. She burst into tears and buried her face in her hands. Cole hadn't known until that moment that he'd come to care about her. He didn't want to care about her, however.

Without warning or word, he turned from the cabin and walked away as quickly as he could without actually running.

"I won't feel anything for her or any other woman," he muttered. "I can't afford to feel anything for anyone."

CHAPTER 23

TWO MONTHS HAD PASSED SINCE THEIR MOTHER HAD BEEN FOUND dead. March was nearly upon them, but still there seemed to be no end in sight to cold weather and snow. Dianne found the days slow and impossible to tolerate. She thought she might go mad except for the company of her Bible. God seemed her only refuge and companion, especially when Zane and Morgan were gone sometimes weeks at a time on the freight route.

More than once she'd begged them to give up the job and find a way to get to their uncle. She felt confident that Uncle Bram would take them in now that their mother had passed away. He wouldn't want them living in the rough mining town alone. Especially if it meant Dianne would spend so much time by herself.

She tried not to be overly troublesome about her fears, but she felt Zane and Morgan needed to understand. One night after supper, when both the boys were home, Dianne had firmly asked them to remain seated at the table while she spoke her peace.

"This town isn't safe for me. I want to go live with Uncle Bram. You two can do whatever you like, but I need your help in getting me settled."

"When spring comes round, we'll get in touch with him," Morgan had told her. "He'll come for his mail and then you'll have a chance to tell him face to face."

"Besides," Zane added, "there's probably no one in town who even knows how to make their way to Uncle Bram's place, much less who would be willing to risk the possibility of a blizzard coming up just to take a message when it's not even a matter of life and death."

Morgan nodded. "Yeah, be sensible about it, Dianne."

"I thought I was being sensible. I can't be confined to this cabin day in and day out until spring thaw, but going to town always presents a risk. Most folks are decent, law-abiding citizens, but there are an awful lot of men whose favorite pastimes are drinking and gambling."

"Well, it's hard to pan for gold in the winter. Some of them are down there working day and night to thaw the tiniest bits of ground in order to sluice a bit for tobacco money and food. Some have given up," Zane told her as if she didn't already know.

"Yes, and some of them have grown desperate—tired of the cold and lack of provisions. There are still plenty of thieves and rowdies. It isn't safe for me to go to town alone, but you two go off for days, even weeks at a time with your freighting duties."

"It's slowed considerably with winter. We're not gone nearly as often," Morgan protested.

"Maybe not as often, but it's certain you're gone for longer periods of time. Do you have any idea how lonely I get?" Dianne asked. "I sit here day in and day out with nothing but memories and the cold."

"We're sorry," Zane said, shaking his head, "but the work is steady and good, and if Morgan and I are to make our own way come summer, we need to have enough money to buy supplies."

"We have money left over from the sale," Dianne complained. "You could take whatever you need from that."

Morgan and Zane exchanged a glance, then Zane replied, "We kind of hoped to use that money to send you back to Missouri."

"Missouri? What would I do in Missouri?" Dianne asked. "We don't even know if Trenton is still in town. It's hardly proper for me to go living by myself, although I suppose I'm doing just that here in Virginia

City." Her tone was bitter, although she tried hard not to feel that way.

"Look, you've got friends in New Madrid. People care about you and would probably take you in. Especially if you had money to give them," Morgan stated firmly. He pushed his dirty hair back and got to his feet. "At least think about it."

Dianne didn't argue with them as they seemed to leave her little room for it. The conversation, now a week behind them, seemed to mark the entire subject as unapproachable.

Dianne grieved over her situation but made the best of it despite her brothers' attitudes. She busied herself with whatever she could find to do—mending, baking, sewing on a new quilt. In spite of her concerns about the rowdies, she daily walked to town, checked in at the post office for letters, then made her way to the dry goods store to see if any new shipments might have made their way through the snowy passes.

Today she felt particularly blessed to find several books, and while they were outrageously priced and obviously used, desperation caused her to buy three. She'd never been much of a reader, but time left to herself had greatly improved her abilities.

"When you're done with them, I'd be happy to buy them back," the shopkeeper told her. "Folks will be glad to have them."

"I'll keep that in mind," she said as she counted out her money.

Dianne put the books in an old flour sack she used as a shopping bag. It made carrying her purchases much easier, although there were times when she would have much preferred a more stable basket.

Exiting the store, Dianne wondered when spring might come to Virginia City. She longed for endless summer days where the sun would beat down upon her. Lifting her face to the sky, Dianne tried to imagine how good it would feel.

"Whatcha lookin' for up there?" a man asked her.

Dianne looked down to see a trio of men standing before her. The one who'd spoken had matted red hair that stuck out from the bottom of his filthy fur cap. He didn't look all that old—probably no older than her brothers.

"I was just looking for the sun," Dianne said.

"If you're lookin' to warm up a bit, I could help you out," said one of the man's equally dirty companions. He laughed as if he'd told a great joke and elbowed the man beside him.

"Uh, no thank you." She moved past the men and continued down the walk.

"Now, wait a minute. We're decent fellows. Maybe we haven't had a bath in a month of Sundays, but it don't mean we can't be sociable. I even know how to dance," the redheaded fellow declared, coming up alongside Dianne.

She might have smiled had she not been painfully reminded of the day her father had been shot and killed. The situation had been much too similar for comfort.

"I'm sorry. I don't have time to talk or dance. I must make supper for my brothers."

"Ah, surely they can spare you," the third of their associates finally spoke. In his bravery, he reached out to take hold of Dianne's flour sack. "I can carry this for you and—"

"Give that back!" Dianne declared, reaching for the bag. The men laughed and tossed the parcel from one to the other.

"If you come home with us, you can have it back."

"She can have it back now."

Dianne stopped immediately at the sound of the voice. She turned to find Cole Selby once again at her defense. She paused, uncertain of what she should do. The three men were close enough to cause her harm if they wished. The redheaded man held her flour sack while the other two seemed quite interested in what Cole wanted.

"You one of her brothers?"

"It really isn't any of your business who I am. Now give her back the sack and get on back to whatever hole you crawled out of," Cole demanded, pushing his brown felt hat back just a bit.

Dianne's skin began to tingle. She thought of her father again. Cole seemed completely at ease with the situation, however. In fact, he moved closer to her, putting himself almost in reach of the men.

Without warning, the red-haired man dropped the sack and threw a punch. Cole easily dodged it while pushing Dianne out of the way at the same time. Dianne fell backward, landing quite unladylike on the boardwalk.

The three men threw punches at Cole without thought to the unfairness of the match. Cole tried his best to duck and bob away from the throws, but from time to time the men made connection with his face. Cole, in turn, landed his own strikes, bloodying the nose of one man and leaving another rather dazed.

Dianne grimaced with each strike, praying that no one would pull a gun. She scooted away from the fight and got back to her feet, all the while watching Cole.

"What's going on here?" a voice boomed.

Dianne looked past Cole to see a big barrel-chested man come forward. "Haven't I told you boys to stay out of trouble?"

Dianne had no idea who the man was, but the three men who'd given her so much grief seemed to fairly tremble in his presence. They immediately stopped fighting and stood at attention.

"They accosted me, and this man came to my rescue," Dianne interjected, hoping Cole wouldn't find himself with a bigger job to handle.

The redhead looked as though he'd just as soon the ground open up and swallow him. "We didn't mean no harm, Pa. We were just funnin' with the lady."

"We don't fun with ladies," the man replied. He turned to Dianne and tipped his hat. "My apologies, ma'am. My boys suffer from powerful poor manners. Their ma, God rest her soul, died young."

He looked back at the three young men and frowned. "I think apologies are in order."

The redheaded man picked up the flour sack and handed it to Dianne. "Sorry, ma'am." He lowered his head and moved to stand behind his father. The other two came in turn, blushing furiously and looking nothing like the rascals they had been only moments before.

"Sorry," they said in unison.

The big man turned to Cole. "Mister, I'm sorry my boys bloodied your lip. You're welcome to have a free throw at each of them."

Dianne wanted to laugh at the shocked expressions on the faces of the man's sons. She watched as Cole frowned, then shook his head. "I'm not much for fighting. Just didn't want to see the lady hurt."

The big man nodded. "You're an honorable sort." He then turned and grabbed two of his sons by their ears. "When I get you three home, we're going to have a discussion about the way we act in town. I swear, if your poor ma were alive to see such things she'd whip you within an inch of your life."

He continued to harangue them all the way down the street. Dianne giggled, but as soon as she turned to Cole and saw his lip was swollen and bleeding, she stopped. "Come on with me. I'll get you fixed up."

"That isn't necessary," he said softly. Reaching up, he wiped at his mouth.

"I'd really feel better if you'd let me clean that up. Besides, you can further your gallantry and walk me safely home," Dianne said, clutching her books.

Cole nodded. "I will walk you home, but . . ."

Dianne smiled. "I have some stew simmering. Maybe you'd like to stay and have a meal with me." It seemed strange to be suggesting such a thing, but Dianne pushed aside any feelings of impropriety.

"You don't need to go to any trouble," Cole replied. "Here, let me carry your sack." He waited while she handed over the bag.

Dianne could tell he really wanted to say yes, so she began walking toward her cabin. "Zane and Morgan are working and it's hard to say when they'll get back. In more cultured environments I'm sure it would never be appropriate for you to take a meal alone with me, but I really don't care what folks think. Are you worried about it?"

"I don't care what anyone thinks," Cole replied, keeping pace with her quickening steps.

"Good. I haven't had anyone to talk to in over two weeks. The freight company can never guarantee whether they'll get through the passes and back to Virginia City. Sometimes the boys are away for what seems like forever."

"One of them ought to be here with you."

"I agree. And I've told them so." As the snow deepened along her street, Dianne slowed her steps. Without questioning her for permission, Cole took hold of her elbow. "The money is good, though. Not only that, but I think Zane and Morgan would go stark raving mad if they had to be stuck in the cabin all day."

"I can understand that. I'm not doing so well waiting for spring thaw myself."

Dianne made her way up the little path to the cabin. "Any idea when the weather will warm up?"

"Nope. I was helping with the wagon train this time last year. At least, I was helping Daniel to get to St. Louis."

Dianne stopped and looked at him for a moment. "You're right. I hadn't realized it's been almost a year since we left Missouri and the war."

"War's about to be concluded," Cole said as she turned to push open the door. "Maybe now we'll be able to see a time of peace and prosperity in this country. Maybe then you'll feel free to return to your home."

Dianne held open the door and waited until Cole stepped inside to answer. "I don't have a home—not really. My only family is here, with exception to my oldest brother, Trenton. I haven't heard from him so I don't even know if he's alive." She took off her coat and motioned Cole to do the same. The aroma of the stew was welcoming to Dianne. She had skipped breakfast that morning and now felt quite ravenous.

"I'll take care of your face first, and then we can eat," she told Cole. "That is, if you aren't afraid of my cooking. I've improved a bit since my days on the trail."

Cole smiled. "You were as green as they come. You had nowhere to go but up, as far as improving was concerned."

Dianne smiled. He really wasn't nearly the ill-tempered oaf she'd once thought him to be. Maybe the winter months in Montana had helped him mature. Or maybe she was the one who'd matured.

"I guess the frontier has a way of growing you up," Dianne said rather thoughtfully.

"Yeah, I guess," Cole said, growing sober again.

Dianne pulled out a chair. She didn't want to give him time to change his mind. They might have had their differences, but she was glad for the company. "Sit here while I get some ice."

She waited until he'd actually taken a seat before going outside. She hadn't bothered with her coat and when the breeze picked up, she immediately regretted her decision. The cold was different here in the mountains. It was a drier cold than what she'd experienced back in Missouri; nevertheless, it had a way of cutting through the skin. Giving a shiver, Dianne picked up a small metal container and hurried back to the house.

Cole sat waiting for her. She smiled and held up the pot. "I keep this outside for just such occasions. Zane and Morgan are always hurting themselves and sometimes the ice comes in handy." She picked up a chisel and hammer and began to chip away at the ice in the pot.

"Speaking of your brothers, how do they feel about Montana?"

Dianne considered the question for a moment. "I don't know if it's Montana in particular or just the big skies and rugged mountains. They both long for their independence and I just can't encourage it—not yet. I still need them."

Cole nodded. "That's for sure. Do you often have trouble when you go to town?"

"Oh, not often. There are times when the rowdies get a bit out of control. They don't mean any real harm—at least I don't think they do." She gathered up the ice chips and put them on a clean dishtowel and knotted the ends together. Next she took up a small bowl and poured in a little of the hot water from the stove reservoir. Taking up yet another clean towel, she came to the table.

"I hope this won't hurt too much," she said, dipping the dry cloth in the water. She touched it to his face gently. "Too hot?"

"No, it's fine."

She continued washing the area around his lips, then smiled with satisfaction. "That ought to do it." She picked up the ice bag and handed it to him. "Put this on your lip while I get us lunch."

"You really don't have to do this. I can grab something to eat in town."

"Nonsense. I have the food ready and I owe you."

"No you don't," he said firmly. "I did what any decent man would do. You shouldn't have to defend yourself."

"Well, there are a whole lot of things I shouldn't have to do," Dianne said, taking down two bowls and a plate from the cupboard. "And a whole lot of things I wish I never had to do again." She smiled to herself more than for his benefit. "But life is what it is."

She dished up the stew and set the bowls on the table. Next, she opened the bread box and brought out a half loaf of bread. After putting this on the plate, she gathered up eating utensils and came to the table. "I have no butter or jam."

"I wouldn't need them anyway," Cole replied, putting the ice aside. "I like to sop my bread in the stew."

Dianne suddenly realized she hadn't thought about something to drink. "I can make coffee, but it will take a little while."

"Water is fine."

She nodded. "Good. That way our stew won't get cold."

She brought the glasses of water and then took her seat. "Do you mind if I offer thanks?"

Cole shook his head and closed his eyes. Dianne murmured a short, respectful prayer of thanks. Her heart seemed suddenly full with gratitude for this reprieve from her otherwise boring day. She wanted to thank God aloud for sending Cole to visit, but instead she only considered her gratitude in silence.

After she'd concluded, Cole surprised her by taking up the knife to slice the bread. He handed her a piece and actually smiled. "Looks good. Did you make it?"

Dianne nodded. "I told you I was improving."

He took a bite of the bread and nodded. "I don't think I've ever had better."

They ate in companionable silence, and only after Dianne refilled Cole's bowl two more times did they revisit conversation.

"I don't suppose there's any chance you know my uncle, Bram Vandyke?"

Cole pushed his bowl back. "As a matter of fact, I do. He hired me on to help drive some cattle to his place last fall."

Dianne felt a new surge of hope. Perhaps Cole could get word to her uncle. It was certain her brothers didn't see the situation as serious enough to consider. "Could you get a message to him for me?"

Cole frowned. "I doubt it. I'm not sure I'd know exactly how to find my way back to his place."

"I could pay you. In fact, I could pay you very well. We've managed to hang on to most of the money we made when we sold the store goods and extra animals."

"It's not a matter of pay," Cole said somberly. "I honestly don't know if I could find the place."

"Would you at least consider it? I mean, I know it's dangerous and I wouldn't want you to even try if there were too great a risk," Dianne began, "but I'm desperate. My brothers don't understand, but I think it's important Uncle Bram know about my mother dying. I think it's also important that he know I'm here alone most of the time. Surely he wouldn't allow that to go on if he knew."

"Why don't your brothers try to get word to him?"

"They think it's a silly point. Uncle Bram can't do a thing about Mama and he can't very well come for a funeral that's already taken place. They think that because he'll be making his way here in May or June to pick up supplies and mail that we should just wait until then. But that's two, maybe three more months."

"I agree you shouldn't be here alone, but by the time I get the message to him and he acts on it, it'll probably be the same difference."

"Please," Dianne said, knowing she sounded like a child begging for her own way. "I'll pay you any amount you ask." She got up and went into her bedroom to retrieve their savings. Coming back, she opened up the small wooden box to reveal their money.

"You shouldn't keep that kind of cash in the house," Cole warned. "Especially not being here alone. Why isn't this in the bank?"

"I don't plan to live here long enough to need a bank," Dianne said. "Look, I just want you to see that I can afford to hire you. I'll just keep asking folks until someone agrees to do it."

Cole blew out a heavy breath. "I'll take on the job, but only if I can get some better idea of how to get to your uncle's place. I know a couple of the cowboys who were working for him on that same drive. They might be able to help me."

Dianne knew then that God had heard her prayers. "Just let me know what you expect to be paid. I'll write out a letter for my uncle and give you money for your expenses as well."

Cole stared at the box of money. "Do you keep a gun in the house?"

"No," Dianne admitted. "Zane and Morgan usually take theirs on the job."

"You need one if you're going to keep this kind of money around."

Dianne shook her head. "I don't know the first thing about them."

"I could teach you. I could pick a gun out for you as well. It isn't like you can't afford one."

She smiled. "Well, if you want to go to the trouble, I suppose it would be fine. Although I seriously doubt I could ever shoot someone— especially over money."

"I wouldn't want you to shoot them," Cole admitted. "It'd be enough if you could scare them off. But if your life was being threatened and no one was around to come to your rescue, you should know how to use the thing and shoot to kill. It might mean saving your life."

Dianne thought about the young men who'd accosted her earlier. She could never have shot any of them, no matter what they threatened her with. "I don't think I could kill anyone, Cole. I'd rather die instead."

———

Cole remembered the serious expression on Dianne Chadwick's face long after he'd left her dinner table. Her declaration that she'd rather die than defend her life was startling to him. Had Carrie felt the same way? Was she happier having died trying to defend her father than to have never tried at all?

He kicked himself mentally for having allowed Dianne to worm her way into his heart. He didn't want to care about her, but it seemed that every time he turned around she was in trouble of one sort or another. How could her brothers be so stupid as to leave her alone to fend for herself? Maybe he should have a talk with them.

"And now she wants to hire me to take a message to her uncle," he muttered under his breath. "And I said I'd do it. I'm ten kinds of fool for that one."

But her sweet smile and desperate pleading were his undoing, and no matter how much Cole thought of Carrie and how he'd sworn never to care about another woman, Cole Selby knew he was in deep trouble when it came to Dianne Chadwick.

CHAPTER 24

COLE STILL COULDN'T BELIEVE HE'D ALLOWED DIANNE TO TALK HIM into taking a message to Bram Vandyke. The trails were fairly open, however, as warm breezes and a week of sun had melted most of the snow. The temperatures were still plenty cold, but Cole used that to his advantage as the land remained frozen instead of muddy and difficult to travel.

With directions from one of the cowboys he'd worked with on Bram's cattle drive, Cole easily found his way to the Vandyke ranch. As he rode into the main yard, Bram waved from where he worked on a corral with another man.

"What in the world are you doing out this way?" the big man questioned.

Cole dismounted and shook the man's gloved hand. "I was looking to have a word with you."

"Well, it's almost lunchtime," Bram said, turning to the other man. "You remember Cole Selby, don't you, Gus?"

"Sure do." The man reached out to shake Cole's hand.

Gus Yegen was Vandyke's right-hand man. Years of working as a cowboy, wrangler, and foreman on a large ranch in Texas made him a valuable companion for the big Dutchman who hoped to build a ranch for himself in Montana.

"Good to see you, Gus," Cole said.

"I'd imagine Koko has lunch about ready. Why don't we make our way to the house and we can talk about whatever it is that brought you all this way."

Cole noted a few changes had been made since he'd been there last fall. Several corrals were in place and a barn had been built out of logs and stripped planks.

"I see you're noticing our handiwork," Bram said proudly. "We barely got that put together before the first big snow."

"It looks good. Solid." Cole thought it looked sturdier than the log cabin they were making their way to just now. He wondered if Dianne had any idea of her uncle's living conditions. Would she find it abominable to be stuck out here in the middle of nowhere, a good twenty-five or thirty miles from any real town?

Cole's senses were assaulted with the inviting aroma of food as soon as Bram opened the door, and concern about Dianne fled his thoughts. He remembered Bram's wife being a good cook, and his stomach rumbled loudly as they made their way into the house. After eating a cold breakfast on the trail, he was more than ready for hot grub.

"Koko, look who's here," Bram announced. "It's Cole Selby. He helped us last year with the cattle drive."

The dark-haired woman smiled and came to meet him. She was dressed as any other pioneering woman might be—simple skirt and blouse, apron to cover both—but her Indian features stood out in a marked way. Her hair was fixed in two black braids, and her high cheekbones and honey-brown skin gave her a rather exotic look. She was a handsome woman, Cole thought, closer to his own age than Bram Vandyke's. He knew a lot of men living in the wilderness were given to marrying native women, sometimes much younger women, but he still found it rather shocking. Back East the mixed marriage wouldn't have been acceptable, but here in the West it seemed almost a common occurrence.

"It's good to see you again, Mr. Selby," Koko Vandyke greeted.

Cole yanked his hat off in respect. "You too, ma'am. I remember your good cooking."

Bram laughed and pulled off his gloves and hat. "Cole, you and Gus can hang your things on the back of the door." Koko came to her husband and took his hat and gloves, then waited for him to get out of his heavy coat.

Gus and Cole did as instructed, then made their way to the table. By this time Bram had taken a seat and Koko was already working to set another place.

"Hope you like elk steak," Bram said.

"I can't imagine anything more welcome after a long ride," Cole replied.

Koko plopped a thick steak down on the plate in front of each man. After this she brought a huge cast-iron skillet of fried potatoes. Bram took the pan from her and began helping himself to the food, while Koko retrieved a platter of sliced bread and a bowl of sweet peas.

After each of them had filled their plates, Bram offered thanks and then instructed them to dig in. There would be no conversation until their hunger was somewhat abated.

Cole watched as Koko lovingly tended to each of them in between eating her own share of food. She poured coffee into their mugs at the first sign of need and went to retrieve more bread when Gus took the last slice from the platter. She was a kind and gentle woman. Cole had never seen such a servant's heart in any person. He remembered from his earlier time with the Vandykes that Koko had never seemed to care whether there were two men or ten to feed and care for. She seemed only to enjoy being needed. How different from his mother, who while happy to take the financial support of her boarders, was less than content in having to actually deal with the people themselves.

As the meal wound down, Bram pushed back and lit a cigar. "So tell me why you rode all this way. Do you need a job?"

Cole put his fork down and shook his head. "Actually, I was hired by your niece, Dianne Chadwick. I have a letter for you." He pulled the letter out of his pocket and handed it across the table to Bram.

"Do you know what's in this letter?" Bram asked, eyeing Cole curiously.

"I know the intent of the letter," Cole admitted. "Dianne spoke with me at length about the situation."

"I see. So why don't you just tell me what's in here." He spoke in such a way that it almost seemed a command.

Cole nodded. "I'm afraid the news isn't good. Your sister passed away just before Christmas. She wandered out in a snowstorm, apparently lost her way, and wasn't found until the next day."

Bram lowered his head and looked at the table. Koko came to stand beside him. She gently touched his shoulder, and he reached up to take hold of her hand. "I thought she would be all right there. I thought she had better sense than to risk her life that way."

"She probably would have, but she was heavily drugged from the laudanum and wasn't in her right mind."

"And the baby?" Bram asked, looking back to Cole.

Cole shook his head. "She hadn't yet delivered."

Bram nodded knowingly. "I suppose it's just as well. Those children would have been hard-pressed to care for an infant."

Cole admired his strength but could see that his eyes had dampened. "Dianne wants to come live with you. Her brothers have a mind to be independent by summer and she's all alone. It's not a good situation for a woman by herself, if I do say so. I had to come to her rescue just last week when she was . . . ah . . . confronted by three men." Cole didn't bother to explain the situation further. He knew Vandyke understood the potential for such an event.

"I'm glad you were there to help. How is it you know my family?"

"I was assistant to the wagon master on the train that brought them west. I was there when Dianne's sisters died. We never did find the older of the two. She was swept downriver. The youngest was kicked in the head by a mule. It appeared she spooked the animal. I was there when Dianne found her."

"That girl has had her share of miseries to be sure," Bram murmured. "Still, I don't have room to have her and her brothers here. Look around for yourself. We have this room and a bedroom. That's it."

"I could help you build on," Gus offered.

"I'd be glad to help as well," Cole replied. "And surely Dianne's brothers would give some time if they knew it meant seeing Dianne well cared for. They might even want to live here themselves. It's a heap prettier here than in Virginia City. Maybe they'd find a heart for ranching."

"I could use their help for sure. I just have a couple of men working for me besides Gus. They're out north of here with the cattle. Come spring thaw, there'll be plenty of work around here and I'll definitely need more hands." Bram sat and sucked on his cigar for several minutes.

Koko moved around to retake her seat. "Bram, you can hardly leave her there to fend for herself. She's from the East. She doesn't know how to live out here. People will take advantage of her. You know this is true."

Bram met her gaze. "Yes, I suppose you're right." He turned his attention to Cole. "It's not that I don't want her here. You have to understand. It's just that I know she's probably not cut out for the life we're living. Her mother wasn't cut out for it—I knew that. It's one of the reasons I told her she couldn't come here. She would have perished after a month without shops to visit and people to talk to. The other reason . . . well . . . she was prejudiced. I knew she could never have lived in the same house with Koko."

"Well, forgive me for being blunt," Cole began, "but you won't find Dianne to be either prejudiced or weak. She's been the backbone of that family ever since I met her. Her best friend on the wagon train was a former slave. Not only that, but no matter what you decide, Dianne has no idea of returning to Missouri. She made that clear to me."

Bram chuckled. "She did, now? Well, she sounds like quite a gal."

Cole started to affirm this, then thought better of it. "She's determined."

"I'll tell you what. If you can get them here, say in May, then I'll have the trees cut and ready to build. Gus and I will have to help fetch the cattle from where they're wintering come later this month or April— that's providing it's not a lengthy winter. We should have the herd settled by May and then we can devote our time to getting those additions put on. Eh, Gus?"

"Sounds about right."

Cole looked to the foreman. He liked Gus Yegen. He was a grizzled, weather-worn man in his forties who had done a lot of living. Even so, he was a friendly sort who had no problem with speaking his mind when the occasion called for it.

"We have those cows to pick up come June," Gus added.

"Right, and it would be good to have Morgan and Zane to help out," Bram replied. "How about you, Cole? Would you consider hiring on?"

"I'm not sure. I'm hesitant to commit because I may well be joining up with another wagon train. I'm to talk to Daniel Keefer next week."

Bram took a draw on the cigar. "I wish you'd consider signing on with me. I intend to build this place into a first-rate operation. I could use a man like you."

"I'll think about it," Cole replied, but he wondered if he could ever take on a position that would put him around Dianne on a daily basis. Then again, maybe he'd be much too busy with the job to concern himself with the boss's niece.

————

"I can't believe you're here," Faith declared as Dianne entered their small shack.

"I can't believe I finally found you! I've looked for you everywhere. I figured because the day was so nice, I'd do whatever it took to find you," Dianne said as she studied Faith's thin face. "Why didn't you come see me?"

"Malachi was so sick for a long time. I couldn't leave him. Then when he started making a turn for the better, there was just so much we had to tend to." Faith pressed a worn red handkerchief against her face. She looked sickly and worn out.

"I brought a few things, just on the hope that I would find you," Dianne said, taking up the flour sack. "I had a lot of scrap material and thought you might be able to use it for rag rugs. Also I have a fresh loaf of bread, some sugar, and a pound of coffee. I remembered how you said Malachi enjoyed a cup in the morning."

"We haven't had coffee in so long, I don't know what Malachi will think," Faith said, sitting on a small crate.

Dianne looked around the room and found very little of any kind of furniture. There was a sleeping pallet against one wall, a couple of crates, and the tiniest of woodstoves. She returned her gaze to Faith, who only shrugged.

"I guess we have it pretty bad," Faith began, "but at least we're free. Malachi says he'd rather live on top of a dung pile in Montana than go back to the way things were before Mr. Lincoln set us free."

Dianne felt bad because she knew she and her brothers had it so much better. "I'm sorry, Faith. I really wanted this to be a new start for you."

"I know. But God has a plan and I trust Him for it."

Dianne noticed that Faith brought the handkerchief once again to her face. "Are you sick, Faith?"

"I'm gonna have a baby." She smiled, but there was no joy in her words.

Dianne returned the smile. "That's wonderful news. I know Malachi must be pleased."

"Yes, he is, but he's also worried. He's out right now trying to find a better place to live. Most folks don't want to rent to people of color, so it's hard to get something."

"A great many people cleared out when the gold strike at Last Chance was announced. There ought to be something better," Dianne said, shaking her head.

Just then the door flew open and Malachi entered. "I swear there be no justice in this—" He paused in midsentence when he spied Dianne. "Why, howdy, Miz Dianne. How you be?" He offered her a broad smile.

An idea came quickly to Dianne. "I'm doing fine, Malachi. But I could do better." Both Malachi and Faith looked at her oddly, but before they could question her Dianne hurried on. "I live in a cabin, most of the time by myself. I get really lonely, but not only that—I need help with the animals and such."

"What happened to your brothers and ma?" Faith asked.

"Mama died around Christmastime. Zane and Morgan are working with one of the freight companies and they're gone more than they're here. I have a small cabin, just two rooms and a mud porch, but you could have the bedroom and I'd sleep in the front room."

"Miz Dianne, folks would talk iffen we was to live under one roof. They wouldn't take kindly to white and black folks livin' together," Malachi told her.

Dianne squared her shoulders, knowing she'd probably have a fight on her hands. "I've never cared what folks thought. You're my friends, and I'd like you to move in."

"We can't be takin' charity, Miz Dianne."

"I'm not asking you to, Malachi. I need the help. I can hardly keep up with splitting wood for the stove. It wears me out something fierce. And then there's the animals. Most of the time the boys take the oxen, but sometimes they don't and I'm left mucking out stalls. Not to mention seeing to the feeding. Added to that, I could use Faith's help with the quilt I'm making. You wouldn't have to stay long if you didn't want to, but I really could use the help. Come summer I'm hoping to go live with my uncle, and then I won't be in this fix."

Malachi exchanged a glance with Faith. Dianne could see he didn't want to say yes, but at the same time he knew it would benefit them both.

"Please." She hoped her pleading tone would be his undoing.

"I guess we could for a spell," Malachi finally said.

Dianne smiled and gave Faith a quick nod. "Thank you. How soon can you come?"

"Guess there's nothing keeping us here," Faith declared. "Why not just go with her now?" She looked to her husband for an answer.

"Sure," Malachi said, nodding. "Iffen that be all right with you, Miz Dianne."

"I think it's perfect."

The next few weeks passed quickly. Zane and Morgan were home only momentarily. They heartily approved of the new arrangement, and while they discussed the news of the war with Malachi, Faith and Dianne prepared dinner. Dianne was glad for Faith's company. She'd missed having a woman around to talk to.

"When is the baby due?" Dianne asked as she checked the potatoes.

"Best I can figure it'll be the fall," Faith replied. "I'm glad it won't be coming in the winter, but a summer baby would have been better. More time for him to grow strong before the winter comes."

Dianne had never considered things that way. They'd always had plenty—a warm secure home and food on the table. Babies were born at all times of the year and one never gave consideration to the season. It disturbed Dianne deeply that Faith had to worry about such things.

On Sunday they went to church together. Dianne had hoped the attitudes of prejudice and condemnation wouldn't extend to Sunday services, but even in God's house she found hearts to be hardened. What she hadn't realized until too late was that a great many of Virginia City's residents were former citizens of the Confederacy. They had no tolerance for freed Negroes and made this clear by sitting as far away from Dianne, Faith, and Malachi as they possibly could.

Dianne felt bad for the couple, but neither Faith nor Malachi said a word about the situation. It wasn't until the next Sunday rolled around and Faith explained that they would not be attending church that Dianne understood how deeply they'd been hurt.

Leaving church that day, Dianne tried to think of how the problem might be resolved when Griselda Showalter approached her.

"What are you doing with those colored folks?" she demanded to know.

Dianne tried to hide her surprise. "Do you mean Faith and Malachi?"

"You know exactly who I mean. How can you have them in your house? Your mother would never tolerate such a thing. She was a proper

Southern lady. She told you not to associate with them."

"She's also no longer with us," Dianne pointed out as if Griselda had somehow forgotten.

"You cannot have them living with you."

Dianne squared her shoulders. "I can do pretty much as I like. My uncle is the one who has provided the house, and he would not disapprove of the situation." She leaned toward Griselda, unable to resist adding, "He's married to an Indian, you know."

Griselda looked rather shocked. "You have no sense of decency."

Dianne could stand the woman's company no longer. "No, you are the one who has no sense of decency. Faith and Malachi are God's children just as we are. They were living in squalor and I had need of their help. We have assisted each other, just as good Christian folk should."

"Well, I never!" Griselda stomped off, leaving Dianne free to head home.

Dianne knew Griselda shared the thoughts of most people around town, but she couldn't understand why such hatred should exist between people. Cole Selby had once commented on how the color of a person's skin seemed to ignite more problems than anything else.

"Too bad God didn't just make us all spotted with a rainbow of colors," he'd said. Then he lamented that even if this were the case, someone would find a way to distinguish between the spots.

A gentle breeze tugged at Dianne's bonnet ties. Thoughts of Cole sent her gaze across the valley to the mountains. Warm, dry winds had melted much of the snow, and she couldn't help wondering when Cole might return. She thought of the man who'd so often rescued her from danger. Had he made it safely to the ranch? Had Uncle Bram said yes to her proposition?

She was still pondering these things when she entered the cabin. All thoughts fled her mind, however, as she found Faith and Malachi packed and ready to leave.

"Where are you going?"

Faith came to Dianne as Malachi made his way outside. "Malachi heard about a gold strike up north. A place called Ophir Gulch. We're heading up that way."

"But what about your condition—the baby?"

Faith smiled. "When my time comes, God will provide the help I need. He always has. Just look at how He sent you into our lives. Just when we needed help the most, there you were. Now both of us have regained our health and we've had nothing but a good bed to sleep on and nourishing food for the last two weeks. We have our strength to move on."

"But I wish you didn't have to go so far away," Dianne said, tears in her eyes. "I don't even know where Ophir Gulch is."

Faith hugged her. "I know. But it's for the best. We aren't wanted around here and folks are talking bad about you. We can't let that go on."

"I don't care what people think," Dianne said, pulling away. "If you think you have to go because of that . . ."

"We're heading north because Malachi says we're heading north," Faith replied with a grin. "And you know my husband. When he gets a thought into his head, that's all there is. Whither he goest, I go."

Dianne wiped her tears with the edge of her coat sleeve. "I shall miss you. You will try to come see me sometime, won't you? I'll be with my uncle. His name is Bram Vandyke and his ranch is somewhere on the Madison River."

"I can't say, Dianne. Only God knows if we'll meet again."

The warmth of her expression caused Dianne's tears to fall anew. The women embraced once more, then Faith moved to the door. Dianne followed and waved to Malachi, who stood at the end of the walk.

"Good-bye, Malachi. Thank you for helping me. I wish you could stay on for a time."

"Bye now, Miz Dianne. Ya take care."

Dianne watched the couple move off down the road. She had no idea how they would ever make it to Ophir Gulch. She didn't know how far away that place might be or what they'd find when they got there. She only knew that her heart was broken for the loss.

CHAPTER 25

ZANE SENT WORD ON FRIDAY TO LET DIANNE KNOW THAT HE AND Morgan would be home for supper. Dianne rejoiced at the news. They'd been gone for so long, it seemed. She wanted to tell them about Faith and Malachi and hear the news they might have picked up on their routes. Her only disappointment was that Cole hadn't yet returned. But that disappointment was short-lived when she opened the front door to find Cole just about to knock.

She laughed at the coincidence. "I was just going to sweep the path." She held the broom up as if to offer proof to her statement.

"Doesn't appear to need it," Cole said, taking off his hat.

"I'm so glad you made it back. Did you have any trouble? Did you see my uncle? Did he say yes?" The questions spilled out like water rippling over stones in a brook.

Cole laughed. "I can see you're not at all anxious to know the details of my trip."

Dianne grabbed him by the arm and pulled him into the cabin. "My brothers will be here within the hour. You can have supper with us and tell us everything, but for now, just tell me what you can."

Again Cole chuckled. "Well, I suppose to sum it up, he said you could come."

Dianne looked at him for a moment. "He said yes?" She sighed, not waiting for Cole's response. "I prayed he would. I wasn't at all sure what I'd do if he didn't take pity on us. Zane and Morgan figured I should go back to Missouri. They even checked into steamboat tickets from Fort Benton so that I wouldn't have to travel in a wagon or stage. They want me to settle in the East, marry, and be a proper lady." She smiled. "But I can't do that."

"Why not?"

Cole's abrupt question caught Dianne off guard. She seemed to remember her manners and reached out for his hat. "Give me your coat as well. You must stay for supper." Cole did as she instructed.

Dianne hung the articles on a peg beside the front door. "As I've told you before, I don't intend to make that long journey back to Missouri. It's not my home anymore."

"But Montana is hard country. There's little out here to interest women."

"There's the land," Dianne said, meeting his intense gaze. "My uncle's desire to start a ranch fascinates me. I'd like to be a part of that."

Cole shoved his hands into his pockets. "Do you know anything about working with cattle and horses? It's not easy work."

"I care for our milk cow and horses every day," Dianne replied, feeling as though he were suggesting the task was beyond her. "I've learned a lot since we left Missouri. You can't deny that."

"I'm not denying anything, but look at yourself. How old are you?"

Dianne felt her cheeks grow hot under his scrutiny. "I turned seventeen last November."

Cole shook his head. "I have a sister around that age. She spends her time with parties and shopping. You shouldn't have to be worrying about difficulties like this."

"It's the life I choose," Dianne said.

He came forward and gripped the back of a kitchen chair. For a moment it seemed as though he'd done this to keep himself from rushing to her side. Dianne chided herself for her wild imagination.

"Women don't fare well out here. You saw how hard it was on the wagon train. You've lost three members of your own family—four, if you count the baby your mother carried. It's a hard country with nothing but hard work."

"Missouri was perhaps more comfortable in its luxuries, but there's something here . . ." Dianne's words faded. What was it she wanted to say? How could she explain that this land was gradually winning her over—taking a place in her heart that she'd never intended to give to anyone, much less a location?

"I feel God's presence here," she finally murmured. "I guess you could say that I hear His voice here."

"I grew up going to church, and I don't ever recall that you had to be in a certain place to be with God," Cole countered.

"No, I don't suppose I ever heard that either." Dianne sighed and moved to check on supper. She opened the oven to find that the biscuits were done. She pulled them out and put them to the side to cool. Then she lifted the lid on the chicken and dumplings she had simmering on the top of the stove.

"It smells good," Cole said. He cleared his throat and added, "I didn't mean to hurt your feelings or make you mad."

Dianne looked up, rather surprised. "I'm not hurt or mad. I just can't think of a way to share how I really feel on this matter. I don't expect folks to understand. Most of the people around here have come with one purpose in mind: gold. I didn't come for that. I pressed for this—I pushed my family to make this move. My mother needed someone stronger than me to help her get through the misery of losing my father. She needed someone to protect her and see to her needs.

"The boys were old enough to get caught up in the war, and I knew Pa didn't want that. I knew to lose one of them in battle would have killed my mother, and yet the very thing I thought would save us all has taken the life of so many I love."

"But still you want to stay?" Cole questioned. He seemed almost eager for her reply, almost as if he had something important to figure out based on her decision.

"Yes." Dianne held his gaze. He was a handsome man. His youth and vigor were evident in his build and stance. But the slight growth of beard and leathered look to his skin made him look careworn, older than his years.

"How old are you, Mr. Selby?" She wasn't sure why she asked or why she questioned him so formally.

"I'm twenty-one. Why?"

Dianne shrugged. "I just wondered how it was that a man such as yourself wasn't already married and settled down somewhere."

Without pausing, Cole blurted, "I would be married by now if my father hadn't killed my intended."

Dianne felt her breath catch in the back of her throat. She tried to speak, but the words wouldn't come. Just then her brothers came bounding through the door, and she knew the conversation would have to wait.

"Smells mighty fine in here," Zane announced, then caught sight of Cole. "Hey, good to see you again. What brings you our way?" He and Morgan both moved forward to shake hands with Cole.

"I figured your sister would have told you." All three men looked to Dianne.

"I didn't want to get their hopes up," she said, turning away quickly to retrieve dishes for the table. "We can discuss it over dinner."

"That sounds ominous," Zane said rather cautiously.

"Yeah, when Dianne gets to plotting, we end up moving clean across the country," Morgan added.

Dianne mused that Morgan didn't know how close to the truth he was on the subject. She thought there might be some further protest, but when the men went back to discussing their own interests, Dianne let out the breath she'd been holding. She could only pray that the twins would see this as a good thing. Maybe they'd even agree to go with her and wait a time before moving off on their own.

Quickly setting the table, Dianne's mind went back to Cole's statement that his father had killed his bride. A shiver went up her spine at the very thought of something so heinous. How had it happened? What could have possessed the man? She wanted desperately to ask Cole more about it but knew it wouldn't be fitting to do so in front of her brothers.

"So I take it the freight business is good," Cole said, following her brothers' lead to take a seat at the table.

"Business is very good. You've no idea. The need for supplies in this part of the country is something you can't even keep up with. Now, if we only had train service, we might be able to make a dent in it," Zane said.

"You have to remember thousands upon thousands have come here for the gold and whatever else they can find. Unfortunately, they figure to live off the land, never counting on the long winters," Morgan threw in.

"That's for sure," Zane agreed. "The freight company could run it so that a wagonload of goods was coming in every day and it still wouldn't meet the needs of those poor fools who came to find their fortune."

Dianne listened as the conversation continued on about the thousands who'd left the new capital of Virginia City to try their luck at other strike sites. She thought of Faith and Malachi and wondered if they would ever be able to find enough gold to survive.

She busied herself by bringing the coffee and cups to the table, then scooted the biscuits off onto a plate and brought them as well. Finally she went to retrieve the kettle of chicken and dumplings and was surprised to find Cole there to help her.

Their eyes met and for a moment Dianne saw raw pain in his eyes. He looked at her as if wanting to say so much, then the moment passed. The hard facade she normally saw was back in place and intimacy was lost.

They came to the table and said grace, then Dianne offered to fill each bowl before the conversation continued.

"Who would have ever thought you'd turn out to be such a great cook," Zane teased.

"Yeah, I remember burnt flapjacks and syrup you cooked so long it hardened," Morgan said, laughing.

"And don't forget that cake she made on the trail. All hard and overdone on the outside and still runny in the middle," Zane added.

Dianne laughed. She knew they were more than a little pleased with the way things had turned out. She could scarcely keep food on the table when they were home. They ate everything in sight and never complained.

Cole dug into the dumplings and nodded as he chewed. He offered her a hint of a smile, but whether from amusement with her brothers or pleasure at the food, Dianne wasn't certain.

"You wondered why Cole was here," Dianne began. "He's here because I sent him on a mission for us—me, really."

Zane looked at her a moment before refocusing on the food. "What kind of mission?"

"I asked him to take a letter to Uncle Bram."

Zane put his spoon down. "I thought we agreed that wasn't necessary. Uncle Bram would have been here in another month or two anyway." Zane looked to Cole. "She's always got to have her own way."

"That isn't true," Dianne declared. "I just felt it was important to know Uncle Bram's answer ahead of time. That way we can be ready to leave when he comes."

"I've got no plans to leave," Morgan announced. "I'm content to stay here."

Dianne squared her shoulders and lifted her chin defiantly. "Well, I'm not. Another few months here and I'll wind up married to one of those no-accounts just for company." The men all laughed at this, but she was more than serious. "Cole, why don't you tell us what transpired at the ranch."

Cole took another couple of bites before he put down his spoon. "Well, at first Mr. Vandyke wasn't at all for the idea. His cabin only has two rooms and he was pretty concerned that you city folk would never be able to endure the hardships of the ranch."

"That's hardly fair to say," Morgan interjected. "He doesn't even know what we're capable of doing."

Cole shrugged. "I'm just telling you how it was. It wasn't for a lack of wanting you there as family, and he admitted that he could use the extra hands helping with the ranch. But he was worried that you'd fall into harm or die from exhaustion. He worried that Dianne would miss the stores and people, and he just didn't want to agree to your coming only to find out that none of you could bear up."

"I'd like to show him a thing or two about bearing up," Zane said angrily.

"Well, you can have your chance," Cole replied. He spooned sugar into his coffee, then took a long drink.

Morgan was definitely interested. "What do you mean?"

"Well, your uncle has agreed for you to come, but he needs help adding on to the cabin. He plans to get the trees felled before you arrive and then he'll need all of us to work on the addition. I told him I wasn't at all sure you fellas would be interested or even know how to go about that kind of work, but—"

"We'll show him," Zane said, banging his fist on the table. "We're cut from the same kind of cloth he is. We're as strong and capable as they come." Zane turned to Morgan. "They'll always hire us back at the freight line."

Cole looked to Dianne and winked. It was only then that she realized Cole had been playing a game with her brothers. He'd known all along that success hinged on convincing her brothers to go to Uncle Bram's. He'd known from what she'd told him earlier that they would never willingly leave their good job and liberty—not without a good reason. And now they had one. Cole had hit them in their one vulnerable place—their pride. She wanted to giggle, but instead she turned her attention to the food. Cole Selby had once again rescued her from certain failure. Dianne hoped she might figure out a way to reward him for his ingenuity.

———

Omaha

Trenton looked at Henry DuPont and knew in his heart that the man's days were numbered. Henry knew it, too, which was why they now stood at the steamer dock.

"Are you sure this is what you want to do, Henry?"

"It's for the best. You're able to see to yourself now, and my daughter will no doubt be surprised to see me, but I think she'll be happy."

Trenton had been more than a little surprised when Henry, after a week-long bout of heavy drinking, had sobered up and declared that he was going back to Indiana to spend out his final days. The parting was bittersweet. On one hand, Trenton would be glad to be rid of Henry's drinking. On the other, he was sorry to lose his traveling companion. When Henry was sober, he was a marvelous friend and source of information, and Trenton knew his days would be sorrier for the loss.

"If she wants nothing to do with you, I'll be here in Omaha for a spell. I plan to write my sister and stay put until I hear from her. That could be months," Trenton told Henry.

"Well, with all that the railroad plans for this town, you shouldn't lack for a game. Just remember what I taught you and you'll be fine."

The final boarding call was given for the boat and with it, Henry picked up his bags. "Take care of yourself, Trenton."

Trenton nodded. "You too." He realized with great sadness that he'd never see the old man again. Henry may have taught him a bad habit or two, but he'd also taught Trenton to have a bit of self-respect—something that had previously been sorely lacking.

Trenton waited until he was sure Henry was safely aboard before heading back into town. The air was heavy and damp. Trenton wondered if they were due a storm. He hoped the rains would hold off. He had a night of gaming planned. Trenton knew his funds were getting short, especially after helping Henry with the purchase of his ticket home.

It didn't matter. Trenton knew there was money to be had. There was always someone willing to gamble away their paycheck or savings. Trenton tried not to feel guilty about it. If he wasn't winning, someone else would be. Weak-willed folks were always bent on doing foolishness. That certainly wasn't Trenton's fault.

Up ahead on the street a commotion was being raised. Trenton edged closer, curious about what was happening.

"It's over! The war is over!" came the declaration.

"We've whupped those slave-loving Johnny Rebs. Maybe ol' Abe will throw them all in prison!" Men cheered and women wept. It was a moment frozen in time; the end of an era, no doubt, for life would surely never be the same again. Brother had fought against brother. The country had been ripped in two, and it would take a mighty big seam to join them back together.

Trenton thought of the news and again his heart was torn. While he was glad to know the war was over, he knew the loss of life had broken his mother's heart. She had never understood why the South couldn't be left alone to live life as they saw fit. It wasn't, as she had said on more than one occasion, like anyone was asking the Northerners to take on slaves for themselves.

Dancing in the street broke out as the spirit of revelry mounted. For the most part, the citizens were clearly Union supporters. Trenton doubted seriously if a Confederate would have dared to admit his standing on this night of all nights.

The liquor would flow in celebration and so too the money. Trenton knew the announcement would give people a sense of elation that would translate into whimsical acts of generosity. And he planned to be in on the take. Making his way to his favorite saloon, Trenton came through the doors into the already crowded, smoky room. The piano player pounded out a lively rendition of "Camptown Races" while the clink of glasses and rowdy shouts acted as percussion for his concert.

"We've got room for one more," Bob Aldersson, owner of the hotel where Trenton held a room, called from a table toward the back.

"Celebrating the end of the war?" Trenton asked with a grin. He took off his hat and tossed it with precision to the hatstand near the back stairs.

"You bet we are," Bob replied and the others nodded enthusiastically. "Come play a few rounds with us. I feel like Lady Luck is with me tonight."

Trenton grinned. "Well, so do I. So deal the cards and let's see which one of us the lady smiles on."

The night passed quickly for Trenton, and true to his assessment, the money did pass around the various gaming tables in a fury of wins and losses. He'd done better for himself than expected. The money would tide him over for some time.

Walking along the darkened streets in the wee hours of the morning, Trenton tried once again to ignore his conscience. He thought about trying a job with the railroad, but when he considered the danger of Indian attacks on the surveyors and the long hours of backbreaking labor in the heat of the Nebraska sun, playing cards seemed preferable.

A woman's scream filled the night air, and for a moment Trenton wasn't sure if it was merely a pleasurable game being played by one of the soiled doves or if someone was genuinely in trouble. The scream came again, only more muffled.

Turning down the alleyway, Trenton caught sight of a group of people. It was dark and difficult to see, but when the woman screamed yet again, Trenton felt he had to intervene.

"What's going on here?" he asked, putting a hand to his gun.

"Get outta here. Ain't none of your concern," one of the men called over his shoulder.

"Help me!" the woman cried as she struggled against the hold of her captors.

"Let her go," Trenton demanded. "Let her go now!"

The men turned from the woman. There were four of them he could see now. They approached quickly, causing Trenton to back up several paces. He wasn't of a mind to shoot them, but he knew he'd have to defend himself.

"I'm gonna teach you a lesson about stickin' your nose in where it don't belong," the man nearest him announced.

By this time one of the other men had managed to slip around behind Trenton. He grabbed Trenton from behind and held his arms fast while the first man delivered a dizzying blow to Trenton's face.

Trenton kicked, but some of his blows didn't connect fully with his assailants and those that did seemed to have no impact. The men must have had a high tolerance for pain. Within moments, Trenton was nearly unconscious. As the man behind him let go, Trenton crumpled to the ground, moaning and spitting blood.

"Where'd she go?" one of the men questioned.

Trenton knew if the woman were still in the area, she'd be doomed to suffer whatever fate the men had in mind. He'd never be able to help her now.

Fighting to remain conscious, Trenton heard another voice announce that the woman had fled. He breathed a painful sigh of relief.

"Well, that's just great." The man came to Trenton and kicked him hard in the ribs. "You're just a know-nothin' do-gooder. You ever get in my way again, I'll kill ya as sure as look at ya."

The men walked away, each one stopping long enough to give Trenton a hard kick. Trenton curled into a ball for protection, but it did little good. Pain shot through him like wildfire and there seemed no relief in sight.

With the men gone, Trenton tried hard to sit up. He was grateful that at least they hadn't been of a mind to rob him. His money was still safely hidden in his boot. Unable to keep from moaning as he attempted to crawl to the wall of the nearest building, Trenton felt as if death would be a welcome friend.

"Are you okay?" came the soft voice of a woman.

She moved out of the shadows and crept along the wall until she'd reached him. "My name is Annabelle. I work over at the Looloo Saloon. Thanks for saving me from them."

"I guess I at least distracted them."

"I ain't never had nobody fight for me like that. Fight over me, sure, but not *for* me."

He couldn't see her face, but she smelled of cheap perfume, smoke, and whiskey. Not exactly the kind of woman his mother would suggest he avenge. Still, a thought ran through his mind as she tried to help him sit up. If he hadn't been out so late gambling, he wouldn't have been around to rescue her. Maybe this act of heroism would set aside the sin of his evening in the saloon.

"Just doing my gentlemanly duty," Trenton said with as much of a laugh as he could manage.

"Well, let me do my duty now," Annabelle said, helping Trenton to his feet. "Let me take you to wherever you're staying and get you fixed up. I know a bit of nursing."

Trenton had no doubt she did but wondered if her type of nursing was the kind he most needed at this point. Having no other recourse, however, he pointed her in the way of his hotel, unable to keep from leaning heavily against her.

"We'll get you put to bed," she said, her breathing labored from bearing his weight.

Trenton felt a moment of panic. What if she were to rob him? He wasn't going to lose all that hard-earned money to a lady of the night. "Don't . . . take . . . my boots off," he muttered. "Not . . . my boots." He was gasping for air but needed to make sure she understood.

"You men," she panted. "You're all alike. Wanna die with your boots on." She reached the front of his hotel and paused to rest against the doorframe. "Well, you aren't gonna die. Not if I have anything to say about it."

CHAPTER 26

DIANNE'S FIRST VIEW OF THE VANDYKE RANCH CAME ON A BEAU-tiful May afternoon. The scene spread out before them on a canvas of rich green velvet. Lush pines and ripening vegetation added character and charm to the landscape, while the Madison River wended along the valley in ripples of liquid crystal. The sight caught her breath. After the barren, stark hills of Virginia City, the artistic masterpiece of her uncle's land nearly brought tears to her eyes.

"It's something to behold," Cole said, halting the oxen. Cole had agreed to drive the team, and the twins had insisted Dianne ride in the wagon. There was no telling what they might encounter along the trail, and they figured her to be safer there than atop Dolly.

Dianne followed Cole's gaze across the landscape and nodded. She then turned to her brothers. They seemed just as captivated. "I've never known anything quite so lovely," she murmured, knowing in her heart that it was so much more than that.

Seeing the dots of cattle in the fields, hearing the birdsong and the music of wind in the trees, Dianne felt as though she had come home at last. A need that had been buried so long deep within her seemed to stretch and awaken . . . slowly unfurling. Her heart soared and for the briefest span of time, Dianne felt herself lifted beyond the present moment. Here, she would live. Here, she would die.

The skies to the west suggested rain, but overhead the brilliance of the sun and the startling blue almost hurt the eyes. Dianne wished that instead of a bonnet she had a wide-brimmed hat, as her brothers and Cole wore. Perhaps she'd check into that once they were settled.

They moved on in silence, reaching the cabin, barn, and stand of corrals. Dianne allowed Cole to help her down, all the while taking everything in at once. It was more than she could have hoped for or imagined.

Bram Vandyke came out of the cabin, his young Indian wife by his side. Dianne thought the woman very beautiful. She was dressed much as she had been that day in Virginia City. A simple skirt and blouse showed her to be a very petite woman, standing a few inches shorter than Dianne and at least a foot shorter than Bram. Koko Vandyke offered her a sweet smile and came to embrace Dianne with a warm welcome.

"I'm so glad you've come to live with us."

Dianne nodded as she pulled away. "So am I. I've never seen any-thing so lovely as this valley."

Bram smiled proudly. "God's handiwork at its best. You can see why I fell in love with it."

"Yes," Dianne replied. "Without a doubt."

The twins stepped forward and shook hands with their uncle. "We've come to help but most likely won't stay," Zane offered.

"I'm glad for the help. As we add to the herd, we'll need more hands, so if you decide to stay, I'd pay you and provide your room and board."

"We'll think on it," Morgan answered.

Cole stepped forward. "I see you and Gus got those trees felled." They all turned their attention to a pile of logs that stood just beyond the back of the house.

"Levi helped too. Matter of fact, here he is now. You folks remember him, don't you?"

Dianne turned to greet Levi Sperry. She knew he'd been sweet on her and wondered if time had diminished his feelings. Brawny and brown, he had filled out with thick muscles and an air of self-confidence that made her smile.

"Miss Chadwick," Levi said, then turned immediately to her brothers. "Zane. Morgan." They all three nodded before Levi let his gaze go once again to Dianne.

Dianne warmed under the scrutiny, even though his look was not leering. "How do you like working for my uncle?" she questioned, hoping it would ease her discomfort.

"It's a good job—good life here," Levi said, pushing back his black felt hat.

Dianne couldn't help but notice the way thick black lashes framed Levi's dark brown eyes. Her mother had once commented that such lashes were wasted on a man. The thought made Dianne smile.

"Well, we've got a great deal of work to accomplish in a short while," Bram said, breaking the spell of the moment. "I figure we men can sleep in the barn. Dianne and Koko can share the house."

"I couldn't put you from your own house, Uncle Bram," Dianne declared.

"No arguing. I've already got this thought through." He smiled to soften the gruffness of his voice. "I figure it'll take us a month to get everything situated. We'll add two rooms onto the side—over here," he said, pointing to the east end of the cabin. "I figure they might as well be good-sized rooms. If you're going to put in this kind of work, might as well make it worth the trouble."

"I agree," Cole announced.

"It sounds reasonable," Zane answered, studying the cabin as though trying to figure out all of the details of the job.

"We can get started tomorrow, after you've had a chance to rest up. Gus and I can show you how this will work out. We've staked out where we'll put the walls. I figure to just build on to the present cabin and then after the rooms are in place, we'll cut a door for passage into the addition. It'll require a little bit of extra work to fit the ends together and keep out the cold, but I've got that all figured out as well.

"It won't be anything special, but in the years to come I hope to build something even better. I figure once the land starts getting settled in earnest, supplies will be easier to come by. They're already getting some lumber mills up and running and stone is being quarried." He stopped and put his arm around Koko. "I plan to build us a grand house. Something to share with my family."

"Well, looks to me this conversation will have to wait," Gus said, pointing to the western skies. "I'm thinkin' it's comin' up rain. Best get this wagon unloaded and unsaddle these horses."

They all worked quickly, but Dianne couldn't help but think on her uncle's words. He planned to create an empire ranch—one to rival the big ranches of Texas. Cole had told her that Bram Vandyke owned a great deal of land. It was hard to imagine just how much space the Van-dyke ranch actually encompassed, but Dianne was fairly confident that for as far as she could see, she stood on her uncle's land.

Lightning flashed across the valley and Dolly spooked, dancing away from Dianne as she untied her from the wagon. "Easy, girl," Dianne whispered softly. She drew the mare close and gently stroked her head, whispering all the while in Dolly's ear. The mare calmed and followed Dianne to the barn stall.

"You have a natural way with her," Koko said, coming beside Dianne as she worked to free Dolly from her bridle. "The Blackfoot believe animals are messengers between humans and divine forces. People who are accepted by animals are honored."

"She's a good-natured horse. We fit together, to be sure."

"You enjoy animals, don't you?"

Dianne looked to Koko and smiled. "I love them. I didn't think I would. I was terrified of the milk cows when I first learned to handle them. Chickens scared me too." She laughed at the thought. "I remember the first time I had to gather eggs. I was determined to do a good job, but the hens seemed just as determined to keep me from their nests. I was pecked and scratched until I gave up and decided I would never eat eggs again."

Koko laughed. "What happened to change your mind?"

Dianne stroked Dolly's nose and grinned. "I came to understand just how much eggs played a part in my life. I've always been the determined sort, so I went back to those hens, shooed them away, and gathered their eggs. It was really all about setting my mind to do it."

"Just as you set your mind to coming here?" Koko asked.

Dianne felt suddenly embarrassed. "I didn't mean to impose myself upon your house and life."

Koko looked momentarily confused and then shook her head. "No, not here. I meant Montana. You are very welcome to be here. Please know that." She glanced over her shoulder, then lowered her voice. "It gets lonely here without another woman. When we lived north, near the great falls, my mother's people were close enough to visit. But here, there are few who will speak to me, much less call me friend."

"Well, I'm hoping we shall be great friends," Dianne declared. "When we moved here, I gave up my dear friends in Missouri. Then after losing my mother and sisters, I thought I might never feel like sitting and talking with women, but I find that the loss of female companionship is so hard."

"We have much in common," Koko said. She drew back a small gate that opened out onto the corral. "There, now she can spend her time right here or go on outside."

Dianne stepped from the stall and Koko followed. They secured the gate with Dolly looking at them as though they'd slighted her with this dismissal. Dianne reached into her pocket and pulled out a piece of dried apple. "Here you go, girl. I wouldn't forget your treat."

With the mare satisfied, Dianne and Koko walked back to the house. The men seemed caught up with the last crates from the wagon—sending some of the Chadwick possessions to be stored in the barn and taking others into the house.

"I'm so glad you don't mind that we're here," Dianne told Koko as they stepped to the cabin door.

"You are a blessing to me. In some ways, an answered prayer," Koko replied.

Dianne was startled for a moment. "You . . . you pray?"

Koko laughed and the sound was delicate and light like wind

through chimes. "Of course I pray. Your uncle helped me to know the Lord Jesus as my savior. I pray all the time."

Dianne nodded, wisps of blond hair falling into her face. "Then we truly are sisters."

———————

The month passed quickly and except for intermittent rain showers, the progress of the rooms went on without pause. Day by day the men stripped logs, notched them, planed, and filed where needed. To Dianne's delight, they even cut in holes for windows. Of course, they would be empty of glass for a time, but with the nice shutters Uncle Bram built, Dianne would still be able to open the windows and let in the sunshine and view the beauty of the mountains and close them to keep out the chilly night air.

A camaraderie developed among the men. Often in the evening after supper, they would sit around and tell stories, joke, and tease each other about the work yet to be done. For the first time in years, Dianne felt at ease and completely happy. Well, maybe not completely. She still worried about Trenton and where he might be. She'd stopped writing letters to him after her friend Ruthanne wrote to say that word had it he had left town for parts unknown. Ramona wrote to say her folks had heard he'd gone to Texas, but Dianne couldn't be sure of any of the stories.

Sometimes she thought about her sisters and missed their laughter and animated excitement. When the emptiness seemed particularly acute, she would go to the trunk and pull out their dolls. There was something about seeing those toys, just touching them, that allowed Dianne to move forward.

It was hardest to think of her mother. Dianne used to figure her mother would outlive them all. She had been such a genteel lady, but at the same time Susannah Chadwick had a strength and determination about her that would have made any Southern person proud. No one had counted on her growing weak in the head. It just hadn't seemed likely, given the woman's nature.

There were days when Dianne felt the loss of her mother more acutely than others. Sometimes Uncle Bram made a gesture or told a story from his childhood that Dianne recognized as something her mother had done or said. Sometimes, Dianne could even see a hint of her mother's expression in Uncle Bram's face.

Even so, there wasn't a great deal of time for sorrow. Dianne spent most of each day working with Koko. The woman knew incredible things about tanning hides, gardening, trapping, and canning. Dianne found each day a new experience in learning, and where book learning had been hard, this practical knowledge came much easier.

"You are quick to learn," Koko told her as they worked to scrape a deer hide.

"I want to be useful," Dianne admitted. "And the work is so very interesting."

"Most of what we do here is necessary for staying alive so far away from civilization."

"I can definitely see that," Dianne agreed. "Even during the war, because of the alliances my father made, we generally had a ready supply of goods in the store. Of course, we did without certain things. Everyone did, but it was nothing compared to this." She grew thoughtful. "It's hard for me to remember a time when we weren't at war, and now that it's over with, I wonder what will happen."

"Bram says there will be a great many people who move west. The territories will offer an escape from the pain of what happened in the East. The brokenhearted will move to the frontier, along with those who desire a new start."

"Yes, given the Homestead Act that Uncle Bram was talking about, I'm sure they will."

"You ladies look mighty busy today," Bram called as he and Gus rode up from the west.

"Are you leaving today?" Koko asked.

Dianne looked up rather surprised. "Leaving? For where?"

Bram dismounted. "I've talked with your brothers and with Cole. They've agreed to go with Gus to Virginia City and bring back the cattle and horses I ordered last winter."

"My brothers agreed to that? They said nothing to me."

"You've hardly had much time with them," Bram said. He handed the horse's reins to Gus and came to stand over his wife. "What will you make from this one?" he questioned.

Koko continued scraping. "Work gloves," she answered without missing a beat. "The new men will need them, and your gloves are wearing out fast. I'll get as many pairs as I can and then you'll just have to get me another hide." She looked up and smiled.

Dianne got to her feet. She barely came up to her uncle's shoulders. She dusted her skirt and raised her hand to block the sun from her eyes as she lifted her face. "Are you leaving us too?"

Bram shook his head and pulled a handkerchief from his pocket. He wiped the back of his neck as he spoke. "No. Someone's got to stay here and see that things keep running. I'll be here and so will Levi and a couple of the other boys. They're actually out taking down more trees as we speak."

Dianne nodded. She felt better knowing there would still be quite a few men around. Zane, Morgan, and Cole came from the barn leading their horses. They were deep in discussion about something, but from this distance, Dianne couldn't hear what they were saying. Cole looked up and fixed his gaze on her for several moments. Dianne smiled. She had wanted to know him better and to have the chance to ask him about his father and bride-to-be. But as if he purposefully had avoided that possibility, Cole was never around her without one of her brothers or Uncle Bram present at the same time. It was infuriating.

"You boys ready?" Bram asked as they approached.

Zane nodded but looked to Dianne. "Sorry we didn't get a chance to tell you about this."

"Me too. Guess I'm the last to know." She tried not to sound upset over the situation. She didn't want Cole to think her a baby about the whole thing. Work had to be done and cattle had to be fetched. If she was going to prove her mettle in this isolated land, she would simply have to bear the burdens that came her way.

"Don't forget to look into buying us another wagon," Bram said to Gus.

"I'll do it, boss." Gus looked back at the boys while Bram came up and took the reins to his horse. The animal was a beautiful bay gelding that Dianne had immediately liked upon their first meeting. Her uncle found the horse to be feisty and full of fury, but Dianne thought him amazingly calm-tempered and gentle. Koko said the horse had never responded to anyone else the way it had to Dianne—even Uncle Bram had been impressed.

"I'm going to head out and see how those boys are doing with the trees," he told Koko. He mounted the bay, and the other men took this as their cue to take to their own animals.

"I can pack you a lunch to take if you wait," Koko said, putting aside her scraping tool. She stood and waited to see what Bram would have her do.

"Nah. I'll be back before you know it, and the boys took food with them. If I'm too hungry, I'll just make them share." He laughed at this and the others joined in. Everyone knew Bram Vandyke was a gentle soul who'd deny himself first if it meant someone else's needs were met.

Dianne met Cole's gaze once again. He nodded, then nudged his horse down the long drive. "Be careful," Dianne called out to her brothers but meant it for Cole as well. She didn't know why, but she felt Cole was less cautious about his own care.

———

The men had been gone no more than three hours and yet Dianne felt their loss in a way she couldn't explain. She worked with Koko to make mattresses for the rope beds that the men had put together before leaving. When the boys came back, she hoped they'd be pleased to find that they had nice beds to sleep in.

"Where do the hired hands sleep?" she asked Koko, suddenly realizing she'd never given it any thought.

"Mostly they sleep in the barn. For now. That's why they're cutting more trees. Besides clearing the land and getting wood for the stoves,

Bram figured we needed to add a bunkhouse before winter. Levi and the others will work on this with Bram. Hopefully they'll have a good portion of the needed lumber together before Gus and your brothers get back from Virginia City."

Dianne nodded. "I suppose that makes sense." She looked at the material spread out on the table. "We'll have to make more mattresses."

Koko laughed. "Yes. I suppose so. There will be plenty of work for all of us. We get so few months in which to secure things before winter."

"Have you always live in this area?" Dianne questioned, forcing her hands back to work.

"My father was a white man who had a trading post up north. I grew up there with him and my mother and my brother."

"I didn't know you had a brother."

"Just one, but one is enough. He's rather wild," Koko explained.

Dianne understood. "I have a brother back in Missouri . . . well, maybe Texas. Anyway, he was always the wild one in our family."

Koko nodded. "Yes, Bram has told me about him. He is the one called Trenton."

"Yes. I miss him a great deal. We were always closer to each other than to any of the others. The twins were always together, and my little sisters were too young to understand some of our frustrations and difficulties." Dianne sighed. "We thought we had so much to worry about then." She shook her head. "We were so naïve."

"A person can only know the things they are exposed to," Koko said. "Our hardships always seem harder than anyone else's and our sorrow more deeply felt. It's the way we are."

"I suppose that makes sense." Dianne paused and stretched to ease the ache in her back. She so admired the petite Koko. She seemed so content to work with her hands and labor for the betterment of those around her. Dianne also thought her appearance so neat and orderly. Koko almost always wore her hair in two braids bound with rawhide strips. It gave her a decided Indian appearance but kept her hair under control. Unlike Dianne's wavy blond hair. No matter how much she worked with it, she always had bits of it falling before the end of the day.

In their discussions, Dianne learned that Koko's mother was of the Pikuni or Peigan tribe of the Blackfoot Confederacy. There were many tribes of Blackfoot—Bloods or Kainai, Pikuni, Siksika, and even a tribe called Blackfeet, who were still members of the larger family of Blackfoot. Some claimed the Siksika and Blackfeet were really part of one group, but others argued they were strictly separate. It was both confusing and fascinating to Dianne. She found that she wanted to know more and more about Koko's heritage.

"You mentioned that the twins will have a birthday soon," Koko said, interrupting Dianne's thoughts.

"Yes, the ninth of June. They'll be nineteen, and I don't suppose they'll stay around with us for long. Both of them crave their freedom."

"I suppose I shouldn't say this, then, but Bram has gotten them to pledge one year on the ranch."

Once again Dianne felt a sense of betrayal. Why hadn't her brothers spoken to her about this? It wasn't that they needed her approval, but she would have liked to have known their plans. "I'd love to see them stay here," she finally said.

"We need the help, that's for sure. As Bram adds more cattle, we'll have more and more trouble."

"What do you mean?" Dianne asked.

Koko looked up. "There are always problems when you double the workload or, in our case, triple it. There are bears and puma, storms and forest fires. And you can't get away from people and their desire to take things that are not rightfully theirs to take."

"What about the . . ." Dianne paused, feeling uncomfortable given Koko's family ties. "What about the Indians? Will they steal cattle?"

"If they're hungry and the cattle are handy, they will. I can't say that all Indians are trustworthy, just as I can't say all white men are trustworthy. There are tribes that are warring with the whites. The Crow are very angry at the white man for being here. Bram tells me they have killed many travelers to the east of here."

Dianne shuddered. "We were afraid of Indian attacks when we came west. The wagon master seemed to know a great deal about keeping us safe, however. He said there was no sense in antagonizing the Indians by crowding them. I guess I have to remember there are people with evil intent on both sides and that maybe the tribes are sometimes justified in their attacks."

"That's true. Before the whites starting moving west, the various tribes were fighting one another. Fighting is inevitable. Growing up with a white father and Indian mother and living at the trading post, I had quite an education in the ways of people."

"You also seem to have had a decent amount of schooling," Dianne added. "Your speech is so good, and I know you read and write."

"My mother desired for my brother and me to be able to live in the white world. She begged my father to bring in a teacher, but he always thought it foolish. He taught us a good deal and then one day an older man came from the East. He was an educated man who had gotten tired of his former life and had come west to be free. My father allowed him to stay as long as he schooled us. He agreed and for almost five years he gave us lessons every day. At least every day we were at the store."

Koko's expression took on a faraway look. "At times when my mother's people were nearby, we often went and stayed with them for weeks on end. I loved those times, and that's where I learned much about the old ways. Of course, my mother was always teaching me something. She said one day I would be a wife, and I would need to know much in order to make a good home."

"How did you meet Uncle Bram?" Dianne asked.

Koko laughed. "He was the man who came from the East. He was my teacher until my parents were killed by a raiding party of Assiniboin. After that Bram tried to help us with the trading post, but my brother had no interest. He was fifteen and wanted only to join our mother's people so that he could avenge the death of our parents. He came and went and finally two days after my twentieth birthday, he rode away for good. Bram and I married the day after that. We ran the trading post for a time; then he decided it would be better to sell it and come live here."

Dianne was stunned. She'd had no idea of how her uncle had come to marry or what he had done during his years in the West. He'd written her mother marvelous letters, but not even once had he mentioned this little family he'd taken on for his own.

"I'm glad that out here you were able to marry my uncle. They would never tolerate such things back East."

"They don't always tolerate them here either," Koko admitted. "In fact, most people would say we aren't married at all, because no Christian minister would perform the ceremony." She smiled a rather sad smile. "I hope you don't think us wrong, but we married in a Pikuni ceremony."

Dianne pondered the matter momentarily. "My father's people were English and my mother's people were Dutch. I know they didn't marry in the same ceremonies or with the same rules put on their families by the old country. My mother said as much once when we were discussing their wedding. And I'm sure very few marry in the manner that Mary and Joseph or others in the Bible would have married." She was trying to reason away any argument she could imagine by her white friends and family but knew it was probably useless. Legally they wouldn't be recognized as husband and wife. Not in a white man's world.

Later that day as evening was coming upon them, Dianne was still pondering these issues as she groomed Dolly. She tried to imagine the hardship of having a different colored skin like Faith or Koko.

"It isn't right, Dolly. People should be valued for just being people. And if two people are in love and want to marry, it shouldn't be the business of anyone else."

Dianne heard a rustling behind her and felt the skin on the back of her neck tingle. Dolly whinnied softly and moved toward her mistress. Dianne looked up quickly and whirled around to prove to herself that it was nothing more than the wind.

But she was very wrong.

Standing no more than ten feet away, a gathering of a half dozen Indian warriors watched her with expressions of great interest—even curiosity—on their faces. Dianne had no idea who they were or with which tribe they were associated. Without giving thought to what she was doing, Dianne let out a scream and climbed through the corral fence. Not bothering to look behind her, Dianne ran as fast as her legs would carry her.

CHAPTER 27

DIANNE HADN'T QUITE REACHED THE CABIN WHEN KOKO CAME bursting out the door. She held a double-barreled shotgun in her hands, and Dianne quickly dove behind her for protection. Stunned when she realized who the intruders were, Koko stopped in midstep. She looked across the yard, then back to Dianne.

Dianne peeked out from behind her and pointed to the group of leather-clad warriors making their way toward the cabin.

Koko began to laugh and lowered the gun. "Don't be afraid! That's my brother, George—or Takes-Many-Horses, as he likes to be called. The others are his Pikuni friends."

Dianne straightened and came from behind Koko as the leader of the group stepped forward. He had long black hair, braided loosely and pushed back over his shoulder. His ebony eyes scrutinized Dianne with an intensity that made her wish she could run and hide. These men were nothing like the Indians she'd seen on the plains. Those people had been either old and sickly or very young. The strength and appearance of these seven men—healthy, strong men—was quite intimidating.

"Are you on the buffalo hunt?" Koko asked.

Dianne edged away from her, trying her best to look brave. It was difficult at best, however, to look casual when facing such an impressive group.

"We aren't on the hunt," Koko's brother finally answered. "Actually, we need a place to stay tonight. I can explain it all to you later. Can you help us?"

His tone was ominous, and Dianne got the distinct impression they were in trouble. She tried to covertly study the men. They were dressed in leather, some with robes, and all held weapons.

"You can sleep in the barn. When Bram gets back I'll let him know you're here. Have you eaten?"

Takes-Many-Horses turned and said something to the men. Dianne was fascinated with the language. She'd not heard Koko speak in her native tongue even once.

One by one, the men filed off to the barn. When they'd gone, Takes-Many-Horses turned back to face his sister. "We're in trouble— the white seizers are after us."

"White seizers?" Dianne questioned without thinking.

"Soldiers," Koko said, not looking at Dianne. "What have you done to bring the army after you, George?"

Her brother looked chagrined. "Does it matter?"

Koko crossed her arms. "Yes, it matters. If you bring trouble upon this household, you'll have me to answer to. I want to know every-thing—now."

Dianne had never seen Koko so determined. The little woman was full of fire. Dianne glanced at Koko's brother, waiting to hear about his problems and why he'd suddenly appeared on the Vandyke ranch.

"We were part of a war party. We killed some white woodcutters up by the Marias." He said it so matter-of-factly that Dianne couldn't help but gasp. She took a step back, stunned by the news. Takes-Many-Horses met her gaze, his expression hard and cold. Dianne held the look, unable to do otherwise.

"Why?"

Koko's single-word question seemed so inadequate. Dianne wanted to hurl wordy diatribes at the man, but his sister merely asked why. It seemed unreasonable—illogical.

Takes-Many-Horses looked back to his sister. "It started in Fort

Benton. Some whites were angry because of some missing horses. They blamed the Pikuni, and rightfully so, but they had the wrong band. We were heading out to hunt buffalo as we do every year at this time. The whites found our camp and ambushed us there. They killed three of us and left the rest badly beaten. After that, there was no talk of peace between the whites and those responsible.

"We came upon the woodcutters and took our revenge."

"I see." Koko's voice had taken on a deadly calm. "And having blood on your hands, you come here. To stain my door and bring shame upon the man who took care of you after our loss."

"There's no shame in avenging my brothers." Takes-Many-Horses' eyes narrowed and his jaw clenched.

"Sleep in the barn and be gone in the morning," Koko told him, then turned to head into the house.

Dianne wanted to follow her, but her legs were much too heavy to move. She looked at Takes-Many-Horses, her heart pounding in fear. Would he storm after his sister and hurt her? What would Dianne do then?

To her relief, the man simply turned and headed to the barn. The minutes ticked by and he was completely out of sight by the time Dianne finally found the strength to move.

Koko prepared dinner in silence and when Bram hadn't returned by seven, the two women sat down to eat without him.

"Do you suppose Uncle Bram is in danger?" Dianne asked.

"He sometimes runs into problems. He's told me never to worry about him unless he's gone more than a week."

"A week! But a person could be . . ." She let the words go unsaid. It was obvious both women were well aware of the possibilities.

Dianne ate a few more bites before she said, "I'm sorry I made such a scene earlier. I was so afraid."

Koko shook her head. "It's all right. You didn't know anything about them. You couldn't have expected it, and I'd just told you how the Crow were murdering whites in the east. If anyone should apologize, it's me."

"Nonsense. I should have been calmer about it." Dianne tore off a piece of bread and nibbled on it thoughtfully. "Has he ... well ... has he killed before?" Dianne had never known a man who openly admitted to killing people.

Koko nodded. "It's all about being a warrior—about a war he perceives he must fight."

"But killing innocent men . . ."

"But you must understand, no white man is innocent to them. The white man has come upon their territory—their land—their herds of buffalo. The white man has taken charge and has pushed the Blackfoot from his home. The whites have killed their women and children—their old men and young. So the Blackfoot, the Crow, the Sioux—they've all declared war in their own way."

"So you see nothing wrong with what Takes-Many-Horses has done?"

Koko pushed her plate away. "It's obviously not the life I would have chosen for him, but Dianne, please do not judge him too harshly. He has been falsely accused and treated as less than a dog. Not once but many times. He cannot live in the white man's world, even though our father was white. No one there will have him because of his blood. The Pikuni accept him as our mother's son. His way is chosen for him."

Koko shook her head. "It's not so different from your war back East. Bram told me all about the fighting. He read to me from the newspaper, when he could get one. Whites fighting one another because they disagreed with the way people were living their lives. Out here the tribes fight each other for much the same reasons. In the East you had the blacks who were scorned and hated. The whites were harsh and cruel—you told me as much when you talked about your friend Faith."

Dianne knew it was true. She'd just never looked at the situation with the Indians as an honorable war. Was there any reason to hold Takes-Many-Horses and his friends any more responsible for being murderers than to charge the Union and Confederate soldiers guilty of the same thing?

Dianne didn't wish to hurt Koko, so she let the matter drop, but that night she slept very little as she thought of the men who rested in the barn. Murderers. Warriors. Men who hated whites.

The next morning, Dianne realized she'd never gone back to finish caring for Dolly. The poor horse had been left in the corral, curry comb and brush abandoned in the dirt. No doubt Dolly was unnerved by the Pikuni guests in the barn, as well, for Dianne found her pacing the ground in the corral when she came to check on the horse.

"Poor girl," Dianne said, setting aside the rifle she'd chosen to bring along. Koko might feel comfortable with her brother and his friends in the barn, but Dianne did not.

Stroking Dolly's neck, Dianne let her gaze go to the barn door. Were they gone? Were they still sleeping? She longed to know the truth but didn't want to go inside and find out for herself. So, pushing her fears aside, Dianne located the brush and comb and tried to refocus her mind on Dolly.

"You have good horse," a voice called out behind her.

Dianne turned to find one of the warriors watching her and Dolly. She stared at him for a moment, wondering what he might do next.

"I take horse," he said, folding his arms against his chest.

"Oh no you don't," Dianne declared. She marched to where the rifle leaned against the fence post and picked it up. She had no plans to shoot anyone, but the rifle made her feel more secure. "You cannot have my horse."

"It good horse—I need horse."

Diane shook her head. "No!" She nearly yelled the word.

The man moved forward and Dianne moved between him and Dolly. She jumped up on the stump of wood that Bram had purposefully left for her to use as a mounting block.

Standing on the block with her gun raised high was how the others found Dianne. Takes-Many-Horses laughed out loud at the sight and commanded the men in his Blackfoot tongue. The men left one by one, including the man who'd wanted Dolly.

"You are not afraid anymore?" Koko's brother questioned.

Dianne gave a nervous laugh. "I'm terrified. Right down to my toes. But you won't take my horse. She's become a good friend to me." As if to stress this, Dolly came up alongside Dianne and nuzzled her gently.

"What is your name?" he asked, relaxing his stance.

"Dianne. Dianne Chadwick. Bram Vandyke is my uncle."

"Well, I will call you Stands-Tall-Woman," Takes-Many-Horses declared with a wry grin. "You are a very fine woman." He turned with that and left, marching off toward the forest to join his friends.

Dianne waited for several minutes before climbing down. She took in a deep breath and let it out slowly. She thought of how her brothers wanted her back in Missouri. At least in Missouri she wouldn't have to worry about invasions by tribal warriors.

That afternoon, Bram and Levi showed up. One of the mares had foaled the night before. She'd had trouble and Levi had just happened upon her in the nick of time.

"They're both doing fine now," Bram told his wife and niece. "Shouldn't be any more problems, but Levi is going to help me keep an eye on them."

"George was here while you were gone," Koko said, following her husband into the house. Dianne decided to go with them. She was anxious to hear what Koko would tell Bram and how Bram would react if Koko divulged all of the details.

"Would you like me to fix you something to eat?" Koko asked.

Bram sat down to take off his boots. "Nah, I just want to wash up and get some sleep. I ate plenty with the boys. They packed enough for an army. Now tell me about George. Why was he here?"

"He's in trouble. The soldiers are chasing him and his friends. They killed some woodcutters up near the Marias River."

Bram tossed his boot aside. "Why?"

Dianne stood listening to the exchange as though they were discussing a wayward child who'd broken the neighbor's window. Uncle Bram didn't seem at all unnerved or angered at this news.

Koko relayed the entire story, then added, "I made them leave this morning. I told them not to come back if it meant the soldiers would be right behind them. I told them they weren't to bring trouble upon us."

Bram nodded. "It won't go well for them. This thing of Indians killing whites is going to stir up more and more difficulty for them. The government is already at odds with them and it wouldn't take that much for someone to get a wild hair and suggest that all the tribes be locked up—put away where they can't hurt whites anymore."

Dianne couldn't help herself. "Would they actually do that, Uncle Bram?"

"I'm afraid it's already going on." Bram yawned. "We'll talk more about this after I get some sleep."

If her uncle and Koko did have a further discussion about Takes-Many-Horses, Dianne was not privy to it. Two weeks later her brothers and Cole returned, along with fifty head of Texas longhorns, five draught horses, and a new wagon loaded to the brink with supplies.

"Well, you're a sight for sore eyes," Bram declared. Gus dismounted and came to greet his boss.

"I've brought you three more boys to help. I figured with building the bunkhouse, we could probably use them."

"What did you tell them we'd pay?" Bram asked, watching as the men drove the cattle on past the main yard and into the largest of three corrals.

"Told 'em room and board to begin with," Gus admitted. "Figured we'd know after a month or two whether they were worth wasting cash on."

Bram gave a deep, boisterous laugh and slapped Gus on the back. "You always know the right thing to do."

"They were desperate enough—been a long time since any of them ate decent. They didn't appear to be drinkers, either, so I figured them to be a good risk."

That night Bram invited Cole and Gus to join the family for supper. Dianne was happy about the arrangement but couldn't really explain why. She knew she would enjoy hearing all about the trip, but her brothers could have just as easily told her about it and left Cole relegated to supper with the rest of the boys.

Cole looked a bit browner than when he'd departed, but it was the weary expression on his face and the sorrow in his eyes that drew Dianne's attention. Perhaps that's why she wanted him to join them for the evening meal. He seemed so lost. So completely left out.

"The ladies had a bit of excitement while we were gone," Bram began, pausing only long enough to light one of his favorite cigars. "Koko's brother and a band of Pikuni warriors came to the ranch."

"What happened?" Zane questioned. Dianne knew he'd been keeping up as best he could with the Indian conflicts on the plains. Indian problems of any kind interested the young man.

"They pert near scared your sister half to death for one thing," Bram explained. Dianne felt her cheeks grow hot. She knew Koko had probably shared all the details of her screaming escapade. "She handled herself well, however," Bram continued. "When one of the warriors declared he would take her horse for his own, our little Dianne grabbed a rifle and made her stand on the mounting block. Waving the gun and her fist like that abolitionist John Brown, she told him in no uncertain terms that he would not take her horse."

Everyone except Dianne burst into laughter at this. "I did not shake my fist at him," she said defensively. This only caused everyone to laugh all the harder. Even Cole couldn't keep from chuckling. Finally she couldn't help but join in their amusement.

"My brother gave her a new name," Koko said as the laughter died down. "He called her Stands-Tall-Woman."

"He probably should have called her Bluffing Woman," Zane said, shaking his head. "I can't imagine she would have ever had the gumption to shoot anyone—even for Dolly."

"You might be surprised what this little gal can do when she sets her mind to it," Bram said proudly.

"I don't doubt it," Cole said, winking at Dianne in support. He pushed back from his plate. "I'd best take my leave. I'll be heading out early in the morning."

"You aren't staying?" Koko asked.

"No, ma'am. I promised I'd get back to town. My father has some business he wants to discuss—said it was urgent."

Dianne straightened and squared her shoulders. She wanted to ask him a million questions but said nothing. How could she ask with everyone else sitting there watching—listening?

Cole got to his feet. "Good night."

Dianne watched him go, fighting the urge to run after him and demand information. Why was he going back to his father? It was completely unfair to tell her that his father had killed his intended, then never allow her to know why or what had happened.

———

Cole hated the very sight of Virginia City—even more so the mining claim where he and his father had worked to make their fortune. There were fewer people here now but more makeshift equipment. With gold being harder to find, many of the whites had moved on. Now quite a few workers were of Asian descent. It was the way of things, Cole had been told. The Chinese were forever coming in behind the impatient whites. They seemed not to mind taking up the leavings of others. They made out well enough for themselves, Cole surmised, noting the improvements.

Of course, there were no improvements when it came to his father's claim. It was still the same rundown shack they'd traded their tent for. Securing his horse, Cole didn't even bother to knock on the door of the rickety building. A stiff breeze might well topple the thing over. What would an angry knock do?

Hallam Selby turned from the small tin stove where he was pouring himself a cup of coffee. "Cole! I didn't expect you back so soon."

Cole strode across the room. "I couldn't see putting this off any longer. What do you want from me?"

"Would you like a cup of coffee?" His father held up the pot.

"No," Cole said, taking up a chair. He turned it around backward and mounted it as he would a horse. "I don't have a lot of time. I want to know what was so all-fired important that I had to come. You said it was a matter of life and death."

"And it is," his father declared. He brought his cup of coffee to the table and took his seat opposite Cole. "I've done a lot of thinking since you've been gone. I know you hate me, and I don't rightly blame you, but I want to state my case, and for once I want you to hear me out. If you still want nothing to do with me after that, then I won't bother you again."

Cole had no desire to hear anything his father had to say, but he figured there was little choice. "Say your piece."

His father nodded. "I never meant for anything bad to happen to that girl."

"Carrie."

"Yes, Carrie. I never thought it would come to that or that innocent blood would be spilled. There isn't a day that goes by that I don't think of my own girls and how I'd feel if someone . . . if someone . . ."

"Cut them down in cold blood?" Cole filled in.

Hallam nodded. "I never meant to take her life, but I'm guilty as charged. I can't bring Carrie back. I would give my life in exchange if I could."

"Well, that's an easy enough thing to say since you know there's no chance of it," Cole said in disgust. "Are you done yet?"

"Show me some respect, boy. I tolerate your attitude because I know if I were in your boots, I'd probably say even worse—maybe do worse. The truth is, I want your forgiveness. I recently started going to the Methodist church in town, and the pastor there spoke to me and made me see that without God, I'm nothing."

Cole refrained from saying that in his mind Hallam Selby was already relegated to that category. He seethed at the suggestion that he should offer his father forgiveness. The man deserved nothing.

"I want to go back to Topeka and make things right with your mother but not without making things right with you."

Cole stood up. "You can't make things right with me, so forget it."

Hallam toyed with his cup, staring at the contents. "I'd like you to come with me. I'd like us to make a new start as a family."

Cole balled his fists but kept his arms at his sides. "I'm not going anywhere with you. So you got a case of conscience. So what? What possible difference can that make to me? God may forgive and forget, but God isn't the one who planned to marry Carrie. God isn't the one who cradled her as she breathed her last." Cole stormed off toward the door, then halted and spun around. "God may forgive and forget, but I can't. Not now—not ever."

Guilt ate at Cole's heart as he mounted his horse. Turning the beast for town, Cole knew he should go back and apologize. He knew he should forgive his father; after all, it was an accident. Still, the thought lingered in his mind that it would never have happened had his father and friends not taken the law into their own hands. Carrie would still be alive if they would have just left well enough alone.

"Carrie," he whispered. But Cole realized he felt very little. Time had dulled the aching in his heart and stilled the memories of better days.

He couldn't even remember what she looked like—not wholly. Her image had faded a little more with each passing month, and in its place came the outline of a vivacious blond whose eyes seemed to pierce his very soul.

"Dianne."

He straightened in the saddle as a wash of determination came over him. "I won't do it," he declared. "I won't love her. I won't see her again. If I have to go all the way to Texas, I won't put myself in a position where I have to deal with her again."

CHAPTER 28

MAY WAS A MONTH OF CHANGE IN MONTANA. IT COULD BE LOVELY and warm one day and bring six inches of snow the next. In the three years since leaving Missouri to come west, Dianne Chadwick had also done a good deal of changing.

Washing up the breakfast dishes, Dianne considered her life in Montana. She was now nineteen years old. It seemed as though a lifetime of events had taken place since coming to her uncle's ranch. The ranch itself bore witness of that. Dianne could see that this much was true from the window of the newly added kitchen.

When they'd first arrived on the ranch they were blessed to have a nice-sized barn and three corrals. Now they had two barns—one having become a stable and smithy for their growing herd of horses. The other had been given over to the milk cows with an extension added off the side for a chicken coop.

Beside this, there were bigger corrals and two small bunkhouses. Bram hadn't stopped there. He'd added a porch onto the cabin so that Koko could work outside even when it rained. She hated being cooped up, especially now as she faced the final days of her first pregnancy.

Dianne could hardly wait for the birth of the baby. The house needed children. She needed children. In the years since losing her sisters, Dianne had come to realize that children had a way of looking at life that cheered the soul. What frightened Dianne about the arrival of Koko's baby, however, was that there would be no midwife—no other person to help with the delivery. Koko had been training Dianne, telling her what would happen and what she would need to do to help, but the task seemed overwhelming. This was a matter of life and death, and Dianne had no idea of whether she was up to the challenge.

Of course, Uncle Bram and the twins would be here. Dianne had been pleasantly surprised that Zane and Morgan had chosen to stay on with Bram for so long. However, Zane had again been dropping hints that he might sign on with the army to fight the Indian wars, while Morgan was fascinated by everything he could read about Lewis and Clark's expedition to the Pacific Northwest.

They're grown men, she reminded herself. *Grown men who deserve to live their lives, marry, and start families. They certainly aren't going to be able to do that here. At least not find wives. They'll need to go elsewhere, and then there's always the chance they won't come back.*

The idea of losing them hurt Dianne, but no more than the loss of Trenton. In three years' time there had been only two letters. One from Omaha, where he wrote to tell of how he'd nearly been killed by a group of cutthroats when he tried to rescue a saloon girl. The woman nursed him back to health, charging him nothing and taking no pay from him. The second letter came from Texas. Trenton told her the bitter cold in Nebraska had driven him south and that once he got headed in that direction, he just kept going. He'd seen the Gulf of Mexico and had been quite impressed. For three weeks he'd slept out on the beach, falling asleep every night to the sound of the water crashing upon the shore. Dianne thought the idea very appealing and wondered if she might someday see the ocean.

Trenton had been sorry to hear about the death of his mother and sisters. He'd been sympathetic about the way Dianne had been forced to grow up so quickly and wondered if she'd found a man to settle down with and raise a family.

Dianne had to smile at that memory. She washed the last of the coffee cups, then set to drying the entire load. Toweling off the plates, she couldn't help but think of the men Uncle Bram now had working for him. Of course there was Levi, and he seemed ever interested in Dianne, but the truth was she had no desire to return his feelings. The other men were kind and considerate—Uncle Bram would have had it no other way. But while they were respectable and often made her laugh, Dianne had room for only one man in her heart.

"Are you daydreaming?" Koko asked as she came from her bedroom.

Dianne smiled. "I suppose I am. I've been thinking about my life here—about coming west and all that's happened." She put the dishtowel down and pulled out a chair at the table. "How are you feeling?"

"Tired, but I think the baby will come soon, so I'm trying to save my strength."

Dianne bit her lower lip and turned away. "Would you like some tea?" She reached for one of the clean cups.

"I know you're worried, but don't be. We'll do fine. I've watched my mother's people give birth. God will bring us through this."

Dianne came to where Koko sat and took the chair beside her. Reaching out to take hold of Koko's soft brown hands, Dianne spoke. "I know God will bring us through. I feel the truth in that. I just feel so inadequate to the task. What if I do something wrong and end up causing you more pain or even hurting you?"

"Trusting God requires walking forward into the unseen places," Koko said, her black brows rising as she shrugged. "We can't avoid what will come. Babies won't be put off. So no matter what our fears might be, we cannot change things now."

Dianne considered her words and nodded. "I'll try to be as helpful to you as I can."

Koko squeezed her hand. "I know you will. We are sisters now—time and love has made it so."

"Yes," Dianne said, meeting the woman's warm gaze. "We are sisters."

Koko got to her feet and pressed her hand against her swollen abdomen. "I think the baby will come by nightfall."

Dianne felt all of her calm diminish. "By nightfall? You said soon, but I didn't think you meant today." There was an edge of hysteria to Dianne's tone and she fought to keep it down.

Koko patted Dianne's shoulder. "I didn't want to frighten you. My pains started in the night and my water passed this morning. Now the pains are getting stronger."

"How can you just stand there and tell me this?" Dianne questioned. "Come on, let's get you to bed."

Koko laughed but allowed Dianne to help her. "Lying about waiting for the baby is not the way of the real people. My mother was making a buffalo robe when my brother decided to be born. I remember it. She put the robe aside, then gathered her birthing tools and had my brother."

"You must have been quite young," Dianne said, leaving Koko's side to pull down the covers of the bed.

"I was only three, but I remember it well."

Koko sat on the edge of the bed while Dianne fetched her night-gown. "I'll help you get this on, then gather the things we'll need. Should I send someone for Uncle Bram?"

"No. He has his work and I have mine. He'll be here soon enough."

Dianne put Koko to bed despite the woman's protests. A woman having a baby deserved to do it in the comfort of her own bed, Dianne believed. After all, it was hard work, and rest would not come easy.

Koko napped throughout the afternoon and into early evening. When the men returned from their chores, Dianne had supper ready but shooed them all outside to enjoy it in the great outdoors.

"We don't need you fellas underfoot," Dianne declared. "We have important work to do."

Bram seemed stunned to be put out of his own house, but then he laughed at her bossy attitude. "You'll make a good wife someday," he teased. "Or else a good trail boss."

Dianne didn't take offense at his joke. She smiled and handed him his plate. "If we need you, we'll call." He went without protest.

Dianne came back inside and drew up hot water from the stove. Koko had explained they would need it for cleaning up. When she brought it to the room, Dianne nearly dropped it at the door. She found Koko squatted on the floor at the end of the bed, bearing down for all she was worth.

"What are you doing?" Dianne questioned, her tone almost accusing.

"Having the baby," Koko said between gritted teeth.

And then before Dianne could ask her anything more, Koko gave birth to a squalling baby boy. The baby's lusty cry brought Bram from outside. He respected the closed door but called out, "Boy or girl?"

"It's a boy," Dianne declared.

Bram gave a loud whoop and yelled, "It's a boy!"

Koko gave a laugh that sounded more like a moan. "He told me it would be a boy."

"Well, I wonder what he would have done if he'd been a girl—sent her back?" Dianne said, washing the baby gently with warm water.

The baby calmed and looked up at Dianne with wide dark eyes. She couldn't help but smile. "Aren't you a wonder?" Something inside Dianne came alive in that moment. The softness of the baby's skin, the delicate structure of his little body . . . it was all so appealing—so marvelous.

Hours after James Nicolaas Vandyke's birth, Dianne sat on the porch, rocking. Thoughts of the baby and his birth were still heavy on her mind. She longed for a family of her own—for a husband to care for and share her life with. She longed for Cole Selby to return.

How can I feel this way about him when I know he cares nothing for me? How can I spend the rest of my life wondering what it would be like to share his life and love?

She hadn't seen him since that day in May two years earlier. There was no way to know where he'd gone or what he was doing. Uncle Bram had offered him a job, but he'd refused and that had been the end of it. Cole had gone back to Virginia City to meet his father, and Dianne had never seen him again.

Gazing out across the moonlit valley to the snow-capped mountains, Dianne tried not to think of her misery. A new life had just come into the household—there was no reason for sorrow. In fact, there was no reason to continue pining over Cole Selby. If Dianne wanted a husband and family, then she needed to put Cole out of her mind and heart and redirect her attention elsewhere.

"That's a mighty fine boy you helped bring into the world," Uncle Bram said as he came to sit beside Dianne.

"None better." Dianne grinned at the beaming look of pride on her uncle's face.

"So why are you out here all by your lonesome?"

"I've just been thinking. Little Jamie is so sweet, so special."

"Jamie, is it?" Bram said, rubbing his chin.

"I hope you don't mind. James sounded much too grown-up for such a little guy."

"I like Jamie. It's got a good ring to it."

"I'm sure Mama would have been pleased that you gave him Grandfather Nicolaas's name as well. You know my brother Trenton has the same middle name."

"Yes, I recall that now. Our father was a fine man and he deserves the honor," Uncle Bram said thoughtfully.

"You're a fine man too. I want to thank you for letting us come to live with you. I love it here. I love this ranch and the land. I love working with the animals. But most of all, I love you and Koko. Losing Mama and Papa was so hard, but you've made that much easier to handle."

"I'm glad you're here. Koko loves you so. I've often wanted to thank you for being so kind to her. She's got such a gentle heart. I knew your mother would break it over and over, and I just couldn't let that happen."

"I don't blame you," Dianne said softly, remembering her mother's anger. "I think Mama was afraid—afraid of what she didn't understand or know to be familiar."

"Yes, I believe you're right. Susannah never did abide those who were different. Be they people with skin of a different color or people of higher means or lesser."

"But she loved you, Uncle Bram. No doubting that. She used to talk about you all the time. Your letters were like cold water on a hot day."

"I loved her too. I'm sorry we parted on bad terms. I never meant to hurt her, and I feel responsible for what happened." He paused for a moment, as if seeking the right words. "I don't know if you will understand this or not, but when a man marries, I believe he owes his allegiance to his wife. I believe that's what God calls us to do—calls us to leave our mother and father—or sisters, for that matter. Your ma wanted me to put Koko aside, to hold my blood family in higher esteem. I couldn't do that. It wouldn't have been fitting in the eyes of God. I hope one day you'll understand and forgive me."

"There's nothing to forgive, Uncle Bram. I already understand, and I can only hope that I will one day find a man as loving and devoted as you."

Bram leaned forward and grew serious. "Promise me something."

"If I can."

"Promise that if anything happens to me, you'll be there for Koko and James."

"Of course," she said, not understanding his concern. "They're family now and family endures together."

Bram let out a heavy sigh. "I just need to know that you won't let them . . . well . . . that they won't have to resort to . . . going back to the Pikuni."

Dianne shook her head. "No, not unless Koko honestly felt that was better. But why would she? She'll have this wonderful ranch and the new house you plan to build her."

Bram said nothing, so Dianne took the opportunity to ask him a favor in return. "I'd like to go to Virginia City with you next week. If you aren't worried about Koko being here without me, I'd appreciate getting to come along."

"I think that can be arranged. It has been a long time since you've been away from here. Do you miss the big cities back East?"

Dianne chuckled. "Not really. Sometimes I miss the convenience, but nothing more. I love my life here. I can't imagine ever wanting to live anywhere else. I hope, if and when I find a man to marry me, that he'll be content to remain right here. In fact, maybe I'll find a man in

Virginia City. One who will work for you and show an interest in me all at the same time."

"In case you haven't noticed, missy, I've got a whole crew of men who'd do nothing but show you interest if you gave them the time of day."

Dianne laughed and got to her feet. "I've looked that herd over, Uncle Bram. There's nothing there that strikes my fancy."

Bram stood and gave Dianne a gentle hug. "Then we'll go looking elsewhere. If you find one that fits the bill, we'll bring him home and get him molded into shape."

Dianne leaned up on tiptoe as Bram bent down. Kissing him gently on the cheek, Dianne whispered a prayer of thanks for her uncle's love.

"I love you, Uncle Bram."

"And I love you, darlin'. Now you'd best get to bed. We're gonna start working with that sorrel gelding in the morning, and I know you want to be a part of that."

"Absolutely. I'll see you in the morning." Dianne headed into the house, the trip to Virginia City rapidly overrunning her thoughts. *I'll put flowers on Mama's grave, and I'll look into buying some more fabric. Then I'll find me a husband of first-rate quality.*

CHAPTER 29

Virginia City had grown some in buildings and civility, but to Dianne it seemed that the population had diminished considerably. She couldn't help but wonder if the lure of goldfields farther north had robbed the territorial capital of its residents. It was to be expected, she thought. After all, most of the people had wandered in from the California goldfields, restless and desperate to find that place where they might get rich easily—without ever having to work for it. It seemed only natural that they should wander once again after learning that the tales weren't true.

The stories Dianne had heard on the trail west had been enough to keep people entertained for hours. The very idea of picking up nuggets the size of your fist had people changing their destinations from Oregon to Montana in a heartbeat.

"Looks like they've gone and got citified," Bram mused as he eased the wagon along Wallace Street. "Less of the riffraff in the streets to be sure, although I see they've added a new saloon."

Sitting beside her uncle, Dianne looked left and right, taking in the sights and making mental comparisons. He was right. The streets seemed much more orderly, and there were many lovely clapboard homes, homes that certainly hadn't been there when she had lived in town.

"Looks like the sawmill is doing a booming business," Morgan said, seeming to note the focus of Dianne's thoughts. Zane and Morgan had accompanied them, Zane to get information regarding army enlistment and Morgan to hear all the news that could be had about the territory.

"We'd best check out the hotel and see if we can get some rooms," Bram said. He then motioned to the back of the wagon. "I know you're anxious to get those flowers on your mother's grave, so why don't you go ahead on up to the cemetery and I'll take care of the hotel."

Dianne nodded. "Should I take the wagon or ride Dolly?"

"The road's pretty steep. I'd take Dolly if I were you. You boys go with her so she's not alone."

Zane and Morgan nodded. "We'd figured to pay our respects," Zane added.

"Good. Then I won't worry about our girl. Who knows what kind of ruffians she might run into." Dianne wasn't all that concerned. The town seemed much calmer than when she'd lived here and spent considerable time by herself. "You boys go on down to the livery and let them know what we'll need."

"Sure thing, Uncle Bram." They turned their horses in unison and headed to the stable.

Uncle Bram pulled the wagon up in front of the hotel. "I'll check on whether they have any rooms available while you get Dolly saddled," he told Dianne as he helped her down from the wagon.

Dianne went immediately to work, hoisting her saddle from the back of the wagon as if it were no heavier than a picnic basket. She'd grown strong over the past years. She was able to do a great many things that she'd found impossible when they'd first arrived. Saddling her own horse was just one of them.

"They have plenty of space," Bram announced, coming back just as Dianne was gathering up the wildflowers she'd picked for her mother's grave. "You go ahead, and when you come back, just ask for your room. It'll adjoin the room the boys and I will share."

Dianne took up Dolly's reins. "We won't be long. I'm getting pretty hungry, so I'm betting the boys are feeling fairly done in. I notice the hotel also has an eatery; do you suppose it would be all right to get our supper there tonight?"

Bram grinned. "I had the same thought myself. How about you see to your delivery, then come back and wash up. I'll let them know we'll be planning on a meal posthaste." He glanced down the road. "Ah, good. Here come Zane and Morgan."

Dianne mounted Dolly. "Come on, boys, we'd best get to it."

They rode to the cemetery, commenting about the town and all its changes. Dianne found the place a bit more appealing than when they'd lived there, but only marginally. There still weren't any trees of substance, although it appeared several folks had planted small saplings in the hopes of regrowing the forest that had once surrounded the town.

The tiny cemetery was nestled up in the hills north of town. The roads there were indeed steep and not very accommodating. Dolly, as surefooted as ever, handled the trip easily, however, and Dianne had little trouble keeping her seat and balancing the flowers across her lap.

"It's such a lonely place," Morgan said as they approached the collection of graves.

"Yes, but the view is quite impressive from this high up," Dianne said as she dismounted. Dolly whinnied softly as if agreeing. Dianne dropped Dolly's reins, knowing the mare would not wander. Dianne had worked hard for two years to teach Dolly this was her signal to stay put. The mare had learned quite well.

Morgan and Zane, taking the hats from their heads, remained mounted and quiet as Dianne took the flowers to their mother's grave. She brushed away the bits of debris and noted that the new headstone, ordered on their previous fall trip, had been put into place.

"It looks nice, doesn't it?" Dianne asked, looking to her brothers.

"It looks good," Zane murmured and Morgan nodded in agreement. Both seemed most uncomfortable with their task.

Dianne took pity on the boys. She placed the flowers at the foot of the stone and whispered a prayer before climbing back atop Dolly. The wind picked up and blew her wide-brimmed hat from her head, but the loose rawhide straps under her chin kept it from going any farther than her back. Wisps of blond hair blew delicately across Dianne's face.

She sighed and looked down across the town. "I guess we'd best head back."

They moved back down the hill at a leisurely pace. Dianne wanted to say something more, but she didn't. The twins remained silent as well. It was as if a door had so completely closed on that part of their lives that they had no desire to reopen it. Dianne wondered if they felt guilty over what had happened. They'd never talked about it. Never once since their mother had died.

"You know," she began, "I think in spite of all that happened, losing the girls and Mama, it was still right to come west."

The boys said nothing, so she continued. "I used to feel really guilty about Mama dying, but I came to realize that everything is in God's timing. I can't keep a person alive if the Lord is calling her home. And I can't change things once everything is said and done."

"But sometimes it's hard to understand God doing things like He does," Morgan said. "I can't say that I'd do it all over again if I had the chance. I might have come on my own, but I would never have voted for bringing you girls."

"Me either," Zane said in a barely audible voice. "Montana doesn't seem like a good place for women."

"Well, I beg to differ with you," Dianne said. "I feel like Montana is a home I never knew. It feels right living here, and I'll be just as content to die here as well."

They reached the hotel and the boys took the horses to the livery while Dianne made her way inside. Someday she'd show the twins that Montana was the perfect place for her. She wasn't sure what it would take to convince them, but she'd show them.

"I'm Dianne Chadwick. My uncle arranged a room for me," she said in greeting to the hotel clerk. "His name is Bram Vandyke."

The clerk, probably ten years her senior, smiled and leaned forward. "He did indeed, but he didn't tell me what a purty young thing you were. Are you married?"

Dianne knew that for every available woman in Montana, there were at least fifty bachelors lined up to court her. She didn't want to hurt the man's feelings, but he definitely did not fit her idea of husband material.

"No, but I am in a hurry to wash up and get something to eat." She smiled and added, "So if you'd give me the key and direct me to my room, I'd be much obliged."

The clerk looked at her for a moment, as if trying to decide if it was worth his trouble to try sweet-talking her again. Apparently he figured her to be determined. He reached behind him to the cubby box and pulled the key out for her room.

"Do you need help with your things?" he asked, his tone sounding hopeful.

"No, my uncle should have seen to my bag. Besides, my two brothers are right behind me. They'll bring anything we've forgotten."

He nodded but looked very disappointed.

Dianne hurried to her room and unlocked the door to find that Uncle Bram had already opened the door between the two rooms. Her bag was on the floor at the foot of her bed and the draperies had been pulled back to let in the light.

"Uncle Bram?" she called, peering around the adjoining door.

"I'm here. Just washing this grime off my neck." He was bent over the washbasin, water dripping from his neck and beard.

"I'd probably better do the same," Dianne said. "Give me a few minutes and I'll be ready."

She closed the door between the rooms and went to her bag. Pulling out a fresh blouse, she bemoaned all the wrinkles. For all her care, there was very little she could do on the trail to keep herself neat and orderly. Koko had told her that's why buckskin was so nice, and in truth, the jacket Koko had made for Dianne from doeskin needed a dusting but otherwise looked just fine.

Dampening the blouse a bit helped to pull some of the wrinkles out, but it still wasn't to Dianne's liking. She quickly rid herself of the blouse she'd worn on the trail, however, and after washing up, donned the new blouse, wrinkles and all. She was just combing out her hair when a knock sounded on the adjoining door.

"Come in," she called.

"Are you ready yet, sis? I'm famished."

It was Morgan, and he looked at her with such a hangdog expression that Dianne had to laugh. "I'm ready." She took up a rawhide strip and tied her hair back in a loose tail at the nape of her neck. "I won't even bother to pin my hair up," she declared as she joined her brother. "I wouldn't want to be accused of starving you to death."

They found seats in the small hotel eatery and ordered the beef stew and biscuits. The meal was quickly laid before them, along with hot coffee that Dianne found much too strong for her liking.

"I've already heard some news," Bram said as they dug into their meal. "The hotel clerk told me the town is looking to get itself federal patent. That will require resurveying the city boundaries. Don't know how long it will take, but they think it necessary with the growing number of people moving to the territory."

"But there are fewer people here now than before," Dianne said. "At least it appears that way."

"Well, granted, a lot of the miners have moved on, but the city fathers are hoping to draw in folks who will stick around and not be given over to leaving every time a new strike is discovered."

"Well, after supper, I intend to go see what I can find out about joining the army," Zane announced.

Dianne opened her mouth to speak but instead found a familiar voice offering a greeting.

"Evening, Mr. Vandyke, Zane, Morgan." Cole Selby paused as Dianne looked up to meet his eyes. "Miss Chadwick."

"Cole! It's good to see you," Bram said as he stood up and shook his hand. "How are you faring? We haven't heard from you in . . . what . . . two years?"

"I guess at least that," Cole admitted.

"Are you here for supper? If so, why don't you join us?"

"I wouldn't want to intrude."

"Nonsense. Pull up a chair."

Dianne listened to the exchange, never once saying a word. Cole looked a bit thinner, his hair a little longer, but he was still the same handsome man. She swallowed hard but felt like her mouth had turned to cotton. She thought of her ambition to come to Virginia City to find a man who might have the potential to be her husband. Here she was face to face with the only man who'd ever caused her thoughts to go in that direction, yet he apparently had never been inclined to think like-wise toward Dianne.

Cole did as Bram instructed and positioned himself between Morgan and Zane. "Have you been in town for long?" he asked, his gaze once again going to Dianne.

"No. We just pulled in. Needed to come for a few more supplies and to find some men who might like to work for me."

"I'd like to be considered for that job," Cole said, surprising Dianne so much that she gave the tiniest gasp.

Everyone looked to her as if she were choking. "I'm sorry," she man-aged to say. "That was rude, but I must say I was surprised."

"I am too," Bram declared. "I always told you I'd hire you back on in a heartbeat, so what made you stay here in Virginia City, knowing I'd give you a job?"

Cole looked to the table and shook his head. "I haven't always been right here in Virginia City. But either way, I guess I figured you would have forgotten about that by now or else had enough men to help."

They paused the conversation long enough for Cole to put in his order for food and coffee, and then Bram immediately started in again. "Do you have any friends who might like a job? They'd need to be dependable and not given to just hanging on until the next strike."

"I might know some," Cole said, his expression thoughtful. "I figure there might be three or four who could give you an honest day's work."

"I'd like to meet them. Could you bring them by here tomorrow morning?"

Cole nodded. "Sure. If that's what you want."

A small man who reminded Dianne of Percy Showalter served Cole his supper, then offered more coffee to Bram and the boys. Dianne thought about asking for tea but decided against it. She didn't want Cole to think she was less than capable of bucking up under the circumstances. She didn't know why his good opinion mattered to her, but it did.

As they ate, she thought of all the time that had passed since she'd last seen Cole. How often she had watched the horizon, hoping he might return to the Vandyke ranch. She'd even prayed he might come back, but to no avail. Yet here he was now. Sitting there eating and talking as if no more than a day had passed.

"So what news have you heard?" Bram asked Cole.

"Well, there's Indian troubles aplenty on the plains. A company called the Union Pacific is trying to put in a railroad from Omaha—it's going to be part of the rail system that goes all the way to the Pacific. When it's finished it will allow travel from the East Coast to the West."

"That will be a wondrous thing," Bram said, shaking his head. "I remember how tedious and long the trip can be."

"Well, the tribes aren't taking kindly to their land being infringed upon. They're afraid the railroad will drive the buffalo away, as well as any other food source. They also understand the rails will bring a permanency to the relocation of whites to the territories and states involved. They're causing no end to problems. They've been murdering surveyors and wreaking havoc with supplies."

"I'm sure it's hard to face the coming changes," Bram replied sadly. "We knew it was coming, though. Koko's father and I talked about it on many an occasion years ago. I suppose I'm just as guilty with my ranch and cattle, but the changes will come with or without me. I might as well benefit if I can and benefit those I love." He smiled at Dianne in particular.

Cole looked again at Dianne, searching her face as if trying to learn something from her expression. She met his gaze, holding it for a moment before her uncle broke the spell.

"What of the Indian problems here in the territory? Have you heard anything new on those?"

Cole nodded. "Had you heard about John Bozeman getting killed?"

Bram shook his head. "No, I'd not heard a thing about him since he got that town started east of the Madison Range."

"Rumor has it that he and his companion were attacked by five Peigan. Mr. Bozeman was murdered and his friend shot."

Dianne looked at her uncle, remembering Koko's brother, Takes-Many-Horses. No one had heard from the young man in two years. Not since he'd shown up at the ranch after he and his friends had killed a group of woodcutters on the Marias. She couldn't help but wonder if Takes-Many-Horses was also responsible for the attack on Bozeman.

"Folks are clamoring for a real fort instead of that local militia post Governor Meagher set up. They don't feel safe. Rumor has it the Blackfoot will make an alliance with the Sioux and Cheyenne and begin a large-scale war."

"I thought maybe we'd have some peace since they closed down Bozeman's trail."

Zane had perked up considerably at the talk of the fort. "Has word come as to whether they'll get approval for the fort?"

Cole shook his head. "No. As I hear it, President Johnson doesn't take Governor Meagher seriously. Apparently our governor is always firing off telegrams to the president. Explaining the impending doom. But no one believes him."

"But what about the Fetterman Massacre?" Zane questioned. "Captain Fetterman and his entire command were killed last December by Red Cloud and his Sioux. Surely that proves a threat."

Cole shook his head and pushed back his bowl. "They don't see it that way, as I hear tell. The Fetterman Massacre took place near Fort Phil Kearny, hundreds of miles away. Bozeman was killed just east of Livingston, but the circumstances are suspect."

"Why do you say that?" Bram questioned.

Dianne could still not get past the idea that Koko's brother, with his dark brooding eyes and casual admittance of murder, might very well have had something to do with this attack.

"Bozeman's friend Thomas Cover stated that they were come upon by several Indians whom Bozeman at first believed to be friendly Crow."

Dianne finally spoke. "But I thought the Crow were hostile to whites."

"Actually, some of the Crow have settled down to a friendly, even helpful, relationship with the whites. Since they have essentially closed down Bozeman Trail, they seem to feel the white man capable of goodness. However, that may not last long. I've heard there are plans to put all of the Indians on reservations—Crow included."

Dianne looked to Bram, wondering what it might mean for their family. Surely Koko and little Jamie wouldn't be forced away from them. Koko was half white and Jamie was three-quarters. Would it matter to the government that they had lived as whites? Or would it be no better than the way the blacks were treated with their rule of a single drop of Negro blood constituting them to be black? Koko and Bram's marriage wasn't legitimate in the eyes of the law. What would happen to them?

CHAPTER 30

The years had hardened Trenton Chadwick. He'd lived a fast and furious life, gambling to keep himself well fed and clothed, avoiding confrontation wherever possible to keep himself alive.

Thoughts of his life in New Madrid were little more than hazy memories as the months away became years. With the war over, a sense of euphoria was spreading. People were daring to dream again—to hope in the future. The influx of wagons moving west brought more and more settlers to the lonely plains, while progress on the transcontinental railroad promised them a means of rapid travel for the future.

Coming back to Omaha hadn't really been Trenton's plan, but it suited his needs well enough. He rode down the dusty street that Fourth of July morning remembering his previous times here. Grimacing, Trenton couldn't help but remember the beating he'd taken on account of Annabelle, the saloon girl. He'd thought to look her up at the Looloo Saloon, then decided against it. Why bother? She probably wasn't even working there anymore—girls like Annabelle had a penchant for moving around.

Hunger drove him to the first restaurant he could find. A placard outside the door promised they had the best beefsteaks in town. Trenton dismounted and looked around for a moment. The town's growth was evident. Omaha bore an atmosphere that spoke more than ever of change and post-war prosperity. They were apparently not at all hindered by the fact the government had been arguing for months to move the capital south. Statehood had energized them and whether they retained the capital or not, Omaha was slated for expansion.

Trenton secured his mount, dusted off his clothes, then made his way to the eatery, still managing a sidewise glance down the boardwalk at the bevy of new stores. New stores meant new money. Who could tell how profitable this trip might turn out to be.

He was shown to a table by a middle-aged woman clad in black from neck to toe. She greeted Trenton with a forced smile.

"Good day, sir."

Trenton took his seat, noting a full table of gentlemen to his left and a moony-eyed couple on his right. "What's your special?"

The woman sighed as if annoyed by the question. "We have the finest steaks this side of the Mississippi. They're served with vegetables and fresh bread." She named the price and Trenton nodded.

"That's fine. Bring me that and a cup of coffee. Oh, and don't cook that steak clear through."

She gave a curt nod and slipped away without another word. She brought the coffee in the same stilted fashion, then disappeared again until the meal was ready.

Trenton had to admit that the steak was the best he'd tasted, and he'd eaten steak from Nebraska to Texas. Settling in to enjoy his meal, Trenton was rather annoyed by the vigorous and noisy conversation taking place on his left.

"Then we force them to build a permanent bridge," a balding heavyset man declared. The man sat closest to Trenton but would have been the loudest no matter where he sat. His voice held a booming quality that very nearly rattled the windows.

"They've assisted with the pole bridge," another man commented. "They won't see the need to do more."

"We must make them see the need, perhaps." This from a soft-spoken man who sat to the left of the booming voice.

"They'll see the need, all right," the heavyset man declared. "Otherwise we'll threaten to move the railroad. The capital is moving—we can move too. We'll build a bridge across the Missouri elsewhere."

"Now, now. Let's not be hasty. A great deal of work has gone into this road. We can't simply pluck it up and move it across the state. I suggest we propose a meeting and explain the situation. I believe we can make it worth the while of the city fathers to push forward support," Mr. Soft-spoken explained. "They're merely cautious because of the amount of money involved."

Trenton thought the whole thing rather amusing. When he'd been in the town years before, he'd heard other people arguing the very same thing. At that time they were hampered by war; now the suggestion was that money held them back.

"The Indians aren't helping our cause any," a fourth man threw out. "The wars to the west are not looked upon favorably by those in the East. Perhaps the Omaha city fathers are being discouraged from supporting the proposed bridge. After all, it would give the Indians an easy means of attack. It would allow them simple access across the Missouri River."

"To what purpose?" the boomer questioned. "What possible use would they find with Iowa?"

Many of the men broke into laughter, but not the man who'd raised the question. A quick glance proved to Trenton that he was not amused by the suggestion.

The couple to Trenton's right got up and left. The woman smiled sweetly as she caught sight of Trenton, but just as quickly she returned her attention to the man with whom she appeared so obviously in love.

Trenton wondered what it would be like to have someone care about him in such a manner. The devotion was obvious.

I'm a loner, he thought, picking at the remains of his meal. *I would be a poor companion for any woman. I'd never be able to settle down to one place for long, and I'm hardly suited to do anything but play cards.*

The summary left his food souring in his stomach. Trenton took a gulp of the tepid coffee, hoping it might settle the turmoil. Instead it brought back a memory of his father. Standing with a cup of coffee in his hands, Trenton's father had considered his son as he worked behind the counter at the store.

"I hate being a clerk," Trenton said as the last customers of the day exited the store.

"You just hate committing yourself to a job," his father declared after a long draw from the mug. "If I paid you to lounge around down at the river with your friends, you'd take well enough to it." Ephraim Chadwick slammed down his mug, shattering the cup into several pieces, causing coffee to soak into the wooden counter and floor. "You'll never amount to anything if you don't set your mind to it."

Trenton forced the memory from his mind and got up just as the man with the booming voice declared it was time to put an end to government telling free enterprise what to do. Trenton couldn't agree more. After all, he was about the free enterprise of gambling, and more than once he'd felt the confines of government as it declared laws against his trade.

He smiled. The men at that table would no doubt give little consideration to Trenton's line of business, although Trenton would be willing to wager money that he'd see these men in a game or two before the week was out.

He paid for the meal, then made his way outside. He mounted his horse, a black gelding he'd bought in Texas, and rode silently to the more advantageous part of town. A collection of saloons and bathhouses was interspersed between hotels and other businesses. Choosing the classier establishments, Trenton urged the horse to the left.

"Trenton Chadwick! Trenton!"

The feminine voice sounded from behind him, and shifting in the saddle, Trenton found Annabelle Tevis waving and calling to him. She wore a more respectable cut of dress than he'd seen her in the last time they'd shared company.

"I didn't realize you were back in Omaha," she declared breathlessly as Trenton dismounted.

"I just got here. It's good to see you." And it was good. In spite of his need to refrain from commitments and relationships, seeing a friendly face was always comforting.

"Are you still working at the Looloo?" he asked as he tied the black to a hitching post in front of the hotel.

"Oh no. My brother makes a good living and he's helping me to get respectable," she announced, tilting her chin up as though she had just assumed some finer quality by merely mentioning respectability.

Trenton pushed back his hat and eyed the young woman. "I guess I didn't realize you even had a brother."

"Geoff's a good man. He'll be here in just a minute and I can introduce you. He was mighty happy to hear what you'd done for me." She pushed an annoying piece of frizzy red hair back into her bonnet and smiled. "There he is. Geoff! Geoff, I'm over here!" she yelled out.

Geoff Tevis looked like the kind of man Trenton had tried to avoid most of his life. The stocky man had the facial set of a bully who would take great pleasure in tormenting his victims. He appeared well muscled but agile, as was noted when a carriage went streaking down the street, nearly running him over. He easily dodged the conveyance, hurling a stream of insults, then crossed to join his sister.

He eyed Trenton suspiciously. "Who are you?" he asked without waiting for an introduction.

"Geoff, this is Trenton Chadwick. He's the man who saved my life a couple years back."

Tevis's expression softened. "So you're the man. I owe you a big thanks. I appreciate what you did for my sister."

Trenton relaxed a bit. "No thanks are necessary. I would help any lady in distress."

"Most wouldn't have seen my sister as a lady," Geoff replied. "Most still don't."

Trenton didn't know what to say, so he offered the first thing that came to mind. "I wish I could have given those men as good as they gave me. I've always wondered what happened to them."

Geoff twisted his face into an almost grotesque demonic smile. "That's easy to tell," he replied. "I killed them."

Trenton had been so dumbfounded by Geoff's casual statement that it wasn't until later, when he was seated across from the man in Annabelle's meager home, that the reality of his situation began to sink in.

Annabelle told proudly of how her brother had hunted and gunned down each of the men responsible for the attack. She felt it was the least they could do for Trenton's troubles, and it was only fair punishment for what they had intended to do to her.

Trenton could scarcely believe his ears.

"Don't look so surprised," Annabelle laughed as she poured Trenton a glass of whiskey. "Geoff's a gun for hire. He makes a good living that way."

Trenton tossed back the contents of the glass without giving it a second thought. He wasn't much of a drinker, but at times like this he felt the whiskey helped to boost his courage.

Geoff studied him for a response. Trenton met his eyes and found them cold, lifeless. The man appeared to have no regret for his actions.

"I've never known a gunfighter. Not personally," Trenton finally managed.

Geoff laughed at this and Annabelle giggled. "I s'pose most folks wouldn't have a daily encounter with my kind. Annabelle tells me you're a gambler."

Trenton nodded and offered a smile. "Seems safer than what you do."

Geoff roared at this, but the laughter was cut short when the sound of glass shattering sent them all to the floor. Trenton noticed the rock first. It was about the size of his fist and a note had been tied to it with a bit of twine.

He picked it up and considered it a moment as Geoff rushed to the window. "They're gone—whoever they were." He made his way to where Trenton stood. "Gimme that," he demanded. He tore off the twine and looked the note over. "Those lousy, no-account . . ." He stopped as he realized Trenton was watching him. "I'll be back, Annabelle." He tossed the note aside and stalked out the door, muttering.

Trenton picked up the note as Annabelle began sweeping up the glass. "That's the second time this has happenèd, and I've only got the one window. Glass ain't cheap. Don't know why they can't just throw the rock at the door."

Trenton read, *Get out of town by midnight or this will be your last Independence Day celebration.*

"Some folks just don't know how to deal nice with other folks."

"Maybe Geoff killed someone they cared about and they're after revenge," Trenton offered.

Annabelle shrugged. "They ought to know better. Geoff will kill 'em now for sure."

Trenton felt weak in the knees at her lack of concern for the lives of those her brother deemed unnecessary. "Maybe he'll calm down and rethink things."

Annabelle reached out to take hold of his hand. "It's when Geoff calms down and rethinks that he takes action. He don't like folks messing around here. He feels like they blame me for his actions and in truth, some do. It gets pretty lonely." She rubbed his hand gently.

Trenton didn't care for the way Annabelle was cozying up to him. She seemed to imply a relationship between them that wasn't now nor ever had been in existence. "Ah . . . here . . ." he said, pulling away. "Let me help clean up that glass." Trenton went to where Annabelle had swept the shards into a neat little pile.

"Don't bother with that," Annabelle said softly. "Geoff won't be back for some time. Don't you think it would be nice if you and I was to just have some time to ourselves?"

Trenton felt his breath catch in his throat. The last thing he wanted to do was offend the sister of a gun for hire. He tried to steady his nerves, glancing wistfully at his empty glass.

"Maybe we could talk over another drink," he suggested.

She smiled. "I can manage that just fine, Trenton. Now, why don't you sit yourself right down while I get the whiskey."

Trenton felt much like a fly being coaxed into a spider's web. He took his seat, his mind spinning in a hundred different directions. His ability to bluff his way through the game completely failed him. Of course, he'd never played this game before. Apparently the rules were quite different.

CHAPTER 31

DIANNE LOVED LATE OCTOBER IN MONTANA—ESPECIALLY THIS day. The skies were cloudless and painted in the palest shade of blue. The air held the taste of snow—the promise of winter—yet the valley was splashed with the colors of autumn. It exhilarated and excited Dianne.

Unwilling to pass up the chance to enjoy the day, Dianne had ridden Dolly to the place where she'd first gazed down upon the Vandyke ranch. The valley spread out below, while the Madison Range jutted above. The mountains had been dusted with snow only the night before, and it wouldn't be long until snow fell in earnest and covered the land.

In another month Dianne would be twenty. It seemed a milestone in her life, but she wasn't really sure why. In another year, when she turned twenty-one, she would put in for homestead land that adjoined Uncle Bram's land. That way they could continue to expand the ranch. She'd hoped her brothers would do likewise, but they were both growing restless, itching to leave and seek their own ways.

The breeze whipped at Dianne's brown felt hat, but she remained fixed on the hill. There was no reason to hurry back. It was moments like these that gave Dianne a sense of purpose and understanding. She'd fallen in love with this land, much like most women fell in love with a man. She loved every ravine, every tree, every twist and turn of the

Madison River. There wasn't a part of the ranch she hadn't explored or taken into her heart.

Ranching in Montana, as with most places, required changes with each season. Summers were short, though they had more daylight than they'd had in Missouri. Autumn was a strange blend of changing leaves, often mingled with heavy snows. The reverse could be said of spring. While new buds and blooms came to life across the landscape, they were often buried by inches of late snow.

Winter seemed the one thing a Montanan could count on. Varying degrees of cold set in and the days grew dark and oftentimes depressing. Still, Dianne loved winter as much as any other season. She found the cold invigorating, and while the shorter days were sometimes frustrating, Dianne honestly didn't mind the extra time in the house. Winters allowed for much more reading, sewing, and conversation with Koko. Dianne would also enjoy this winter in particular because there would be hours to play with baby Jamie.

Of course, there were still animals to take care of, but the cattle would soon be moved north to a more open valley where the snows would blow off to leave open range grass for feeding. Uncle Bram said their own valley was much too prone to heavy winter snows for them to run the cattle year round.

Realizing quite a bit of time had passed during her contemplation, Dianne made her way back to the ranch. There was to be a meeting that afternoon on the very topic of moving the herd, and she didn't want to miss it. It was her hope that Uncle Bram would allow her to help on the drive. It would be the last time she'd get to see Cole for several months, and she wanted the extra time to get to know him better.

It shouldn't bother me that he'll go away and be gone for months. Dianne searched her heart and knew she couldn't deny, however, that it did affect her. It troubled her a great deal, in fact.

He obviously doesn't feel anything for me, she mused. *Not that I feel anything for him—other than friendship. Oh, all right. I feel something more, but it's silly. He doesn't even look at me when he's around, and most of the time he's not even here to care.*

But he would be at the meeting. Cole had already volunteered to stay with the cattle come winter. Gus and Levi had gone north earlier in September to scout out a site and build a range shack for the boys who would stay to keep an eye on the herd. Cole seemed almost eager to take up the duty, whereas some of the other fellows were just as happy to head back to Virginia City and be done with their jobs for the winter.

"Where have you been?" Zane asked as Dianne rode into the main yard.

"Just giving Dolly a bit of exercise." Dianne slid down from the horse's back and offered her brother a smile. "So are you still determined to go through with your plans for the army?"

Zane pushed back his hat, allowing blond hair to fall across his left brow. "It's all I can think about." He grinned. "The new fort east of Bozeman will keep me in the area. You'll be able to come visit me when we aren't out on maneuvers or fighting the Indians."

"I wish you wouldn't go. There's so much here that needs your attention."

He frowned. "I'm not a rancher, Dianne. You may love all of this, but I don't. I've only stayed because Uncle Bram made it to my advantage to do so and because I knew it was the right thing to do. Now that problems are heating up with the Sioux and Cheyenne, I'd just as soon be with the army."

Dianne twisted Dolly's reins in her hand. "But what if you get killed?"

"We've all gotta die sometime," he offered with a shrug. "Might as well die doing what you love."

"But you've never been a soldier. You have no idea whether you'll love it or not."

Zane nodded. "True enough, but I have a good idea. I used to talk at length with Captain Seager. Remember him? He and Pa hit it off so well; he was always coming around talking."

"I remember him."

"Well, he told me about army life, and I guess it charmed me. I haven't been able to get it out of my mind ever since."

"Well, at least you'll be close," Dianne said, realizing she wasn't going to change Zane's mind. "I hope you know you'll always have a place to come back to. I plan to sign up for my homestead land next year. I have to live at least part of the time on the land, and it would be just as nice to live there with you and Morgan."

"I appreciate that," Zane replied. "Who knows? You may be right and I'll get into the army and hate it. But I doubt it." He reached out and tweaked her earlobe. "Don't worry about me, baby sister. I'll be just fine. Besides, by this time next year—you'll probably be married."

Stunned by his words, Dianne watched her brother walk away. What did he mean by that comment? She took Dolly to the barn, shaking her head as she went.

"You look perplexed," Levi said as she entered.

Dianne started at the voice. She found him smiling at her surprise. "Didn't mean to scare you," he added quickly. "Here, I'll take Dolly. I know they're expecting you for the discussion."

"Thanks. I'd rather do it myself, but Uncle Bram told me not to be late." She handed Levi a piece of apple. "Give her this and she'll love you forever."

Levi took the apple but refused to let go of Dianne's hand as he did. "What's a fella gotta do to get *you* to love him forever?"

Dianne gave a little laugh, trying not to let the matter become serious. "A fella doesn't have to do much at all, but it has to be a match the good Lord puts together. Otherwise, it doesn't make sense for either party. Attraction is all well and fine, but God has a purpose in putting folks together for life. I'm not going to try to interfere with that."

Levi let go and pulled Dolly along. "Well, at least I'll have *you* lovin' me, eh, girl?" Dolly gave a whinny as if in protest.

Dianne giggled and headed back to the house. Levi was such a sweet guy. He would make someone a good husband, but not her. She felt toward Levi the same kind of love she felt toward her brothers. Nothing more.

Bram and her brothers were already assembled when Dianne came in. Koko bustled around serving the men coffee while Jamie played on a buffalo hide nearby. Dianne couldn't help going to her little cousin and picking him up. Jamie cooed and smiled as Dianne talked softly to him.

"Hello, my fine little man. How are you?"

The baby reached out to touch Dianne's face as she drew him close for a kiss. "I can't believe how he's grown."

"He's gonna be big like his pa," Bram said proudly.

Koko nodded, adding, "And his grandpa. My father was no small man."

"That's true enough," Bram admitted.

The front door opened, admitting Gus and Cole. Dianne looked at the men and smiled, while Jamie tucked his head against Dianne's neck. Cole halted in midstep while Gus began talking of the weather.

Dianne held Cole's gaze, wishing fervently that she could read his thoughts. Koko came to Dianne and reached out for Jamie. "It's time for his nap and then I have laundry to do." She took her son and added, "I've made you a pot of tea."

Dianne lowered her head as if embarrassed by her attention toward Cole. She felt such a growing sensation of confusion, mingled with fascination, and there seemed to be no answers for the questions those feelings brought. "Thank you," she murmured, then went quickly to take her seat at the table.

"Gus and I both think the winter is going to be a hard one, so we need to get the cattle moved as soon as possible," Uncle Bram began.

Dianne poured herself a cup of tea and listened as her uncle continued. "There's good open range to the north. We won't have any trouble getting the herd through winter—at least that's my hope.

"Gus also arranged a deal with the man in charge of Fort Ellis. They're going to buy thirty head from us. They have the opportunity to buy additional beef from some of the men in the area, which is good, because we can't really afford to send more than thirty off for sale."

"Who will drive the cattle to Fort Ellis?" Cole asked.

Bram took a long drink of his coffee, then answered. "Zane, Morgan, and Gus will take them east. The hardest part will be dealing with the river. If we keep crossings to a minimum, it shouldn't be too bad, but otherwise I'm afraid that herd will give you a bad time of it."

"We can handle it, boss. Don't you worry none about us," Gus replied. "While we're over Bozeman City way, we'll check out to see if there's any supplies they've got that we could use. Maybe I can pick up some hayseed."

Bram nodded and pulled a cigar from his vest pocket. "With the problems that seem to be springing up with the Indians, I think we'll do well to keep the herd guarded through the winter. It's completely accept-able to trade off one or two to the Indians," he said, looking to Cole, "especially if it keeps you alive and them from coming back to steal five or six head. But don't encourage it."

Cole nodded. "So when do we leave?"

"Day after tomorrow," Bram replied.

Dianne had held her tongue for as long as she could. She'd been planning for days to interject the idea of going along on the trip to help drive the cattle and to go to Bozeman. Now seemed as good a time as any to make the suggestion. "I want to go along. Would that be all right?"

Everyone at the table turned and looked at her as though she'd just suggested President Lincoln had come back to life. She held her ground, however. "I can ride as well as my brothers—shoot as well, too. I could be good help in driving those cows and I would have a chance to look at the supplies that might interest Koko and me."

"No, you'd best stay home. Koko is going to need your help with winter preparations," Bram declared.

"Besides, the trail is no place for a woman," Cole threw out. He eyed her quite seriously. "Your place is here, in the home."

Dianne tried not to let his words get her dander up. This was the first time in months Cole had uttered much of anything concerning her. Why did it have to be so negative?

Dianne got up abruptly, afraid that if she didn't leave she might say something foolish. Storming out of the room, she made her way out the back door, a luxury added only the previous year. Seething, she tried to calm her temper.

"To use one of Bram's favorite sayings, you look as if you could bite the head right off a rattler," Koko said, straightening from where she stirred laundry in a huge iron pot.

"I'm mad, that's for sure. I just wanted to go on the trail with the boys. I wanted to go to Bozeman with my brothers and Gus. Uncle Bram said no, and that was bad enough, but then Cole had to jump in with his opinion."

"And what was that?"

Dianne plopped down on a stump. "He said the trail was no place for a woman—that my place was here." She sighed in exasperation. "It's not that I don't agree with a woman's place being in the home—but this isn't my home. I'm no man's wife or child's mother. It seems to me I should be able to come and go at will."

"Is that truly what you want?" Koko asked softly.

Dianne considered her words for a moment. "No, I suppose it isn't. But to be honest, I don't know what I want. I don't know what God wants for me. I have all these feelings inside—feelings for people and places, and I don't know what to do with them."

"Have you tried asking God about it?"

Dianne huffed indignantly. "Well, of course I have."

Koko smiled at her defensive response. "So your prayer life is strong?"

Dianne knew she couldn't lie. "No . . . well . . . I try to pray. I do pray—quite a bit. When I can."

"You don't have to convince me," Koko said with a laugh. "God's the one who knows the truth of it."

"Oh, I suppose I don't pray as much as I should. I get busy, to tell you the truth," Dianne admitted. "I guess when things are going pretty well, it's easy to forget about praying."

"But how will you grow closer to God if you don't talk to Him?"

"I don't understand."

Koko nodded and came to squat beside Dianne. "You have become a dear sister to me. We talk about everything—just like now."

"That's true." Dianne could think of no better friend than Koko.

"If you never talked to me, never asked me about my life, my people, how would you come to understand me? How would I understand you? To be close—to truly love each other—we must get to know each other better. The same is true with God. How can you know Him if you never read His Word—hear His voice to you? How can you grow closer if you never talk, never share your heart?"

"I see what you mean," Dianne said, her gaze fixed on Koko's delicate brown face. "I need to open the lines of communication, just like when they strung the telegraph wire from Virginia City to Salt Lake."

Koko laughed and got to her feet. "Exactly," she said as she retrieved a few more chunks of wood for the fire. "It's a marvelous thing to take Jesus as your savior, but don't stop there. Let Him also be your friend."

"I will. I'll start right now."

Cole Selby came out the door, halting abruptly. He looked to Koko and then to Dianne. "I . . . uh . . . I . . . can we talk a minute?"

Koko smiled. "I need to go check on Jamie. Dianne, would you stir the clothes?"

"Of course." Dianne got to her feet and took up the long-handled paddle.

Once Koko had gone, Cole came to stand across from Dianne at the fire. "I'm sorry. I shouldn't have said what I did earlier. You've got just as much right to go to Bozeman or any other place. I was just thinking of your safety."

Dianne looked up and met his dark brown eyes. "You were right too. If I were a wife and a mother, then my place would be at home."

Cole said nothing for several minutes. They simply stared at each other over the steam of the laundry. Dianne felt her heart give a lurch and butterflies seemed to flitter in her stomach.

"I didn't mean to hurt your feelings," Cole finally said.

"I know," Dianne whispered, feeling the words stick in her throat.

Cole moved from his place as if to head back to the house. Instead, he stopped as he came up even with Dianne. Reaching out, he let his hand rest momentarily on her arm. Dianne held her breath, uncertain as to what would happen next. A strong desire arose inside her . . . a desire to experience his kiss. She leaned forward just a bit. *Kiss me. Please kiss me.*

CHAPTER 32

But he didn't kiss her. Cole had wanted more than anything to take Dianne in his arms, but he held those feelings in check, knowing the danger of such things. Now as he sat atop his horse, waiting for Gus to give the signal for them to move the cattle out, Cole tried hard not to remember the longing he'd seen in Dianne's eyes. She had wanted him to kiss her as well. He knew that and had almost given into it.

He watched her even now as she stood beside Bram and Koko. She called out something to one of her brothers, then laughed at whatever reply he'd given. Dianne had grown into a handsome, capable woman. Instead of being defeated by the frontier, as Cole thought she might, Dianne had blossomed and thrived.

She was quite amazing, and he knew she'd captured a special place in his heart. But Cole fought against that as much as he fought against forgiving his father. Only last week one of the men had gone to Virginia City and brought Cole a letter from his mother. She spoke of the changes in his father—how he held steady work and attended church faithfully. She was blessed by the changes and wished that Cole would make his peace, as that seemed to grieve her husband daily.

Cole had thrown the letter into the fire, not caring about his father's grief. Thoughts of Carrie flickered through his mind even now as he watched Dianne. The two women were very similar. Carrie had loved the territory too. She hadn't minded that she was one of only a handful of women in the area. Instead, she had taken pride in her femininity, and Cole had taken pride in her. Just as he took pride in Dianne.

These feelings are dangerous, he warned himself. *There's no room for them out here. She's the boss's niece—nothing more.* But even as he told himself this, his heart declared him to be a liar.

"You boys ready?" Gus called out.

The chorus of affirmative replies was all Gus needed. He gave Bram and the ladies a nod, then moved the men out.

"Be careful!" Dianne said as Zane rode past. "Don't forget to send word to us from time to time—and visit when you can."

"I will. Stop worrying," Zane replied.

Cole caught her eye, and her gaze seemed fixed to his for several moments. He wanted to say something—to at least tell her good-bye—but the words were frozen in his throat. It seemed that she had the same problem.

Finally Cole looked away. There was no sense in tormenting them both. He didn't know what to do with his feelings, didn't know how to live with the knowledge that he'd lost his heart to yet another woman.

Didn't I swear that would never happen? Didn't I make Carrie a promise to never love another? The questions flooded his mind, but none of them mattered. He couldn't stop what had already happened.

They moved the cattle slowly to the north. The herd seemed content, not at all bothered by the gathering clouds. Gus felt certain they'd run into snow, so when the first flakes started falling, Cole merely raised the collar on his coat and hunkered down. The bad thing about being in the saddle for long hours was that it gave a man a lot of time to think. There were things to keep watch for and work to do, but Cole had no trouble doing that while contemplating what had become of his life.

He knew he'd made a mistake in taking the job with Bram Vandyke. He'd known up front that he'd have to see Dianne on nearly a daily basis.

But he'd told himself this would purge her from his system. In fact, Cole had been convinced of that.

It didn't work that way, however.

Instead of feeling better about putting Dianne aside, the pain of her nearness was acute. Cole couldn't help but see her as she worked with some of the horses in the corral or earlier in the summer as she tended the garden and picked vegetables for canning. It seemed she was always outdoors, just as he was.

Cole had volunteered to sit in the range shack all winter just so he could distance himself from her. He figured it would help him clear his head once and for all. He'd spend the winter away from her and that would be that.

Then Dianne had gone and asked to accompany the men on this trip, and he'd nearly felt his resolve undo itself. There was no way he could handle her being there—riding alongside him—just as he envisioned she might do when he dreamed of her every night.

"Wind's picking up and that snow's getting heavier," Gus said, interrupting Cole's thoughts. Cole hadn't even noticed that the older man had ridden back to meet him. "We'll get the cattle settled in a canyon I know up the ways. Otherwise, I figure we'll be drivin' them in a blizzard."

Cole respected Gus's opinion. The man seemed to know exactly the right thing to do at just the right time. "How will we keep them together?" Cole asked, raising his voice above the wind.

"I'll put a few of you at one end of the canyon and the rest on the other end. The walls are too steep for them to go climbing much. Besides, I think they'll be just as happy to stick this one out together.

"I'll let the others know. Just keep sharp. No more daydreamin'," Gus said with a hint of a smile. "This weather is about to get mean."

———

"I don't like the look of things," Bram declared as he peeked out the front window. He took up his coat from the peg by the door. "I'm going out to check on the horses and make sure the barn doors are secure."

"I'll help you," Dianne said, taking up the new coat Koko had given her as an early Christmas gift. The buckskin coat was lined with warm wool fleece. Dianne was never cold when she wore this. She pressed her hat down hard on her head, then secured it by tying a long wool scarf over it. This way her ears would stay warm.

"I'll bring in some extra water," Koko told them as Bram opened the door.

"No, you stay put. I'll bring in extra wood and water," Bram told her. He smiled as Jamie began to cry for his supper. "See—my son agrees."

Koko shook her head. "No, he is telling you that wood and water are women's work."

Bram laughed heartily. "Maybe on most days, but today it's my job."

Dianne enjoyed the bantering between them. Bram and Koko were definitely in love. Dianne couldn't have imagined it when she'd first arrived. Koko seemed so much younger, and Uncle Bram . . . well, he was Uncle Bram. To imagine him with a wife and then a child had been something that had never occurred to Dianne.

They headed out the back door, buttoning their coats as they went. Wind blew crusty bits of snow into Dianne's face. It stung and she lowered her head against the wind and let her hat take the brunt of it.

"I can see to the animals," she said, taking hold of her uncle's arm.

"All right. You go ahead. Just make sure all the doors are secured. I'll get the wood." Bram turned to go, then stopped. "Hold on," he commanded.

Dianne waited, confused by his actions. She watched him go back into the house. Moments later he returned with a long rope in hand. "What's wrong?" she asked.

"Take this," he said. He gave her one end of the rope while he tied the other end of it to the cabin door. "Tie it to the barn door when you get there. That way if the snow gets too bad, we can follow this back and forth and not get lost."

"Sounds wise," Dianne said.

Dianne hurried to the barn and fixed the rope to the outside latch.

Heading inside, she breathed the mingled odors of manure and hay. Here, the horses' stalls offered the animals protection from the weather, but first she'd have to gather them in.

It was to Dianne's benefit that she worked with the horses on a daily basis. They came easily to investigate her appearance—no doubt hoping for some kind of treat. Dianne ushered each animal into the barn, securing them away from the storm.

Next, she checked their supply of hay and water. She was relieved, on one hand, that many of the horses had gone north with the cowboys. But she also worried because if the weather was also bad where they were, the poor animals would suffer through the full force of the storm out in the open.

Then Cole and her brothers came to mind. Dianne was already shivering from the arctic winds, and she was inside the barn. How would it be to endure the blizzard from a saddle? Dianne whispered a prayer for the safety of each man on the drive. "Bring them back to us, Lord, without injury or harm."

After the horses were cared for, Dianne made her way to tend to the chickens and milk cows. Because of a recent grizzly attack in which they'd lost one of their stock, Bram had moved the remaining cows to a small corral off of the second barn. This made it easy for Dianne to see to their needs.

By now the wind was moaning through the trees, and the snow was so heavy that visibility was limited to less than twenty yards. Dianne pressed on, however. The animals couldn't fend for themselves, and it was up to her and Uncle Bram to make sure all was well.

Closing the shutters on the coop, Dianne felt confident the chickens would endure the cold just fine. They were a tough little breed. Animals in this territory had to be, she decided. People too. If you weren't of enduring stock, you simply couldn't make it in Montana.

Dianne made her way back through to the horse barn, grateful they'd worked so hard in preparation for winter. Everything would be just fine. This would no doubt be the first of many coming storms. Securing the barn door, Dianne turned to face the full impact of the wind. The storm's intensity was now a force to be reckoned with.

Taking hold of the rope, Dianne worked her way along the corral, using the rope for guidance and the fence to steady her against the wind. She stumbled more than once as she fought to keep her balance. Snow quickly piled up, drifting against anything solid, including the fence posts. Her plan was to follow the fence until it ended at the drive and turned back to the east and trust the rope to bring her safely back to the cabin.

It seemed a good plan, but the cold was numbing her face and fingers, and her vision was obscured by the blowing snow. Reaching the end of the fence, Dianne knew there was no other choice but to let go and set out for the house. The rope gave her marginal confidence.

"Lord, watch over me," she prayed aloud.

Her tiny frame, although well muscled, was no match for the wind. Dianne had staggered no more than two or three steps when she lost her footing and fell backward. The fall took the breath out of her momentarily; it also wrenched the rope from her hands. She struggled to sit up and to breathe. Gasping, she drew in mouthfuls of cold icy air, which only made her cough and gasp again.

Getting to her hands and knees, Dianne thought perhaps it was a better choice to just crawl the remaining distance. Her dress would be soaked by the time she made it back to the cabin, but at least she wouldn't fall. Dianne looked up to get her bearings, but there was nothing she could see to take sight on. Reaching up, she tried to find the rope, but her arms batted uselessly at the snowy air.

"Lord, I need some help here," she said, forcing herself to keep moving. "I need help. Please send Uncle Bram to find me." Immediately Dianne felt guilty. If Uncle Bram did worry about her and came looking, he could put himself in jeopardy as well. Koko and little Jamie needed him too much. "Lord, I'm just as happy if you would help me."

Without warning, Dianne felt herself being lifted into the air. Someone had a firm grip around her waist and was helping her to steady herself as they moved forward. Silently, Dianne thanked God for His intervention, but it wasn't until they reached the back door and were safely inside the cabin that Dianne realized who her rescuer was.

Her eyes widened as she fixed her gaze on Takes-Many-Horses. His black hair was wet with melting snow, but his smile seemed to indicate he'd not minded the inconvenience.

"Now you are Stands-Tall-Woman again," he said, his grin broadening.

"Thank you," Dianne whispered. "I don't think I've ever seen a storm quite like this. Where's Uncle Bram?" Dianne pulled off her gloves and stuffed them into her pockets. She then tried to force her cold fingers to work the buttons on her coat.

Koko rushed forward to fuss over her. "He's changing his clothes and so should you. Now you go on. Just leave your boots here at the door and I'll take care of them." She helped Dianne out of her coat and took the scarf and hat.

Dianne looked back at Koko's brother as she kicked off her boots. "When did you get here?"

"In time to help Bram with the wood and water. He sent me to find you while he finished with the last load."

"It's a good thing," Dianne said, feeling not in the least bit embarrassed by her dilemma. Now was no time for pride. "I doubt I would have made it had you not come and helped me."

He shook his head. "You would have made it just fine. You are strong—like my sister. No storm could stop you."

Dianne took his praise warily. Takes-Many-Horses still unnerved her. Where Koko looked like nothing more than a darkly tanned white woman, Takes-Many-Horses looked every bit the part of Pikuni warrior.

"Come on," Koko interceded, "you need to go change and then sit by the fire. I don't want you coming down sick."

"I'm coming," Dianne told her friend, but her gaze was still fixed on the dark-eyed Blackfoot who'd rescued her.

CHAPTER 33

DIANNE QUICKLY CHANGED HER CLOTHES, PULLING ON A BROWN wool skirt and yellow blouse. She glanced in the mirror, noting that her hair was still fairly neat and deciding against doing anything more. She felt nervous about rejoining Koko and her brother. Dianne knew Uncle Bram would be there, as well, but it was still rather unnerving.

Takes-Many-Horses had the same upbringing as Koko, Dianne reminded herself as she reached for her doorknob. *He's not that different.*

But he was different. He was Pikuni and proud of that fact.

Dianne went into the kitchen, where Koko and her brother were talking in hushed whispers. Uncle Bram had still not returned.

"I'll set the table," Dianne said, hurrying to gather the needed utensils and plates.

Jamie began to fuss and Koko smiled as he struggled on the buffalo robe. "He gets mad when he can't do exactly what he wants."

"And what does he want, sister?" Takes-Many-Horses asked as he moved to better view his nephew.

"He wants to crawl and walk and run, all at the same time," Koko declared. "Much like his uncle."

Dianne smiled to herself. She knew it was true of Jamie. The baby seemed very strong and very determined, and Dianne had no doubt that Koko's brother had been the same way.

"Well, it doesn't look like it'll be letting up anytime soon," Bram declared as he joined them. "It might snow like this for days."

"I hope not," Dianne said, thinking of the men on the cattle drive.

"I'm sure Gus will see everyone to safety. He's been ranchin' for a long time. He was foreman for almost twenty years down Texas way and then up in the Dakota Territory. He knows how to deal with the snow—even when it's like this."

"I'm glad to know that," Dianne replied.

"I'll bet you're glad you stayed behind now too," Bram declared.

Dianne straightened as she finished with the last plate. "I suppose I am. It wasn't very pleasant out there."

"I'm just glad you're all safe," Koko said, positioning her son so he could better see what was happening. "I can remember many times when people were lost up north when my father had the trading post. We'd hear about it come spring. Some poor fool would set out to walk to the post and winter would catch him unaware." Koko pulled out the chair for her husband. "Supper is ready if you are."

"I'm starved!" Bram exclaimed. "Besides, I know you've fried us up some chicken, and my mouth is watering just thinking about it."

"And Dianne made an apple pie too," Koko announced. "And of course we have green beans and potatoes."

Bram took his seat. "Let's stop talking and get to eating. Dianne, would you say grace tonight?"

Dianne turned from the stove where she'd just retrieved the coffee-pot. "Sure, Uncle Bram." She wondered what Koko's brother would think of them praying. Dianne knew Uncle Bram had been instru-mental in teaching Koko about Jesus, but had Takes-Many-Horses had the same lessons? Did he care about such things?

They all took their seats and Dianne was rather surprised to find that Takes-Many-Horses had chosen the seat beside her. The table was large enough to seat eight, and he certainly needn't have crowded her.

They bowed in prayer and Dianne tried hard to steady her voice as she asked for protection for those on the trail as well as blessings on

338 —— TRACIE PETERSON

the food. All the while her mind was well aware of the man sitting at her right.

The meal began with lively conversation, and from the very start Dianne found herself drawn in when she'd expected only to listen.

"The Blackfoot are in trouble," Takes-Many-Horses told them. "The white man has decided there is no room for us. They push us away and kill the buffalo for sport."

"That grieves me as well," Koko said sadly. "The Blackfoot use the buffalo for their very existence, while the whites seem to make a game of hunting."

Dianne knew this to be true. She'd seen examples of it on the wagon train. Kills were made even when there was no hope of keeping all of the meat or butchering the entire animal.

"The white man can keep pushing, but the Pikuni will just push back. If we push hard enough, the whites will go back to where they came from."

Dianne shook her head vehemently. "Don't believe that. The harder you push the whites, the more tenacious and determined they will become."

"She's right, George," Koko said, reverting to his Christian name. "You know our father was that way. As hard as it was to keep a trading post in Indian country, he was only strengthened by the adversity."

Takes-Many-Horses leaned back in his chair and eyed Dianne, quite serious. She met his gaze and squared her shoulders. There was a raw, unspoiled wildness about this man that held her captive yet terrified her at the same time.

"You think the whites will stay. Even with the Sioux and Cheyenne killing them? Even with the Blackfoot taking as many lives as they can?"

"Yes, I do," Dianne replied. "Think of your father for an example. Or Uncle Bram." She looked to the older man for confirmation.

"It's true. The whites will force the Indian out, just as they have in the East. They'll come with their superior weapons and numbers and little by little have every single Indian driven off the land."

"We won't let them," Koko's brother declared. "We'll all die if need be."

"Sadly, that's what it will probably come to," Bram said. "Why do you think I've tried to convince you to come join us here? At least if you're living with us, living as a white man, you won't be rounded up with the others."

"But they're my people," Takes-Many-Horses declared.

Koko put her fork down. "So are we."

"It's not the same. I've taken the life of a Blackfoot. I'm accepted there. Any other white man would see me as a Pikuni. You know it's true."

"I know that," Koko admitted, "but I also know that what my husband says is true. I don't wish to lose you. I don't wish to see you dead on the battlefield, believing in your heart that you had to kill or be killed."

"That's all that's left to us. The whites will never allow us to be a part of their world."

The conversation halted for several minutes. Dianne took the opportunity to cut the pie and offer it for dessert. Takes-Many-Horses took a piece and ate it quickly. He asked for a second before Bram or Koko had even begun to eat their first.

Dianne smiled and dished him another slice. "I'm glad you like it."

"Some white man's food is worth eating," he said, grinning. "This meal was definitely one of those."

"So stay with us awhile and eat like this every night," Koko said.

Takes-Many-Horses laughed and declared, "I'd get as fat and lazy as a white man."

Dianne pondered his words as the meal concluded and Koko left to put Jamie to bed. Takes-Many-Horses' attitude toward whites was much the same as the white man's attitude toward blacks. She remembered Faith talking about how no one wanted to hire her husband, a gifted and experienced blacksmith, because he was black and everyone believed he would be lazy.

"The two words go together," Faith had once told her. "*Black* and *lazy.* They've come to almost mean the same thing, and whether we prove our worth or not, the branding follows us."

Dianne had been saddened by that declaration, but now she thought of how the Indians viewed her own people. They saw the whites as marauders. Thieves. The whites would trespass upon the Indian lands, steal the buffalo, kill the people, and never face any retribution for their actions. The whites were lazy to the Indian—choosing to take what didn't belong to them rather than working to make better what they already possessed. The whites were nothing more than opportunists in the eyes of the Indian.

Yet at the same time, the whites perceived the Indians as ignorant savages who knew nothing of the real world. She'd heard men on the wagon train discuss it. *"If you treat them like children and give them a little candy or a small trinket, they'll generally go away happy,"* one man had told them. *"I had to deal with them in western Kansas—before it became a state. They're just simple-minded and not capable of deep thinking."*

But Dianne knew that wasn't true. Koko, though only half Pikuni, was amazing in her depth of thought and intelligence. And the stories Koko offered about her people were fascinating and proved to Dianne that they were skilled and considerate.

It's all about passing judgment based on ignorance and misinformation, Dianne reasoned. *The whites blame the blacks for the War Between the States. The Indians blame the whites for the wars on the plains. The Indians believe the whites to be indifferent and without compassion, and the whites believe the blacks to be shifty and lazy, hardly worth the trouble of considering. What a vicious and ugly circle.*

"You seem awfully deep in thought," Bram said as he got up from his chair.

Dianne started. "Sorry."

Yawning, Bram scratched his stomach. "It's completely all right. I think I'll leave you to your contemplations. It's been a long day and I intend to turn in for an even longer sleep. With that wind howling outside, I'll probably think the wolf is at the door for sure." He grinned as if amused with himself. "George, you're welcome to stay with us for as long as you like."

"As soon as the snow stops, I plan to rejoin my people. I just wanted to come let Koko know that I'd be away for a while."

Bram nodded. "Well, don't leave without saying good-bye."

"I won't."

Dianne got up and started clearing the table. She said nothing as she worked, but her mind was overwhelmed with thoughts.

"You're very quiet. Are you always this way?" Takes-Many-Horses asked as he poured himself another cup of coffee.

"No, not truly. My brothers would tell you I'm very opinionated and happy to speak my mind. You know that as well."

He smiled. "Yes. I know that." He sat back down at the table and watched her for several more minutes.

Dianne was rather unnerved by his appraisal but forced herself to continue with the task at hand. Koko returned and began to assist Dianne with the dishes. "When we're done here," she said, "I'm going to bed too."

Dianne saw how tired Koko was and reached out to still her hands. "Go ahead now. I can take care of this."

"No, I don't want . . ."

Dianne pushed her gently in the direction of the bedroom. "Go. I'm fine. Uncle Bram will be freezing in there and need your body warmth."

Koko laughed. "He makes enough warmth all by himself. That man is never cold." She turned to her brother. "Dianne can show you to her brothers' room. I'm sure they won't mind if you sleep in there tonight."

"I'll bet they wish they were sleeping here," Dianne said as she put the last of the pie in the pie keep.

"Yes, I'm sure," Koko said. "I wish they'd waited to go, but I'm also certain the snows will be worse here than where they're headed. Hopefully they made good time." She gave Dianne a kiss on the cheek. "Thank you for all your hard work." Then without giving him time to protest, she kissed her brother on the cheek as well. "I haven't had a chance to do that since you were little. I miss you and wish you'd stay."

Dianne turned away, not wishing to further embarrass Takes-Many-Horses. She washed the dishes and left them to dry on the counter before turning back around. The entire time she could feel Takes-Many-Horses watching her.

"So, are you ready to . . . uh . . . well . . ." She felt embarrassed, unable to figure out how to word her question without sounding provocative or bold. "I can show you to your room if you're ready."

He chuckled at her nervousness. "You know," he said as he got up, "I believe I am. I've traveled far today, and tomorrow, if the snows have stopped, I'll go even farther."

Dianne took up the lamp and led the way to the addition where her brothers shared a bedroom. "There are plenty of blankets in the trunk at the end of the bed," she told him. She opened the door to the room and shivered at the cold. "I'll light the bedside candle for you." She went quickly to the task while Takes-Many-Horses leaned casually against the doorframe, watching her.

"If I didn't feel it was my duty to put an end to white men taking over my people's land," he said softly, "I would steal you away for my wife."

Dianne straightened abruptly, the lamp and candle trembling in her hands. She saw the seriousness along with the teasing in his expression. She hastily put the candle in its holder and wondered at how she should respond.

Humor, she thought. That would make the situation less uncomfortable. Gathering her wits, she smiled and walked slowly to the door and eased past his unmoving body.

"I can make a very good moccasin," she began, "but I absolutely refuse to chew leather. So, you see, if you took me for your wife, your clothes would always be hard rawhide and the other braves would laugh at you."

She moved down the hall to the door of her own room, hearing his soft laughter. She swallowed hard and entered her room, firmly closing the door behind her. A part of her wanted to believe he was merely joking about stealing her away. Another part was absolutely convinced it could very well happen.

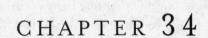

CHAPTER 34

THE SNOW STOPPED SHORTLY AFTER MIDNIGHT, AND COLE WAS relieved to see the clouds clear and the stars appear. He couldn't remember a time in his life when he'd been colder. Everything was covered in snow, and with no tents to take cover in, the only thing they could do was hunker down and wait out the blizzard. Short of throwing on a slicker over his winter coat, there wasn't any way to avoid the bone-chilling dampness of the heavy wet snow.

"The herd seems content to stay where they are," Levi muttered as they worked to clear a small campsite. They cut a long evergreen branch and used it as a broom to push through the drifts.

Cole noted the way the cattle bunched together in the canyon. No doubt it was the best way to keep warm. "Hope they stay this quiet through the night."

"Me too."

"Boys, I'll have us a fire made here shortly. I've managed to pull together some dead brush. Sent a couple of the other boys to bring in some more," Gus declared. He went right to work getting a decent size fire going. The flames provided not only warmth but added light.

"Douse that lantern. We'll light it up if we need it, but hopefully this will do us," Gus said.

Before long Cole was sufficiently warmed on the outside, and Levi's hot coffee helped warm his insides. They ate supper at a little past one in the morning, then those who weren't on guard turned in and tried to get comfortable on the cold Montana ground.

That night Cole dreamed of owning his own ranch. He found himself at the top of a hill, much like the one overlooking Bram Vandyke's ranch. For as far as he could see the land was his. A sense of peace washed over Cole as he watched his cattle contentedly feed on lush green pastures. He awoke feeling refreshed and for the first time in his life seriously considered that he might very well want to take up ranching as a career.

Why not? He could stake a homestead claim and work the land. Maybe add to it as the years went on. It was hard work, but it was a whole lot more certain than mining. The thought invigorated him. Yawning, he sat up and wondered at the time. He needed to take his turn with the cattle and figured even if it was a little early he was fully awake and might as well go to it.

Cole went to saddle his mount and met up with Gus doing likewise. "Doesn't feel half so cold without the wind blowing," Cole said.

"That's a fact. Storms like that make a fella consider going back to Texas."

"What was Texas like?" Cole asked.

"Hotter than you can imagine most of the time. Hot and dusty, that's what I mostly remember," Gus said, tightening his cinch. "Nothing like Montana."

Cole mounted his horse and looked down at Gus. "Did you ever think of owning your own spread?"

Gus looked up at him rather oddly. "Why do you ask?"

Cole shrugged. "Guess I was considering what it might be like to do something like that. Maybe get a homestead nearby."

"Settle down and raise a family?" Gus's tone was teasing, but his expression was serious.

Cole smiled. "Could be. Mainly I was just thinking of how I wanted to spend the rest of my life."

Gus nodded. "Well, it seems to me you've come to the right place for it." He mounted and pulled his collar up. "Might be particularly interesting what with Miss Dianne takin' such an interest in the same kind of thing. I doubt you'd have to work too hard to win her hand."

Cole shook his head. "No sense jumpin' the gun. It'd be better to see to the land first, then worry about what follows." He nudged his horse forward, ignoring Gus's chuckle.

———————

The next morning dawned bright and clear. Gus had them break camp and get ready to head straight out. Knee-deep snow slowed the progress for the first mile or so, then the valley opened up and revealed rangeland where the wind had blown most of the fields clear.

The sun's brilliance hurt Cole's eyes as he gazed out across the herd. Still, he wouldn't trade the clear skies and warming temperatures for what he'd experienced on the previous day. The herd appeared to agree.

After having little feed and water on the previous day, the cattle were restless. They'd reach their destination by nightfall, however, so Gus wouldn't let them stop for long. He told the boys to keep pushing them north and soon they could eat their fill.

As the sun began to set in the western skies, dipping out of sight behind the Tobacco Root Mountains, Cole was more than ready to be out of the saddle. The range shack didn't boast much comfort, but it looked like a palace to Cole and Levi. The one-room cabin would be their home for the next few months, and Cole hoped the time away from the ranch might give him a chance to seriously consider his new ideas about land ownership.

"You boys will find supplies stacked against that far wall. Stove works good," Gus said. "But we didn't manage to get enough wood cut to take you through winter, so you'll need to be considering that. When you have good days, take advantage of it and lay in a supply. There's some good wood to be had in that stand of trees to the west."

"Sounds simple enough," Cole declared.

"I know of a hot spring not far from here," one of the boys offered. "Sure would feel good about now."

"Maybe we can reward ourselves with a bit of a swim," Gus said, smiling. "I'm kind of partial to such adventures myself."

"Do you think we'll have Injun troubles, boss?" one of the men asked Gus.

"Could be. The Blackfoot aren't real happy with the white man. I wouldn't be surprised at all to see them start attacking in full force."

One of the younger cowboys in the group appeared to pale at this news. Cole knew Gabe couldn't be much older than sixteen. He'd come to them from the mining fields, explaining that he'd been in an orphanage in the East but was turned loose after the war because of his age and the influx of younger children. Somehow he'd drifted west and ended up in Virginia City.

"Gabe, don't you go worryin' none," Gus said as he gave the boy a hearty pat on the back. "Cole over there is a dead eye with a gun. He can surely take care of any Indian attacks, now, can't you, Cole?"

Cole smiled. "You bet." But he had to admit he had his own misgivings. The rumors from town weren't good. Whenever one of the boys went to Virginia City for their Saturday night constitutional, they came back with stories of scalped settlers and burned-out homesteads. It was enough to make a man sit up and take notice. Cole hoped that the winter weather would keep the Indians from being too eager to make war.

———

Zane Chadwick hadn't slept a wink that night for thinking of the Indians as well. The Indians were the real reason he was joining up with the army. Fort Ellis was to be his new home and a uniform his only manner of dress. His father would have been gravely disappointed in him. The family did not pride itself on making war against anyone, but Zane saw the western frontier as a different situation. The westward expansion of white settlers had brought out the complication of Indian removal.

Since meeting his uncle's wife, Zane had come to have a better understanding of the Indians, at least of the Blackfoot. He and Dianne had enjoyed learning the Blackfoot language and Zane knew that such a skill would probably come in handy in the army. He'd taken to the language rather easily, just as he had picked up a fairly fluent capability in Spanish during his freighting days in Virginia City. Languages seemed to be something he was gifted at.

Before first light, Gus had roused them, and Levi and Gabe had set to fixing breakfast. Zane and Morgan worked with Gus and Cole to cut out the thirty head from the herd that would be taken to the fort. As they prepared to leave, Cole gave Zane a wave.

"Take care of yourself. Your sister wouldn't forgive us if anything bad happened to you," Cole said.

"I don't intend for anything bad to happen," Zane replied. "Dianne told me she'd be praying for my safety, and she's pretty set about getting what she goes after. God and me don't stand a chance."

Morgan leaned over in the saddle toward Zane. "He doesn't stand a chance either. If our little sister has her way about it, Indians will be the least of Cole Selby's worries."

"What was that?" Cole called.

Zane smiled. "He's just warning me about the future. Not to worry." Morgan laughed and reined his horse back toward the cattle.

Cole shrugged as Gus rode up beside him. "We'll be headin' out now. You should see me back here in a week. I'll check in before I head to the ranch."

Cole nodded and Zane gave him a wave, then turned to move out and corral a steer that seemed intent on wandering back toward the larger herd. He liked Cole and seriously hoped that things would work out between him and Dianne. It would be good to have a man like him in the family. It would certainly make it easier to leave Dianne behind if Zane knew she'd have someone besides Uncle Bram to see to her needs.

They reached Fort Ellis without any real obstacles. The rivers weren't frozen and passage was easy, albeit unwelcome by the cattle. Bozeman City had grown considerably and Zane was actually sorry he wouldn't have a chance to explore the town. Perhaps there would be time for that later, however.

Gus handled the exchange of the cows with the fort personnel. This left Zane and Morgan free to say their good-byes.

The twins stood beside their horses facing each other. "I don't know why you want to be a soldier," Morgan began. "Seems like it would be awful to have to answer to someone all the time."

"I want to be a soldier for the same reasons you want to go out exploring," Zane replied. "It's my calling. I think about it more than anything else. I thrill to the stories told about it. That time we spent at Fort Laramie convinced me beyond anything else. Soldiering is something I have to try my hand at."

"I can understand that," Morgan said, looking off across the post. "But you've never had to kill anyone before. I don't see you as a killer."

"I don't either," Zane agreed. "But I am a defender. I will defend the right of people to move freely as they choose, whether they are Indian or white. But I'll also defend the law, and if the law says the Indians cannot come into an area because they refuse to deal in peace with the whites, then I will uphold that law."

"Seems like you've thought this through," Morgan said. "I guess there's nothing left to do but say good-bye. I hope I'll see you again soon."

"It's not that far to come for a visit. From either direction. So maybe you'll come see me come spring."

"Could be," Morgan admitted. "Might be if Bozeman keeps growing like it has, we'll come this way for supplies instead of Virginia City."

"I can see the time coming."

"You ready to head into town?" Gus asked Morgan as he approached atop his horse.

Morgan looked at Zane momentarily. Zane felt an odd sensation in being parted from his twin. It would be the first time they'd not been at each other's side.

"Take care of yourself," Zane whispered and embraced Morgan in a powerful bear hug.

"You too," Morgan replied.

They pulled away and nodded, as if knowing all the unspoken things they might have said. Zane looked up to Gus and smiled. "Take care of yourself, Gus. I'm much obliged for all that you taught me."

"Keep your head down and your arm steady," Gus advised. "You'll find it helps to keep you alive during attacks."

Zane laughed. "I'll do just that."

Morgan mounted his horse and together he and Gus rode off toward town. Zane felt an emptiness inside him at their departure. *Maybe I'm crazy for this,* he thought. *Maybe I should mount up and follow them out.* But before he could change his mind, a soldier approached him.

"Your friend tells me you're here to sign on."

Zane looked the man in the eye and nodded. "Yes, sir. That's what I'm here for."

———

"Since I won't see you before Christmas," Koko declared, "you should take these things now."

Takes-Many-Horses took the small bundle from his sister and smiled. "Presents?"

"Yes. I made you a new buckskin shirt and moccasins."

He nodded appreciatively. "I'm sure they are of the best quality. Thank you."

Koko bit at her lower lip for a moment. Dianne could feel her friend's anxiety. "I wish you would stay," Koko told him.

Takes-Many-Horses shook his head. "I can't. There are hard times coming for our people. I need to be there to help them."

"And if you're killed?"

Takes-Many-Horses shook his head. "I won't be. I saw myself as an old man in a vision. I'll live many years before I die." He tucked the gifts into his pack, seeming completely unconcerned with his sister's worries.

Dianne felt like an intruder, but Koko had asked her to hold Jamie while she fetched the gifts. Now standing there with the baby, Dianne didn't know what to do but wait out the departure scene.

"I'd better go," Takes-Many-Horses declared. He headed for the front door, but Koko took hold of his arm.

"No, come this way. Bram has a gift for you too."

Takes-Many-Horses raised a brow and looked to Dianne, as if to ascertain her knowledge on the matter. Dianne knew what the gift was, but she wasn't about to spoil Bram's surprise. Instead, Dianne turned to walk toward the door herself.

Outside the sun was shining brilliantly and the reflection against the snow was almost painful to the naked eye. Bram stood just outside the barn with a fine black gelding. The animal had been equipped with a rope hackamore and blanket but no other tack.

"We thought you could use a strong mount," Bram said, bringing the horse forward.

Takes-Many-Horses seemed genuinely stunned. He said nothing for several moments, then looked to his sister and finally back to Bram. "It is a gift of great value. I don't know what to say."

Bram chuckled. "You don't need to say anything. I hope he'll keep you on straight paths. Dianne helped to train him, but he's still a little green. I figure you'll have your hands full and maybe that way you won't be so interested in getting into mischief."

Takes-Many-Horses slung his pack around his neck and took up the rope reins. He catapulted himself onto the horse without any need of stirrups or help. The horse whinnied nervously and backed up several paces as if to protest, but Takes-Many-Horses soon had the animal calmed as he stroked the neck and spoke to him in Blackfoot.

"Good travels, George," Bram said, coming to stand beside his wife.

"Good life to you," Takes-Many-Horses replied.

"Oh, I almost forgot!" Dianne declared, handing Jamie over to Koko. "We packed some pemmican for you."

She hurried to the house and found the food bags. Hurrying back, she handed the pouches over to Takes-Many-Horses.

"These are very soft—good quality work—chewed soft," he said, taking up the bags. He grinned at Dianne and she smiled as she remembered their conversation last night.

"I didn't make them, although I did help make the pemmican."

Takes-Many-Horses laughed softly. "Sister, you need to teach Stands-Tall-Woman to chew leather. She may have need of such skills in the future."

With that he gave a little yell and nudged the horse's sides to head him off down the road.

"What did he mean by that, I wonder?" Koko asked, looking to her husband.

Dianne bit her lip to keep from laughing out loud. She knew exactly what the implication was, and she had no desire to share it and face further teasing by her aunt and uncle.

CHAPTER 35

"WHEN WILL YOU HEAD OUT TO BRING THE CATTLE HOME?" Dianne asked her uncle as they watched Morgan work to saddle break one of the horses.

"I'm planning for the end of the week. A few of the boys we let go last winter have come back looking to be rehired, and I think I've finally got enough hands for the roundup."

Without warning, the agitated horse swung around, catching Morgan off guard. A swift kick of the gelding's hind leg sent Morgan slamming into the dust. Dianne couldn't restrain a gasp and jumped up on the fence to go in and rescue her brother.

"No, you wait here," Bram declared. He opened the corral gate and went inside with slow, deliberate steps. "Whoa now," he called as he walked to the horse. Morgan was already getting to his feet, though his hand was on his lower back.

The gelding bobbed its head up and down as Bram approached. Dianne watched as the horse shied away, ears flattened against his head. Bram seemed undaunted. Two other hands came to help Bram while Morgan made his way out of the fenced enclosure.

"Are you hurt?" Dianne asked as she hurried to his side.

"My back is twisted something fierce. I can hardly take a step without it shooting pain down into my hips."

"Come on, I'll help you to bed. Koko will know how to ease the pain."

Morgan nodded and allowed Dianne to put her arm around him for support. He leaned on her heavily, leaving Dianne little doubt that the severity of his wound must be great. They'd all suffered their fair share of bumps and bruises in working with the animals—especially the horses. Dianne herself had been thrown a half-dozen times.

"What happened?" Koko questioned as Dianne and Morgan came into the cabin.

"The black gave him a kick in the pants," Dianne said, trying to sound lighthearted.

"More like the back." Morgan pointed and Koko nodded.

"Let's get him to bed. I'll get hot compresses and make some tea to help relax those muscles."

Moments later Bram joined them. "You going to be all right?" he asked Morgan.

Morgan moaned in pain as Dianne stripped him of his shirt. "Feels like I was hit by a bolt of lightning."

"Koko, don't forget that great salve you made for me that one time." Bram turned back to his nephew. "Had me up and running before I knew it."

Morgan clenched his teeth and nodded. Dianne felt awful for her brother. He'd never made a good patient. Being confined and in so much pain was probably more than Morgan could bear.

By the end of the week Morgan was better but still in no shape for the roundup. "You stay here with Koko and the baby," Bram told him. "That way I'll know they'll be taken care of." He turned to Dianne and smiled. "Why don't you ride along with us and help cook for this band of no-accounts." He laughed, adding, "They'll be so grateful for the sight of a pretty gal and a good meal that they'll work twice as hard for me."

Dianne didn't care what the excuse, she was delighted. "Truly, Uncle Bram? I can help with the roundup?"

"Well, nothing dangerous. Just cooking."

"When we first came west, that was danger enough," Dianne laughed. Her heart was as light as a feather. She'd been so anxious to do something—anything—to break the monotony of being cooped up on the ranch all winter.

Since they would be gone for as long as two weeks, Bram loaded the wagon with food supplies and bedding. Dianne made the hard decision to leave Dolly behind. The mare was due to foal in a few weeks and needed the extra rest. Dianne was excited about the new arrival. It would be wonderful to raise the colt from birth.

The mount Dianne chose for herself was a gray-and-white gelding that she'd worked with throughout the winter. The animal seemed to have a natural affection for Dianne and worked hard to please. He was also a good cattle horse, having proven himself the fall before when the herd had been gathered to drive north.

Dianne called the horse Pepper, but the men in her family thought it a silly name. She didn't care, however. The animal's coat reminded her of finely ground pepper, and no other name seemed appropriate.

"Come on, boy," she encouraged, leading Pepper from the barn. Dolly whinnied in protest, but Dianne pressed on. "I'll see you soon, old girl."

"You about ready?" Bram asked. "I've sent the boys ahead with the wagon. Figured that'd give them some extra time in case the road's muddy. Besides, we'll have some time to talk, just you and me."

"I'd like that," Dianne declared. She positioned the horse beside one of her mounting blocks, then quickly climbed atop.

"There've been some things on my mind and I figured now would be as good a time as any to share my concerns."

Dianne eyed him suspiciously as she came up alongside. "Sounds serious."

Bram nodded. "It is, but it's nothing I want to get all maudlin about."

"All right."

They urged the horses into a slow walk past the house. Morgan sat in a rocking chair on the porch. Koko had wrapped him in a blanket and stood beside him with Jamie in her arms.

"Be careful," she called.

"We will," Bram replied, bringing up his horse to pause. "Don't forget you have Jake to help with the milking if you need him. He won't like it, but I've told him to help if you need it." Jake was one of their older hands, whom Bram declared in no shape for taxing roundup work. He'd given the old man a job because he felt sorry for him, but Jake had quickly jumped in to pull his weight.

"I'll be just fine. Morgan can watch Jamie for me, and I can tend to the milking." She waved to Dianne. "Have fun."

Dianne returned the wave. "Don't take any trouble from Morgan. He's never been good about being sick or laid up. When he starts getting mean, that's a good sign that he's almost well."

Koko and Bram laughed, while Morgan shook his head. "Very funny," was all he said.

Bram and Dianne finished their good-byes and turned the horses down the drive. Dianne felt a surge of exhilaration wash through her. Soon she'd see Cole again, and she could only wonder what the meeting might hold in store for them. Throughout the winter she'd thought a great deal about him. Had he put his past to rest, whatever that past might be? Had he thought about her? About them together?

She couldn't help but realize that something troubled him deeply, and while she didn't feel she had the right to intrude on those feelings, Dianne often prayed for Cole's release.

"Well, now is just as good a time for our discussion as any," Bram began.

Dianne pulled herself from thoughts of Cole and turned to her uncle. "What do you have on your mind?"

"Quite a bit, actually. I suppose the best way to lay it out is just to tell you what I'm thinking and let you decide how you want to deal with it."

Dianne frowned. "Is there a problem?"

"In a sense. You know this ranch is important to me," he began, "but certainly no more important than Koko and little Jamie."

"Of course not," Dianne interjected. "That's easy to see."

"My concern, however, is for them. You see, I own all of this land. I have a good-sized herd, and with the money you gave me years ago, I've been able to gradually increase that stock, both in numbers and quality. We've been able to add permanent hands to help with the work, and we've built a good many additions to the ranch itself.

"Furthermore, you know it's my desire to build a fine house. That's something I plan to begin this summer."

"Wonderful!" Dianne declared. "I know it will be lovely."

Bram nodded. "I want to give Koko good things. She's had a hard life."

"I know. She's told me about much of it."

"There are many things she won't speak of," Bram said softly. "She's a good woman, Dianne. I've appreciated that you've never seen her as less than that because of her being Blackfoot."

"She's not held it against me for being part Dutch," Dianne said with a smile. Her uncle sounded much too serious for such a beautiful day. She worried that something troublesome was afoot.

Bram smiled at his niece, then looked down the road thoughtfully. "I will make this house the finest in the land, big enough for you and your family as well as mine."

"That's kind of you but not necessary. I still plan to put in for my homestead come fall."

"That's part of why we're having this discussion, Dianne." He pulled up on the reins and stopped the large bay gelding. Dianne halted Pepper and waited for her uncle to speak.

"If you homestead, you'll have to live at least part of the year on the land. The nearest tract will put you a good distance from the house, even though the land will adjoin. And given what I'm about to tell you, you won't need the property anyway."

Dianne knew her puzzled expression was probably more than enough to prompt Uncle Bram to continue, but still she asked, "Why?"

"I've talked it over with Koko, and I plan to add your name to the deed for the ranch."

"I don't understand. Why would you do that?"

"Because when I die, I want to know that the property will stay in the family. Your brothers certainly have no interest, but I know your heart. You love this place as much as I do."

"But what of Koko and Jamie? This is their home."

Bram nodded and replied, "Yes, and I'd like it to stay that way after I'm gone. But you see, Indians cannot inherit—they can't own land. They aren't even deemed citizens of this country."

"But Koko is half white." Dianne couldn't imagine that the government would force a wife, even a wife of Indian blood, from the home of her dead husband.

"I don't think it will matter to anyone, so long as she's also half Indian. Believe me, I've discussed this with the authorities and this is the counsel they've offered. Laws may well change, but they may not. I want to make certain my family is provided for, and you are the only way to ensure that."

Dianne felt almost sickened by this news. "How awful for Koko. How terrible that a man can't leave his own son a legacy."

"But through you, I can leave him a legacy. I'd like to see that the land is shared. I'd like to see that Koko is allowed to live out her days in comfort. She's a young woman; if I die and she chooses to remarry and go elsewhere, that's up to her. But if she desires to stay here, then I want that to be an option. Do you understand?"

Dianne nodded. "Of course."

"And will you do this for me?"

The weight of responsibility fell heavy on her shoulders. "Yes. I'll do whatever you ask."

He smiled as if her words suddenly made everything all right. "Good. I'll have the papers drawn up after we get back from roundup."

———

The men were already hard at work when Dianne and Bram made their way to the camp. Most of the herd had been gathered into a manageable collection, and the mothering up of calves and cows had already begun.

Dianne watched in fascination as Gus and the men would rope the calves by the hind legs and drag them to the fire for branding. She had thought this part of the job would upset her or even sicken her with the smell of burnt hair and flesh, but in truth she wasn't bothered at all. It seemed she had ranching—all aspects of ranching—in her blood.

Cole seemed surprised by her appearance but said nothing. He was too busy to stop and talk, but it didn't keep Dianne from watching his every move. She thought him more handsome than she'd even remembered. She loved to watch him work with the calves, his arm muscles straining against the flannel of his shirt. He needed a haircut, to be sure, and a shave. Both he and Levi had grown beards over the winter. No doubt it offered their faces added warmth.

If Cole noticed her watching him, he didn't respond, and for this Dianne was grateful. She wasn't sure how to handle her feelings for him. She'd hoped that in his absence she might be able to let go of her consuming thoughts, but that hadn't happened. And now, with dreams of Cole Selby mingling with the news her uncle had shared, Dianne wasn't at all sure what she would do.

She longed to discuss the situation with Cole. She longed to let him know what her uncle had said and see what Cole thought about his plan. Then she wondered if she should say anything at all. *What if he doesn't have feelings for me but when he hears that I'll someday inherit the entire ranch he pretends to care so that he can take control?*

"Have you heard the news?" Bram asked Dianne. "We've got fifty new calves. Fifty!" He was so excited about this that he didn't even wait for Dianne's response. She laughed as he rode off, calling out for Gus. The herd was growing more rapidly now. Most of the new cattle he'd brought in the previous year had made it through the harsh winter, and now the calves were showing great promise as well.

"Well, in another ten years your uncle will have a herd to be reckoned with," Levi said, pausing to get a drink from the water barrel.

Dianne nodded. "To be sure. I've never seen Uncle Bram this excited."

"We lost only two calves and one cow over the winter," Levi

declared. "He's got reason to be excited."

That evening as the men and cattle rested, Dianne cleaned up the supper dishes. She'd been pleased that her elk stew had gone over so well. The men had come back for seconds and before she knew it, every bit of stew was gone. She'd not even had a chance to have a bowl for herself. But it didn't matter. The men were well fed and happy, and that blessed Dianne in a way she couldn't explain.

"Good supper," Cole said, coming to where Dianne stood at the back of the wagon.

"Thank you. I'm glad you liked it. Did you get enough to eat?"

"Sure did. Had three bowls."

Dianne already knew this but said nothing. She continued washing the dishes as Cole stood casually beside her. She wondered what he wanted—if there was something more he intended to say. She might have asked, too, but her hands were trembling so much that she worried her voice might well do the same if she opened her mouth to speak.

"You didn't bring Dolly," Cole commented.

"No . . . ah . . . she's due to foal. Did . . . you forget?"

He shifted to lean back against the wagon. "I suppose I did. Hope she'll wait until we get back."

Dianne finished the last of the dishes and started to lift the basin to dump the water. Instead, Cole swept her aside and lifted the pan himself. "Where do you want it?"

"Anywhere," Dianne said. "I was just dumping it."

Cole tossed the water aside and handed the basin back to her. Dianne quickly dried it out and then began drying the other dishes. By the time she finished and Cole hadn't said another word, Dianne thought she might scream. What did he want? Why was he here?

Nervously she began to chatter. "You should see Jamie. He's crawling everywhere and getting into everything. I can't wait until he's walking. He's already trying to do just that. He pulls up to everything and . . ." She ran out of things to say the minute she glanced up to look at Cole's face.

Oh goodness, why do I have to be so flustered? It's just Cole. I've talked to him a hundred times. I've even yelled at him a couple of times. Her cheeks grew hot at those memories. She looked away quickly.

"Remember the blizzard the day you left with the cattle?" She didn't wait for a response but hurried right along. "Well, it got really bad at the ranch and I was out checking the horses and milk cows while Uncle Bram got extra wood and water. Next thing I know the wind is so fierce, I've fallen. I had no choice but to crawl and before I knew it, I was being lifted up. You'll never guess who had come to my rescue."

"Bram?" He finally spoke.

Dianne laughed nervously, now wishing she'd never brought up the story. "Ah, no. It was . . . Koko's brother. Takes-Many-Horses."

"I thought he was on the run from the law," Cole said, not sounding in the leastwise happy to hear the news.

Dianne finished putting away the dishes and hung her towel over the side of the wagon. "I don't think he was running from anyone this time," she said. "He was very pleasant. Very nice to talk to."

Cole pushed off from the wagon. "What did you talk about?"

Dianne shrugged. "He talked about the Indians and conflicts with the whites. He also loved my apple pie." She bit her tongue, wishing she hadn't said that. There was no sense in it.

"You do make good apple pie," Cole admitted. "What else did you talk about?"

Dianne's face grew hotter. She looked to the ground. "Well, really not much."

"You seem upset. Did he say something that upset you?"

Cole sounded angry now. Dianne looked up abruptly. "No, not at all. He was very kind. He even teased about marrying me." Cole's eyes widened and Dianne decided then that perhaps that hadn't been the best thing to mention. "I assured him he wouldn't want me for a wife," she continued, trying her best to sound lighthearted. "I can't chew leather." She smiled, hoping Cole would relax his rigid stance.

"Would you walk with me?" Cole asked.

"What?"

"Walk with me," he said, almost making it a command. Quietly he added, "Please."

Dianne took off her apron and hung it alongside the dish towel. "All right." She pulled on her wool-lined coat, as the evening had grown chilly. She couldn't imagine what had come over Cole. He was acting like a nervous schoolboy one minute and a jealous husband the next.

They walked away from the camp, strolling at a slow pace as if they were visiting a park. In truth, Dianne had never seen a lovelier park anywhere. The grandeur of God's splendor was vastly superior to anything man could order or create.

"My father and I came to Montana in search of gold," Cole began softly. Dianne almost had to strain to hear him. "Instead, I found true love. Or what I thought was true love. Her name was Carrie. She was young and sweet and totally unspoiled. Her father had come for his fortune, as well, but before long his ways led to breaking the law and he found himself on the wrong side of the vigilantes."

"The ones who went around hanging highwaymen?" Dianne asked.

Cole's expression grew pained. "Yes. My father was a member. He wanted badly to prove his mettle to his peers. He forced me to come along with them on the day they went to confront Carrie's father. It had already been proven by several eyewitnesses that the man was a murderer and a thief, and because the sheriff would do nothing about it, this group of men felt they had to act.

"I didn't want to go, but my father made it clear that I would go and assist or that I was no son to him. He would send me back to my mother. Well, that wasn't what I wanted to hear. I wanted to make him proud— to please him. But I didn't want to do it this way. I didn't believe in taking matters into my own hands. I felt confident something else could be done. I went along hoping to change their minds, but that didn't happen."

Dianne nodded, still not understanding why Cole was suddenly telling her all of this. She'd wanted to know the truth for a very long time, but now without warning here he was telling her everything without being prompted to do so. She couldn't help but wonder why.

"I learned when they planned to hang Carrie's father and arranged for her to be in town with a friend. I didn't want her to witness the ugliness. So with that taken care of, we went out to her place. The men accused Carrie's father and prepared to hang him. Then there was a noise in the brush. It appeared to be an ambush. The men drew their weapons, and as Carrie came screaming into the clearing, my father shot her. She died in my arms." He said it all so matter-of-factly that Dianne wasn't at all sure how to respond.

Cole reached out and took hold of Dianne's forearms. Her eyes widened and she swallowed hard. In spite of the thick coat, his touch sent tingling charges up her arms. She met his eyes, watching, waiting for what would come next.

"I promised Carrie I'd never love another woman. I determined in my heart to spend my days alone."

It wasn't at all what she'd expected him to say. But then again, she really didn't know what she'd expected him to say.

"Dianne, I've had a lot of time to think out here this winter. I can't keep my promise to Carrie."

"Oh?" Dianne barely uttered the word. Her mind was running in a hundred different directions as she tried to understand exactly what Cole was trying to get across.

Cole closed his eyes and drew a deep breath. He let it out slowly, mesmerizing Dianne with his action. He opened his eyes and fixed his gaze on her face.

"I want to spend the rest of my life with you, Dianne. In case you haven't figured it out before now, I've fallen in love with you."

CHAPTER 36

"You what?" Dianne asked in disbelief. She had often dreamed of hearing Cole's declaration of love, but now that it'd come, she was stunned.

Cole took hold of her chin. "I love you, Dianne. You're all I could think about out here. I didn't plan to fall in love with you, but it's happened, and I need to know how you feel."

Dianne swallowed hard. Cole's touch was doing strange things to her stomach and knees. She felt her breath quicken. "I . . . uh . . . I . . ." Dizziness gripped her like the time when they'd found Betsy's lifeless body. Dianne fought against it this time, however. She didn't want to faint and miss out on the very moment she'd longed for.

"I feel the same," she whispered.

Cole grinned. "The way you lost all your coloring just now, I wasn't sure what you were going to say." He hugged her close, then quickly released her, totally catching Dianne off guard. "Sorry," he murmured as if embarrassed, "I shouldn't have done that."

"Why not?" Dianne said, not in the least bit sorry for the embrace.

"Well, we aren't engaged and even if we were, it would be a bit forward of me. I wasn't raised to be a cad about these things."

Dianne grinned. "Good thing. I've no interest in cads."

"How about simple cowboys?" he asked, his gaze boring into her soul.

Dianne reached up and tenderly touched her fingers to his face. "I have a fascination for them. Especially one in particular."

Cole closed his hand over hers. "So should we talk to your uncle?"

Dianne felt her entire body tremble. She nodded slowly, then remembered the conversation she'd had with Uncle Bram about the ranch. "But there's something you should know first. Something that might change your mind about everything."

"What?"

Dianne pulled away. "My uncle just informed me this morning that he's putting my name on the deed to the ranch. Koko and Jamie can't inherit it because in the eyes of the law, they're Indian. I told him I'd stay here and make a good home for them if anything happened to him. I gave him my word, Cole, and I can't go back on that."

"I wouldn't expect you to," Cole replied. "It's a surprise to be sure, but I'd already decided after spending the winter thinking things over that I would get me a piece of homestead land and build my own ranch. I'd be just as happy to help your uncle—if he agrees to it."

Dianne sighed in relief. "I'm sure he'll be delighted, Cole. Probably happier than you or me about this whole thing."

"That isn't possible," Cole said, his expression growing quite serious. "No one could be happier than I am."

"Nor I," Dianne whispered. And in her heart, she knew the truth of it as joy washed over her in waves.

———

Trenton had hoped for a nice quiet dinner at his hotel, but at the first sign of Annabelle and her brother Geoff, he knew that wasn't to be. Grimacing, he raised a glass of wine to his mouth to keep from allowing them to see his displeasure.

"I told you we'd find him here," Annabelle said to her brother as they ignored the waiter and pushed their way to Trenton's table.

Trenton stood, setting his glass aside. "Is something wrong?" He hoped whatever the problem, they would state it quickly and leave. People were already staring at them, and it made Trenton most uncomfortable.

"Is it true you plan to leave town?" Geoff asked, his voice holding a serious tone.

"Tell him what you told me," Annabelle demanded.

Trenton hoped to put an end to the encounter as soon as possible, but having them stand there questioning him was only drawing additional stares. "Won't you sit down?"

Annabelle smiled sweetly and took the chair beside Trenton's while Geoff took the one opposite. "I ain't never been to this place before. It's sure pretty."

Geoff grunted. "Expensive too. That's why you ain't been here before."

Annabelle ignored him and turned her attention back to Trenton. "You look upset. Are you mad that we came here?"

"I hate to draw attention to myself," Trenton said honestly. "I didn't like folks gawking, that's all."

"Well, we had to come. I told Geoff what you said about leaving."

"Why would that be of interest to your brother?" Trenton asked.

Annabelle shifted her gaze to Geoff, then to her hands. She nervously twisted a handkerchief that had seen better days. "Well, given how we feel about each other, I thought it only fair to tell him your plans."

Trenton shook his head and met Geoff's hard stare. "How we feel about each other? I don't think I understand."

Annabelle sniffed. "Now, don't be pretending our time together meant nothing to you. You told me otherwise."

For months on end, the only thing Trenton had felt for Annabelle and her brother was complete contempt. They fought constantly, came to him for money whenever things were tight, and generally made a nuisance of themselves. Annabelle seemed to believe she could somehow be found to be more respectable through association with Trenton. Why she figured that was beyond Trenton. Sure, he frequented more upscale hotels and restaurants than Annabelle could afford, but he was still a gambler. No matter how he painted himself, facts were facts and his social standing was no better than hers.

Trenton leaned back in his chair and waved the waiter off when the man started to approach the table. Annabelle took note of this.

"Ain't you gonna buy us dinner?"

Trenton shook his head. "No. In fact, as soon as I pay my bill, I'd planned to retire for the night."

"You ain't playing tonight?" Geoff asked.

Trenton wondered at his motive. "No. I never travel with much money."

"See, I told you he planned to leave," Annabelle wailed.

"Where are you headin' and when do you plan to be back?" Geoff asked.

Trenton began to feel as though they were backing him into a corner. "I don't know. I don't have a destination in mind. I may go visit my sister in Montana Territory. I've been telling her I'd do that for a long time now. As for returning, well, I really don't have any plans of returning soon. I've had my fill of Omaha."

Annabelle began to sob into the handkerchief, totally baffling Trenton. Again other patrons began to stare, and Trenton longed only for the quiet solitude of his hotel room.

"So you were just plannin' on leavin' her like this?" Geoff asked coolly.

Trenton looked to Geoff, then back to Annabelle. "I don't know what you're talking about."

Geoff leaned forward rather menacingly. "You've been makin' my sister promises, and now you're just gonna head out of town, easy as you please. I think you better reconsider."

"I've never promised your sister anything. I'm not in any position to make promises."

"You did too," Annabelle declared in a loud obnoxious cry. "You promised to marry me and make me an honest woman."

Trenton's mouth dropped open. He was flabbergasted. "I . . . well . . . you . . . I never made any sort of suggestion." Trenton couldn't begin to see himself married to a whining, argumentative woman like Annabelle Tevis.

"You callin' my sister a liar?"

"Both of you need to calm down and listen to reason." Trenton turned to Geoff. "I have nothing to offer your sister. I don't have a good name. I don't have a steady job. I don't even have a horse. I sold him a few days back to get money for a game. I gamble when I can get a game and move on to another place when that town is tapped dry. What kind of life is that for any decent woman?"

"I don't care. I wanna go with you. You promised we'd always be together," Annabelle said, dabbing at her eyes.

Trenton could see now that she wasn't crying real tears at all. She was merely giving the pretense of tears to convince her brother and drive home her point. Feeling the heat of Geoff's gaze, Trenton shook his head very slowly.

"I did not promise any such thing. Annabelle, you have to be fair and tell the truth."

"You *are* callin' my sister a liar!" Geoff declared, his raised voice again drawing stares from the people around them.

"I'd prefer to think Annabelle is simply mistaken."

"Well, she ain't and I expect you to do right by her."

The waiter approached the table. "Sir, the management would appreciate it if you would take this discussion elsewhere. You are disturbing the other customers."

Geoff got to his feet. "Well, ain't that a shame."

Trenton immediately stood as well. "Here," he said, handing the man more than enough money for his bill, "I was just leaving."

"No you ain't," Geoff called after him.

Trenton continued walking through the restaurant and into the hotel lobby. He walked past the clerk at the desk and went to stand by the front door while Annabelle and Geoff caught up with him.

Once the trio was again together, Trenton led them outside. "Please hear me out," he said, trying hard to stand his ground and pacify Geoff, knowing the man's penchant for losing his temper and killing his adversaries. "I have never made any promises to Annabelle, and if she thinks I have, then she's mistaken. I do not ever plan to marry—not Annabelle or anyone else. I have no reason to consider my conduct toward your sister as anything but honorable. In fact, my conduct with both of you has been above reproach. I've given you money when I had extra to spare. I've paid for many a meal and even helped pay for repairs to your house.

"Added to this, I've helped to keep Geoff out of the reach of the law on more than one occasion, lending you my horse so that you could get away and even hiding you in my hotel room. I've been the best friend I knew to be, even though you two aren't the easiest folks to be around."

Geoff and Annabelle looked rather surprised at this declaration, but Trenton was feeling brave and continued. "I don't know why you think I would want to stick around for the constant fights and draining of my purse. I'm just as tired of the both of you as I am of Omaha—maybe more."

Geoff had taken all he was going to. Stepping forward, he grabbed Trenton by the collar. "You'd better stop right now before you say something you're really gonna regret. You've made my sister promises of marriage, and I intend to see you go through with those promises. I'll give you a couple of days to think it over, but you'd better come up with the right answer and a ring for my sister's finger. She's got her heart set on being respectable." He released Trenton with a backward push. Trenton landed with a loud plop on the boardwalk.

Staring up in silent fear, Trenton wasn't sure how to deal with the situation. He wasn't about to marry Annabelle, but on the other hand, he really didn't want to encourage her brother's wrath.

"We'll be here day after tomorrow with the preacher, Chadwick. You'd best not try to get out of this either. Otherwise, I'll hunt you down and put a bullet in that thick skull of yours."

Trenton got to his feet as Geoff led Annabelle down the street. He knew he would have to leave Omaha tonight in order to give himself as much lead time as possible. Hurrying to his hotel room, he took only what was absolutely necessary. That way if he ran into Geoff on the street, it wouldn't appear he was headed anywhere but to a game. Of course, he'd already told Geoff he wouldn't be playing tonight.

Well, if he sees me tonight, I'll just tell him that given the change of events, I need more money and will have to play a game or two. It seemed reasonable to Trenton. What didn't seem reasonable was anything else that had happened in the last hour. How had his life managed to get so convoluted?

Memories of running from Jerry and Sam Wilson came to mind and Trenton shuddered. He could still feel the fear of stealing away in the dead of night—listening for footsteps in the dark. He broke into a cold sweat. Again he was on the run. There was no time to plan his moves—no time to buy a horse and gear. He'd have to see about catching a steamer. He knew there were boats that went to Fort Benton in the Montana Territory. He'd researched that much. The trip ended there, however, and he'd be completely on his own to find a way to Uncle Bram's ranch. The idea of traipsing around in Indian country, especially given the most current reports of problems, didn't appeal to him in the least.

But then, neither did staying in Omaha.

Then there was the money factor. He didn't have that much on him. As he'd told Geoff, he never traveled with much. It just wasn't prudent. There were too many occasions for contact with thugs and pickpockets in Trenton's line of work.

I just need to get out of Omaha and then get a game, he told himself as he exited the hotel by way of a back door he'd discovered only the day before. Cautiously, he peered down the alley and drew a deep breath. This would work—it had to work.

Trenton went to the river and finally found help in the form of a freight boat bound for Kansas City. It didn't matter which direction he headed as long as it was away from Omaha. He paid the captain an outrageous sum and slipped aboard. Hiding amongst the tarp-covered load, Trenton could only hope Geoff Tevis had caught no sight of his getaway.

The miles drifted by and Trenton began to breath easier. By the time they reached St. Joseph nearly three days later, Trenton felt his confidence and strength return. When they docked in Kansas City two days after that, Trenton felt as if he could conquer the world. The first thing he needed to conquer, however, was finding a room and a decent poker game. After that, he'd keep moving. He'd have to avoid ever returning to Omaha if he wanted to stay alive.

Securing a room at a hotel he'd never used, Trenton counted his remaining cash and smiled. It was enough to get him into a game. He tossed his jacket over the end of the bed and stretched out for some much-needed sleep. It would be hours before he could square away a game, and he figured this would be the most beneficial way to pass his time. Exhausted, Trenton dozed off with memories of the terror that had sent him on the run.

———

It was nearly nine-thirty that evening before Trenton awoke with a start. He lay awake in the dark, listening and hoping that there'd be no sound to betray an intruder. All seemed quiet. Sitting up, he steadied his nerves and yawned. Under his door came the tiniest shaft of light. Apparently the hall lamps had been lit.

Trenton dusted off his clothes as best he could, then opened his hotel door. The light allowed him to find his coat and hat before heading downstairs to search out a game. Several other people moved about in the hallway, but Trenton didn't recognize any of them. With a sigh of relief, he closed the door behind him.

It's going to be a good night, he told himself. He always started his gaming nights this way. Henry had told him more than once that a man who exuded a positive attitude could work his way into just about any circle of gentlemen. It was as much a part of the game as the actual card playing. Confidence was everything.

After making some discreet inquiries, Trenton made his way to a suggested gambling house. It wouldn't be as lucrative as a game with refined businessmen, but it would still provide him diversion and money. A light rain began to fall, but Trenton refused to let it dampen his spirit. *Things are going to be better*, he promised himself. *I'll get enough money together and then I'll go to Montana.*

Trenton quickly found his way into a game and before long began winning just enough hands to give him a good pot without attracting too much attention about his luck. It was his turn to deal when someone called him by name.

"Well, well. If it ain't Trenton Chadwick. Just look at you all growed up and fancy like."

Trenton would have known the voice of Jerry Wilson anywhere. He looked up and met Jerry's menacing stare. Sam stood to his left and Mark was on his right. The Swede was the only one who seemed to be absent.

Trying to appear unmoved, Trenton nodded. "Good evening, boys."

Jerry laughed. "It's a good evening now. That's fer sure."

Trenton dealt the cards, trying hard not to even glance up. He wanted to show Jerry that his presence meant nothing, but it was hard. Trenton's insides felt like they were churning. He was afraid it wouldn't take much effort to be sick.

The round went to the man on Trenton's left. With this win, the man decided he'd had enough of poker and gathered his winnings to leave. Jerry quickly took the man's chair.

"Deal me in," he said, tossing a coin into the center of the table.

"Me too," Sam declared, motioning for an old man to vacate the table. He sat down before the man could even reach to finish his drink. Sam tossed back the whiskey and smiled. "I always like a drink with my game."

Mark pulled up a chair and nodded. "I do too. Why don't you order us a round for old time's sake, Trent."

Trent nodded and ordered the trio whiskey. Thoughts flooded Trenton's mind as he dealt another hand. How in the world had this happened and what was he to do about it now? Getting away from Jerry and the others would be no simple feat.

They played cards for two hours, all the while Trenton continuing to wonder how he would manage to separate himself from Jerry. Jerry insisted on telling anyone who joined the game that they were the best of friends from southern Missouri. Trenton hated the association, but to keep Jerry from being too suspicious he went along with it. It was close to midnight when Jerry finally stood and announced he'd had enough.

"Well, it was mighty good playin' with you again, Trent, but you know, we've got business first thing in the morning and will be headin' out. It wouldn't do for us to be stayin' up all night."

Trenton felt a sense of relief. Maybe Jerry honestly didn't care about him anymore. Maybe he'd just go away and leave Trent to his own business. "Good night," Trenton offered, dealing cards to those who were remaining.

Sam and Mark got up and followed Jerry from the room, leaving Trenton to exhale in an audible sigh. The remaining men at the table gave him an odd look but said nothing. After all, the cards were dealt and it was time to play.

Trenton won enough money that night to pay for an extra day at the hotel and then some. He settled with the clerk and went back to his room, feeling like a burden had been lifted from his shoulders. That night he slept better than he had in years. With any luck, Geoff still believed him to be in Omaha and now Jerry no longer held any interest in his whereabouts. If all went well, Trenton would be in Montana by fall. The thought filled him with genuine peace. It seemed the right thing to do.

Trenton rose late the next day. He had a leisurely lunch at a café down the street, then took a long walk around the town to enjoy the day. By the time evening came around, he made his way back to the same gambling house. A surge of excitement filled him as he came into the room. Many of the tables were empty, as the night was still young. He made his way to the bar, hoping to order himself a strong cup of coffee, but before he got that far, a plump man stepped into his path.

"Say, I saw you here last night."

"That's right," Trenton admitted. "You did. What of it?"

"Hey, Bruce, this is one of 'em," the man declared, taking hold of Trenton's arm. His steel-like grip took Trenton by surprise.

"What's this all about?" Trenton questioned, trying his best to pull away from the man.

"Send for the police. This is one of the fellas who robbed the First National this morning."

Trenton shook his head. "I did no such thing. I don't know what you're talking about."

"I'm talking about three dead men and a bank that's short of about five thousand dollars," the man said, giving Trenton a sharp jab with his elbow. "Now settle down or I won't even save you for the hangman's noose."

Trenton's head began to spin. *Hangman's noose? He wants to hang me? But why? I haven't done anything wrong.* A sickening thought came to mind. He recalled the man's words. *"This is one of the fellas . . ."*

Dread washed over him as they waited for the officer to arrive. Jerry and his boys had no doubt pulled a bank job, and Trenton, like the fool he was, had allowed himself to be associated with them just in time to take the blame.

CHAPTER 37

THREE WEEKS LATER, TRENTON FOUND HIMSELF BEING DECLARED guilty and sentenced to hang for the death of three men. Despite his declaration of innocence, the judge and jury quickly assigned his guilt by association.

The hanging was set for the following Friday, May 8. Trenton was taken back to his cell at the jail, completely baffled as to how all of this could have happened. The first week his emotions had been raw. He'd screamed himself hoarse, declaring his innocence. The second week he'd grown sullen and silent, despair overwhelming him. After that had come the numbness. What good were feelings, after all?

Sitting in his cell, Trenton tried to write a letter to Dianne and explain how wrong things had gone. He debated on whether or not to tell her that they planned to hang him, then thought it only fair that she know the truth. He'd hold the letter until they walked him up the gallows, then ask the guard to post it for him.

> I don't know why this has happened. I've always tried to stay on the right side of the law—to do the right thing. I was accused of robbing a bank and killing three people. I didn't do it. I swear to you. Still, I find myself facing an end to my life. They plan to hang me on Friday.
>
> Dianne, I wish things were different. I wish I'd come to Montana with

you and never fought against it. I never did feel like I really avenged Pa.
Never saw a way that made any sense. Even when I tried to do things,
there was no satisfaction.

I'm so sorry for all of this. Sorry to be such a disappointment to you.
Please forgive me. I want to make my peace with you and Morgan and
Zane. I need to make my peace with God, as well—but I don't know
how.

Trenton reread the words he'd written and felt a deep, debilitating sorrow. Folding the unfinished letter, he stuffed it into his pocket and stretched out on the cot. Staring at the ceiling, Trenton couldn't help but think of what he'd said to Dianne about making his peace with God. How did a person go about making peace with someone he'd completely ignored for so many years?

He slept restlessly that night, thinking about the hanging and what it would feel like to die. Just as Trenton would manage to doze off, he'd feel the noose around his neck. His breathing would become strained and he'd wake up gasping. Each night it was the same and by Thursday evening, he was half mad with exhaustion and his own wild imagination.

Taking out the crumpled letter to Dianne, Trenton decided to finish it.

I'll go to my death as sorry as a man can be. I don't mind that I've
suffered in life for the wrong I've done, but feel it's terribly wrong to pay a
price for something I had nothing to do with. I love you, little sister. My
last thoughts will be of you and better days.

Trenton

He read over the letter and decided it was the best he could do. There were no words to explain his sadness or regret. There was no possible means to tell Dianne how much she meant to him. How he longed to see her and the twins again.

Lying down, Trenton tried to keep the tears from his eyes. Fear ate at him. He wanted to scream at the guard to just get it over with—to just shoot him and put him out of his misery.

As if thinking of the man had conjured him, the guard approached the cell door and inserted the key. He had a strange look on his face—an uncomfortable, questionable look.

"Come with me, Chadwick," the man said.

"Why? What's going on?" Trenton asked. He came to the door nevertheless.

"We're breakin' you out of here, that's what," Jerry Wilson said as he popped around the corner. "Now you get in there," he said, pushing the guard inside the cell.

Trenton stood in dazed surprise. "What?"

"I said, get out here." Jerry reached in and grabbed Trenton and pulled him out the door. Slamming the cell door back in place, Jerry turned the key.

"I can't leave," Trenton said, backing away from Jerry. "I can't break out of jail."

"Sure you can. You just did. Now come on."

Trenton shook his head. "No. I can't do that." He looked to the guard and then back to Jerry. "Look, I had no great desire to die for something I didn't do, but this is wrong."

"Hanging you would be wrong too. Do you want to die?"

Jerry's words hit him like a sledgehammer. Trenton looked again to the frightened guard. "I didn't rob the bank. I don't want to die for something I didn't do."

"You don't get much of a choice," Jerry declared. "Besides, I've already gone to all this trouble. Now come on. You owe me, and I intend to collect."

Trenton kept his gaze fixed on the guard. The turmoil was acute. "I don't want to die," he told the man again. He could see in the guard's eyes he felt the same way. Perhaps the best thing would be to get Jerry out of the jail where he couldn't hurt anyone.

"All right, Jerry. I'll go with you—for now. But I intend to clear my name."

Jerry laughed all the way down the hall. "There's no chance of that. You're one of us now."

Late August

Dianne watched as Cole expertly cleaned the hooves of his horse. Buddy had been his horse since their days on the wagon train, and the two had become quite accustomed to each other. She liked the way he meticulously cleaned and clipped then filed the hoof smooth.

Watching him, Dianne imagined this was how they would spend the rest of their lives. They would share the work and the love, each one finding strength and hope from God, each other, and even the land. There was something so powerful about this vast land. This was God's country, Uncle Bram had declared more than once, and Dianne had come to understand why he felt that way.

Still, there were troubling thoughts in Dianne's heart. Since Cole's declaration of love and Bram's blessing on their courting, there were times when Dianne felt as if something were wrong. Cole seemed to be keeping something from her, and no matter how Dianne tried to encourage discussion on the matter, Cole would have no part of it. Dianne wondered if it had to do with Carrie and the past. That idea frightened her and kept Dianne from being able to completely abandon herself to the idea of becoming Cole's wife. If Cole didn't feel comfortable sharing his heart with her, Dianne couldn't marry him. And if he hadn't really purged his heart of his love for this other woman, Dianne wouldn't live with a ghost between them.

Bram had suggested they spend at least a year courting, reminding each of them that they'd never really had a chance to get to know each other outside of the ranch work they'd shared. But, as the summer passed, it was generally the ranch they discussed and shared ideas about, even when they were walking together or taking an evening ride. Perhaps that's what bothered Dianne the most. Cole seemed less than eager to talk about himself or his family.

Dianne had taken Koko's advice and had begun to pray in earnest about her relationship with Cole. She longed for marriage and his love, but every time she opened her mouth to speak about it to Cole, something held her back. It was almost as if the Lord were putting a guard over her lips.

She'd sought the Bible for answers and when her eyes had come upon Psalm 141, she felt as if God were speaking directly to her. David had prayed in that psalm, baring his soul and his heart before the Lord.

Set a watch, O Lord, before my mouth; keep the door of my lips. Incline not my heart to any evil thing. . . .

The words were stirring in her heart even now. How could she explain them to Cole? She loved this man. She was convinced of that. But there was a wall between them that Dianne couldn't quite grasp, and she didn't want to incline her heart toward evil even for the sake of better understanding.

What's wrong with us, Father? she prayed in silence. *I've wanted his love and attention for so long, but things aren't right.*

She considered all of the problems they'd overcome already. Arrogance and pride on both sides had blinded them to the need for self-satisfaction. Dianne had detested Cole upon their first meeting because of his smug attitude and condescending ways.

They'd overcome that as Dianne had matured and had begun to see her own flaws as well. Pride had been a miserable companion to her, and working to put it aside had greatly improved her personality. Maturity had also changed Cole.

Together they had endured painful loss and conflict. Cole had been there through the deaths of her sisters and mother. They'd even shared their dreams of working the land, of building a fine herd and owning magnificent horses.

"You're awfully quiet," Cole said. He finished nailing the preformed shoe. After inspecting it, he dropped his hold on the horse. "Something wrong?"

Dianne shook her head, then thought better of it. "I don't know what's wrong."

Cole grinned and walked to where she stood. Without warning he gave her a quick kiss on the cheek. "Does that make it better?"

Dianne thrilled to his touch and returned the smile. "It certainly didn't hurt."

"Let me gather my tools and we'll go for a walk," Cole said. He picked up his hammer, rasp, and hoof cutters and secured them.

Dianne waited in silence, wondering if this would turn out to be a good idea or a bad one. She really did love this man, but she felt she didn't know him at all.

They walked toward a stand of pine, Cole gently holding her hand, his thumb stroking the edge of her hand. Dianne couldn't imagine loving him more or having any deeper desire to be with him.

Please, God, please show me what's wrong.

Cole stopped and pulled her into his arms. "So what's got you so preoccupied?"

Dianne shrugged. "I'm not really sure. There's just something . . . well . . . I don't know. Maybe it's the fact that it's already September and soon winter will be here and there's so much to do."

"I can't imagine that's what's making you all quiet. Usually you want to talk about things like that."

She remained quiet for several minutes. "Well, I do miss my family. I miss Zane and my sisters. I wish I knew where Trenton was. I haven't had a letter from him in so long. I worry about him and wish he'd just come to Montana. And of course I miss my mother and father."

Cole stiffened but didn't release her. Still, his actions made Dianne take note. "It overwhelms me sometimes to realize," Dianne continued, watching him for further reaction, "that those I loved so dearly are gone. I'd love to see them again—just to share my heart and dreams."

"They might not even care. Did that ever cross your mind?"

Dianne was surprised by this turn in the conversation. "Why do you say that?"

Cole dropped his hold and started walking again. "People don't always care about each other. And some folks come to realize that just because people are a part of the same family, that doesn't mean there's any love lost when they're separated."

"I don't understand. Are you saying you don't miss your family?"

Dianne asked, working hard to keep stride with him.

"We don't need to talk about my family. You're the one who was upset."

"I want to know about your family—about you," Dianne said without thought. "You always do this—you always close up. Why is that? Why is it that you'll discuss calving and horse breeding, saddles and feed, but you won't talk to me about Cole Selby?"

Cole glanced her way but kept walking. "Fine. What do you want to know?"

Dianne reached out and stopped him. She felt as though she were panting as she asked, "Do you miss your family?"

"I think I miss the illusion of what I thought was my family, but otherwise I don't miss them that much."

"Why is that?"

Cole met her gaze, his dark brown eyes narrowing slightly as he spoke. "Because I just don't. I don't have to have a reason."

"Yes, I think you do." Dianne suddenly felt as though she were about to get the answers she needed. She trembled slightly as she pressed him. "I'd really like to understand."

"My place is here. It's better that I put the past and its people where it belongs—in the past."

"Is that what you'll do with me when you tire of our love?"

Cole looked at her incredulously. "Why would I tire of loving you? What makes you even think that's possible?"

"Why does a child tire of loving his mother and father—his siblings?" she asked softly.

Cole pushed away from her. "You know the truth. You know what my father did. And I've told you of my mother's indifference toward me. Although our last visit was decent, I don't think she holds any real concern for my whereabouts or needs."

"Of course she does," Dianne replied. "She's your mother. She will always love you."

Cole crossed his arms and fixed his jaw. Dianne could see that he was angry, but she couldn't let the matter drop. Something inside her pushed for answers, answers to explain the wall she felt she had to hurdle in order to reach the man she loved.

"Cole, have you forgiven your father for what he did to Carrie? Have you forgiven your mother for her lack of nurturing?"

"Why should I forgive them? They don't deserve it. Besides, they've gone on with their lives. They couldn't care less whether I forgive them or not."

"But I care."

"Why?"

"Because holding in this anger is putting up barriers between you and me," Dianne said, trying to help him understand. "Don't you see? Until you learn to forgive those who wrong you, how can you love anyone?"

"That doesn't make sense."

Dianne could see he'd balled his hands into fists. He was more than a little irritated with her line of questioning and comments. Still, it seemed as though God were guiding her very words.

"Cole, you say you love me—want to marry me. But how can I marry a man who won't forgive?"

"I'd forgive you—if you needed me to," he muttered.

"How can I be sure of that? The only examples you've given me—examples with people you once loved dearly—is that there is to be no forgiveness for bad judgment and behavior. Why should I believe that you'd forgive me if I made a mistake?"

"Dianne, none of this makes sense."

"But it does, Cole. If you weren't so mad at me right now, you'd be able to see it for yourself. I'm sorry, but this is serious. I don't see how we can get married until you've learned to forgive your father for his mistake."

"It wasn't a mistake!" Cole yelled.

"You mean to tell me your father intentionally killed Carrie? That he knew it was Carrie and purposefully set out to end her life?"

"Well . . . he . . . oh, just leave me alone. You don't understand." Cole began to storm off toward the barn.

Dianne ran to catch up with him, hoping against hope that she might help him to understand. "Cole, I do understand. My father was accidentally killed in crossfire in New Madrid. I blamed myself for a long time for his death. My mother wandered away while under my care and froze to death." She paused. "I know what it is to feel responsible for someone dying. I know how it weighs on you day after day, even when you know you didn't pull the trigger. I can only imagine how awful it would be if I had been the one to shoot him."

Cole stopped walking but said nothing. Dianne looked at him, praying he might understand her. "Please forgive him, Cole. Forgive him and your mother and anyone else who has wronged you."

"What if that someone else is God?" Cole asked. "Do you suggest I forgive God, as well, because I hold a grudge against Him just as surely as I do my father?"

Dianne was so stunned by this declaration that she didn't know what to say. Her mouth opened but words wouldn't form. He held God a grudge? How could he just say it like that—like God was no more important than the man next door?

Cole shook his head. "Maybe I'm not the man you should marry after all. Love is obviously not enough for you."

With that he walked away. Not in the same stalking manner, but rather a defeated one. Dianne was frozen to the ground. She couldn't have moved if she'd had to.

"Oh, Lord," she whispered, "help him. Please help him."

CHAPTER 38

"I'M SORRY YOUR HEART IS SO HEAVY," KOKO SAID TO DIANNE AS they worked to make bread together. "But I'm glad you've finally told me what happened. These last few days have caused me great concern for you."

"It's just that I never realized that the problem between Cole and me was God. I just figured that because we gathered every Sunday for Uncle Bram to share Scripture and pray for us Cole believed in God and had his own faith in God. Now, after all this time, the truth is hard to take."

"Better now than after you were married," Koko declared. She punched down the dough and smiled with great satisfaction. "This will be fine bread. I know the men will enjoy it. Of course it won't last long into their stay at the range shack, but it will be pleasing for the time."

Dianne nodded. She and Koko had agreed to make as many extra loaves of bread as possible. Uncle Bram had already announced they would move the cattle north within the week. Gus also had plans to head over to the fort with an additional few head for sale. He also promised to bring back word from Zane.

"I hope you and Cole can work everything out," Koko said, giving Dianne's arm a gentle pat. "I want you both to stay here and be happy. I liked knowing that it would be you and Cole who would run the ranch after Bram was gone."

"Well, God willing, Uncle Bram won't die for many, many years. As for Cole and me . . . well . . . only God knows." She sighed and covered the bread to rise again. "I hope Cole will make peace with God. I know there can be no future . . . for us . . . without that." Her voice broke and tears came to her eyes.

"God knows the best way of things," Koko said, embracing her friend. "We must trust Him. We will keep praying about this, all right?"

Dianne sniffed back her tears. "Yes. Oh yes."

———

Cole worked alone to round up strays. He'd had little luck in finding any of the missing cattle, however. The isolation had calmed his anger. Here he could just ride and ride and not have to feel guilty for his feelings or thoughts.

Why does she have to be this way? Why does it matter how I feel about Pa or God or anyone else but her? Women are such peculiar creatures. He was ready and willing to make a life with her—to support her by the sweat of his brow. To give her his heart and be faithful to her until death. Why wasn't that enough?

"How's it going?"

Cole turned his horse to find Bram Vandyke approaching from behind. He hoped the man would respect Cole's privacy and refrain from bringing up anything related to his disagreement with Dianne.

"I haven't found any of the strays," Cole said, waiting for Bram to draw his horse up alongside.

"I wonder if we could talk for a few minutes. Seems like a good place for a discussion," Bram said, smiling. "No one to interrupt."

Cole grimaced. "I suppose, if that's what you want."

"I think it'd do you some good. Why don't we head over to those rocks?"

Cole nodded and led the way. He knew Bram probably had heard everything from Dianne. No doubt she'd spilled her heart and told Bram that Cole was the same as a heathen. Maybe Bram wanted to let him go.

Dismounting, Cole tried to justify his feelings. Somehow in preparing to discuss matters with Bram, he seemed less certain of his right to hold this anger. Truth be told, he'd been less certain since his talk with Dianne. He couldn't help it. Anger and rage toward his father and even toward God had been his companion for so long now, he wasn't sure there was even hope for resolution.

He hobbled the horse and left Buddy to feed on the grass while Bram did likewise with his own mount. The big man lumbered up to the rocks as if he didn't have a care in the world, while Cole felt as though he were about to go on trial for murder.

"I can see by the expression on your face that you figure I'm here to give you a good dressing down, but in truth, that's not why I came," Bram began.

"No?"

"Not at all. I know you're unhappy, but I don't know why. I know Dianne is troubled as well."

"You mean she didn't tell you?"

Bram shook his head. "No. Should she have?"

Cole sank onto one of the rocks and shrugged. "I don't know. We had a fight. I got pretty mad and walked away saying that maybe we shouldn't marry."

"Why is that?"

Cole toyed with a rock. "Dianne felt like something was wrong between us, and yet it wasn't between us at all." He paused and sighed. "I tried to tell her that, but she doesn't see it that way."

"Can you explain it to me?"

Bram's gentle nudging disarmed Cole's heart. Without meaning to, he blurted out the entire situation until finally he'd said it all. Taking off his hat, Cole struggled for words to conclude. "I guess you're pretty shocked to hear someone say they hold God a grudge."

Bram chuckled. "No, not really. I've been there before, son. You aren't the first one to be angry with God and you won't be the last one."

Cole turned and looked Bram in the eye. "You were mad at God?"

"I think everyone goes through a time in their lives when they have at least a tiny spark of anger. They may not get as mad as you or me, but they still question why God would put them through something bad. They still get upset to think that God could have stopped bad things from happening but didn't."

"Dianne said I had to make my peace with God and my father—that I had to learn to forgive before I could love her."

"I think she's right," Bram replied. "I think that when a man's heart is hardened toward God, he can't give anything of value to anyone else. He must first deal with his hard heart—let God make it supple again."

"Maybe God doesn't want to make it supple again. Maybe I'm beyond help."

"I've felt that way too. I've never told Dianne why I came west. My own sister never knew. The fact of the matter was my father and I had a horrible argument. He wanted me to take over his business of making and repairing clocks. I wanted no part of it. He had presumed for all those years I helped him that I would naturally stay and be a part of the business. I told him, however, that I wanted only to go west and explore the country, live my own life and make my own way.

"He was enraged. He'd planned for years how it would be. He'd drawn up the paper work and was ready to add my name to the business. And there I stood, shoving this gift back in his face. Now I can see that by rejecting the business, he felt I was rejecting him. But it was never that way." Bram grew very thoughtful. "He told me if I left—if I walked away from this opportunity—that he'd never speak to me again. He told me he'd disown me and settle everything on Susannah. I told him to go right ahead and walked out. I didn't even tell him good-bye. I simply went to my room, packed my bags, and left. The only note I offered was to Susannah and my mother, explaining that I had chosen a different life for myself but that I loved them both. I said nothing about my father."

The silence hung between them for several minutes after Bram concluded. Cole didn't know what to say, but a part of him desperately wanted to know if Bram had ever sought his father's forgiveness.

Bram cleared his throat. "For years, I was angry at God."

"At God?" Cole questioned without thinking. "Why?"

Bram smiled. "I figured God could have let my father see reason. I figured God could have interceded and stopped the whole thing from becoming such an ugly affair. I convinced myself that God was surely against me because nothing went right for years after that. So I became hard and angry toward God. I remember even telling Him, 'Fine. If you don't care about me, I won't care about you.' I somehow felt vindicated by that outburst."

"So what happened?" Cole asked.

"A lot of things. No matter how far I tried to run, God wouldn't leave me alone. I'd find myself in the company of missionaries or traveling preachers. I'd wander across the countryside for days and when I was down to my last ounce of strength, happen upon some isolated house where they'd take me in. Only to find out," he said with a grin, "that the family was completely devoted to God. Not just religious, mind you, but rather filled with all kinds of loving joy about being a part of God's earthly family. It just about drove me insane."

Cole couldn't help but smile. "I think I understand how that is."

"I finally met a man who talked to me without milking it down for me. He wasn't in the least bit concerned about sparing my feelings. He told me I was acting like a selfish sinner. Of course at first I was offended and decided I wouldn't hear the man out. Then he said something to me that drove a knife right into my heart."

"What?" Cole couldn't imagine anything being that powerful.

"He told me I could go on being a lost sinner, living my life as I chose, ignoring the offer of eternal life and the peace that only God could give me. But, he told me, 'You will literally have to step over the broken, bleeding, nail-pierced body of Jesus in order to enter the gates of hell.'"

Cole shifted uncomfortably at this. The image in his mind was vivid. "I don't understand," he murmured, afraid that he really did understand more than he wanted to.

"Cole, you can go on with your anger at God and your father. You can go straight to hell when you die and never look back. But to do so, you'll have to make a decided choice to reject Jesus and what He did for you."

They were quiet for several minutes while Cole tried desperately to collect himself. He wanted to do the right thing, to have peace in his heart and soul. God knew—He completely and totally knew the misery that Cole had carried around these last few years.

Bram turned once again to Cole. "I never had the chance to make things right with my father. He died before I could send a letter back to him seeking his forgiveness. I've always carried that heartache with me. I'd give anything if I could see him just one more time and ask him to forgive me."

Tears blurred Cole's vision. "But my father killed the woman I loved. God let her die in my arms. Let her die."

"He let His Son die too," Bram said softly. He reached out and put his hand on Cole's shoulder. "He let Him die so that you might live."

Cole felt a dam release somewhere deep inside. It was as though years of pent-up emotion and rage came pouring out in the form of pain-wracked sobs. "I'm so worthless. He can't possibly want me. He can't possibly forgive me."

Bram hugged Cole close. "Son, He's always wanted you—and He stands ready to forgive you. But you have to ask."

"Do you really believe that?"

Bram nodded. "With all my heart."

Cole fought back his tears. He wanted the peace that Bram talked about—he wanted things to be right again. "Please," he whispered, gazing heavenward, "oh, God, please."

Dianne saw Cole ride into the yard and wondered if he'd ignore her as he had the previous days since their fight. She continued combing Dolly, hoping and praying that somehow Cole might find peace.

In the corral beyond where Dianne worked, Dolly's colt, Petra, kicked up his heels and sprinted in youthful exuberance. Dianne watched him for several minutes, laughing at his antics. He bore markings that suggested he'd be a buckskin like his mother, but Dianne knew that could change as he grew older. She'd seen it happen before.

"Can we talk?"

She startled at Cole's low voice.

"Of course," she replied, continuing to comb the horse.

Cole climbed atop the fence and settled himself on the rail. "I want first to apologize for the way I've behaved. I was angry, but more than that, I was afraid."

Dianne stopped at this. "Afraid? What in the world were you afraid of?" She hoped her question didn't sound too harsh.

He smiled. "I guess I was afraid of you being right."

Dianne moved away from Dolly and put the curry comb away. "Right about what?"

"That I needed to forgive my father—that I needed to make things right with God. See, I knew that if I faced up to that and did nothing about it, I would be making a choice to turn my back on all I believed and had been raised to know as truth. I wanted to put a veil over the truth so that I could make it what I wanted it to be. So that it wouldn't hurt so much. But instead of finding peace and easing the pain, it just hurt all the more."

Dianne swallowed hard. "And now?" The words were barely audible.

Cole jumped down and came to where Dianne stood. "I had a long talk with your uncle and he helped me to see the truth again. Without the veil."

Dianne felt her throat tighten and tears came to her eyes. She didn't want to make a big scene, but this moment was so important to her—to them and to their future.

Cole took hold of her hands. "I've made my peace with God. I've asked Him to forgive me for my arrogance and foolish pride. And I've asked Jesus to direct my steps for the rest of my life."

Dianne broke down and fell into his arms. "Oh, Cole, I'm so glad."

Cole held her close, saying nothing for several moments. Dianne thrilled to his touch and to the safety she felt in his arms. The walls had come crumbling down. Nothing would ever come between them now.

"I don't know what I did to deserve a good woman like you," Cole whispered against her ear. "I feel like your perseverance, your willingness to stand your ground and trust God for the outcome, saved me in a way."

"I think God knew we'd need each other," Dianne said, pulling away. She grinned. "You've saved me on so many occasions. You kept me from catching fire, being bit by a snake, and accosted by ruffians on the streets of Virginia City."

"Yes, but you kept me from losing my soul."

"No, only God can do that," Dianne countered.

"But not unless someone is willing to show a fella the error of his ways—set his feet in the right direction. A direction of truth. You were willing to stand your ground with me—to help me understand what was wrong and how to go about fixing it. I think that proves we'll make a good team."

Dianne gazed into his eyes and felt her heart beat faster as Cole put his hand to her cheek. "Don't ever change, Dianne. Don't ever be afraid to maintain your stand for what's right." He stroked her cheek, then gently touched his fingers to her lips. "I love you with all of my heart."

"I love you, Cole. More than I thought possible."

"Will you wait for me?" he asked. "Will you wait for me while I go back to Kansas and make things right with my father?"

She nodded slowly. It was the right and perfect thing to do. "If it takes forever, I will wait for you."

Cole drew her into his arms once again. "It won't take that long. I'll leave tomorrow and be back by the spring. And when I come back, I'll be a better man—a man more worthy of a wife like you."

Dianne knew the days would seem an eternity, even if Cole said it wouldn't be forever. He had awakened her heart to the promise of love, just as Montana had awakened her to a promise of home. It was this promise to come that would keep her hoping, believing, trusting for all the days ahead. For all the days that would pass until Cole came back safely to her arms.

Historical Fiction
AT ITS MOST POWERFUL

Loss United Them, Hope Sees Them Through

Brought together when their families were lost in the Civil War, two Southern girls must rely on each other to stay safe. One the daughter of a plantation owner, one the daughter of a slave, they fight against everything they'd been taught about the other in order to trust, survive, and see the better day ahead. A challenging new historical series from bestselling author Michael Phillips.

SHENANDOAH SISTERS by Michael Phillips

Angels Watching Over Me
A Day to Pick Your Own Cotton
The Color of Your Skin Ain't the Color of Your Heart

A Heartwarming New Series From Lauraine Snelling!

Ruby and Opal Torvald's estranged father has left them an inheritance. Leaving the comfort of New York for the unknown wilds of Dakotah Territory, the sisters soon discover what he left is something quite different from a gold claim. With nowhere to turn and a scandal brewing, Ruby and Opal face a journey that is lighthearted, heartwarming, and inspiring.

DAKOTAH TREASURES by Lauraine Snelling

Ruby
Pearl